CW00541576

DARCY
A Pride and Prejudice Variation

Alice McVeigh is a London-based author previously published by Orion Publishing in contemporary fiction (*While the Music Lasts* and *Ghost Music*). A professional cellist, who performed for over fifteen years with orchestras including the BBC Symphony and Royal Philharmonic, she is married to Professor Simon McVeigh. They share one daughter, two long-haired dachshunds, an addiction to tennis, and a bolthole in Crete.

Darcy: A Pride and Prejudice Variation is the third standalone novel in the award-winning Warleigh Hall Press Jane Austen Series.

McVeigh's *Susan: A Jane Austen Prequel* was a quarterfinalist in *Publishers Weekly*'s prestigious BookLife Prize (rated 10/10), and an editor's pick ('outstanding') in *Publishers Weekly*. It won Gold Medals in the PenCraft, eLit, Global, Entrada's Incipere, and Historical Fiction Company Book Awards. It was also a finalist in many other book awards, including Chanticleer's Goethe Book Award, the Indie Excellence Book Awards, and the Wishing Shelf Book Awards.

Harriet: A Jane Austen Variation was also an editor's pick in *Publishers Weekly* and won a bronze IPPY (Independent Publishers Book Awards) and a Gold Medal (Historical) in the Global Book Awards. *Shelf Unbound* magazine chose *Harriet* as one of its 100 'Notable Indies' of 2022. An Honourable Mention in Foreword Indie's 'Book of the Year', *Harriet* was also a finalist in Chanticleer's Chatelaine Book Award and the International Book Awards.

Also by Alice McVeigh

Novels

Susan: A Jane Austen Prequel
Harriet: A Jane Austen Variation
Last Star Standing (by Spaulding Taylor)
While the Music Lasts (from www.alicemcveigh.com)
Ghost Music (from www.alicemcveigh.com)

Short Stories

Capturing Mr Darcy: A Pride and Prejudice short story
All Hallows Eve at the Bennets
Valentine's Day at the Bennets
A Highbury Christmas: A seasonal Austenesque short story
From Mr Perry's Diary: A Jane Austen-inspired short story

Plays

Beating Time (Lewisham Theatre, London)

DARCY

A Pride and Prejudice Variation

Alice McVeigh

Warleigh Hall Press

This edition first published in 2023

Warleigh Hall Press
24 Holborn Viaduct
London EC1A 2BN
www.warleighhallpress.com
All rights reserved

This book is a work of fiction and, except in the case of historical fact,
any resemblance to actual persons, living or dead, is purely
coincidental. The author certifies that absolutely no AI was used in
the writing or plotting of this novel.

ISBN (eBook): 978-1-9168823-6-2
ISBN (Paperback): 978-1-9168823-7-9

Cover design by designforwriters.com

Cover portrait (Eugène Delacroix, *Léon Riesener, peintre cousin de
l'artiste*) courtesy of the Musée du Louvre, Paris

For Simon

Cast of characters

The Bennets of Longbourn, near Meryton in Hertfordshire
Mr Bennet: a gentleman of entailed property
Mrs Bennet: his wife

Their daughters:
Miss Jane Bennet (21)
Miss Elizabeth Bennet (Eliza, Lizzy) (20)
Miss Mary Bennet (19)
Miss Kitty Bennet (18)
Miss Lydia Bennet (15–16)

Their other relations
Mr Gardiner: Mrs Bennet's brother, a London businessman
Mrs Gardiner: his wife
Mrs Philips: Mrs Bennet's sister, a widow in Meryton

The Bingleys and their connections
Mr Fitzwilliam Darcy (28): a very rich gentleman with an estate in Derbyshire (Pemberley)
Mr Charles Bingley (21): a rich gentleman whose fortune was acquired by trade, close friend to Mr Darcy
Miss Caroline Bingley (20): sister to Mr Bingley and Mrs Hurst
Mr Humphrey Hurst (30): a London gentleman
Mrs Louisa Hurst (27): elder sister to Miss Bingley, married to Mr Hurst

The Lucas family of Lucas Lodge, near Meryton

Sir William Lucas: knighted during his mayoralty

Lady Lucas: his wife, friend to Mrs Bennet

Their children:

Miss Charlotte Lucas (27)

Master Timothy Lucas (20)

Miss Maria Lucas (18)

and several younger children

In and around Hunsford, Kent

Lady Catherine de Bourgh, of Rosings: a very rich and well-born
   widow, aunt to Mr Darcy and Colonel Fitzwilliam

Miss Anne de Bourgh (20): Lady Catherine's only child

Mr Collins (25): Mr Bennet's cousin and heir, a clergyman

The Darcys' other connections

Mr George Wickham (27): childhood friend of Mr Darcy, son of the
   Darcys' steward, godson of Mr Darcy's late father

Colonel Fitzwilliam (mid-thirties): second son of an earl, cousin to
   Mr Darcy and nephew to Lady Catherine

Miss Georgiana Darcy (20): wealthy sister to Mr Darcy

Chapter 1

London

'May we waken Mr Hurst, Louisa?'

As Mrs Hurst had not the smallest objection, Miss Bingley sat down at the pianoforte, pushed back her sleeves, and began to pound upon the instrument.

Mr Hurst started. 'Save the women and children! What is happening?'

'Nothing at all,' said Louisa, 'except that Caroline is practising.'

Mr Hurst rubbed his brow, yawned, and said, 'Well, I cannot see the point.'

The point, thought his wife, was that Caroline was not yet wed, that music was her most persuasive claim to accomplishment, and that there was precious little point in her having tuition if she was never to practise – but she said not a syllable of this, for her husband was quite as well aware of it as she.

'Where are Charles and Darcy gone to?' was his next plaint.

Louisa sighed. 'Charles has gone into Hertfordshire – as even *you* must remember – to look at some place or other. As for Mr Darcy, he is visiting the Admiral at Eaton Place.'

She did not mention that Darcy's absence was the reason for her sister's practising – but so it was, because it was her admirable policy not to attempt any work in Darcy's hearing until it was fit to be listened to. And then, the sonata she was practising – really, she seemed resolved to attempt one bar a thousand times! – could not be said to have attained any level of fitness at all. Somewhat to

Louisa's relief, Mr Darcy then entered, and the semiquavers jangled to a halt.

'What, back so soon!' cried Caroline. 'Was the Admiral so desperately dull?'

'The Admiral,' said Darcy, 'was not within.' And he crossed to the table on which he had left his book.

Caroline, fluttered, thought how very good-looking he was, and how well his new coat fitted his strong shoulders, and how she rather liked his frown, as it increased the distinction of his profile. Closing her music, she said, 'What a nuisance for you! Would you care to walk, Louisa?'

'If you wish,' said her sister, perfectly aware – first – that it was cold and gloomy, and second, that *she* had only been asked in hopes that Darcy might be persuadable. However, as he continued to frown at the fire and as Caroline had no real desire for exercise, the notion was dropped. Not long afterwards, there was a bustle in the hall, through which Bingley's fresh voice could be distinguished.

Louisa cried, ''Tis Charles, I vow – I was not expecting him this long age!'

'I suspect he took one glance at the mouldering great ruin, and turned about without stopping,' said her husband, curling himself more comfortably upon the settee. 'He cannot have been gone long enough to inspect a Pembroke table, let alone a country house.'

But when Bingley appeared, he had a very different tale to tell. 'Friends, I am returned, to tell you that Netherfield, near Meryton, Hertfordshire, is the prettiest place I have been privileged to see, in the entire course of my life!'

'So much, my dear Mr Hurst, for your ruin,' observed Caroline, but Mr Hurst's eyes were most peaceably closed.

Charles removed his gloves. 'I cannot pretend that it has, of course, the maturity of timber, or indeed of architecture, of places such as Pemberley – it is in an altogether lighter, more modern, style. But the entrance is delightful, with gravel all new-laid, an open aspect, and a curved frontage – I was rather taken with the frontage – while the servants' quarters alone are twice the size of the place in Buckinghamshire!'

'But what of the society?' inquired his sister Louisa.

'Do not fret – I recollected your advice and it seems entirely unexceptionable. A Sir William Lucas and family are settled within a mile – there is a well-maintained hunt – the market town of Meryton is within a *very* easy distance – and there seem no end of excellent properties nearby. I passed at least five very decent-looking houses. The shooting –'

Caroline wrinkled her nose. 'But who would *live* in such a market town as Meryton?'

'At the moment, a great many soldiers, for the — regiment is quartered there. As I passed through, I observed any number of redcoats – as well as some pleasing shops and a few barouches. In addition, there are balls – though the housekeeper was too discreet to vouch for these. She is a Mrs Emmerson, a solid, sensible soul. I have asked her to stay on, as she received a famous recommendation from the Ibbotts and must know every tradesman in the country.'

'And you have truly taken it!' marvelled Caroline, while Louisa teased, 'Why, for someone as hasty as Charles, to have inspected it for ten minutes must count as the most devout consideration!'

But their brother defended himself. 'I was not hasty to no purpose, I assure you, for there was another family wishing to inspect the property had I not secured it. Besides, if one deliberates too tediously, one never gets anything!'

'My concern,' said Caroline, 'is merely that the society might prove unendurable.'

'Then *you* may stay in town, and allow Louisa to organise my dinners at Netherfield, instead.'

'My dear,' came from Mr Hurst, in the depths of the settee, 'my advice is that you not touch that idea with the far end of a bargepole. It will only involve you in a great deal of trouble and exertion.' And, in proof of his distaste for either, he began almost immediately to snore.

Darcy inquired sardonically, 'And so, you have taken it on a 24-month lease, with the option of continuing thereafter?'

'Nothing like it, and I can quit it at any time, so the solicitor said. Should we find that it does not answer, we can be off in a moment!'

'What, you had enough time to call upon a solicitor, as well?'

'Nay, for he was good enough to ride over from Meryton, for the purpose. There is a splendid drawing-room, with French windows and a charming view of open country.'

'I suspect that not a soul has asked to view the place since Michaelmas,' said Louisa.

But in the end, they agreed that it would be amusing to inspect 'Charles's folly' at the weekend. Once Darcy had assented, Caroline could entertain no possible objection – and so, to Netherfield they were to go.

Chapter 2

Longbourn

'So, what think you of Mr Bingley, Jane?'

'Why, what should I think of him? – except that he is inspecting our neighbours' house, with a view to renting it.'

Eliza laughed. 'No, for it is already decided that *he* is to take it and *you* are to marry him! Mama is entirely convinced and – of course – her instinct can never err!'

'What, has she said so?'

'She has not – but she is having her embossed gown altered for you, the one with the green ribbands. And as she declared her intent, the gleam of maternal calculation was glittering in her eye!'

'My dear Eliza, your imagination –'

'No, not at all, and – judging from the pursing of her lips on the subject of Mrs Long's nieces – she will push you at this Bingley as hard as she can… And it is not so hare-brained a scheme, at that. A spoilt young bachelor rarely looks farther than the nearest beauty, and your equal in *that* regard is hard to find.'

Jane cried, 'Oh heavens! For the last person Mama wished me to marry –'

'You mean Colonel Watson, I suppose?'

'I have never been more embarrassed!'

Lizzy, imitating her mother's tones: '"And here is Jane – the beauty of the family – and no creature could be better-natured, besides! What a delightful wife she would be, for the right young man!" The poor Colonel could scarcely keep his countenance!'

'But Lizzy, how can Mama be so certain that Mr Bingley will take Netherfield? Or, should he take it, that I should like him?'

'Why, as to that, you are obliged to like him! We are obliged to like any man of good fortune, you know – be they bat-witted, beetle-browed or bow-legged. But *you* need not fret, for you like almost everyone. Indeed, you are celebrated for it, almost as much as for your divine complexion and your annoyingly obedient hair.'

'Do not tease me, Lizzy! – There is a very great difference between liking a man and – and *marrying* him!'

'I am afraid you will find that, to Mama, there is almost no difference at all.'

'And you say she is depending on it? Even though we have no means of knowing whether Mr Bingley might not be already attached – or might not *choose* to be attached – or might prefer someone slender and clever, like you!'

Lizzy laughed. 'No, *that* could never happen, for I should certainly – within the course of a single morning – offend so rich a man's entire acquaintance! Instead, I shall die an old maid – residing with Mary, or perhaps with Charlotte Lucas – condemned to good works and morning visits, along with a quite frightening amount of embroidery. But perhaps you might occasionally invite me to Netherfield, when no one more exalted might be expected!'

'Such a fate,' said Jane warmly, 'might happen to Charlotte – though I hope it shall not – but never to *you*.'

Elizabeth smiled. Secretly, she did not believe her prospects quite as bleak as she pretended. Somewhere, there must exist a gentleman willing to overlook her lack of fortune in consideration of her quicksilver wit... For the moment, she was perfectly content as she was.

Chapter 3

(From Mr Darcy's diaries)

I was rather impressed with Netherfield, though Bingley's sisters kept up a remorseless flow of banter concerning Charles's little 'folly'.

Having said which, if Netherfield *is* a folly, it is not a little one, and will prove costly to maintain. And yet, its aspect is not at all bad, the furniture acceptable and its drawing-room commendable. Though Louisa had teased Charles about his fancy for its façade, it is very pleasing, and I found myself feeling sorry for its owners who – excessively in debt – have been obliged to quit it.

We arrived during a light shower, and after tea Mr Hurst – as ever – preferred to rest, but the remainder of the party rode around very agreeably. Charles however remained restless.

'Why do we not take out the dogs, Darcy?'

Louisa said drily, 'Perhaps because they are not yet come?'

'Nay, I thought they were to be delivered on Thursday!'

'That was the plan, indeed, but nothing could be arranged till tomorrow.'

'Very well. Sir William Lucas might be still in London, but we have yet to see Purvis Lodge or Longbourn – not even from the road.'

Mrs Hurst said slily, 'Is not Longbourn the house with all the beautiful young ladies?'

Charles had the grace to look self-conscious, while I recollected his housekeeper's commending the young ladies' looks, though allowing that, 'they were permitted somewhat more freedom than *she* would have advised, had she the charge of them.'

As I had no desire to be introduced to slews of bold young ladies, Charles rode out to Longbourn alone, returning with the observation that Mr Bennet was rather a droll fellow, with a famous library.

'And the five beauties?' teased his sister.

'– were nowhere to be seen. Indeed, I find that I do not entirely believe in the beautiful Bennet sisters. Instead, I suspect good Mrs Emmerson of wishing us to consider Hertfordshire as rich in pretty women as it is in pleasing rides… Will you play at chess, Louisa? As Darcy seems obsessed by his new book?'

Then Caroline uttered an exclamation.

'What is it, Caroline?'

'Oh! 'Tis nothing, really. It is merely that Lady Lucas's note has a postscript. "I cannot pretend that the Meryton ball will be anything extraordinary, but we would be most honoured to meet you there, should you have nothing else planned."'

Charles was charmed. 'A ball! What say you, Darcy?'

As I had no wish to become acquainted with the good people of Meryton, I discreetly made my preferences known, and the ball was not mentioned again. But at breakfast on Friday, Bingley felt bored, as he so often does, and he boldly declared his intention of weathering Sir William and his neighbours on his own. Thus, in the end, we all consented to accompany him, though Caroline, whom I took care to engage for a dance, for fear of worse – did complain about 'Charles's ungovernable good nature'.

With which I was secretly obliged to agree.

Chapter 4

Netherfield

'What you want,' said Louisa, 'is to efface yourself.'

'Efface myself!' cried her sister Caroline. 'But why? And how? And in what regard?'

'With regard to Darcy. I feel for him most sincerely.'

'But why?'

'Because you are, subtly – yet constantly – pressurising him.'

'I? Little I?'

DARCY

'Little you, indeed! Why, you never let the poor man be. You are like Ruth, in the Old Testament, for "whither he goest I wilt go" – though Mary and her lamb would do quite as well, for you trot along at his very heels… When, I beg, can the poor fellow ever say, "Thank God, I am alone!" with you bustling about him?'

Caroline sniffed. 'I may be attentive, I grant, but not obtrusively so.'

'You think so, do you? – But what you fail to consider, my dear Caroline, is that Darcy is a most private fellow. He has no desire to be hounded – he is far likelier to be beguiled by mystery. You present him with more than he wishes for. You should wait till he petitions you, instead.'

Caroline grappled with this a moment and then asked, 'You think me rather too busy?'

'Intolerably so. You should attempt to mirror his own moods.'

'But – he is so provoking – he has no moods to observe! He is always the same!'

'He has more moods than you are aware of, despite making it a point of honour to obscure them.'

'Truly? And what do you mean by mirroring?'

'I mean that, should he be engaged in reading, you ought to appear to be equally entranced by your own book. And when he moves about might be the best moment to propose a change. When *he* is thoughtful, you should give over prodding him to share whatever he might be thinking. While you should wait till he lays his correspondence aside to propose a ride – for supervising such a place as Pemberley might be as demanding as some professions.'

Caroline pursed her lips. 'You think I dog him?'

'Like a Pekingese.'

'And that it fails to gratify?'

'*Quite* the opposite.'

9

'Well, I am grateful for your candour,' said Caroline gloomily. 'Was it so with Mr Hurst, when he was wooing you?'

'No, for Humphrey rather pursued me, in his fashion. Which is to say, he teased me, chose to sit by me, and most perseveringly sought my opinions. I have yet to see Mr Darcy pursue anything beyond a fox, and *that* without any remarkable attention.'

'And yet, here he is,' objected her sister, 'as old as twenty-eight – with every possible advantage – divinely handsome, excessively clever, impossibly rich – and his every relation undoubtedly urging him to wed, for the sake of the line.'

'Agreed. And yet his *riches* are not in your favour, for the richest are the hardest to tempt, and the quickest to scurry away.'

Louisa was amused to observe the effect of this sisterly advice, for Caroline most obediently paid almost no attention to Darcy at luncheon, while *he* seemed entirely unconscious of any affront... However, as she dressed for the ball, she complained to her husband, 'I cannot conceive how we are ever to get Caroline wed! She has no more notion of what men are like than does the cheese we had at luncheon!'

'True,' he consoled her, 'but she is not ill-looking, and has a bit of money, besides. I imagine some young idiot will feel he might do worse.'

'What said Darcy, last night, after we left?'

'Oh, this and that.'

Louisa sighed. 'I mean, about women.'

'Why, nothing at all! He is a well-bred fellow. If pressed, he will admit, "This one is handsome" or, "That one is clever" – but that is all. It is your brother who is forever admiring women! Be they flat-footed, thick-witted or plain as a board, he will find something pleasing to say.'

'Well, as far as Darcy is concerned, I cannot imagine that Caroline possesses the slightest chance.'

'Darcy may put off the business of marrying as long as he can. And no bad notion either, since' – he added hastily – '*you* are no longer available.'

'Well, *I* suspect Caro of being fifteen thousand shy of it – and there is the little de Bourgh cousin, as well.'

'What, Miss de Bourgh? There is nothing in *that*, I am sure.'

'And I am not as convinced as you that Darcy is not thinking of marrying *somebody*. There has been a difference lately – he is restless, somehow.'

'If you think it,' said her husband peaceably, 'it must be so. But now I must have a nap. Else I shall nod off in the cardroom, and never hear the end of it.'

Chapter 5

(From Mr Darcy's diaries)

Following the Meryton ball, and finding it impossible to sleep, I have again caught up my diary.

Most of my doubts were perfectly borne out by the Meryton ball. The musicians were execrable, Sir William obsequious and the food inedible – but no more jokes, I believe, are likely to be made at the expense of the Bennet sisters. The master of ceremonies lost no time in introducing them, favouring – as well he might – the eldest, a demure, blushing beauty in a glossy cream gown with green ribbons, with whom an entranced Charles spent most of the evening.

For once, I could not blame him. Jane Bennet possesses modest manners, silvery-blonde curls, delicate features, a lovely voice, a breathtaking complexion – just enough colour – and a figure almost Grecian, a figure impossible to fault. But why in heaven's name am I dwelling on the exquisite Miss Bennet? Had I danced with her, she would certainly have bored me. Here, despite unusual beauty, was no trace of Giuditta's fire!

Beyond the astonishing Miss Bennet, the gathering was precisely as anticipated. Every woman I met instantly blushed – the luminous Miss Bennet included – barring one. Only her slighter, darker sister, who possesses a neat ankle and a satirical eye, dared meet my gaze, before coolly dropping it.

As for Caroline Bingley, she was intolerable. Of all her variations – and I believe I am beginning to know them all – her coquettish is the one I most detest. She is not a stupid woman, as a rule; however, entrap her in a ballgown, cement her braids into place and she becomes quite impossible to deal with. I have mentioned before, in these pages, that I sometimes suspect she might be a little in love with me. I am usually equal to managing such nuisances and yet, as we took our places in the set, she said, with an archness that sank my heart to my boots, 'And so, you dared ask Louisa to dance before me! Well!'

'I did, for she was a good deal nearer.'

'And is *that* all you think of, when wondering whom to dance with?'

Now, all that I can generally think of, in such circumstances, is whether I can contrive to escape – but I had not the heart to say so. She added, 'And what think you of my new gown?'

'I failed to recognise it – thus, it must be considered a triumph.'

She pouted. Absolutely pouted. Now, here is my true complaint about balls. *Sans* ball, Caroline Bingley – a genuine-enough woman, in her fashion – would never have dreamt of perpetuating a pout. But she was pleased that I had noticed her gown – though now, I find that I cannot recall a single detail, while Miss Bennet's cream dress seems imprinted on my memory.

She tossed her head – an error, as her elaborate concoction of braids was loosened. 'You never take me seriously!'

This, of course, was perfectly true – but it is dangerous to remove all hope from a woman. So I said, as earnestly as possible, 'I do. Indeed, Miss Bingley, you are the person at Netherfield whom I take *most* seriously.'

Which would pass as a fairly stately compliment, under normal circumstances. Yet she shook her finger at me and cried, 'I shall tell of you – to Louisa, of course!'

Now Louisa Hurst – who boasts the strongest and most interesting mind of all the family – is rather a favourite of mine, something I trust Miss Bingley will never be quick enough to understand. At this point, the slighter, darker Bennet girl was dancing opposite, and I caught a swift, almost mocking, glance in our direction, as if to say, 'Just the kind of witless chatter one might have expected!'

Just then, a fellow I vaguely recognised tapped me on the shoulder. 'Good Lord, Darcy! Are you here?'

As I considered this obvious enough not to require affirmation, I informed him that I was visiting with Mr Bingley.

'Aye – an excellent fellow! But, man, surely you know that George Wickham is in Meryton?'

Wickham! If true, this was exceedingly unwelcome intelligence – and almost unbelievable, for what is there to bring him into Hertfordshire? Here there is no gaming, to speak of, and comparatively little sport. My informant – I had recollected him, a fellow called Thorpe – then amended his statement: 'Or rather, he is every moment expected. He has accepted a commission in the —— regiment. I am sorry to be the bearer of ill tidings – and in such a hole, besides! I say, why should we not meet on Thursday? We might command a decent dinner at The Hound.'

After I feared that this was impossible, he wandered away to plague others of his acquaintance. Then I found it exceedingly difficult to manage Caroline Bingley, for she had heard Wickham mentioned, and had always longed to learn the tale. (Which I have no intention that she should. What chance would my own sister Georgiana have with Bingley, in such a case?)

I finished my two dances with Miss Bingley feeling unusually hot and ill-tempered, but Bingley himself was as enchanted with his evening as ever. Dismally, I imagined a long procession of similar events, should I remain in the country. With town unendurable, I even found myself toying with other routes of escape – with going down to Rosings, or to Fitzwilliam's in Somerset… Though I could not help thinking, 'Why should I escape Wickham? Surely it was he – though with nerve sufficient for ten – who should be avoiding *me*!'

Having distinguished both of Bingley's sisters, I resolved to dance no more. When Bingley quizzed me on the subject, I objected, '*You* are dancing with the only handsome woman in the room' – for he had just petitioned, for the second time, the lovely Miss Bennet.

'Oh, she is the most beautiful creature I ever beheld! But observe her sister – just there – who is also very handsome and, I daresay, very agreeable.'

I glanced again at the sister and replied, somewhat louder than I had intended, 'She is tolerable, but not handsome enough to tempt me, and I am in no humour to distinguish young ladies who are slighted by other men.'

I then endured the mortification of observing that young lady deliciously amused at my expense. Furious at myself, I removed to play cards rather than be plagued by Charles – quite the king of the company – dancing every dance and chattering without reserve to every creature in the room.

Chapter 6

Longbourn

'Well,' said Charlotte Lucas the next day to Elizabeth Bennet, 'all Meryton speaks of nothing beyond your not being handsome enough to dance with. Yet you truly hold no grudge?'

'None at all! What care I for Mr Darcy's opinion? And besides, did he not suppose Mrs Hurst handsome enough to dance with?'

'She *is* heavy, to be sure – but I thought he seemed more at ease with her than with her sister.'

'Between ourselves, my dear Charlotte, *my* only concern is for my own sister Jane.'

'I thought her wonderfully collected – for not only did Mr Bingley seem to have eyes for no one else, but she was distinguished by all that party. What did she say about him?'

'She was discretion itself, yet those great eyes of hers said more than enough. The moment he approached her she began to glow, as if lit inside by tiny candles.'

'She *did* look charming, indeed! But why should you fear for her?'

'Lest she care too much. Such a man as Mr Bingley might amuse himself for an evening with a pretty girl, never to recollect her again. While Jane – I think Jane truly liked him.'

'As did your mama, I expect?'

Eliza laughed. 'She is a caricature of herself, scolding, bustling, praising, dreaming – dreaming that such a promising start might be carried through to its most delightful possible conclusion. That, in short, it will be a match, despite his great wealth, and our down-at-heel style of living, her own importunities, and Papa's indolence! When a few dances, to the *ton*, might mean nothing at all!'

Charlotte hesitated, partly because she believed that to dance twice with a stranger was truly somewhat unusual, and partly because she believed herself to have observed a glance from Bingley towards Jane Bennet of no common meaning. 'Well,' she said, 'I think Jane's placid manner rather a drawback than otherwise. Nine times out of ten, a woman should display more interest than she feels. Most men need a great deal of encouragement to fall in love.'

'Perhaps,' said Eliza, 'but it is not Jane's way. If she *does* like a man, he will simply have to have enough sense to divine it for himself.'

Chapter 7

(From Mr Darcy's diaries)

At breakfast the next morning, I learned that Caroline had given over teasing me in favour of teasing her brother, instead. She said archly, 'And so, I suppose we might expect Mr Bennet at any moment, with his gun and his dogs.'

'Why?' asked Charles.

'To inquire as to your intentions, of course!'

Bingley had the grace to look self-conscious. 'I only danced with her, after all. One is expected – unless one is Darcy – to dance with young ladies at balls.'

'But to dance with her *twice* – and to spend half the evening by her side…'

'Nay, let him be, Caroline,' urged Louisa. 'His ears are turning pink, which is never a good sign. Besides, I thought Miss Bennet quite sweet.'

In confirmation of the locals having been charmed – by Bingley, at least – there were so many callers that I took my horse out rather than be obliged to revisit every incident of the ball. Though I secretly applauded the judgement displayed by the Bennets, who chose *not* to appear, their eldest's triumphs notwithstanding. And as I rode, I comforted myself with the notion that admiration of Charles was natural enough, what with his being excessively sociable, new to the country and so fine a fellow.

The next few days, however, saw no falling-off in the neighbours' clamorous delight, and so numerous were the visitors that I elected to return briefly to town. Before I left, I made inquiries at the officers' mess and learned that Wickham had indeed accepted a commission in the militia, something that I had been doubting before. Not that I was astonished at his decision, for he has – God knows – few enough options left to him… I *did* regret his choice of regiment however, for we are certain to meet at some point – something I would give a great deal in order to avoid.

On my last evening in town I again fell into company with Thorpe. We had been at school together, though he was some years my junior. I had not intended to leave the club with him, and I liked him still less when he again mentioned George Wickham: 'Your father's godson, I believe?'

'Quite.'

'And – or so it is said – a famous shot.'

'So I believe.'

I threw a chill into my tone but, on such as Thorpe, such subtleties are thrown away. He continued, 'And such a favourite with the sex!'

I had nothing to say to this. It has always astonished me how many women look for nothing more than a pleasing face and a decent figure in a man.

'Mind,' he added lightly, 'you can have no difficulties in that direction yourself, I am sure!'

'I cannot pretend to be in Mr Wickham's class,' said I – just as he added, 'I believe that in Rome, or perhaps Florence –'

'I advise you,' said I, 'to say no more.'

The mortified Thorpe apologised. ('I never intended – 'twas just in sport, I vow!') Yet as I bade him farewell and left, I found myself growing steadily more furious. So, my time in Rome had become the subject of London gossip! I hated to imagine what my sister Georgiana might think, were it to reach her ears – though it was far likelier to reach the ears of other men, as gentlemen tend to shield ladies from such insinuations. I felt helpless as well as angry though, for what could I do, what could *anyone* do, in such a circumstance?

Later, I wished that I had pressed Thorpe rather harder, as I have generally found it best to know the worst at once, and to deal with it accordingly.

Chapter 8

Longbourn

The next Wednesday Miss Bingley sent a note inviting Jane to spend the day at Netherfield, as the gentlemen were dining with the officers. ('The gentlemen dining elsewhere!' repeated Mrs Bennet. 'How unlucky!')

Jane had refused to beg her father for the carriage. However, as she mounted her horse she glanced up at the sky, concerned. Perhaps she had been a little hasty. Lizzy's droll prediction that she would catch cold and be obliged to remain at Netherfield, did not seem entirely unlikely... She had never seen more threatening clouds in all her life! And she urged her mare into a canter, from the moment she left the stables.

Halfway to Netherfield, the rain truly began to descend. Jane lowered her chin and tightened her cloak around her, thinking, 'Heavens, what a storm!'

Chapter 9

(From Mr Darcy's diaries)

When the outdoor bellpull again resounded, I assumed it was Sir William Lucas – the fellow is indefatigably social – coming yet again, to assure us that he was, remorselessly, at our service. But when the butler opened the door, 'Miss Bennet' – and Jane Bennet alone – was announced. Only then did I recall that Caroline Bingley had invited her to visit, before our own plans had changed.

Charles brightened directly and busied himself with finding her some refreshment – though she protested that she was not in need of anything. It was Louisa who, observing that she had been caught in a shower of rain, insisted upon removing her upstairs to borrow dry stockings and a gown. When she descended – ironically enough, as it transpired – she looked very well indeed. Her hair is so fair that it had an almost glittering cast, her eyes were fired with – what turned out to be – actual fever, while the flames in her cheeks and lips set off her every feature to admiration.

Bingley would not stray from her side, as hopeful as a puppy (I shared a smile with Louisa Hurst). I suspected that Louisa, like myself, was recollecting Bingley's infatuation with Miss Richardson – or perhaps those hours he dawdled in Grosvenor Square, in hopes of the most casual acknowledgement from Lady Diana. Truly, he is susceptible enough!

It was perhaps twenty minutes before Miss Bennet admitted, with embarrassment, to being 'a trifle tired'. Touching her hand, Louisa cried, 'Good heavens, the child is burning!'

Rather than taking offence – she *did* look child-like, with that flaming colour – Miss Bennet disclaimed, but to no avail, as Mrs Hurst bustled her upstairs for a second time. A note having been dispatched to Longbourn, and the rain having passed over, Bingley then proposed that we ride to the farthest extent of his domain, for which he had vague but ambitious plans for improvements.

As we rode, I could not help observing that, given his quick impatience, and given that he was committed to only a short lease, I doubted that he would be in a position to reap the rewards of his efforts. Bingley decapitated a weed with his whip and said, 'Perhaps not, but my sisters think it time for me to settle. There is potential here, you must concede, and interest.'

'Do you refer to the property, or to the eldest Miss Bennet?'

Charles started and said, very frankly, 'Good Lord, you are quick, Darcy – you are quick, indeed! Do you suppose the others have noticed?'

'Your eldest sister misses remarkably little.'

'Yet even you admitted Miss Bennet to be handsome at the ball!' he said accusingly.

'Oh, she is certainly handsome.'

'Even handsomer than your goddess in Rome?'

I said icily, 'I believe that we agreed never to mention –'

Charles instantly apologised, 'but *that* was long in the past.' Though, of course, it was not. And upon our return we learned not only that the local apothecary was expected, but that Mrs Bennet appeared to have not the slightest objection to parting with her daughter – for months, if need be. The curl of Louisa Hurst's lip was not lost on me.

Chapter 10

Longbourn

At luncheon Mr Bennet said drily, 'Well, my dear Mrs Bennet, if Jane should become very ill, should she waste away and die, you will, at least, have the satisfaction of knowing that it was by your desire and under your orders, for it was you who proposed she ride through rain and storm.'

'Nonsense! People do not die of such trifles!'

Elizabeth's own conscience was not easy. She said, 'I should feel more at ease if I were with her. Her acquaintance with Miss Bingley is so very trifling!'

'There is indubitably some truth in what you opine,' observed Mary, who prided herself on her vocabulary. 'Yet I believe, exertion should ideally be expended in proportion to the seriousness of the situation concerned.'

'I shall not be easy, unless I go.'

'Is this a hint to me, Lizzy, to release the horses?' inquired her father.

'Not at all. I can walk – to be sure, the clouds will have all passed over by this time.'

And, as she was not to be dissuaded – despite her mother's fear that she might prove an incumbrance – she set off. The dirt was worse than she had expected, but Elizabeth hooked up her skirt, sacrificed her petticoats, and walked on.

It was not until sighting Netherfield that she felt any doubt. Perhaps her mother had been right – perhaps her arrival would only cause confusion – while her petticoats were truly a disgrace. Also, she had no desire to encounter Mr Bingley's superior sisters. But she felt unequal to combatting her father's witticisms if she did *not,* so she released her skirts over her ruined petticoats and resolutely rang the bellpull for admittance.

In the Netherfield drawing-room she found the gentlemen – and whatever were *they* doing there? – and ladies variously engaged. Mr Darcy was reading, Mrs Hurst sewing, Mr Hurst dozing, and Caroline attempting a sketch. Mr Bingley had appeared lost in thought, but he rose at once, equally delighted at her arrival and discomfited by her sister's fever. ('It happened so quickly! One moment she was admiring my sister's new tambour frame, and the next she was unwell indeed!')

'I expect you will wish to go straight up,' said Miss Bingley, and rang the bell for the housekeeper.

Elizabeth had long known Mrs Emmerson by sight but had never spoken to her before. ''Twas good of you to come, Miss, for she does seem poorly... Are you not the youngest Miss Bennet, and very often visiting at Meryton?'

'No, I am the second,' said Elizabeth, thinking, 'Here is proof that half the village is laughing at the youngest Bennet girls!'

'And *here* is Miss Bennet. Miss Bennet, here is your sister come!' As she turned and left, Jane turned a languid gaze towards Eliza and said, 'Oh Lizzy, you are too good!'

'Not at all, but I have brought you some jellies,' said Elizabeth.

'I am not in need of anything. But I am so glad you have come! How is Mama?'

'Quite as usual.'

'And how do they do downstairs?'

'Upon my word, as I have no notion how they generally do, I could not say. Only that Miss Bingley is sketching – rather badly – and that your admirer seems to be missing you already.'

'Oh, Lizzy, do not tease me. My head aches so!'

'Forgive me. But why are the gentlemen still here? I had understood – I had taken comfort from the fact – that they were to dine with the officers. Was that not why you were invited?'

'I expect you will learn why, at supper.'

'I have no wish to go down to supper. I shall ask for a tray, instead.'

'I should like nothing better – yet it might look odd, should you *not* be there.'

Elizabeth detested the notion. She found Bingley's sisters arrogant – and arrogant without justification, as their wealth had been amassed by trade. She had also believed herself to have caught a contemptuous glance towards her petticoats... However, she would not oppose Jane's wishes and so, after tidying herself as best she could, she descended the long staircase at Netherfield.

'What? Feverish!' Bingley repeated, frowning. 'Cannot a fever be the forerunner of something still more serious?'

Louisa said tolerantly, 'My dear Charles, the rate of taxation is serious, as is the situation in France. I should be vastly surprised, however, if Miss Bennet's fever had not abated by tomorrow.'

Caroline said, 'I suppose this part of Hertfordshire has altered a great deal of late, Miss Elizabeth?'

'It has grown, certainly.'

'And Netherfield is not its only new estate?'

'No – nor even its newest.'

'And *you* do not much care for it, or so your tone might suggest?'

'Nay, I like it very well, your frontage particularly.'

'Do you, by Jove! – but what is your sister's opinion?' asked Mr Bingley eagerly.

'Upon my word, I could not say, but no one could dislike so lovely a view.'

'True! True indeed! – but you would not credit the amount of grief which I endured, Miss Elizabeth, when I chose to rent the place quite off my own bat – but I am glad that you do not dislike it.'

As soon as she was safely upstairs, Caroline said spitefully, 'What pretentions the poor creature has! One would imagine she had attended Mrs Stowe's academy for young ladies – or Mrs Ansruther's, at least.'

'I cannot imagine Mr Bennet affording either,' observed Louisa. 'Which is a pity, as she has a spirited air. I think I prefer her to her sister.'

'Oh, never – for Miss Bennet has such captivating softness – and with looks such as hers, requires nothing beyond! Do you not agree, Mr Darcy?'

'Miss Bennet is the prettiest, beyond a doubt,' said Darcy, 'but Miss Elizabeth's eyes are unusually fine.'

Caroline, displeased, dropped the subject. At three, the apothecary having been and 'a violent cold' diagnosed, Elizabeth proposed returning home. Miss Bingley was on the point of sending for the carriage when her brother cried, 'You said that she was still feverish?'

'But I do not wish to impose,' said Eliza.

'Impose! You must not think of it as imposing! I shall have the next room made up at once, that you may stay, and improve her comfort as much as anyone can.'

Eliza, relieved and grateful, thanked him from her heart. Had she not been so concerned about Jane, however, she might not have thought Caroline particularly delighted. As soon as she had run upstairs again, that lady remarked, 'What odd manners she has – what a curious mixture of pride and impertinence! And really, this morning, she looked almost wild!'

Louisa laughed. 'She did indeed! And her petticoat – I hope you saw her petticoat. Ankle-deep in mud, I assure you, and the skirt let down not doing its office.'

'I thought Miss Elizabeth looked remarkably well this morning,' said Bingley. 'Her dirty petticoat quite escaped my notice.'

Caroline murmured to Darcy, 'I fear that the episode might have affected your admiration of her "fine eyes."'

'Not at all. They were brightened by the exercise.'

Caroline sighed affectedly. 'I have a great regard for Jane Bennet. What a pity she has such low connections! I understand that there is an uncle at Cheapside.'

'And – ha! – one who was in business in Meryton.'

'Had they uncles enough to fill all Cheapside,' cried Bingley, 'it would not make them one whit less agreeable!'

'But it must make it less likely that they marry men of any importance in the world,' said Darcy – to which not even Bingley could find anything to say.

Chapter 11

(From Mr Darcy's diaries)

I rather wish that Miss Elizabeth Bennet had never come because, as if as recompense for doting on her sister, Miss Bingley appears to have conceived a near-immediate dislike to her. Though for that I might be partly responsible: I was foolish enough to admit to admiring her dark eyes – and Miss Bingley has enjoyed teasing me ever since.

She returned downstairs after dinner, while we were playing at loo, but declined to join us. 'No,' said she, 'I should disgrace your high standards – I shall amuse myself with a book, instead.'

'You prefer reading to cards? How very singular!' observed Hurst.

'Eliza Bennet despises cards,' said Caroline. 'She is a great reader and has no pleasure in anything else.'

Miss Bennet looked surprised and said, 'I deserve neither such praise nor such censure. I am *not* a great reader, and I have pleasure in a great many things.'

Later, after Caroline had lauded my sister Georgiana's accomplishments, Bingley said, 'It amazes me how young ladies can have the patience to be so accomplished as they are! They all seem to paint tables, cover screens and net purses. I scarcely know any young lady who fails to do all this – and I am sure I never heard a young lady mentioned for the first time without being assured that she was very accomplished.'

I said, 'Your list of common accomplishments contains only too much truth. The word is often applied to those who merely net a purse or cover a screen. But I cannot agree with you in your estimation of ladies in general. I cannot have met more than half a dozen whom I consider truly accomplished.'

'Then,' observed Miss Elizabeth, with a smile, 'you must comprehend a great deal in your idea of an accomplished woman.'

I acknowledged as much and Caroline cried, 'Indeed, a woman must have a thorough knowledge of music, singing, drawing, dancing and the modern languages to deserve the word – and must possess a certain something in her air and manner, besides.'

I agreed, but could not resist *this* tweak at Miss Bingley, who too often pretends to have read books which she has never opened – 'and yet to all this she must add substance in the improvement of her mind by extensive reading.'

Miss Elizabeth said, 'I am no longer surprised at your knowing only six accomplished women – I wonder at your knowing any! *I* never saw such a woman – *I* never saw such capacity, taste, application and elegance united!'

At this, there was an outcry from both sisters, and this from the aggrieved Hurst: 'Am I alone in paying the slightest attention to the game at hand?'

Miss Elizabeth took the hint, and took her leave – only to return, much subdued, just as the scores were being tallied. Addressing herself principally to Louisa, she said, 'Forgive me – but Jane is worse. She is so unwell that I know not what to do!'

Bingley instantly proposed sending for the apothecary, but Louisa objected, 'for in darkest Hertfordshire one is as well-off without the local surgeon as with their assistance!'

Caroline was urgent that their town physician be sent for, as he was 'so clever and obliging!' but Mr Hurst shook his head. 'Aye, but *that* was when he had but two miles to traverse. I cannot think he would be agreeable to being summoned from his fireside at such a distance, and at such an hour. And, having delivered this pearl of wisdom, I shall now retire.'

'There is naught amiss with Mr Jones,' said Miss Elizabeth, once he had gone, 'though it is late – it is late, indeed! But how her forehead burns!'

And, in the end, it was decided that Mr Jones be summoned in the morning.

Two things struck me about the business. First, how distraught Charles seemed at this setback and second, how excessively pretty Elizabeth Bennet had looked as she rushed into the drawing-room. However, I had enough sense to keep both these thoughts to myself.

Chapter 12

Netherfield

After a night by her sister's side, Eliza rejoiced to find her very much better in the morning. Having requested that a note to Mrs Bennet might be substituted for one to the apothecary, she descended, in hopes of an early breakfast. As the Netherfield breakfast table was not yet laid, she dawdled about the rockery until ten. There, one of the Netherfield maids found her.

'Begging your pardon, Miss, but the ladies wish to know how Miss Bennet was – and the master, too.'

Eliza returned a courteous response, though reflecting that the 'master' was probably the only one truly concerned.

Returning to the breakfast room, to her utmost dismay, she found Mr Darcy alone. How she wished she had lingered longer about the rockery – even Miss Bingley would have been preferable! He bowed, as if quite as dismayed as she. Then they were entirely silent, but so unnatural did it seem – and before so many servants, too – that she finally suggested, 'Another pleasant day.'

'Indeed.' How stiff and formal he was! But after a moment he added, 'I suspect Miss Bingley will be taking out her new horse.'

'Is she very fond of riding?'

'Nay, is not every young lady fond of riding?'

'Many are, I believe – I do not ride, however.'

'And did not your own sister choose to ride from Longbourn, despite the storm?'

Elizabeth could not endure the implication – particularly as there was more than a grain of truth in it – that Jane had been obliged to ride in hopes that she might be detained at Netherfield. She said, 'Jane had been engaged to spend the day with the ladies, as the gentlemen were supposed to have been absent.'

He acknowledged as much as she added, 'How fortunate it is for Mr Bingley that your family can spare you so often!'

'I fear that I have no family left, beyond my sister, my aunt, and two cousins.'

'I am sorry,' she said, rather struck. His strong, shapely hands were resting lightly against the table. She was reminded of the hands of a well-known pianist whom she had once heard at the Gouldings'. Indeed, with the sun from the window just fingering his dark hair, he was really very well-looking altogether. What a pity it was, for such wealth, breeding and looks to be wasted on so cold and superior a fellow!

Just then, he was delivered of a letter and excused himself.

✦

Shortly after breakfast at Netherfield was concluded, Mrs Bennet, Lydia and Kitty arrived, by carriage, in a great bustle. At the end of their visit, Lydia boldly taxed Mr Bingley with his earlier promise to host a ball, remarking that 'it would be the greatest shame in the world' were he to break his promise.

'I have not the slightest intention of doing so,' said he, 'and I shall soon be sending round my cards. However, you would not wish to be dancing while your sister is ill.'

Elizabeth, catching a glance pass between Miss Bingley and her sister, returned upstairs as soon as she could.

Chapter 13

(From Mr Darcy's diaries)

The letter that I had received at the breakfast table, as I instantly recognised, was from my cousin, Colonel Fitzwilliam. And after I had read it... But first, I must finally commit to paper what happened in Rome. Whether this will relieve my feelings must be doubtful – however, I hope that it might clarify my mind.

I first met Giuditta thanks to Sullivan. An opera enthusiast since our days at school, he had latched onto me, almost gleefully, at the opera in Rome, and from that moment, I could not shake him. I have rarely met a creature so entirely deficient in tact or one more brimming with self-assurance. He even boasted that he had 'led' the applause for Giuditta Menotti's first-act aria – a boast I found entirely credible, for the applause had begun well before the aria was finished.

His arrogance irked me more than it should have, probably because her performance had already undone me. Her *presence* I had been prepared for, but the voice! – from her first note, I was transfixed – and afterwards, transported. I could only recall feeling a similar sense of ecstasy one evening at Pemberley, standing motionless as the sun was setting, transcendently, over the Peaks. And yet there were those in London who called her singing 'earthy' or even 'coarse'!

At the interval, after meeting Sullivan, I should have left – then none of this could ever have happened. But the truth was, I was lonely – I had stalked through galleries till my brain was weary, and admired architecture till even I was sated. It had been a week since I had met with a fellow countryman or spoken anything beyond my own imperfect Italian. For that reason, and despite my reservations, I agreed to meet him after the opera. (I did not commit myself to coffee though, lest his company prove unendurable.)

The final chords having been played and the final curtain calls taken, I found him in a state of high excitement. 'My dear fellow, come with me!'

As I dislike being termed anyone's 'dear fellow' I considered escape, but shortly afterwards found myself at the rear of the theatre – I presumed, from the hurtling past of musicians, at the stage door. I felt a rush of excitement but, strangely enough, much more dismay, at the thought that Giuditta Menotti herself might soon be there. I could not bear for the impression of that voice to be diminished. And then, there were so many others crowding around! Sullivan, still buoyant, seemed to feel very differently.

'I believe I shall go,' I told him.

'Are you mad? I should remain, should the little lady's change of dress take all night!'

'In that case, I must bid you adieu.'

'Do not be such a fool, man!' And then, 'And there she is, indeed!'

And there she was, to rabid applause from her admirers, a silken black cloak gathered about her throat, but with those dark eyes imbued with such fire and spirit that I felt momentarily unable to move.

Not that doing so would have been easy. There must have been any number of admirers there – some perfectly well-behaved, others positively leering – I was secretly appalled at my impulse to crush one fellow to the ground. (Had I lost all common sense in the spiraling colours of that voice?) – And all the while her eyes flashed round, as if impatient for yet another admirer – presumably someone tardy, but still privileged, expected.

Finally, turning to her maid, she murmured something, and appeared prepared to retreat. But then she seemed to notice me – perhaps the only person entirely motionless, silent, and reserved in all that company – and said entreatingly, *'Mi giuterai per favore?'*

Do her a favour? I could only bow, but the elated Sullivan was 'only too delighted, most honoured, indeed!' and within half a minute he had not only procured a municipal carriage but ushered her and her maid inside. It was a very down-at-heel sample of the species, but what was that, when Giuditta Menotti was within? For perhaps the first time in our long acquaintance, I accepted the usefulness of Sullivan's existence!

But only momentarily. After officiously acquainting the coachman with the lady's address, and without the smallest encouragement from herself, he elected to dissect, in order, the opera, the production, the costumes and the conducting – being particularly scathing with regard to the last. Once, she glanced over at me, half-laughing, as if to silently protest, 'But it was *you* I chose, not *he*!'

I felt myself flushing, as if the fault were my own, but the second time it happened I dared to hold her gaze, during which my own heart seemed to crash headlong into the side of my chest. I had thought her beauty terrifying on stage – off-stage, it silenced me.

As we drew up outside the property, we both leaped down to assist her. She had the choice – Sullivan or myself – but he took his defeat in very good part, bowing low as her glove briefly clasped my hand.

'Chiamami,' she told me, very softly, before sweeping away, her maid scurrying after her.

Call on her. *Call on her!* I felt shocked, almost shaken, but Sullivan was exultant. Anyone would have imagined our circumstances reversed, as we ordered the coachman to turn his horses around. Never in all my life had I been more tempted to boast, for what did she know of me? Nothing – and yet, that look! That soft, *'Chiamami'*!

But had she meant it? Distrustfully, I recalled all that I had ever heard of continental ladies, their lack of inhibition, their liveliness, their mockery of English habits. So celebrated a singer might be accustomed to mix with well-dressed foreigners. Or she might perhaps have supposed that I was one of those English aristocrats who make a habit of sponsoring opera singers – a thing I have never attempted, being the first male in my family to care for music, and no aristocrat, besides. And yet that look, the soft pressure of that gloved hand within my own!

Meanwhile, Sullivan babbled on: 'I cannot suppose that you observed it, but it was most apparent that she liked me very well indeed. The smile in her eyes, the dimples in her cheeks! Her every glance pregnant with allure! I believe, my good Darcy, I shall try my luck and call on her tomorrow. After all, what is the very worst that could happen? – she might send word that she was not at home!'

'Nay, if you are as confident as that, why delay? Why not tonight?'

'I assure you,' he said crossly, 'the signals, to anyone possessing the slightest instinct, were clear enough!'

'To what signals do you refer? Do instruct me, for I am sure I lack your insight.'

Sullivan preened. 'The arts of the feminine have long been a study of mine, of musicians most particularly. As for female singers – they are the maestras! The way in which, of the two of us, she privileged *you* rather than myself spoke volumes!'

'Did it, indeed?'

'Of course. It was you whom she first implored for assistance, and you to whom she confided that adorable little hand, at the close. But this was all a blind, a game, a tease – for she was directing that burning gaze at me, all the while! She could not trust herself so near to me!'

There was a good deal more in the same vein, which – I must confess – did divert me, for I could not believe myself to have been mistaken. But I excused myself as soon as I could, and strode back to my hotel, vowing to call on the lady the next morning, as she had suggested.

The next day dawned gloriously, the air as crisp as the pines and cypresses about the Coliseum, as I returned to the diva's house. At the gate, I hesitated, for was there any excuse beyond her whispered invitation? – while I had no wish to appear Sullivanesque. In fact, I might very well never have called had not a passing footman, observing me, offered assistance. I thought of pretending to have mistaken the address. Instead, I heard myself saying, 'Is this the residence of Miss Giuditta Menotti?'

A minute later I was in the vestibule, and being shown into an ornate reception room, where she reclined, fiddling discontentedly with her rings. 'Marietta! Where in heaven's name is – oh! So you are here, *Signor*!'

I merely bowed as she regarded me.

At last she said, with just the slightest tilt of her chin, 'And so, *Signor,* why do *you* not find my garnet bracelet?'

Yes, that impudence marked our beginning.

Forgetting – for surely, she must be the most forgetful creature alive – her antique bracelet, we sat down together. Omitting introductions, she quizzed me with the greatest impatience about my family, my home, my background, my schooling… Sometimes she cut me short with her answers – at others she chided me for cautiousness. I have never received so powerful an impression that ours was an acquaintance *resumed* rather than embarked upon – or felt such confusion, besides.

'And your mother?'

I said, 'My father –'

'I am not interested in your father. They are always most boring! What was she like, your mama?'

'It is difficult to –'

'Try,' said she, that black-eyed gaze bending deeply into my own.

'My mother – my mother was rather delicate, but clever, accomplished, musical.'

'So,' she said. 'Rather like you.'

35

I had nothing to say to this. Instead, I mentioned Georgiana – and was again fiercely interrupted. '*No, no*, so young, so dull – Tell me of your *amanti*, instead!'

But I had no lovers of whom to tell. Nor would I have mentioned them if I had.

'Come, my handsome English milord,' she whispered, leaning forward, 'if you cannot even find my poor bracelet – *Marietta, non dimenticare il bracciale!* – then you must pay for your omission. There must have been *someone*! There must have been the moment, the encounter, the –' And then, regarding me, she unleashed those dimples again. 'But – ha! – perhaps there are things even the handsome milord has yet to learn?'

My half-hearted objections were dismissed: 'No, demi-gods do not arrive at my home every day!' And to her faithful Marietta – whom I was to know so well – *'Marietta, il bracciale!'* And with that, she locked her warm hand inside my own and said, very firmly, 'But first, we must eat.'

It was the beginning of the most extraordinary fortnight of my life. After which – entirely unwillingly, for her manners were impossible and her language outrageous – I found myself not only passionately in love, but entirely unable to determine what to do about it.

For a start, we quarrelled constantly, and I cannot think that I am a naturally quarrelsome fellow. Giuditta had, along with her perfections, obstinate ideas, mostly imbibed either from her upbringing – she had emerged from a tempestuous family – or from her temperament. She could quarrel with an oyster – she could quarrel with an ornamental cushion. After sharpening her claws on these, she would reach the summit of fury with me.

The fourth night I attended her – I was *obliged* to attend her, I could never be excused, lest her witchcraft fail – she introduced me to some Venetians as 'her English milord'. I endured this at the time but rebuked her in the carriage: 'You cannot conceive my embarrassment – and it was untrue besides, for I am a commoner, as well as no plaything of yours!'

'And yet *you* are only playing with *me*!'

'Believe me, Giuditta, I am in no mood for play.'

'What, not at all?' (Those warm little fingers!)

'Nay, do not test me.'

'It is *you,* milord, who is testing me…' But only a moment later, very mournfully, 'You do not care for me at all!'

'How can you tell such lies?' I returned – and truthfully too, for I was very far gone by that point.

'*Bugiardo!* Because you do not say soft and pretty things to me, as you did before!'

I longed to say that, if I could contrive to get a word in edgeways, there might be a better chance of this occurring. And also, that I am not the kind of man to flatter a woman. Perhaps my silence enraged her, as she began to upbraid me – under her breath, though I suspect that her servant heard every word. But perhaps it was not unusual for her to curse her admirers, or even to whisper, in order to spare that glorious voice?

I felt that I owed it to my reputation to halt the carriage, and to descend from it without a word. I secretly swore that I would never see her more – but I called the next morning, just the same.

Why? How many times have I asked myself this question! I was no laggard at school, regularly coming first in my class; while I did so well at Oxford that I was advised to publish my thesis. Why, then, could I not extricate myself – why did she thus over-master me? Why, with Giuditta alone, was I so helpless?

DARCY

I had never been in love before – that might have played some part in the business. There are those who claim that the first fall, as from a horse, is the hardest. But I suspect it was the music.

In music, I had never been encouraged. My father held strong views on its being a distraction from the business of life, and only suitable for foreigners and young ladies. It was for my mother's sake that he attended the opera – which was, as it remains, a place to be seen. But I had always secretly longed to play, and sought for any excuse to learn the violoncello or the violin… but it was not approved for one of my rank, beyond the quirks of royalty, for even the Prince Regent attempted the violoncello!

In compensation, perhaps, I have encouraged my sister all her life – the best masters, the best instruments – and she sings very prettily, though her pianoforte playing is probably superior. Yet to compare Georgiana to Giuditta would be like comparing a wood pigeon to a nightingale. Giuditta's voice is, to my mind, perfection. She can conjure up a note, from the softest hint, and enable it to resound in the farthest depths of a theatre. She can warm it from within, and colour it gold! I cannot count the times when, fired up and furious, made miserable by her mockery, I heard that voice and felt my entire being, my entire soul, vibrating in sympathy. It was less a kinship than a collision – sometimes, a violent one. And yes, I *did* occasionally wonder if I was not in love with the voice.

Of course, the voice was also a curse. It could be destroyed by the smallest possible difficulty – whether emotional, physical or even imaginary – her every servant stood in awe of it. I found it entirely mystifying how someone who – only a moment before – might be as thoughtful and generous as any creature in the world would – the next moment – snap my head off, from fear of losing her voice! The tiny beauty could storm like a madwoman – and how she treated me then is not to be told.

The ninth evening we spent together – the second week of our acquaintance – was after a performance during which she sang bewitchingly enough to drive an entire regiment mad. Still, she wept against my shoulder because she could feel the voice going. 'It is fading, failing – there was a moment in the second act… Oh, no one can imagine what I suffered! Silvio was pushing me, too fast, too fast on the semiquavers – ah! He does not know what he does to me, and to my voice!'

The exquisite sensation of her heart so near my own, as she wept, 'It goes, it goes, the timbre, the floating high notes, the pianissimo – I can feel it – every moment, it is slipping away! I wish that I was dead!'

I assured her again and again, over and over, that her high notes were as arrow-like yet soft-edged as ever – but she remained inconsolable. While her warmth – even through her cloak – was so disquieting that it was all I could do to control my impulse to kiss her. She surely guessed my feelings, for she said, in low and urgent tones, *'Stai con me stanotte!'*

If only I could have 'stayed the night'! But – had I done so – had I dared – could I have faced myself in the morning? I had been brought up an English gentleman, though no English 'milord'. Thus, I did not – and she was affronted.

Perhaps that was why Sullivan's jealousy so rankled, for when I met him on the way to Giuditta's the next morning he attempted to be witty on the subject. 'I hear – ha! – that you have muscled in on my *amour*. Not the best form, would you say, my dear fellow?'

'I have not the pleasure of understanding you,' I said coldly.

'Nay, you need not pretend, 'tis only too clear! She has been "out" – the impudent creature – to everyone ever since, and I paid her maid to learn the rest. An English milord, she said – so you have been pretentious about your birth, to cap all!'

'I have never, in the whole of my life, pretended to be of noble birth.'

'And so, is it true, as one hears, that she is as inventive in the bedchamber as she is on the stage?' After which he added so coarse an addition that I cannot record it here. I probably coloured as I retorted, 'I would advise you to apologise for that implication – and without loss of time.'

But Sullivan only said, 'If I were you, I should take good care all the same, for the lady's relatives are mostly Sicilian. And I happen to know a bass-baritone who adores her – and whilst on stage the tenor prevails, in real life it is always the bass who triumphs!'

I continued towards Giuditta's, greatly discomposed, not because of any Sicilian (or indeed, bass-baritone) but instead because of Sullivan's own reputation, as one of the greatest rattles in London. In his current mood of curmudgeonly disappointment, whom might he not tell? For one mad moment I very nearly called him back, with some notion of bribing him to silence, just as he had bribed Giuditta's maid to disclosure.

This thought so appalled me that I had to restore myself in a dark and dingy coffee house. There – where I was one of only two customers – I vowed that I would part from her. I even bought an antique brooch, of amethyst with inlaid pearls, for her to remember me by... Yet still, I could not do it.

That evening, Giuditta was in sparkling mood. She teased me most delightfully, laughed the way only a singer can laugh at Sullivan's displeasure and – despite one moment of dangerous discontent – confided, '*Mio dio*! Your friend must have wasted a great deal of money, for Marietta is so faithful, in general! And so, this was your fat froggy friend – the *rosto*! As if I should have him, even for a footstool!'

And walking home, I found myself meditating on the unthinkable.

She had been so serene, so piquant, so confiding, that I found myself wondering – yes, and dreaming too. I kept imagining her, in the same gown that she wore in the third act, walking down the aisle of St George's, Hanover Square – or down the shorter aisle in the chapel at Pemberley, a few soft tangled ringlets escaping onto her temple, giving me that dark and thrilling look from underneath her lashes.

I imagined her sitting across from me at the breakfast table in Grosvenor Street, ridiculously demure in one of her day dresses. I reminded myself that there *were* married women who still performed as singers or actresses – though few indeed.

It was all madness, of course. I could not imagine what people would say. An Italian *noblewoman* might be acceptable, but Giuditta was undistinguished either by birth or by fortune. If one inclined towards the brutal, she was a beauty with a voice. I recollected hearing Lady Catherine maintain that opera dancers – by whom I presume she meant the ladies of the chorus – were no more respectable than ballet girls, though I cannot imagine her encountering either.

Still I continued to daydream, although knowing that daydreams were all that they could ever be. For I knew, all along, that any serious candidate for the post of Mistress of Pemberley would require wealth or an ancient family – or else a name of some political renown.

Yet in the stillness of that hot Italian night – as I could hear, from the courtyard, strolling players, sudden bursts of folksong, someone hallooing in the distance – I found myself wondering, was not *I* the failure? Given her astonishing gifts, who and what was I? How was a moneyed wastrel reckoned worthier than she, who could

41

tussle a high B-flat into submission, and in pianissimo besides? I, who had nearly lost my sister to a reprobate? – I, who had done, since my university days, nothing of any note at all?

I had even failed at wickedness, for – despite every indication of her willingness – I had steadfastly withstood her every effort at seduction. Yet how sweetly, how beguilingly, had she recently behaved! Was it possible that Giuditta herself might have heard of Pemberley? – or had she simply despaired of inveigling me into her bed in any other fashion?

In short, I was dreaming of impossibilities – of Giuditta performing for the Prince Regent – of Giuditta, surrounded by darkly pretty children, riding across the grass of Pemberley. While meanwhile still enjoying, as I always did, the colourful disorder of the Roman streets – the colonnaded buildings surrounded by broken marbles in neglected gardens, the ragged organ-grinders outside the opera house. Also, at times, the conjunction – of Giuditta and London – seemed too wild for even my imagination. Instead, I imagined a *palazzo* in Rome, or Venice – I imagined Giuditta on a gondola along the Grand Canal: I imagined long and languorous Italian nights.

Most of all, of course, I dreamed of being no longer alone, as I had always felt myself to be. I remember, when very young, asking my mother whether everyone felt lonely all the time. She had sighed and said, 'Why do you always ask such strange things? How my head aches!'

Nor had I felt less alone when sent away to play with 'young Wickham' for there was no natural sympathy between us. Once my sister was born, I preferred to read to Georgiana, for – almost from birth – she had a soft air that was very soothing. But as a companion, at ten years my junior, she was still unsatisfactory. No, whether at school or at home, books were my closest companions, and music my secret solace. Small wonder I dreamed of the passion that Giuditta so powerfully expressed each night in the Opera House!

I was still thinking of impossibilities the following morning as I knocked on the door to Giuditta's house. I was surprised when Marietta appeared, instead of Luciano or Tomas, and felt a swift pang of misgiving. Was that pity in those wide eyes? She curtseyed then and said, '*Per favore, devo dirle, dalla signora, che è impegnata.*'

Too busy to see me – and at so early an hour? How I longed to inquire! but pride – or the avid curiosity in the maid's gaze – prevented me. Instead, I turned and walked down the path without a word.

Yet something told me, in that moment, that Sullivan had been right. The only part I could not fathom, the part I most longed to know, was whether she was closeted with the bass-baritone in hopes of driving me mad, or because he had truly succeeded me in her affections. Because she *had* wanted me – I had felt the oppression of her longing from our first meeting. She had tested me – and severely, too – but I had kissed nothing beyond her temple, and that burning hand. What a strange tempest of feelings possessed me then, of jealousy and exhilaration, of pride and misery! For she had broken me, yet never broken me. Where almost every other man would have failed, I had remained steadfast. We had been lovers – but never lovers – and, though I passionately envied the bass-baritone, my regret was almost equalled by my relief.

My feelings about the bass-baritone himself were less conflicted. I had never seen the fellow, so I was unaware of his personal attractions, but the fact that he was Italian, with a fluency in the language and – most likely – in the language of seduction as well, was enough to inflame me. Hardly knowing what I did, I walked from her house, which was not far from the Teatro Argentina, straight past Gerolamo Theodoli's superb façade and then along a series of narrow and odorous lanes towards the River Tiber. I was besieged by urchins and beggars and even hailed by an English acquaintance, whom I politely refused to join for a meal. What I wanted, in addition to fresh air – or for what passed for fresh air in Rome at the time of year – was time to think.

I sat by the river – then as now, impossibly dirty but still majestic – with a view of the Castel Sant'Angelo.

I had two choices – to wait and to learn, perhaps from Marietta, perhaps from Giuditta herself, what had occurred in my absence. (Or had nothing occurred, and she was merely hoping to push me beyond endurance? – She was incalculable!)

The wind had a stormy feel and, as I gazed out on the Tiber – grey, ruffled – I decided not to linger, but to accept my dismissal at face value. Watching the river rushing past, I vowed that I would never tell a soul what had happened in Rome, or the reason why I had delayed my return, or the reason why I would – and so suddenly – soon be leaving.

I returned to my lodgings and directed my man to pack at once. This admirable fellow asked not a single question, but set to immediately, with a view towards leaving in a few hours, which we did. I half-expected, every moment, for Marietta to rush in with a message, but I have never seen her since.

And so, that is the whole – I swear it – of the whole, sorry tale.

Yet the letter from my cousin – the letter which had driven me from the Netherfield breakfast table – was nothing more or less than this: the lady was suing me for breach of promise. Yes, she had sufficient effrontery to sue, despite my never having asked for her hand – for though a fool, I was never quite an utter fool!

DARCY

My dear Darcy,

Forgive my importuning you but it is a matter of some moment. I called on Jameson yesterday and found him exceedingly concerned. He has received a communication from the lawyer of the famous opera singer, Miss Giuditta Menotti, complaining that you offered to her whilst in Rome, and then departed. Of course, neither of us give the slightest credence to her unsupported word, but I promised to see you, to discuss the business, as soon as may be. You may expect me, therefore, on Thursday, which I trust will be acceptable to Bingley and his sister. If it is not, the nearest inn will suffice, as I cannot stay above a few days, in any case. Yours etc. Fitzwilliam

At first, upon reading this, everything went black. I stood looking sightlessly over Netherfield's sloping lawn, seeing nothing, receiving nothing, half-drowning in a silent storm of fury and humiliation. Jameson is, of course, our lawyer, while the Colonel has access to all of my affairs – and to Pemberley's, besides. But what in heaven's name could she be thinking of? For I had never, even in my maddest moments, even when she had so feared for her voice that she had wished for death – never had I mentioned marriage! (I admit that I did think of it. But only in these pages.)

I recalled all the times I had heard of such things ('Bunyan's got into a spot of trouble with Miss Percival, have you heard?'… 'They say he is all to pieces, and being taken to court by Lady Elliott for breach'… 'Not even his brother knows what he is about! He cannot stop offering to such women, and *they*, as everyone knows, have nothing to lose.')

I had heard such rumours with scant attention – and with scant sympathy, as well. Secretly, I always thought, 'I never rated Bunyan very highly' or 'What kind of a fool would get himself in quite such a mess?' And even, 'That's Sir Hubert done for. Who

45

would marry him, after this?' The idea that *I* might ever be spoken of as a fool, or as some species of cad, made me writhe. And yes, I have been called proud, but the thought of 'Darcy of Pemberley' on everyone's lips at Brooks's and at every other gentlemen's club in London was unbearable. Whatever she wanted – beyond marriage, of course – why, she must have! Anything so that Georgiana and indeed all my acquaintance might not consider me a fool!

But then my spirit revolted. How dared she imagine that I could be so imposed upon? She had no proof that I had ever offered to her (how glad I was, that I had kept the brooch of amethyst and pearls!) And how I longed for Fitzwilliam's steady presence, even as I shrank from telling him all that had occurred, for how could my cousin ever respect me again, after opening myself to blackmail?

With my mind thus whipped into a fiery mix of fury and impatience, Caroline Bingley's making up to me was astonishingly ill-timed. Dinner was bad enough – 'Of course, our plate cannot equal yours at Pemberley, but Charles did do rather well with this set. I fancy the tiny roses not inelegant. What is *your* opinion, Mr Darcy?' She also tested my patience that evening as I wrote a short note to Georgiana ('How ever can you contrive to write so even?') – At that, I even detected a momentary contempt in Miss Elizabeth's pretty countenance… It was a relief when the sisters favoured us with a duet – though one possessing an unfortunate association, as I had once heard Giuditta sing it. But I was so determined to appear unaffected that, when Caroline chose to follow it with a Scottish dance, I obliged myself to suggest, 'Do you not wish, Miss Bennet, to take this opportunity of dancing a reel?'

When she made no response, I assumed she had not heard and repeated my offer – whereupon she released so impudent a smile that I was rocked back on my heels. 'Oh!' said she, 'I heard you perfectly the first time, but I could not immediately determine what to say in reply. You wished me, I know, to say "Yes," that you might have the pleasure of despising my taste. But as I delight in overthrowing such schemes, I have made up my mind to tell you that I do not wish to dance a reel at all – and now – you may despise me if you dare.'

'Indeed, I do not dare,' I returned – and very nearly meant it. What a piquant wit!

But I was in no humour for company all the same, and went upstairs as soon as I could, to re-read the Colonel's note and to recollect all that I must tell him on the morrow.

Chapter 14

Longbourn

Mary sat back to inspect her handiwork. Very nice – very nice, indeed! – She had created as charming a cover as anyone could desire. The title – *The Wisdom and Wit of Miss Mary Bennet* – was particularly pleasing, with an identical flourish on both 'Ws'.

Its subtitle – *A Consideration of the Great Truths Contained Within Fordyce's Sermons to Young Women* – looked rather less perfect. She had miscalculated the size, and the final letters looked a trifle crushed, in consequence. But her publisher would resolve such matters in the final edition – once she had procured a publisher, as she most certainly would.

Despite her being constantly underestimated, even ridiculed, by her family at Longbourn, the world would one day awaken to her philosophical genius. Unlike such trivial-minded lady scribes as Mary Wroth, she had no interest in genealogies – and very little in novels. A steely passion for the great truths was her watchword, and she often wished that young ladies were as encouraged to be as fond of philosophy as of music, for she secretly preferred the former to the latter… With a sigh, she re-read the opening of her last entry:

As Fordyce so ably comments: 'There is in female youth an attraction which every man of the least sensibility must perceive. If assisted by beauty, it becomes in the first impression irresistible.'

In other words, thought Mary gloomily, men care for nothing beyond looks. Really, as a species, men were quite hopeless. She picked up her pen and continued.

For proof, one need look no farther than upon the last Meryton assembly. There, I assure you, were gathered gentlemen of all types and of every station, from the disdainful Mr Darcy – related by blood to Dukes and Earls though no nobleman himself – down to poor Mr Hartley, who is never truly at ease in society.

Yet every person of the masculine persuasion appeared equally smitten by my eldest sister, Jane. And what is there in Jane, to so smite them? Does she display unusual brilliance in conversation, or dance more prettily than the rest of us? Is she capable of deep observation? Or does she, perchance, convulse the company with the brilliance of her repartee?

She does not. Yet despite this it was – and on every side – 'Miss Bennet's complexion… Miss Bennet's air… A goddess! She is all perfection!' – even though the simplest book fatigues her and she has not a tithe of such information as even Lizzy possesses. Yet even Mr Darcy described her as 'the only handsome woman in the room'

– meaning, the only creature in the room handsome enough to dance with.

But – and this is the point I must stress – after hearing this opinion, Mr Bingley should have rebuked him, saying, 'But, in terms of worth, my friend, you should consider such solider assets as accomplishments, intelligent action and good works.' Or as Fordyce puts it, 'the result of gentler feelings, and a more elegant humanity.' Instead, Mr Bingley abused his friend's taste and recommended Lizzy, as being both 'quite handsome and probably agreeable.' (Please note! Not well-principled or well-read! Note – too – that Lizzy's 'handsomeness' was stressed, even above her character.)

Thousands of young ladies would never have noticed this but, as my father once said, 'Mary is deep. She is so deep she may sink altogether, one of these days.'

But to return to my argument, my two elder sisters are very pretty – prettier, at least, than my younger sisters or myself. Thus, whenever we are in company, Jane, and (after Jane) Lizzy, invariably receives the most attention. This is evidenced by the amount of time that men choose to speak to them, chat to them or even glance in their direction. It does not signify how brilliant a comment I might make, or how silly a joke Lydia might produce… Men seem curiously impervious to a well-turned phrase – at least, in comparison to a well-turned ankle. I might be instructing the company on the philosophy of music, perhaps, and never receive more than a nod – while if Jane but drops her handkerchief, every male in the room is falling over themselves in their zeal to restore it.

So, looks are everything, to men – and to some ladies, likewise. My own parents' marriage stands as proof, for my father was entirely beguiled before he realised that poor Mama cannot add up, can play only two tunes on the pianoforte, and is incapable of following a serious line of thought.

As Fordyce might well have said, had he thought of it: *Est quodcumque est*. (Or: It is what it is.)

Yet I submit that such superior and long-lasting attributes as character and abilities ought to be preferred, instead. I am myself intensely musical – I am probably more musical than all four of my sisters combined, for Eliza rarely practises, and can make the most terrible muddle of the left hand. But Eliza is naturally witty, which I am not. (I have even heard Mrs Long say, 'La! What drudgery it is to engage Miss Mary in conversation!')

In short, I have endeavoured to be witty but without signal success, so I have determined upon increasing the depth of my knowledge instead. This must be the likeliest way in which I might attract some man to marry me – an important consideration, given that Longbourn is entailed. Though I am only nineteen, which is rather too young to despair, the utter unsuitability of anyone in Meryton – at least, for one of my intellectual cast – remains a serious concern.

Though I have *this* consolation: should I really be doomed to spinsterhood, this can only benefit the already substantial depth of my thinking. In the stilly watches of the night, I cannot decide whether I would prefer to be a famous philosopher or an important poet, but I am confident that my true and immortal destiny will become clear – to myself, if not to the family with whom an all-seeing God has seen fit to try my patience. To quote Cowper:

I see, or think I see
A glimm'ring from afar,
A beam of day, that shines for me,
To save me from despair.

Nil desperandum!

(Partially excerpted from *The Wisdom and Wit of Miss Mary Bennet*. Part the first. Edition the first, likewise.)

Chapter 15

(From Mr Darcy's diaries)

While awaiting the Colonel's arrival the next morning – with what impatience might be imagined – I agreed to walk with Miss Bingley. The weather was fine and the Netherfield flowerbeds remarkably so – but she continued to harp, in a manner she probably considers amusing, on my supposed passion for the second Miss Bennet. While I could not help thinking, 'If she only knew of the breach of promise suit, how shaken she would be!'

'I hope,' said she, as we were walking in the shrubbery, 'you might perhaps give your mother-in-law a few hints, when this desirable event does take place, as to the advantage of holding her tongue – and, if you can compass it, cure the younger girls of running after every officer in Meryton. And, if I might mention so delicate a subject, you might also endeavour to check that little conceit and impertinence, which your lady's own manner possesses.'

'Have you any other advice for my domestic felicity?' I inquired.

'Oh! Only this, as for your Elizabeth's portrait, you must not attempt to have it taken, for what painter could do justice to those beautiful eyes?'

I was surprised to catch, in Miss Bingley's expression as she glanced up at me, a sudden reminder of Charles's, when smitten. Utterly dismayed, I thought, 'Could it really be true that Miss Bingley is not, in reality, the artificial creature I have always thought her, but – in some fashion – has come to care for me?' How ardently I hoped I was mistaken! – But just then, emerging from behind the great hedge – could they possibly have overheard us? – we encountered Louisa Hurst and Elizabeth Bennet, herself.

Miss Bingley instantly began to upbraid her sister for choosing to walk without telling her. (They often had minor spats, in which Charles wisely played no part.) At the end of this one, Mrs Hurst dropped Miss Elizabeth's arm, and took my own.

This surprised me for, though Louisa can be forthright, she is very rarely rude. I attempted to soften the offence by proposing that we turn into the avenue, but Miss Bennet only laughed, disclaimed, and slipped past, observing that we 'appeared to uncommon advantage' grouped as we were. It is rare for a woman to run with grace but – I must admit – her light figure sustained it perfectly.

'Apparently,' said Louisa, in an undertone, 'Jane Bennet is rather better, and they are to return home. Whereupon poor Charles will doubtless go into a decline and perish, regretted by all.'

'Not he,' said I, 'for he failed to perish when Lady Diana was wed.'

'Well, let us hope he can recover his manners, at least, and become conversable again.'

But when Miss Bennet did come downstairs – looking pale but very lovely – Bingley was devout in his attendance. He told her, 'I do hope, when our ball here *does* take place, that you will dance with me again.' As she confusedly agreed, Miss Bingley cried, 'Surely, Charles, you are not serious in meditating a dance? For I am much mistaken if there are not *some* amongst us to whom a ball would be more of a punishment than a pleasure.'

'If you mean Darcy, he may go to bed before it begins – but as for the ball, it is a settled thing. I told Mrs Emmerson that I shall send round my cards next Tuesday.'

'I should like balls infinitely better,' said Caroline, 'if they were carried on in a different manner. It would be much more rational if conversation instead of dancing was made the order of the day.'

'Much more rational, my dear Caroline, I daresay, but not nearly so much like a ball.'

Shortly afterwards, while I was growing impatient for the Colonel's arrival, I was surprised to observe Miss Bingley perambulating about the room, arm-in-arm with Miss Elizabeth. She instantly invited me to join them, but I observed that I could admire their figures very much better seated by the fire.

'How abominable!' she cried delightedly, adding to her companion, 'How shall we punish him for this?'

Miss Elizabeth said, 'Nothing could be easier, I am sure. We can all tease and plague each other – Intimate as you are, you must know how it can be done.'

'I assure you that intimacy has not taught me *that*. Tease calmness of temper and presence of mind! Nay, Mr Darcy is not to be laughed at.'

'Mr Darcy is not to be laughed at!' she repeated. 'That is an uncommon advantage – and uncommon I hope it will remain, for I dearly love to laugh.'

And when I observed that even the wisest of men could be made ridiculous by those whose first object in life is a joke, she returned lightly, 'That there are such people I admit, but I hope I am not one of them. I hope I never ridicule what is wise or good. Follies and nonsense, whims and inconsistencies, *do* divert me, I own – but these, I suppose, are precisely what you are without?'

'Perhaps *that* is not possible,' I said, uncomfortably. 'But I have always strived to avoid those weaknesses that might expose a strong understanding to ridicule.'

'Such as vanity, or pride?'

'*Vanity* is a weakness indeed. But, where there is a real superiority of mind, pride will be always under good regulation.'

Caroline then requested the result of her examination, upon which Miss Elizabeth said lightly, 'I am perfectly convinced that Mr Darcy has no defect. He owns it himself, without disguise.'

And here, I could have let the matter drop, yet somehow, I could not. I said, 'Nay, I have faults enough, but they are not, I hope, of understanding. My character is too little yielding – I cannot forget the follies and vices of others as soon as I ought. My temper might be called resentful. And my good opinion, once lost, is lost for ever.'

The lady said, '*That* is a failing indeed – implacable resentment is a shade upon a character! But you are safe from me – you have chosen your flaw well – for truly, I cannot laugh at it!'

For the next ten minutes, I found myself unable to concentrate on my book. Instead, I kept recollecting her impish turn of phrase ('That is an uncommon advantage, and uncommon I hope it remains... I am perfectly convinced that Mr Darcy has no defect. He owns it himself, without disguise.') It was not merely the elegance of her wit – it was the mixture of impudence and sweetness in her countenance. Truth be told, I have learned to relish that tilt of chin, that flash of fire in those dark eyes. I will be sorry when the Bennet sisters are gone, for the loveliness of the first, and the quickness of the second, are such an addition!

As for the elder Bennet sister, I cannot deny that Bingley is attracted, but that is as far as the business will go. Louisa's intuitiveness, for once, has led her astray, but it is not my place to set her right.

＊

The Colonel arrived, and made himself as agreeable as ever, but my longing to speak to him privately was frustrated at every turn. First, Bingley insisted upon showing him around his new domain. Later, Caroline begged him to play her at chess, 'for' – looking teasingly at me – 'Mr Darcy first gave me a pawn and then a rook and then pretended it was chess no longer!'

Anxious to get on, I said, 'The Colonel, I am sure, would love nothing better, but might you postpone it for an hour? He has come, not only to enjoy your company, but also on business, and I shall not be easy till the business is done.'

She agreed, of course. I took the Colonel out of doors, for fear of our being overheard, and he thanked me.

'Well done,' said he. 'The Bingleys are wonderfully hospitable, but really, we must speak. And, my dear cousin, please forgive me if I speak bluntly, as well. The news is worrying. Mistress Menotti says, and her own maid also, that you visited her every day, and attended her every evening, for weeks altogether! Yet you assert that nothing occurred?'

'Nay, a very great deal occurred – at least, on my side. But I never offered to her. In the entire course of my life, I have never offered to anyone!'

We walked on. 'I understand,' said he, 'that she can act any actress off the stage, while the voice –'

'She is an actress, indeed! – for I believed that she cared for me. But is it so impossible that she merely intended to – to draw me in, and then to sue for breach of promise?'

Fitzwilliam hesitated, and then, 'It is not impossible, Darcy. But let us proceed in a more orderly fashion. I imagine that your fascination was with the voice, primarily?'

How I hate discussing feelings – or being obliged to confess to weakness! It was all intolerable! – yet, as I had no choice, I said, 'Not at all, I desired her deeply – and how I resisted, I still cannot conceive.'

'Forgive me – and yet you *did* resist?'

'I did.'

'Consistently? Unambiguously?'

'I swear it.'

He breathed out a great sigh and said, 'You did wonderfully well then, and – and, I hope, we ought to see our way clear. But how did you resist?'

'Partly, I resisted because I feared her. She is of low birth, of great impetuosity, of careless habits. Who knows what disease such vitality might disguise that could have blighted myself, or even stained our progeny? – But there was more. I feared her character, her fire, even as it fascinated me. I was captivated, nearly enslaved – the power she wielded was almost terrifying. I could depart from her villa, from her carriage – I could tramp through the streets of Rome vowing that I would never see her more – yet she drew me back with her music, with her... It was a bewitchment, almost a torture – I was no longer entirely sane!'

Fitzwilliam shook his head. 'It sounds like a *coup de foudre*, and that you had a most fortunate escape! And you may still comfort yourself that you never stained the family honour, as I did with that infernal duel.'

'But –'

'But that is all by the bye. I still fear that you might, despite the most honourable intent, have imperilled your reputation. First, I must ask, were you ever alone together with the lady in question?'

'On the continent, as you well know –'

'I mean, quite alone, and in her private chamber?'

'In the garden, in the drawing-room – and yes, in her chamber. There was one evening after we had had words –'

'You argued?' prompted my cousin.

'We were continually arguing, if it can be termed an argument, when *one* party is mostly silent. Yet even in her furies there was a fascination, in the tone of her voice, in the poise of her head, in those glorious eyes! She could cast abuse more musically than most women can compliment!'

'But you attended her in her chambers, and entirely alone?' And, when I nodded, he could not refrain from expostulating, 'Good God, man! Why did you not leave Rome?'

'Why, indeed? Can you imagine that I did not tell myself to, day after day and night after night? I would have given my very soul to leave, but I could not. She was messy, taunting, late, even rude, but I endured it all. She cherished her voice as if it were a baby – I indulged her in everything. She teased me – she berated me – she threw her little shoes at my head – and I *returned* them to her!'

'You were in love, Darcy. A variety of love, at any rate.'

'If it was, indeed, love, then I would not wish it on my most fervent enemy! I have been so cured of the sickness as to wish to never endure it again.'

'Nay, you are not even thirty!'

'And yet I hope to have left such intensity of feeling behind me.'

57

'I should hope, as your senior, that you have plenty of feeling left, at such an age as yours! – And so, did you truly never mention marriage?'

'Never – but never did I stop thinking of it.'

'Or pledge undying passion?'

'No – yes – perhaps once, in a way. But I was never *quite* such a fool.' The Colonel frowned thoughtfully as I added, 'But – what to do?'

'Oh, *that* much is clear. You must entrust all this to Jameson, and swiftly too. The lady might not be serious – she might be merely piqued, at your escape. But she might be very serious indeed. She might be in difficulties – or in debt. Does she gamble?'

'Only on myself,' I said bitterly.

Fitzwilliam hesitated, then, 'I think it possible that she has decided to gamble on you again – and on your honour, besides. Which you have already proven means a great deal to you. I did wonder at your unexpected return from Rome!'

'I do not believe I once slept – in tavern, inn or hostelry – till reaching Pemberley again.'

'It will be difficult for a man of your stamp to be entirely open with Jameson – still, I believe you must try. He is trustworthy, experienced, unshockable – and has the best interests of the family at heart. And there is Georgiana to think of.'

'Lately, believe me, I have thought of little else. But is there no other way? Must I confide in Jameson?'

Colonel Fitzwilliam stroked his chin thoughtfully. 'Might you put it down on paper, instead? You wrote a famous thesis at Oxford. And I believe you keep a journal?'

'I do and have done for years. But I could no more write to Jameson than –'

'Perhaps *I* might serve as your representative, instead?'

'What!' I cried. 'You would do that much, for me?'

'I would, and with a good deal less trouble, for I could relate the facts with less distress. And so, if you could commit it to paper, and trust me so far –'

As I silently grasped his hand, he added, 'I am honoured, Darcy, and trust that all will be well. I know enough already to give Jameson strong reason for hope... And now for my chess match with Miss Bingley! Must I truly surrender a pawn and a rook before we begin?'

'From my recollection of your gifts,' said I, with a half-smile, 'and my knowledge of the lady's, you might be well-advised to sacrifice a bishop as well... With her sister you might be rather more challenged.'

Chapter 16

(From Miss Mary Bennet's private papers)

Sometimes, Papa is quite impossible! Why delay till the very day his cousin – a 'gentleman and a stranger' – is to arrive to propose that we have a nicer dinner than usual? The day after Jane and Lizzy returned from Netherfield, he said to Mama, 'I trust, my dear, that you intend to give us your usual immaculate dinner, for I have reason to expect an addition to our family party.'

'Well, as to *that*, I know of no one likely to visit, I am sure – unless Charlotte Lucas might chance to call, and I hope my dinners are good enough for *her*. I do not believe she often sees such at home.'

'The person of whom I speak is a gentleman and a stranger.'

'A gentleman and a stranger!' cried she. 'It is Mr Bingley, to be sure! Well, I shall be extremely glad to see Mr Bingley, but – Good

Lord! How unlucky! There is not a bit of fish to be got today. Lydia, my love, ring the bell. I must see Hill this moment!'

'It is *not* Mr Bingley. It is someone I have never met in the entire course of my life.'

'Your Scottish cousin, Mr Laing?' I inquired.

'It is not.'

'Then it is a mysterious stranger from Barbados, who comes to divide his fortune between us,' Lizzy teased.

'Your imagination, Lizzy, does credit to your novel reading – but Mary is far nearer the mark. We are shortly to be graced by a visit from my cousin Collins – who, when I am dead, may turn you out of the house as soon as he pleases.'

Mama banged down her fork. 'How can you mention that odious creature? You know that I cannot bear *that* to be spoke of! 'Tis the hardest thing in all the world, for any estate to be entailed away from one's own children! – and had I been in your place, I should, long since, have done something about it.'

At this, Jane and Eliza exchanged glances. To be fair, they have often attempted to explain to Mama the nature of an entail. However, she prefers to repine over a law capable of wresting an estate away from a family of five daughters – in default of heirs male – in favour of a man 'whom nobody cares for.' Though how she is so certain that no one cares for Mr Collins, I do not know.

Mama then said, 'It is most hypocritical of this Collins creature to write to you at all! Why could he not be content to quarrel with you, as his own father did before him?'

Papa passed something to Lizzy, saying, 'It is indeed iniquitous, and nothing can absolve Mr Collins from the guilt of being heir to Longbourn. But here is his letter if you care to read it.' Lizzy caught it up and read it aloud:

Dear Sir,

The disagreement between yourself and my late father always gave me great unease and, since I have had the misfortune to lose him, I have often wished to heal the breach, but feared that it might seem disrespectful to his memory to attempt to be on good terms with one with whom it always pleased him to be at variance. However, having received ordination at Easter, I have been distinguished by the patronage of the Right Honourable Lady Catherine de Bourgh, whose gracious beneficence has preferred me to the valuable rectory of the parish here at Hunsford, where it shall be my earnest endeavour to demean myself with grateful respect towards Her Ladyship, and be ever ready to perform those rites and ceremonies instituted by the Church of England. As a clergyman, I feel it my duty to promote the blessing of peace within my reach of influence and thereby flatter myself that my present overtures of goodwill are highly commendable. I trust and hope, therefore, that the circumstance of my being next in the entail of Longbourn estate will be kindly overlooked on your side. I also beg leave to most humbly apologise for being the means of unconsciously injuring your amiable daughters, to whom I am prepared to make any possible amends – but more of this hereafter. If you have no objection, I therefore propose myself the satisfaction of waiting on you and your family on Monday at four and shall probably trespass upon your hospitality till the Saturday following. I can do this without any material inconvenience, as Her Ladyship is far from objecting to my occasional absence on a Sunday, provided that some fellow clergyman is engaged to do the duties of the day. I remain, my dear sir, with respectful compliments to your lady and your daughters, your relative, well-wisher and friend, William Collins (Rev.)

'Make the dear girls some amends!' cried Mama, exceedingly well-pleased. 'Well! I should rather, for the sake of the fish, have known a good deal sooner, but there is good sense in what he says about the girls, and should he be truly disposed to make them amends, I shall not say him nay!'

'Though I am puzzled as to how he could compensate us,' said Jane, 'the *desire* to do so is to his credit,' but Lizzy said, 'Surely, he would not wish to alter the circumstances of the entail, even if it was allowable. Can he be a sensible man, Papa?'

'I doubt it, my dear. There is a mixture of servility and self-importance in his letter that promises otherwise. I am impatient to meet him!'

Mr Collins was punctual as to his time and greeted by us all. He is a heavy-set fellow of five and twenty, neither handsome nor plain. He had not been seated long before he said, looking around with unfeigned satisfaction, 'Mrs Bennet, I must confess myself astonished! I have heard, on all sides, reports of my cousins' beauty, yet – in this case – fame has fallen well short of the truth! I have no doubt that they will all soon be well-settled in marriage.'

'You are very kind,' said Mama. 'It has long been my dearest wish – for things are settled so very oddly!'

'You allude, perhaps, to the entail of the estate?'

'Ah, I do indeed! I have never been able to comprehend –'

'More coffee, Mr Collins?' asked Eliza hastily.

'No, I thank you, Miss Elizabeth. I would say more, madam,' turning again to Mama, extremely politely, 'but that I fear to be precipitate. But I can assure my cousins that I come prepared to admire them.' He then accepted Papa's invitation, to choose a book from the library.

Upstairs, Lizzy cruelly imitated his speeches – even including his bobbing half-bows. While Kitty and Lydia fell about with laughing, Jane said, 'Do you know what I suspect?'

'I believe I do,' said Lizzy. 'I suspect that he intends to choose one of *us* to keep his house, organise his servants and assist him in those duties and obligations that he is contracted by the Church of England to render to the harried citizenry of wherever his famous abode might be. *That* is his notion of consoling us for his inheriting Longbourn.'

'Lord! Marry *that* great lump?' cried Lydia. 'Well, one of *you* may do it, for I could never bear it!' But Lizzy only shook her head, and said, 'And you, my dear Jane, may consider it a warning, for as you outrank us all, in looks as well as age, his choice will likeliest fall on you.'

However, as I moved into my room to practice – it is G major/G minor day, for I practise them in order – I found myself thoughtful, and for several reasons.

The first is that I have always secretly felt it likeliest that I will wed a clergyman. This is because they are sufficiently educated to raise their intellects to a level not unadjacent to my own. I could never marry the rector, for he is old and gouty and he was married before, but I consider our new cousin not unpromising. He is just six years my senior, perhaps a trifle solid and rubicund but not ill-looking, and – as for what my sisters find so comical in his manner, I can see nothing amiss. He might be somewhat over-precise in his sibilants, but that – I believe – is not uncommon in clergymen, while he seems most grateful for all Mama's attentions.

From the first moment of entering the house he was expressing his delight: in the occasion, in the weather, in the food, and in meeting relatives, specifying our family, most particularly. At dinner, he principally dwelt on the glories of his patroness, the Right Honourable Lady Catherine de Bourgh ('For never was there such gentility, geniality, condescension, elegance and taste combined!')

'As for Rosings,' said Mama, 'I long to see it, but Mr Bennet never wishes to go anywhere!'

This, of course, represented a far longer-standing grievance than the missing fish: Bath or Brighton, Tunbridge or Weymouth – our father was equally unwilling to display them to us all. Mr Collins continued to describe Rosings – its furnishings, its china, the numbers of its windows. Whilst he was enumerating its delights, Lydia began to giggle. (She grows less and less tameable – I saw Lizzy give her a nudge with the toe of her shoe.) Of Miss de Bourgh, Her Ladyship's only child, he observed, 'I have more than once remarked to Lady Catherine, that her charming daughter seemed born to be a duchess, and that the most elevated rank, instead of giving her consequence, would be adorned by her. This represents the variety of delicate attentions which I conceive myself peculiarly bound to pay.'

'You judge very properly,' said Papa, winking at Lizzy for some reason, 'and it is happy for you that you possess the talent of flattering with such delicacy. Might I ask whether these attentions proceed from the impulse of the moment, or are the result of previous study?' And, while Mr Collins was good enough to explain, I was shocked to notice Lizzy smiling secretly at Jane. Such disrespect – to a relative and a clergyman! Really, Lizzy can be almost as rude as Lydia, though rarely as loud.

After tea, Mr Collins was asked to read, and, after disgustedly rejecting Lizzy's novel, he selected Fordyce's *Sermons to Young Ladies*. I sat back, and had hardly begun to prepare my mentality for the cognitive stimulation which my favourite invariably excites, when Lydia cried, 'Have I told you, Mama, what Mrs Long said of Mr Denny?'

Our cousin closed the book in a marked manner, saying, 'It astonishes me how little young ladies care for books of a serious stamp, though written solely for their benefit! But I will no longer importune my young cousin.' I felt indignant on his behalf, but Papa proposed a game of backgammon, instead. After our guest had retired, I heard Mama – never sympathetic to those of a higher stamp – complaining to Hill about our cousin's obtuseness, fastidiousness – he had requested a different pillow – loquacity, pedantry, and quality of speaking voice.

I suspect she does not like him.

However, this morning all this was to alter – and instantly, besides. I happened to be in the hall when I overheard Mama saying, 'As to the rest, I do not *know* of any predisposition, however, my *eldest* daughter is likely to be very soon engaged.'

How strange a statement was this for Mama to make to our housekeeper! – though I have observed that she often betrays private matters to the servants, and to Mrs Hill, particularly. Nor was I astonished by her opinion – Mama had determined, before Jane had even been introduced to Mr Bingley, that the family beauty was destined for Netherfield. And, as there is no arguing with Mama once she takes a notion into her head, and as she had taken *that* notion into her head so particularly early, I am convinced that, till she personally observes Mr Bingley in St George's, vowing eternal constancy to some other lady, she will never surrender it.

But I was shocked to then overhear *Mr Collins* making Mama some polite response.

In brief, Mama's confidante was *not* Hill. And it was Lizzy who had read the situation aright! I sat down, feeling rather breathless, thinking, 'Our cousin must have been confiding nothing less momentous than that he has indeed come into Hertfordshire in hopes of choosing a wife!' I then returned upstairs, where I stood pensive before the glass.

Now, I am not ill-looking. I cannot be compared to Jane, of course – my face is too square, my eyes too small, my skin too sallow. But my nose is as straight and as neat as my figure – I am modestly proud of my nose – whilst my extraordinary acuteness is not obvious to outward view. And not only have I long believed myself destined to marry a clergyman, but to wed this particular clergyman would be to save our entire family from expulsion from Longbourn!

'In short,' I thought, 'is it not my duty, at least to try?'

Before I had straightened my gown, I had made up my mind in the affirmative. And here I must add that I made up my mind not for the purposes of duty alone. I believe that a man of the cloth, who appreciates the genius of Fordyce, might become – with advice and encouragement – not entirely unworthy of me. And if I, with my straight small nose and remarkable erudition, succeed in entrancing him, I hereby vow to never be less than kind to those four sisters who have each, in different ways, decried my genius and offended my sensibilities for so many years altogether.

My campaign did not start ill. My cousin beamed at me when I endorsed his observation about the excellence of Cook's boiled potatoes. After he had praised Mama's cabinet ('So fine a maple is rare, and the varnishing quite exemplary!') I kindly undertook to instruct him about its provenance, though Lizzy, with her usual impatience, chose to turn the subject before I was half-finished. And when Papa proposed that Mr Collins accompany his daughters

to Meryton, to Lydia's astonishment – 'La! Even Mary is agreeable!' – I decided to accompany them.

Why? – Because, despite the embarrassment incumbent upon
being attached to so raucous and unruly a party, I felt it my duty to
protect our cousin from his intellectual inferiors. (This includes
Lizzy – though she does not lack ability – as her education has been
so neglected.) Thus, as we walked, I stayed as near to Mr Collins as
I could. He happened to be walking by Lizzy.

'And so, Miss Elizabeth, I understand that you keep your father
company in his passion for books?'

'I cannot follow his scientific interests, but we share a love of
history – and we both dearly love a play.'

'Yet plays,' I observed, 'are often silly. Whereas, in sharp
contradistinction, the study of history can illuminate any age.'

'Quite,' said our cousin. 'As Kant wrote, "Experience without
theory is blind, but theory without experience is mere intellectual
play."'

Charmed by his sagacity, I quoted Kant likewise: '"Two things
awe me most, the starry sky above me and the moral law within
me."'

'Just so,' said he, 'I daresay. So, what so attracts you to history,
Miss Elizabeth?'

'Oh, heavens! I hardly know – but I suspect it is the human side
– the story.'

'Precisely. The ancient Greeks –' I missed the rest of his
observation, though I suspect it was a just one, as Kitty whispered
loudly in my ear, 'There's for you, Mary! Look, coming out of the
baker's. *That* is Mr Denny! Is he not divinely handsome?'

I turned and observed a young officer, uniformed and booted,
emerging onto the street, followed by another young man. At the

sight of the stranger Lydia gasped, 'Be still, my beating heart!' while Kitty cried, 'Heavens! Whoever might *he* be?'

It is a truth universally acknowledged that an exceptionally handsome and agreeable young man, loosed upon a small provincial town, is a rare and glorious thing. In other words, even I was obliged to admit that Mr Denny's companion was unusually well-looking. He owned all the best parts of beauty, including height, a fine physique, curling dark hair, a neat moustache, and a dashing air. His features were as striking as his figure, and I could not wonder – though I still despaired – that Lydia and Kitty could not stop gaping, and that our poor cousin could command no one's attention beyond my own.

In short, the entire scene represented as perfect a demonstration of my thesis – about looks being all – as Fordyce himself could have devised.

'A family of five,' Mr Denny said in a low voice, 'of which *one* would bore any right-thinking fellow to death. But *two* are beauties, while the youngest is lively enough!' I was trying to recall any such family as that when he hallooed to us. He then crossed the street, and begged leave to introduce his acquaintance, Mr Wickham, who had just accepted a commission in the regiment. Mr Wickham bowed and smiled – his teeth are startlingly good – declaring that he had heard much of the beauties of Hertfordshire, but that he was astonished by those he had witnessed thus far.

I was probably the only woman of the party not utterly smitten. He struck me as being almost *too* gallant.

'The half was not told unto you,' suggested Mr Collins good-humouredly – though this reference to Scripture seemed to go over the heads of all the rest. I murmured, 'Kings, Chapter 1,' but no one heard me. Instead, the young soldiers were persuaded to attend us to our aunt's while the fortunate Lizzy found herself with Mr Collins on one side of her and Mr Wickham on the other.

When I had caught them up, our cousin was praising Meryton – tidy, bustling, cheerful and so on. Lizzy said archly, 'I daresay, Mr Collins, that you will come to know every shop in the village, once you inherit Longbourn.' (I was surprised at Lizzy – she is rarely so impertinent with strangers.)

'When that unhappy event *does* occur, I trust that both our minds will be upon higher things,' said Mr Collins gently.

'I suspect,' said Lizzy, 'that our notion of "higher" things might not bear very close resemblance.'

For some reason, Lizzy did seem rather vexed with him – but she is a moody creature, and as likely to offend as to entrance. I have often attempted to advise her to affect a greater sweetness of demeanour – in short, to take *Jane* as her guide in manners and *myself* in matters of mind. But she is generally too impatient to listen. Instead, she asked Wickham, 'In which part of Derbyshire were you born?'

'On a large estate near Lambton, where my father worked as steward.'

'A most pleasing area of country,' put in Mr Collins. 'I was there myself not five years hence.'

'I suppose it is excessively pretty, Mr Wickham?' asked Lizzy.

''Tis well enough, though its charms cannot compare with the loveliness I see all around me.'

He must have been thinking of Jane, but Lizzy still blushed as I observed, 'Derbyshire is the centre of an area long known for its excellence in wool production. The East India Company –'

'Perhaps,' said Wickham to Lizzy, 'we might walk on?'

As this precisely suited my purpose, I said to Mr Collins, 'I believe that your house is not far from the mansion belonging to the Right Honourable Lady Catherine de Bourgh?' But *his* first purpose seemed to be to befriend Mr Wickham, for he bustled to catch up with him, instead of answering me.

(Between ourselves, this flirting business can be quite discouraging, at times. I wonder that Lydia and Kitty are so addicted to it!) As so often, Fordyce put it best, 'In my own humble opinion, there can be no doubt that men worth having will not respect young ladies who lower themselves by flirtation. A discreet, quiet and genteel deportment is what men wish for in a wife.' To which I would only add, 'Huzzah!'

Just then two gentlemen clattered up on horseback: Mr Bingley and Mr Darcy, the one who famously finds Eliza only 'tolerable'. Upon seeing our party they halted, and Mr Bingley informed Jane that they were on their way to call upon Papa – who, I could have told them, would not thank them for it. But I suppose that not even young men can spend *quite* every hour hunting, fishing, shooting or otherwise plaguing animals.

But then something strange occurred, for Mr Darcy, upon observing Mr Wickham, suddenly turned very pale. The newcomer touched his hat, but Darcy barely returned the compliment before wheeling his horse back towards the road. I rather envied the horsemen, as they cantered away, and as the rest of us continued to my aunt's. There we endured an unbearably noisy round game, during which Aunt Philips monopolised Mr Collins while everyone else made up – quite shockingly – to Mr Wickham.

Yet now, as I write, I comfort myself with the recollection that, after all, it was only my very first effort at flirting, and Mr Collins is the sort to look for deeper things. All in all, I am not entirely disheartened.

Thursday sees the long-heralded Netherfield ball and, though that will also be insufferably noisy, Mr Collins has agreed to accompany us – and there is an excellent chance that I might have an opportunity for musical display.

Chapter 17

My dear Darcy, I have taken the papers to Jameson, who promises an early response. I shall hope to have something from him with regard to Miss Menotti by Friday, and then we shall see if the lady dares to continue. As she is not, as you mentioned, a gambler, I think we might modestly hope that she might fail to persevere. My regards to Bingley and his sisters, and of course to yourself. Yours, Fitzwilliam

Chapter 18

(From Miss Mary Bennet's private papers)

I did not *intend* to eavesdrop, but I could not help overhearing Jane and Lizzy's conversation.

'Nay, you must be mistaken, Lizzy. Depend on it, you are mistaken!'

'I am not. Wickham was most explicit.'

'What! Mr *Darcy* deny the poor fellow a living that his own father had bequeathed to him? For what plea? Upon what reason?'

'Why, for no reason at all – beyond ill temper. Though Wickham *did* hint to me privately, at our aunt's, that there might have been some little jealousy, besides. It seems that Darcy's father enjoyed his company a great deal, and even paid for his education.'

'Well, I still cannot believe it,' said Jane, with a firmness most unusual in her. 'I cannot think that Mr Darcy's friends could be so mistaken in his character!' (She was thinking of Mr Bingley, of course. She is forever thinking of Mr Bingley!)

'I can more easily believe in Mr Bingley's being imposed upon than in Mr Wickham's concocting so ingenious a series of untruths – names and dates, all mentioned without ceremony.'

'But surely Mr Wickham could have applied to the law courts, in such a case?'

'Apparently there was just enough doubt in the wording that he could not. Also, as he so nobly put it, "I could never publicly dishonour the son, for the sake of his father."'

'It is distressing – it is most distressing! But perhaps poor Mr Wickham was granted the living only conditionally. Or perhaps Mr Darcy might have been deceived as to the precarious nature of Mr Wickham's situation. For I cannot imagine Mr *Darcy* in need of the money involved.'

'No – though the excessively rich can generally imagine a thousand reasons for believing their income insufficient for their purpose.'

At this point I rose and shut the door. Uniquely in all of greater Meryton – or so it seems – I have no interest in the 'divinely handsome' Wickham – or in Mr Darcy either, though I suppose it might explain their odd encounter in the High Street.

Returning to my papers, therefore, I drew up the following plan of campaign:

DARCY

1. Listen to Mr Collins and attend to him a great deal
2. Agree, as far as my conscience permits, with whatever he says
3. Unobtrusively insinuate that somewhere – and at no very great distance – might exist someone like-minded
4. Quote Kant/Fordyce/Holy Writ? (Though he had not seemed particularly impressed with my knowledge of the Holy Writ, thus far.)

That afternoon, Mr Bingley called, to secure Jane for the first two dances at the Netherfield ball. As Mr Collins was present, I took the opportunity of hinting that I remained available for those self-same dances myself. Though in truth I was – despite the straightness and neatness of my nose – still available for *every* dance.

I said, 'Whilst I can have my mornings to myself, I think it no sacrifice to occasionally join in evening engagements. I profess myself one of those who consider intervals of recreation as desirable for everybody.'

Lizzy laughed. 'But our cousin's situation is very different! Should *he* be tempted into dancing, he might receive a rebuke from his archbishop!'

'Not at all,' said our cousin, with his usual good humour. 'Indeed, I am so far from objecting to dancing, that I hope to be honoured with the hands of each of my fair cousins in the course of the evening, and take this opportunity of soliciting *yours*, Miss Elizabeth, for the two first dances – Something which I trust my cousin Jane will attribute to the right cause, and not to any disrespect for her.'

How annoying! Especially as Eliza looked more nettled than gratified at this honour – possibly because she, Lydia and Kitty are all vying for the attentions of the new regimental favourite, Mr Wickham. Meanwhile, I went up to my room to meditate on what I should say and do, when the time came for my own share of our cousin's kind attentions at Netherfield.

I comforted myself with this consideration: had Mr Collins chosen me for the first two dances – thanks to a lurking suspicion that I might be the cousin best-suited to preside over Hunsford Rectory – it might have appeared disrespectful to Lizzy. I greatly admire his even-handedness ('I hope to be honoured with the hands of all my fair cousins in the course of the evening') – though it is my intention to make him *less* even-handed, if possible.

Of course, Jane is the prettiest and Lydia extraordinarily vital, while Lizzy possesses a rapier wit. I am convinced that my own weapon lies in my intellect and so, though I practised my music diligently, I devoted several hours to the following:

1. Memorising some fragments of Kant, a philosopher we both appear to admire
2. Refreshing my memory of the immortal Fordyce (likewise)
3. Attempting to make my hair curl

This last, I own, is really rather beneath me, but Mr Collins said something pleasing about Lizzy's dark curls whilst at our aunt's, and I remain determined to leave no stone unturned.

I was gratified to learn, from Charlotte Lucas, that her brother Timothy intends to ask me to dance, as well. (Query: might this be due to the prettiness of my nose?) He has been slightly ill of late – he seems to be ill not infrequently, being the only Lucas with any claim to delicacy, as well as the only member of that family remotely interested in books. And so…

Veni vidi vici! (Meaning: 'I came, I saw, I conquered!')

Onward!

Chapter 19

(From Mr Darcy's diaries)

Netherfield looked elegant indeed, with most of the furniture cleared away for the ball. I complimented Louisa Hurst who said, in her admirably blunt way, 'Nothing to do with me, my good friend – but you can have no notion how busy poor Caroline has been.' I was, in fact, already aware of this, while as for their housekeeper, she looked exhausted indeed. Louisa leaned forward then and said very quietly, 'I would give a good deal, between ourselves, for the ball never to happen.'

''Tis a form of entertainment I despise,' I agreed.

'Not because of the dancing, or even the company, though I am exhausted by Sir William Lucas's protestations of unending regard, not to mention the ill-judged giggling of the youngest Bennet girls. Instead, I am concerned for my brother.'

'You refer to Miss Bennet, I presume? But a ball cannot be very material, in terms of furthering his suit. Indeed, I should think almost any other occasion better suited to the formation of a serious attachment.'

'No doubt, but Miss Bennet is quite lovely enough without her finest clothes and half the family jewellery about her hair and shoulders.'

We were interrupted by Bingley himself. Rubbing his hands he said, 'Why, what long faces, with such an evening of pleasure before us! I suppose you shall hide in the cardroom all evening, Darcy?'

'Very likely,' I agreed. 'By the way, did you invite every officer in the —shire?' Upon which he dismayed me by saying that he 'believed' that they were all expected – though I secretly doubted that Wickham would dare to appear.

I remain convinced, though, that Elizabeth Bennet likes him. We had a most singular dance together.

Now I had never intended to dance, except with Bingley's two sisters – *that* must be unavoidable – but, upon noticing with how light a step she moved, I felt compelled to ask her. She looked taken aback at being asked and positively discomfited as I led her to the position at the top of the set which my consequence demanded.

Our dance once begun, she seemed resolved upon hardly speaking, making her responses as short as possible. After a long silence, she said, in a tone more like herself, 'Now it is your turn to speak – about the size of the room, or the number of couples.' Once I had assured her of my perfect willingness to say whatever she commanded, she continued, with a curl of lip that was almost Giuditta-like, 'Very well, that shall do, for the present. *Now*, we may be silent.'

'Do you talk by the rule then, when you are dancing?'

'Sometimes. It would look very odd to be silent for half an hour altogether. Yet for the convenience of *some*, there should be as few words said as possible.'

'Are you considering your own feelings in the present case, or do you imagine that you are gratifying mine?' I inquired with a smile.

'Why, both, I believe! – We are each of an unsociable, taciturn disposition, unwilling to speak unless we might say something to convulse the room, and be handed down to posterity with the éclat of a proverb.'

'This is no very apt description of your own character,' said I. 'How near it might be to *mine*, I cannot say.' To alter the subject, I asked – a comment so inane I can hardly bear to recall it – if she and her sisters did not often walk to Meryton. She admitted it, adding, 'When we met you the other day, we had just been forming a new acquaintance.'

I perceived that Wickham seemed to have made his usual easy conquest – but held my tongue as we moved down the set. Once we reached the end, I said, 'Mr Wickham is blessed with such happy manners as may ensure his making friends. Whether he *retains* them, is rather less certain.'

'He has been so unlucky as to lose *your* friendship,' she said, with sudden warmth, 'and in a manner he is likely to regret for the whole of his life!'

Before I could collect myself, we were interrupted by the tedious Sir William Lucas – soon afterwards, we parted. Deeply angry at Wickham, whose tales of ill-usage at my hands must have deceived her at my expense, I was in no humour to dance more. Unluckily, I had already been engaged to Sir William's Charlotte – though, I am sure, she found me as dull as ditchwater, for I could think of nothing beyond that contempt with which her friend had favoured me.

At the end of my dances with Miss Lucas, I sought out Caroline Bingley and said, as casually as I could contrive, 'Do you, by any chance, recall the circumstances I must have mentioned to you, with regard to my father's godson, Mr Wickham?'

'Oh heavens, yes! Did not your father promise him a living – and did not he renounce it in favour of some great sum? But what of that? – for he is not here – he has not come. Charles felt obliged to invite every officer, but Wickham sent his apologies.'

'I was merely wondering if you might be willing to do me a favour. Miss Elizabeth Bennet has been wrongly informed that I infamously deprived Mr Wickham of the living he had long depended on. And, as he is now based in Meryton, such idle gossip could easily spread.'

'Heavens! But did not Mr Wickham agree to the compensation, instead?'

'He did, and I have the evidence to prove it. But the point is whether he might be conniving to blacken my name – even the name of my father.'

'Dear me! How appallingly unpleasant! But how could *I* assist?'

'If you would be so good, very easily. The Bennets, with the Lucases and Gouldings, form the linchpin of local society. Were you willing to intimate to Miss Elizabeth that she has been misinformed, the rumour will be scotched before it has any chance to take hold.'

Miss Bingley could scarcely have been more compliant. 'I should be only too delighted, Mr Darcy, to tell Miss Eliza exactly how far her imagination has led her astray. Indeed, I shall make a point of it!' I thanked her and moved into the cardroom. For that reason, I could not say how Miss Bingley approached Miss Elizabeth – or how she appeared upon receiving the intelligence.

I was, however, perfectly placed to describe how outrageous her mother's behaviour was at dinner. I was unluckily seated close by, and despite every effort to direct my attention elsewhere, was obliged to hear almost every word, though she spoke not to me but almost exclusively to Lady Lucas: 'I assure you, she is as modest as modest! – Despite my own wishes, she would do nothing intricate with her hair – observe how simple, how unadorned, it is! She refused my every ornament likewise, beyond her gold cross… Such a place as Netherfield – charming as it is, and I did grieve for the Ibbotts when they were obliged to quit it – is no more than Jane deserves!… And he is *such* a delightful young man, of such winning address and manners! His *wealth* does not concern us – it is of no concern at all, though he probably has £4,000 a year – but did not they look enchanting as they danced?… What, truly? – I cannot think that one could have looked at any couple else!… I am glad that you noticed her gown – I have been saving that material for ever and – though Jane needs nothing to set off her exquisite complexion – I daresay it might do for one of the younger girls, once *she* is settled here at Netherfield…'

And as if this were not sufficient effrontery, I then found myself approached by a stranger who introduced himself as cousin to Mr Bennet. 'I have the inestimable honour, sir,' said he, 'to have been distinguished by your aunt, Lady Catherine de Bourgh.' Observing that I did not doubt it, I tried to escape – we had not even been introduced – but he detained me, trusting that I would rejoice at his assurance that my aunt had been 'delightfully well, yesterday sennight.'

I thanked him as briefly as I could – yet *still* the fellow persevered, marvelling at his pleasure in meeting me and, 'had I any messages for Her Ladyship, the honour'– I was assured – 'would be entirely his.' As I could not help doubting his tale, I then inquired in what capacity Her Ladyship had distinguished him. He responded exultantly, 'I have the signal honour, sir, to have been selected as the new rector of Hunsford, in Kent.' I remarked that I believed my aunt incapable of bestowing any honour unworthily, and thereby rid myself of the fellow.

It would be a charity to pass over the rest of the evening: the witless mirth of the company, Sir William's ill-judged toasts, the risible young lady performers – Miss Mary Bennet, particularly – the follies of the cardroom.

But as I write this, I suddenly find myself wondering, 'What is it to me what Elizabeth Bennet thinks of me – or of Wickham, either?' And can find no very persuasive answer.

Chapter 20

(From Miss Mary Bennet's private papers)

I am no very expert dancer, which puzzles me, as my sense of rhythm is so exemplary, but I was relieved to discover that our cousin Mr Collins is still less gifted. Lizzy seemed almost to be wincing during the first two dances, though most of the company was observing Mr Bingley and Jane instead. I hovered in Mr Collins's vicinity as the second dance concluded, methodically rehearsing what I wished to say to him.

He bowed to Lizzy and observed that she danced like a naiad, but Lizzy, with her usual inattention to the civilities, said as little as she could in return. 'Well,' said he to me, 'would you favour me with your company for the next dance, Miss Mary?'

I said that I would be charmed, just as Mr Darcy – Mr Darcy! – offered to Eliza. It is a good thing that Mr Collins has so fine a mind because he really does not dance very well, paying scant attention to the subtleties of the music. It was also too noisy for conversation – however, I did my best.

'What was that, my dear Miss Mary?' he inquired.

'I was mentioning Kant,' said I.

'Who?' asked Mr Collins, who seemed to be puffing a trifle.

'The philosopher!' I shouted.

'I agree,' said he. 'It is indeed a trifle warm!'

After a moment's deep thought, I decided that it was not the time or place for philosophy. The best generals – supposedly – deploy swift changes in tactics. Modelling myself upon these, therefore, I asked, 'Does Lady Catherine have many balls down at Rosings?'

'No,' said Mr Collins, 'the neighbourhood there is unfortunately not on as exalted a level as Her Ladyship's distinction deserves. Indeed, there is a certain family of upstarts, situated quite close, whom she seldom deigns to meet.'

'I am sorry to hear it,' was my observation, to which he said, 'Indeed, it is rather exhausting. I would prefer a quiet evening with the good book.'

'I am extremely fond of reading the Bible,' I shouted, in hopes of his hearing me.

'Indeed. I had never' – (puff) – 'expected' – (puff) – 'it to be quite so noisy.'

Soon it grew noisier still, for Lydia and Mr Denny danced past, in a great fit of laughter. I then understood Mr Collins to suggest that we withdraw from the dance. This I was perfectly content to do, for I was growing tired of the noise. Once we had found a quiet place, I said, 'About Kant's categorical imperative…'

After I had finished, Mr Collins for some reason went off in search of refreshment. As for me, I could not tell whether I had done well or ill. I was watching Jane and Bingley enviously, for surely any woman in the room would look distinguished with such a partner, when Timothy Lucas asked me to dance.

To my surprise, I enjoyed it. Despite his asthma he seemed to manage without any puffing at all, and tolerably in time besides.

'What are you reading?' was his first question. I thought about Kant, but I was feeling rather weary of Kant and so I said, 'I am always reading several books at once.'

'It is the only way,' said Timothy, 'for no one's mood can always be in sympathy with, for example, the Stoics. Indeed, there are some days, Miss Mary, when I find myself out of sympathy with Stoics and Epicureans alike.'

I wished to espouse the Stoics' cause, for it is my own belief that anyone growing up in so chaotic and disorganised a household as Longbourn requires a great deal of stoicism. Therefore I said, 'Perhaps we all ought to be Stoics,' and he countered, 'I think your new cousin inclines to the Epicurean side.' And I wished to defend Mr Collins but could not think how.

'Your dress is very pretty,' said Timothy then, and as Mama had always instructed us that one should blush at any compliment, I tried very hard to blush, but was unable. 'And Miss Bennet's also.' He leaned towards me and whispered, 'It is said that she is likely to marry Mr Bingley, which is the reason for her fine attire. I do not know the reason for your own.'

Now the reason for my wearing the cream muslin was – truly – that, though one of the nicest gowns in the house, it was too slender for Jane, and too short for Lizzy. It was pleasing he had noticed although – in return for the gown – I had been obliged to loan Jane my prettiest shoes. Never could there be more, and more pointless, arguments than amongst five sisters in quest of a ball!

Then Timothy said, 'Would you mind very much, Miss Mary, if we sat down for a moment?'

I agreed, recollecting his asthma, and once he had recovered, he went to fetch me more refreshment, which, by then, I was in want of.

After dinner there was music and here – at last – was my chance to shine. Following a short introduction of perhaps ten minutes, briefly explaining the sonata form structure, I favoured the company with the first movement of the Clementi. And not without success, for as it concluded Mr Collins cried, 'Brava!' so loudly that it made Lizzy jump and Miss Bingley said something to her sister that I could not catch, but which started with 'Thank heavens!'

I sang very well also – perhaps rather *too* well – for Papa stopped me while I was just beginning to introduce my second selection, observing that 'other young ladies should have a chance to exhibit.' Though they did not wish to, beyond poor Miss Goulding, who performed lamentably. I would have been more than willing to resume after she had done, but there was a general movement of the company, and then the dancing began again.

Chapter 21

(From Mr Darcy's diaries)

The events of the ball were to prove crucial at Netherfield. Nothing was said that night, but the next morning I entered the East Room to hear Louisa's low but urgent tones, '*Something* must be done.'

Caroline said, 'I daresay. But what?'

'Forgive my intrusion, I beg,' said I. 'But perhaps you refer, Mrs Hurst, to last night, and to your brother?'

'Precisely.'

'In that case,' I said, 'we are of one mind,' as Miss Bingley's eyes grew larger, 'for poor Charles is as far gone as I have ever seen him. While the family –'

'The family is utterly impossible,' said Mrs Hurst. 'The mother cannot be silent, even by accident. The younger sisters think of nothing but making a great noise and chasing officers from the regiment. I quite feared for the Ibbotts' pianoforte whilst the middle girl was pounding at it – and the father seemed to find it all intensely amusing!'

'Do not omit their cousin Collins,' I reminded her. 'For servile obsequiousness, he has not his equal. How my aunt can endure him, I cannot conceive!'

Caroline said eagerly, 'Oh, I agree – I *do* so agree! And to dare to address *you*, without the slightest excuse – you, of every creature in the room! But what can be done? For Miss Bennet is modest, soft-spoken, charming – and very nearly beautiful. Small wonder poor Charles is besotted!'

'He is worse than he was with Lady Diana,' added her sister, 'though *she* gave him no encouragement. The difficulty with Charles is that, once he has started, he will always be in love.'

'Then we must get him away,' said I. 'He goes to London tomorrow, I believe. We must follow him there, and – somehow or other – contrive to detain him.'

'But how?' breathed Miss Bingley, looking devoutly at me.

'I can think of nothing,' said Mrs Hurst, 'for he is excessively pleased with Netherfield.'

'Given Charles's modesty, I might have an idea, perhaps?'

The plan I had was this: Charles, particularly since Lady Diana's engagement, appeared to possess surprisingly little self-confidence. I reasoned that, were I to tell him that Miss Jane Bennet had no serious feeling for him – for nothing could be calmer than her serene complacency – then he would not wish to see her more. In short, Charles has never had a high opinion of himself – while, by contrast, he had the highest possible opinion of Miss Bennet.

Louisa said, 'It might work. Charles has never been arrogant, perhaps never arrogant enough! – And you would truly be willing to tell him?'

'I would, as I believe it to be true. And while I do not dislike the lady, the family…'

'Precisely,' said Louisa, with a shudder, and thus it was decided. We are to follow Charles to London, and Miss Bingley is to write in apology to Miss Bennet, for our not keeping our dinner engagement.

As I write, my conscience troubles me about Miss Elizabeth, for I admire her arch wit as much as those mischievous dark eyes – while she and Miss Bennet have done nothing of which they ought to be ashamed. But we are doing Charles a kindness by nipping his passion in the bud; and one day, I am convinced, he will thank us for it.

Chapter 22

Longbourn

Eliza found the Netherfield ball, in every respect, the most wretched of disappointments. First, she had understood that all the regimental officers had been invited – despite this, Wickham had not been there. (According to his friend Denny, with a significant smile, 'He might not have been obliged to go to town had he not wished to avoid a certain gentleman here.')

She had endured two appalling dances with Mr Collins before Mr Darcy had asked her. If only she had possessed the presence of mind to pretend to have been engaged! And though she had, at least, managed to imply her disapproval of his behaviour towards poor Wickham, the tax for her zeal was to find Miss Bingley later waylaying her.

'And so, I hear that you are quite delighted with George Wickham! Let me recommend you, however, as a friend, not to give the slightest credence to his information. For as to Mr Darcy's using him ill, it is entirely false. On the contrary, he has always been remarkably kind to him, though Wickham has treated Mr Darcy infamously... As he is merely the son of the Darcys' steward, his coming into the country at all is a most insolent thing – I wonder how he could have done it! I pity you, my dear Miss Eliza, for the discovery of your favourite's guilt – but given his descent, one could not have expected much better!'

'His guilt and his descent appear – by your account – to be the same,' Elizabeth had returned very warmly, 'for you have accused him of nothing worse than of being the son of Mr Darcy's steward, and of *that*, I assure you, he informed me himself!'

'I beg your pardon,' Miss Bingley had sneered, 'I did not mean to interfere – it was kindly meant.'

Bad as this had been, still worse was to follow. During dinner she had been afflicted by her mother's boastful predictions of Jane's marriage, and then by Mary's affected performance at the pianoforte. While throughout the event she had been dogged by the unctuous Mr Collins, who had seemed almost as determined to ingratiate himself with *her*, as with Lady Catherine's nephew himself.

'It was all appalling,' said she, banging her brush down on her dressing table. 'I cannot bear to recollect a moment of it! Lydia, Mary, Mr Collins... but perhaps Mama was quite the worst.'

'Why, whatever did Mama do?' asked the bewildered Jane.

'*That* was at dinner. She was regaling poor Lady Lucas with her regret that her daughters were not as lovely as you, and counting the days till she would be *your* guest at Netherfield. And all this, mind you, with Mr Darcy not ten feet away, and almost too disgusted to eat. Lady Lucas kept pretending to yawn, yet still she yapped on, like a dog enjoying the sound of its own barking, until I wished to scream!'

'But,' said Jane, 'Mr Darcy might never have heard her, for so great was the babble of converse that I could scarcely understand what Caroline was saying, across the table.'

'I am confident that he heard every word, for he looked more and more contemptuous – so much so that I bid Mama to hold her tongue, but she would not.'

Jane was sorry, but she sustained such a sweet glow of happiness from the delights of her own evening that she could not be concerned. 'I am sorry Mama was so unfeeling to Lady Lucas, but Mr Darcy – I am sure – would never dream of mentioning it.'

'What! Even after the sorry exhibition Mr Collins made of himself?'

'Why, whatever do you mean?'

'Disdaining my advice – and I cannot conceive how I could have spoken clearer – he insisted upon introducing himself to Mr Darcy.'

'What, with the intervention of no other person?'

'Indeed – and cringed throughout, like a cur wishing to be kicked. Though I loathe and detest Mr Darcy, even I was obliged to admit that the wonderment in his countenance was entirely justified.'

'Did he cut him, then?' asked Jane, troubled.

'Not he. He simply listened, with much the same expression as when listening to Mama, and dismissed him. While as for Mary – I wished the floor would swallow me up!'

Jane nodded sombrely. 'Oh, yes! To play when asked to was well enough, but to carry on – and at such length – and in such company!'

'Her affected style, her reedy voice, the derision of Bingley's sisters – though Bingley seemed entirely unaffected. He must either possess a mind above such trivialities or else a pitifully poor ear for music.'

'Mary provided my only discomfiture of the evening – except when Lydia laughed rather too loudly. She does not mean to sound coarse, but really, she might be accused of it! Mama ought to advise her.'

'But *that* would be only to waste her breath, for Lydia would pay not the slightest attention.'

'I am sorry,' said Jane, after a moment, 'that you found the ball such a trial. For me, it all seemed perfection, till Mary seized her chance at display – and even *that* did not destroy the evening, because most people hereabouts, I am very sure, must know how she longs to perform, and would be kind enough to make allowances.' After a moment, she said tentatively, 'Mr Collins seemed very often near you?'

Lizzy grimaced. 'I spent the entire evening wishing him away – and, without Charlotte's kindness, might well have disgraced myself, in some fashion or other. I have no notion what he hoped to gain by it, for he admitted disliking dancing in general, and seemed to disdain my every opinion. In desperation, I promised to introduce him to any lady in the room, but he would not choose!'

'I believe he admires you,' was Jane's opinion, but Eliza ridiculed the notion. 'It is merely that he has no other acquaintance here and, for all his self-conceit, seems ill-at-ease in company. He did dance with Charlotte – but she very nearly had to ask *him*!

However, soon he will return to his beloved Lady Catherine and to his humble abode and, after that, we shall never hear of him again!'

Just before she slept, she recollected Mr Darcy – and the astonishment of the company in perceiving him leading her to the top of the set. Secretly, she acknowledged that he danced extremely well, and even that he looked well – though who could fail to look well, in such perfectly-cut coats and waistcoats? But how *dared* he enlist Caroline Bingley to spread lies about poor Wickham? – while his anxiety that she do so only suggested concern lest the truth become known.

Still, how she would enjoy discussing it with George Wickham upon his return! She fell asleep recalling the tone of his voice, the crinkle in his dark eyes, his strong figure, and his misfortunes at the hands of Mr Darcy.

The next morning, however, Eliza found that she had something else to think about, as one distressing scene followed hard upon the heels of another. Upon reaching her bedroom at last, she shut the door and leaned back against it, breathing hard.

Heavens! – that Mr Collins could have been so arrogant, so presuming, as to *assume* that she would have him – that he could have imagined his attentions to have won her heart, instead of arousing pure contempt – Oh! What did he not deserve?

She had told him. She had contrived, as best she could, to keep her countenance, while assuring him that she was as little disposed to toy with his feelings, as to accede to his ponderously stated wishes. She thought: 'Who could possibly accept an offer from such a man? – his palms so sweaty, his eyes so beady, his figure so portly, and his protestations of regard so wildly heightened! Were she as unsought as a widow of thirty, she would never have accepted him! Surely, attractive, lively and scarcely twenty, *she* had no such reason to despair? And he had proven so stubborn, besides!'

She admitted that he deserved acknowledgement for desiring to console her family for his inheriting a property deservedly their own. Beyond that, she could find not a single excuse for him – nor could she accuse herself of having offered him the slightest encouragement. She even suspected that he had only not fixed on Jane when informed – probably by Mama – that her dearest Jane was destined for Netherfield... Then, suddenly, she recollected Mary. Should Mr Collins only be willing to transfer his – entirely imaginary – allegiance to her, and should Mary agree, then Longbourn might remain their home after the death of their father!

Still, her heart misgave her. At the ball, Mary had displayed the most pedestrian musical talents to a level of derision surely not wasted even upon Mr Collins... Had not his own 'Brava!' possessed a touch of sarcasm?

Also, did not Mary deserve a better fate? Her immediate repugnance towards Mr Collins was so strong that Eliza, at least, believed it. Mary was still young enough to mature and to improve. Mr Collins – by contrast – had already congealed into a self-congratulatory, falsely obsequious, self-satisfied caricature of a man.

She shuddered, just recalling it. ('I am not now to learn that it is usual with young ladies to reject the addresses of a man whom they secretly intend to accept'... 'You must give me leave to flatter myself'... 'You are uniformly charming!'... 'I shall hope to lead you to the altar, ere long!')

She recalled too his double chin – a double chin surprisingly well-developed for so young a man – and his pomposity, likewise.

But Mama had been so angry! ('Well! If someone had told me that I should live to hear such ingratitude from a child of mine! That, without so much as a word to myself, she could have refused such an offer – from a near relative, and in such circumstances as we endure, why – Lord bless me! – I should never have believed it!')

Thank heavens Papa had supported her – for in some families, as she well knew, paternal pressure would have been brought to bear, but she could not imagine her father attempting to coerce any person, let alone the daughter whom, perhaps, he might love best. ('Elizabeth, an unhappy alternative lies before you. From this day you must be a stranger to one of your parents. Your mother will never see you again if you do not marry Mr Collins – and *I* shall never see you again if you do.')

But at least, the worst must be over. She would have unpleasantness to endure from her mother, and doubtless some heavy-handed raillery from Aunt Philips, but that her father agreed with her was such a comfort! He, at least, seemed not to doubt that, poor as she was, someone else would wish to marry her – and there was Mary pounding at her arpeggios again. (Perhaps she might do for Mr Collins after all?)

Of course, she could never have accepted him – and not only because of his odious self-satisfaction. Secretly, ever since being introduced to Mr Wickham, she found it difficult to envisage any other person as her husband. It was not only his fine looks. It was the way he would give her private smiles, the way he would make some perfectly ordinary comment diverting or even meaningful, with just a glowing glance in her direction. She really *did* believe, at times, that he felt for her something of what she herself felt for him.

And thus, when Lydia eagerly proposed that they go to Meryton, 'to see how everyone got on,' Lizzy agreed. It would refresh her

91

spirits to leave the house, where Mr Collins made his displeasure so obvious… and was not there a chance that Mr Wickham might already have returned? How she longed to remind herself of his dark eyes, to hear again that deep, well-modulated voice – and to share Miss Bingley's outrageous impertinence at the Netherfield ball.

Chapter 23

(From Miss Mary Bennet's private papers)

He has offered and been refused! What a fuss! Why, even the maids can speak of nothing else! I was not by – I was working – when I first heard Kitty rush into Lydia's room shrieking, 'It is happening! It is! Mr Collins is asking for Lizzy's hand in the drawing-room!'

My first feeling, I must admit, was one of pure annoyance. Heart sinking, I thought, 'So it is Lizzy, after all! Well, it was only to be expected, men being what they are (and had not Fordyce himself predicted it?).

Lizzy – who had never succeeded in finishing Rousseau – Lizzy, who had given up on Gibbon without a sigh ('So many pointless wars!') – was the lucky sister Mr Collins had selected, after all. What a waste – and what a shock as well, for who would have imagined that Eliza would be engaged before Jane? I opened my door in time to hear Lydia cry, 'La! Engaged to Mr Collins, after all! And I should not wonder if we do not have new gowns for the wedding!'

'But those froglike hands!' objected Kitty.

'And that oily voice!' And here Lydia imitated Mr Collins's thoughtful compliments to Mama, at breakfast. ('Delicious porridge – and a chop fit for Rosings, itself!')

In short, not an hour before, we had all been at breakfast and without the slightest hint of Mr Collins having any such intent – but no, there *had* been a hint, for he had said how pretty a cap Lizzy had on, though it was neither as new nor as pretty as Jane's.

Yet I still feel oppressed by what might have been. For, with just a fraction more time, I might have been the lady of Longbourn, and very much calmer, more organised and generally suited to such a position than Lizzy could ever be. But I had insufficient time even for regret before Lydia was rapping noisily on my door again, crying, 'Mary! There is such fun here, for Mr Collins has offered and Lizzy will not have him!'

I felt conscious of a rush of hope, as I repeated, 'Not have him! Is she mad?'

'Well, *I* think it shows a great deal of spirit. At any rate, you must come into our room, for he is in the garden and is striding about in such a funny way, with his hands behind his back!' And I had scarcely time to lament so disrespectful a reflection upon a gentleman and a clergyman before Mama entered, in a great rush.

'Dearest Mary!' she said – which I could never remember her saying before, because it is generally 'dearest Lydia' or else 'dearest Jane' – 'whatever have you got on?'

'Why, my working muslin, Mama. What should I be wearing else?'

'Well! You must change then, and quickly too, for I am going half-distracted! Mr Collins has offered to Lizzy and the silly goose has dared to refuse him – Aye, she has indeed, and refused to listen to reason as well – but *that* is all by the bye. So, you must change into the gown with the purple ribbon that Lizzy gave you at

Christmas. And then you must come with me and make eyes at your cousin Collins.'

As, in this singular instance, her thoughts chimed so neatly with my own, I made no objection.

Instead, I put down my book and silently changed my dress – yes, I did – and I permitted her to put up my hair, though she never even paused for breath, but kept talking, through the hairpins, about how thankless Lizzy was, and how – due to her selfishness – we should, one and all, be out on the streets before our father's body was cold. Though it is, at present, as warm as anybody's, and I could not imagine Mr Collins pushing anyone onto the street. I did not resist her hairpins either, though secretly convinced that Mr Collins was not to be won with vapid fripperies, but with Kant and Rousseau instead.

'And 'twas not two days ago since he confided that he had come here on purpose to find a wife, and what will any man be doing of an evening, with a snug little parsonage, all by himself? And Longbourn awaiting him! And so, what *you* need to do, my dearest child, is to smile a good deal, and to laugh whenever he says anything witty, and to nod and fix your eyes upon him when he does not, and – Oh Lord, here is Charlotte Lucas walking up, as if we had not enough to be thinking of!'

The burden of all was that I was to do my best, for the sake of the family. It was my bounden duty. Thus I descended and first wandered around the garden, in hopes of encountering our cousin. But he had gone to the library, doubtless discomposing Papa a good deal, for he loathes it when anyone else is there. And during luncheon, though excessively polite to the rest of us, Mr Collins would not even look at Lizzy, but kept his head turned the other way.

Lizzy herself was silent – most likely repenting – but Charlotte Lucas most helpful in soothing his ruffled feelings and in engaging his attention. Afterwards, Mama proposed that we all walk out on the woodland path, but Lizzy refused and, though I chose to go, I could do nothing, for Charlotte Lucas chatted to him most of the time, and Kitty and Lydia were as giggling and useless as ever.

And in the evening it was our father's turn to become exasperated, when Mr Collins followed him to his library. I heard him joke to Lizzy, 'I wish you had accepted the fellow after all, for he haunts me like a shadow, and never reads more than a page without wishing to share his thoughts and impressions… Why, here is a happy notion! Why do you not tell Mr Collins that you have changed your mind?'

Lizzy saw no humour in this, but I have noticed before that those with a reputation for wit detest being the butt of wit in others.

But there is still tomorrow, and Mr Collins is not to go before his time. I was sorry to learn, from Charlotte, that her brother Timothy is again poorly. It is a pity as, of all the Lucases, he is the most interesting, and I enjoyed dancing with him at the Netherfield ball.

Chapter 24

Longbourn

The next day, Mary made a plan. No sooner had her sisters departed for Meryton than she put away her pen, having just inspired herself with the immortal Fordyce: 'Women may avail themselves of every decent attraction, that can lead to a state for which they were manifestly formed.' And 'should they, by any neglect of their persons render themselves less amiable than God has made them, they would disappoint the design of their creation.'

Then, after pinching her cheeks as hard as she could, she trotted down the stairs.

She found her mother and Mr Collins in the drawing-room. He, having borrowed a book from his host's library, was busily excerpting quotes for a sermon. It was however an exercise that he appeared very willing to suspend in favour of being flattered by Mrs Bennet. He was just saying, 'Just so. Indeed. Such an attitude as that will win her no friends for, portionless as she is – why, here is Miss Mary. And I had thought you all in Meryton!'

'Nay, *I* have no interest in Meryton. I cannot conceive what entices my sisters there so often!'

'I confess myself quite of your opinion, Miss Mary – though your aunt is most kind, and I was exceedingly grateful for her attentions, upon the occasion of my visit to Church Street.'

'And such a fuss about officers! Really, one would suppose a red coat to cover any number of sins.'

He looked at her then with some attention, at the same moment as her mother, busily poking at the fire, cried, 'If I must be truthful, I well recollect relishing the company of young soldiers when I was a girl – but Mary has this much in common with her father, she always did prefer a book!'

'Do you think it too wet to walk, Mama?' asked Mary earnestly.

'Heavens, child, how should I know? – I have been far too busy even to poke my nose outside the door! What say you, Mr Collins? Have *you* yet ventured?' He had not; but pronounced himself willing to accompany his young cousin on her 'perambulations'. Mary rushed to fetch her pelisse and they set out together.

Fixing her eye rather beadily on him, she said, 'Tell me, Mr Collins, what think you of Fordyce?'

'I think him admirable,' said Mr Collins with alacrity, 'for example, his "When I have seen a woman in a rage, I have always wished for a mirror, to show her to herself. How would she then have started back from her own image, if not an absolute demon!"'

'A powerful passage, indeed,' said Mary gravely, but was then treated to what he considered other noteworthy excerpts from the noble Scot's opinions for another half-hour. Mary had analysed the original source more diligently than her cousin, but she obliged herself neither to interrupt him nor to set him right – though, when he misattributed a quotation, she had to bite her tongue in order to desist.

She tried him next with the Bible, but he seemed far more interested in describing the gold plate at Rosings – though equally pleased to discuss his patroness's opinions on the inequities of taxation, the presumption of the local residents at Warleigh Hall and the dilapidated state of the local school. No other subject seemed to gratify him to anything like the same degree. It was all rapturous adoration: 'Her Ladyship's condescension, Miss Mary, is extraordinary! I find myself – and this, by the bye, is passing rare – at a loss to describe it. So generous in her advice! So discerning in her judgement!' When Mary protested that she was entirely convinced, he wagged his forefinger at her. 'But you, at so delicate an age, Miss Mary, can have no notion just how rare such behaviour is!' And she was treated to another ten minutes of Lady Catherine before she could return to Fordyce again.

Chapter 25

Another day passed, and during the evening and night that followed, Mr Collins thought a good deal, principally about Miss Charlotte Lucas, who seemed to him a most sympathetic person. Upon first meeting her, he had not paid her much attention, though she had made some exceedingly intelligent comments at the Netherfield ball. While the previous day, as they had been walking with the others, he had contrived to converse with her, and the results had been far from displeasing.

He had first remarked on the throaty song of the wood pigeons. Miss Lucas had said, 'My favourite birds. Their cooing falls so soothingly upon the ear!'

'I must say that I agree. I have, in my humble abode,' he had told her, 'a small dovecote. However, as the doves were inclined to be messy, I secured three china doves in their stead. In my opinion, they look quite charming.'

'What a clever idea, Mr Collins!'

'It was, I must admit, Her Ladyship's own suggestion, along with the new cupboards, and the addition of a separate pantry. However, I have other such schemes in mind, not to mention the expansion of the stables.'

'How delightful it must be to have a home of one's own! I can imagine nothing more charming than planning modest improvements and watching them come to fruition.'

How bright her eyes were – really, she was not so very plain! Meanwhile Miss Mary Bennet – she had been trotting alongside them – made some observation on Immanuel Kant. (An odd girl, and one somewhat lacking in the social graces, in Mr Collins's opinion.) He had for that reason elected to ignore the allusion to Kant.

'I consider the maintenance of the property, my dear Miss Lucas, to be almost as solemn a duty as my obligation to abase myself before my lady patroness, in gratitude for my elevation. An astonishing woman! An astonishing woman, indeed!'

Miss Lucas had said – and very sensibly too, 'I have always heard what a remarkable and agreeable woman she is.'

'I am in a position to assure you, Miss Lucas, that she is all that you have heard, and more besides! There is nothing of politics beyond her understanding. As for her generosity, I am invited to Rosings so regularly that another neighbour – a fellow of the name of Johnson – jests that Her Ladyship can scarce endure an evening without my attendance. This, between ourselves, is not strictly true – Johnson *will* have his little joke – but, if there is a joint of meat, I am invariably begged to carve it. And whenever I dine at Rosings, she always takes care to have two full courses – while she is as generous with her advice as she is in every other respect. Indeed, it was she who advised me that my hat was set at rather too rakish an angle for one of my position.'

'I have often observed the same fault,' said Charlotte Lucas, 'in men of the cloth. And indeed, in men in general.'

'I daresay. I expect you have. Ladies notice a very great deal, in my humble opinion – Her Ladyship, particularly. And she is not only perfectly conversant with French and Italian, but has no small knowledge of Latin, besides!'

'I am very fond of Latin,' Miss Mary had interrupted. 'As Hippocrates so aptly observed, "*Ars longa, vita brevis*" – meaning, "Art is long, life is short."'

'Quite. And not merely Latin, Miss Lucas! Her eye for art is just – her ear for music sublime! Sadly, for one blessed with such exquisite taste, she does not perform. But it is a privilege, merely to hear her *speak* of music! As I always say, "Her insights, in every respect, set her far above the generality of her sex."'

'I honour her,' Miss Lucas had said, lowering her eyes, 'for my own talents are only domestic.'

'Excellent, excellent!' Mr Collins had cried – and indeed, it was at that very moment when the magnificent idea had first occurred to him, just as Miss Mary quoted Reverend Fordyce. For was not *Miss Charlotte Lucas* the epitome of what Lady Catherine had long since been recommending for his own happiness?

Her Ladyship's words still resounded in his ears: 'Choose properly, choose a gentlewoman for *my* sake. And for your *own*, let her be an active, useful sort of person, not brought up high, but able to make a small income go a good way. This is my advice. Find such a woman, and I shall visit her.'

She might have had Miss Lucas in mind! 'A gentlewoman, not brought up high' – humble, agreeable, religious, with a docile manner and a sweet smile. Clever, but not obtrusively so. Attractive, but not so attractive that her beauty could prove a distraction. Sensible – and doubtless a very economical manager, as well. Self-confessedly domestic – he imagined his abode blessed with a woman's touch. 'The daughter of Sir William Lucas' did not sound ill! And she was of a sensible age – whilst her modest demeanour must be as acceptable to Her Ladyship as a comfort to himself.

And who *were* the Bennets, after all, that he should be privileging them? – it was scarcely his fault, that he was next in the entail! And while Mrs Bennet was affable enough, Mr Bennet seemed less sensible of the honour of his company. The fellow possessed a most admirable library but Mr Collins had sometimes imagined him not best-pleased to share it.

As for the Misses Bennet, the eldest was already secured and the two youngest impossible, while Miss Elizabeth, in the words of her own mother, was 'a wilful, selfish, ungrateful creature!' He secretly doubted that anyone would ever again offer to Miss Elizabeth. As for Miss Mary, she had assuredly read a great deal, but seemed to lack the slightest intuition about when to speak and when to be silent. A curious young woman – a most curious young woman, indeed!

Whereas Miss Lucas's attentiveness was balm to his wounded feelings: those timidly admiring glances, the way in which she seemed to hang upon his every word, her demure collectedness. Oh, she would make him the happiest of men! By midnight his resolution was formed, and the next morning found him of the same mind.

After giving a final polish to his boots, Mr Collins gave the mirror a last glance. Really, he was a well-looking fellow! – particularly when holding his breath, for he was, as well, an excellent trencherman. But what woman would wish to marry a man as scrawny as the Bennet's footman or Master Timothy Lucas? Then he crept downstairs and out of the main entrance, startling Mrs Hill, who was relishing the fineness of the day from the doorstep.

'Why, Mr Collins, sir!'

'I am exceedingly sorry to startle you. I am – ah – I am merely taking an early stroll.'

'Very good, sir,' said Mrs Hill – but secretly, she wondered. For the man was headed towards Lucas Lodge – was he not? – when the walks in every other direction were reckoned superior. And then, that Miss Lucas had been calling almost daily since he had been visiting. In short, if that Miss Lucas had not set her cap at him then she – Mrs Hill – was a Dutchman! She bustled inside, to canvas Bessy's opinion.

Miss Lucas was tidying the ribbons on her bureau when she noticed a hatted figure in black, boasting a certain heaviness of jowl and a certain portliness of outline, emerging into the avenue. Swiftly retrieving a small leather-bound book, she slipped downstairs and out the side door, past the labyrinth. There she sat, supposedly immersed in it.

'Miss Lucas! You are up betimes! What are you reading?'

'Why, only the psalms,' said she, slipping the book into her pocket, as he smiled approvingly down at her. 'Will you come inside?'

'I would prefer to remain outside, if you might do me the honour of joining me?'

Silently, she took his arm, wondering what Mama would conjecture, were she, in turn, to glance out of an upstairs window. And, as he continued his enumeration of the beauties of the morning, she solidified her thinking, and stiffened her resolve.

She thought: 'My life is not freedom, it is servitude, instead! – the scrimping and saving, the cooking and making-do, the washing and mending, not to mention the teaching and correcting of all my youngest siblings! What woman would not prefer the security of an independent home? Mr Collins is tedious – he is, in fact, perilously, extravagantly and quite astonishingly tedious – but he is immensely eligible, as well: someday, he will be Master of Longbourn. In short, Mr Collins – podgy and greedy, obsequious and sententious – might very well represent my last best chance!'

He cleared his throat and said, 'My dear Miss Lucas, you will no doubt be astonished to learn that, almost as soon as we were

– ah – introduced, I singled you out as the companion of my future life.'

'Why, Mr Collins!' she cried.

'But before I am run away with my feelings on this subject, perhaps it would be advisable for me to state my reasons for marrying – and, moreover, for coming into Hertfordshire with the design of selecting a wife, as I certainly did. My reasons for marrying are, first, that I think it a right thing for every clergyman in easy circumstances – like myself – to set the example of matrimony; secondly, that I am convinced that it will add very greatly to my happiness; and thirdly – which perhaps I ought to have mentioned earlier, that it is the particular advice and recommendation of the very noble lady whom I have the honour of calling patroness.'

Charlotte smiled up at him affectionately, as he strutted along, jowls a-quiver with his own appreciation of his nobility. Heavens, what a speech! But he had prepared it – he had clearly memorised it – let him, by all means lay it out before her: the 'violence' of his affection, his 'conviction' of her suitability, praise for the humble abode where she was to make him the happiest of men, and praise still more ardent for that rather less humble abode near to his own, where she would be summoned, to express gratitude to Her Ladyship, to second her every opinion, and to marvel at her every possession. Charlotte took a long look down the avenue of years – her abode, her hens, perhaps her children – and felt content. She would be relatively independent and, eventually, relatively wealthy. She had relieved her father and brothers of responsibility for her. She had done well.

But Mr Collins had – finally – stopped, and was looking down at her beneficently, beaming. He was waiting for her, so trustingly! She must not disappoint him – she must try never to disappoint him.

'Mr Collins,' said Charlotte steadily, 'I would be delighted – indeed honoured – to marry you.'

He lifted her hand rapturously to his lips. 'My dear Charlotte, you see before you the happiest of men! I shall go to your father, without loss of time. How immensely surprised he will be!'

This, thought Charlotte wryly, was very true, if less than gallant. She crossed to a wooden bench and closed her eyes, imagining the scene: her lover's self-importance, her father's delight… Lizzy, of course, would detest the very idea of the match – Lizzy, who had only just rejected him, herself! – but she would eventually reconcile herself to the idea. Perhaps she might even visit them in Kent?

Charlotte was surprised, far sooner than she had expected, to again hear footsteps on the gravel, and to find her brother Timothy approaching. How thin he looked! But she and Timothy had always perfectly understood each other.

He said, 'I saw him just now – proud, jubilant – and I presume, on his way to Papa.'

'You, at least, cannot have been surprised. You must have perfectly realised what I was about.'

'I had some suspicion, certainly.' He sat down beside her. 'Rather a noble thing to be doing, in my opinion. And thus, very Charlotte-like.'

'You forget that I was never sentimental, like you.'

'Me!'

'And that you love poetry, which *I* cannot abide. And beyond that, I believe that I can manage him. Not all marriages are love matches, as you know. Our parents' was not, nor the Bennets' – nor even the Gouldings', I believe.'

'But mine will be.'

She looked at him – so slim, so straight, so young – and thought,

'I hope that it will. I pray that it will – whoever the lady might be!' And deeper still: 'And how I pray that you live!'

But then, because she could not bear the weight of this last, she rose and kissed him, and said, 'Let us go in, my dearest Timothy, and endure the brunt of our family's joy together!'

Chapter 26

(From Mr Darcy's diaries)

When we surprised Charles in London, I determined to be kind, recalling what it had cost me to leave Rome. But if I felt more sombre than usual, *he* was very light indeed, 'I was never more surprised,' said he, 'than when you were announced! Did you miss me so outrageously that you could no longer endure Netherfield without me? For Louisa looked uncommonly serious, just now.'

'Being serious at breakfast is an admirable fault; Hurst ought to bless his own good fortune. A sensible man does not wish for playfulness in a wife – at least, not in the morning.'

Bingley laughed. 'Nay, be honest with me. Tell me why you, my sisters – and Hurst, of course – are come.'

'I will, if you promise that it will make no difference to our friendship.'

'To our friendship! I should think not, indeed!'

'Then – I came because of the ball.'

Charles helped himself to coffee, and mocked, 'Nay, we all know how much you love a ball!'

'Yet I detested the ball at Netherfield more than most.'

'Why, whatever was amiss with it?'

'Your servants excelled, your sisters did you credit –'

'Then you objected to the company, instead?' he inquired, tensely.

'I did, and to the members of *one* family, in particular.'

At this, Bingley blushed deeper than I had ever seen him. 'Darcy, this is not fair. 'Tis not Miss Bennet's fault that her youngest sisters –'

'It was not only the youngest. Miss Mary –'

'Miss Mary will never set the Thames afire, but she is a good-natured creature.'

'Bingley, all your partiality cannot disguise the fact that the Bennet family is impossible.'

'Not at all!' cried Bingley. 'For Miss Elizabeth, though I cannot always catch her meaning, is as delightful as Miss Bennet, whom even Caroline dotes upon. And their father is formidably well-informed.'

'He is no one's idea of a fool, I concede, but he does nothing to restrain his daughters – or his wife. And as for their cousin' – here, to give him his due, Bingley did wince – 'he is beyond bearing. There was Collins forcing himself upon the party, the youngest sisters drowning out the fiddles with their laughter, the middle sister destroying the comfort of the company with the ponderousness of her introductions, the mother loudly bragging of your passion for Miss Bennet, and the father thinking it all a great joke!'

'But not even you, Darcy, can say a word against Miss Bennet!'

'I cannot, and I do not intend to try. Miss Bennet is charming.'

'Charming!' cried Charles. 'Oh, much more than charming! It is not only her beauty – I hope I can see past mere beauty – it is her sweetness, her kindness, her thoughtfulness, her speaking voice! She would be the toast of London, would only her father bestir himself sufficiently to take her there!'

'It is, most probably, not within his means. And I suspect that she is content and complacent enough, as she is.'

Bingley's eyes sparked. 'Complacent? You find her complacent?'

'Perhaps that seems harsh – I daresay it does. But she has the languid grace of one so accustomed to admiration as to be rarely moved, herself.'

'By which you mean, she does not care a fig for me. Go on, say it. Say it!'

'I cannot say it, Bingley, for I cannot *know*. I suspect, however, that, though flattered by her conquest, her heart remains untouched.'

Bingley was struck. He took a few steps, then turned and asked, 'And your reason? For surely – *you* must know!'

Secretly, I doubted this, for had I not fallen in love, and left the lady, only to be sued and pursued? Aloud, I only said, 'It is only that – that a woman in love has more – variability. Why, she showed no greater pleasure in accepting your hand than she did Goulding's! I find such coolness as admirable as it is rare, but it does not suggest the heart of a woman in love.'

Bingley was silent, then: 'You do not think she dislikes me?'

'Not at all! It is only that I have searched in vain for any symptom of more serious regard.'

'While *I* have never seen her equal!' Bingley strode around the room, immersed in thought. Finally, he said, 'I – I do not wish to put my judgement above yours, Darcy. However, my own impression is different. I believed her to confide her hand to mine with more confidence and greater warmth than she entrusted it to any other man. I could have sworn her eyes were softer, as they gazed into my own, than into yours or Mr Goulding's. But what do I know? – I, who made myself the laughingstock of London over

Lady Diana? What do I know of women's feelings? It is likely only my own wishes, because – of every woman I have ever encountered, Miss Bennet seems – but then, compared to you, I am rather a stupid fellow. And so, if *you* think her untouched and unmoved, then – why, in such a circumstance, there is nothing left for me at Netherfield. Quite the opposite!'

'What! You would give the place up, in an instant?'

Bingley whirled. 'In an instant? – far, far quicker than that! I should hate to go back – it would be odious, noxious, to me, after this revelation! For me, it would always be coloured by – recollections. By places where *she* looked so exquisite, by moments when I was thinking that she – but never mind. You may believe me, Darcy, when I say that I shall never go there more. And yet, advise me, I beg! How might I extricate myself, with any honour, after such proofs of affection as I have given? – for I feel as if we were already bound to each other by every solicitor in London!'

I could only advise – thinking, as you might surmise, of a very different woman – to go down to Netherfield no more, to distract himself as much as he could, and to attempt to believe that the strength of his own feelings had misled him. I could only smile – almost painfully – when he burst out, 'You, who have every woman in the world at your feet, cannot imagine how unbearable it is, when the only woman you care for is indifferent!'

And catching my wry smile – for had not the only woman I had ever cared for disdained me, and for a bass-baritone besides? – he accused me of making light of his suffering. ('You are recollecting Lady Diana, I know, but *she* was only a doll: attractive but empty, and entirely without substance!')

At this outburst, I must own that I felt uneasy. I could have been mistaken in Miss Bennet, of course. But could Louisa Hurst and I *both* have been mistaken? – I could not believe it. Had Miss Bennet ever said anything to Bingley that she would not to any other man, then – but if she had, I never heard it. Her air was so unvarying, her manners so discreet – there was never a slip, never even a momentary loss of composure. She was the opposite of Giuditta, indeed! – for *her* temper fluctuated with the wind, and it was all her own maid could do to keep windward of it!

Later, I confided my worries to Louisa, but she dismissed them.

'If ever I could conceive any lady without ambition,' said she, 'it would be Jane Bennet. She has shown nothing for Charles beyond pleasure in the attention. I am as convinced as ever that she cares for him not at all... The difficulty is that he is every bit as likely to fall in love with someone greatly his superior, such as Lady Diana, as with the inferior Miss Bennet. I shall never be easy till he is wed, for only such an event will see the end of it!'

And Caroline, who had understood only in part, said, 'The end of it, indeed! But I must write to Miss Bennet with our apologies with regard to the dinner engagement, as soon as may be... How surprised she will be, to receive it from town!'

Chapter 27

Longbourn

Jane was at first silent, and later distressed, after receiving Miss Bingley's pretty note, but Lizzy ridiculed her fears.

'Nay, he will soon return – next week, or the next. The *beau monde* cannot bear to be from town for long, you know, for fear of being forgotten by their grandest acquaintance. But Bingley will soon have quite enough of concerts and theatres and yearn again for the freedom of the country and the rides around Netherfield. While

Miss Bingley has only followed him, I am persuaded, on Mr Darcy's account.'

'But she says they may not, in her own words, "return this winter" – and then, that line about her hopes that Miss Georgiana Darcy might become her sister!'

'*That* is only Miss Bingley indulging in her own hopes and wishes. As if Miss Darcy would demean herself to marry lower than a duke! – But I expect our aunt and uncle will invite you to return to town with them after their Christmas visit. In which case you might well see the Bingleys there, instead of here.'

That afternoon, at their Aunt Philips's, Lizzy teased Wickham about the Netherfield ball. 'You were missed by many,' said she.

'But not by you,' he said knowingly, 'as much as by all the rest.'

'Why would you think so?'

'Because you – and, to some degree, your eldest sister – must have been far too sought-after to notice, of course!'

Elizabeth blushed. 'My cousin refused to leave my side – but no one could take such a man as *that* seriously.'

His gaze sought hers as he said, in an undertone, 'I am delighted to hear it – else I should feel a jealousy better left unexpressed.'

How strange it was that she could, almost, feel a kind of heat emanating from him as he spoke. Surely, he did not mean… Then, with relief, she recalled Miss Bingley. 'You were however a topic of conversation,' she said, as lightly as she could.

'But that would only be Denny, making quips at my expense.'

'As to *that*, I could not say. But while I was dancing with Mr Darcy –'

'Dancing with Darcy! Did I not tell you that you would be too sought-after to miss me?' he said, laughing.

'Do not tease me, I beg – I had not the presence of mind to pretend to be engaged. But when I mentioned your ill-treatment at his hands, he persuaded Miss Bingley to harangue me, with regards to his innocence.'

Wickham frowned. 'What, Miss Bingley harangued you?'

'She did, claiming that *I* had been misinformed, and that you were not to be trusted – but *she* would take Darcy's part in everything!'

Wickham took her hand and – just – squeezed it, making her pulse speed. 'You, my dear Miss Bennet, are a true friend, to a man with very few. How I honour you!'

Eliza blushed deeply and then asked, 'Why does he hate you so?'

'Truly? Well, truly then, I do not know! All I do know is that, wherever I find myself, Darcy tries to bring me down. He had me dismissed from school, by pretending I had done something that I was perfectly guiltless of… He tried to persuade his father that I was too intellectually inferior for university, and nearly succeeded! Despite which, I completed my degree. I guessed, the moment I heard that Darcy was in Hertfordshire, that he would attempt to blacken my name – but to be honest, I had very little money, and precious little choice.'

Lizzy thought, 'How refreshing such honesty is!' But all she said was, 'It is likely only jealousy.'

'Yes, had his father liked me less, Darcy might have liked me more. But 'tis a sad case when such a fellow – a man possessing riches, property and influence – chooses to misuse all the power he commands!'

'It is more than sad,' said Eliza warmly. 'It is quite wicked!'

'But how can I thank you for standing – and so staunchly – in my cause?' he inquired, with that crinkling-eyed smile she so admired. 'I know how I would *wish* to thank you,' and again, she felt a wave of heat, 'but *that* must be impossible.'

She thought confusedly, 'Ought I to pretend to be offended?' – though she was not, in fact, offended. But the conversation then became general, and the other ladies permitted their share of Mr Wickham's attention.

Late that night, she recalled two other moments she thought significant. While describing that famous beauty, Lady Diana, he mentioned having only twice seen her equal, and his gaze had strayed towards her. The other moment had occurred at the end of the evening when, as the party was boisterously breaking up, he had held her hand a moment longer than usual, while the expression in his eyes almost overpowered her.

Recollecting it, she thought, 'It felt, in that moment, as if I was falling into his eyes. Is this what is meant by "falling" in love?'

Chapter 28

At Christmas, the Gardiners arrived at Longbourn, with their children. Mr Gardiner was an intelligent and thoughtful man of business, very different from his sister, Mrs Bennet. No less different was his petite and elegant wife, a particular favourite of her eldest nieces. Lizzy took care to introduce Mr Wickham to Mrs Gardiner, as soon as opportunity offered. She had grown up not far from the Pemberley estate where he had been born, and they had acquaintances in common. Mrs Gardiner was as delighted by his manners as was every other lady – but after watching Lizzy carefully over several meetings, took it upon herself to advise her.

'First, my dear Lizzy, I am so sorry for poor Jane! It seemed such a desirable match, and I am exceedingly sorry that it went off. But these things happen so often! A young man, such as you describe Bingley, so often falls in love with a young girl and, when accident separates them, so easily forgets her, that these inconsistencies are very frequent!'

'An admirable consolation, in its way,' said Eliza drily. 'But it will not do for *us*. We do not suffer by accident. It is not often that the interference of friends will persuade a young man of independent means to think no more of a girl with whom he was violently in love.'

'Poor Jane! If it was really so, then her case is hard indeed! – but perhaps she might be persuaded to come back to London with us? A change of scene might prove of use, and I trust that no consideration with regard to Mr Bingley will concern her. We live in such different circles, all our connections must be different, and thus it is almost impossible that she and Mr Bingley should meet – unless he might come to find her, I suppose!'

'But *that* will never happen, for Mr Darcy would not allow it,' said Lizzy. Despite this, though, she could not resist a rush of hope on Jane's account. Was it truly so impossible that Jane and Bingley might meet again in town, and that their mutual affection might prevail? But her aunt had something more to say. 'And now, another thing. You are too sensible a girl, Lizzy, to fall in love simply because you are warned against it and yet – seriously – I wish to warn you to be on your guard against Mr Wickham.'

'My dear aunt, this is serious indeed!'

'I am serious, and I mean to engage you to be serious likewise. He is a most interesting young man and – had he the fortune he deserves – I believe that you could not do better. But as it is, you ought not to involve either yourself or him in a connection so imprudent. You must not let your fancy run away with you. You have sense, and we all expect you to use it.'

'Well then, he shall not be in love with me, if I can prevent it.'

'Lizzy, you are not serious now.'

'I beg your pardon. I shall try again. At the moment, I am not in love with Mr Wickham. But he is, beyond comparison, the most agreeable man I ever – and if he was to become attached to me – I believe it will be better if he does not. Oh – that deplorable Mr Darcy! – In short, my dear Aunt, I will try not to be too encouraging. When in company with Mr Wickham, I will try not to be wishing. In short, I will do my best. And now, I hope that you are satisfied.'

Chapter 29

London

'Oh heavens, it is she – it is Jane Bennet. It is indeed!'

'Do not look in her direction,' said Louisa Hurst levelly, 'but, instead, if you please, tell me in which level she is sitting.'

'The second, near the front, and on the left. But it is certainly she!'

'Ah, there she is, between her aunt and uncle, I suppose. I cannot think that Charles will notice, however, for it is such a crowd.'

'But she might call on us!'

'I expect she will – and, if she does, why then you must receive her.'

'And then?'

Louisa sighed. 'Heavens, Caroline, must I tell you every single thing? – And then, you must be very polite but rather chilly, and talk about the weather.'

'What, in heaven's name, is the point of discussing the weather?'

'Because the weather leads to nothing and ends nowhere.'

'How I wish you would speak sensibly!'

'I fear – but it *is*, after all, my only fault – I can speak in no other fashion! What I mean is that you must say nothing of any importance, and then, if Miss Bennet has still not departed, pretend to another engagement. You must be perfectly polite but exceedingly formal, and thank her a great deal for coming, without showing the slightest interest in anything she says. Miss Bennet, after all, is not a stupid creature. She will realise that, though she was acceptable enough while we were buried in darkest Hertfordshire, here in town why, the Bennets simply will not do! And, with any luck, she will not call a second time.'

'But *that* does not signify, for I shall be obliged to return her call.'

'Indeed you will. But during the visit, in whichever godforsaken corner of Cheapside her uncle might reside, you will talk, and quite remorselessly, about the weather.'

'I do not think,' said Caroline doubtfully, 'that it is possible to talk about the weather as much as that.'

'Nay, there is no limit to the uses of the weather: at court, I believe, they speak of little else. But the point is that Charles is not to hear that you have seen her.'

'But she is not two hundred feet away!'

'Oh, indeed. Tonight, we must simply trust to luck.'

Chapter 30

(From Mr Darcy's diaries)

Colonel Fitzwilliam arrived yesterday – nothing has yet been heard from Rome, so I am in great hopes that our solicitor's letter has sorted the matter – and today we travelled down to Rosings for Easter. It will not be necessary to stay above a week, but Her

115

Ladyship would not be satisfied unless we came. I dislike leaving Georgiana – she has been delightful lately, so affectionate and settled. In fact, I wished for her to accompany us here, but she had promised to attend Miss de Lille during her nuptials, which I shall not be sorry to miss.

As Fitzwilliam and I travelled down to Kent, I found myself recalling the occasion when Georgiana had – very nearly – been seduced at Weymouth, five years before.

I had, on an impulse, decided to go to Weymouth, as the weather was set fair, and I had finished my business in town earlier than expected. I found the inn where Georgiana was staying easily enough – the Red Lion – and decided to surprise her. Therefore, without being announced, I knocked on the door to her suite. When she opened it, I instantly noticed that she looked skittish, almost nervous – and with me, of all people! I kissed her brow and she cried, 'I – oh, Fitzwilliam! I never expected you!'

'It seemed so long since last I saw you that I could not resist.'

'How delightful! And – and how is your horse? I thought your horse was injured?'

'It was not a serious fall – but, of course, I came in the chaise.' She seemed strangely restless, yet blooming, as blooming as the posy on the table. I inquired, 'I expect I am wrong – but is not that a new gown?'

'It is fairly new. I ordered it from – but *that* would not interest you!'

'My dear Georgiana, is something wrong? You seem distracted.'

'Not at all! I am perfectly well! I have just had a few nervous headaches lately, that is all – as if I was obliged to perform before someone of great importance, and yet I could not do it.'

I removed my gloves. 'I have never been able to comprehend how only the most gifted performers are so concerned with their performance. Had you endured Miss Bingley's playing last week –'

'Ah, poor Miss Bingley! You have no idea how devoted she is to you.'

'Nor do I wish to know,' I said, rather discomfited.

I supposed that I had startled her, by arriving so unexpectedly, yet her agitation only seemed to increase during the meal that followed. Mrs Younge, her chaperone, seemed exactly as usual – which is to say, worthy if rather officious. But I could not prevent myself from thinking Georgiana disordered in spirits, one moment vivacious, the next withdrawn, and at times in an almost pitiful state of exhaustion. I questioned Mrs Younge, once my sister's high sweet voice could be heard engaged in some vocal exercise in the next room.

'I do not know why,' I said, 'but to me Georgiana seems – ill-at-ease.'

'Ill-at-ease! In what respect, I beg? For she eats well – today was quite the aberration – sleeps well, and rides most days, with great enjoyment, while the doctor gave her the most flaming report!'

I was struck by a chilling thought. 'Do you ride out with her, Mrs Younge?'

'No, sir. Instead, Hawkes attends her. A most reliable young fellow.'

I knew nothing of this Hawkes, though his father had run the stables at Pemberley for at least ten years. But when I offered to accompany Georgiana on her ride that afternoon, to my astonishment, I watched her face fall. 'No, no, I shall not go far enough for your pleasure!'

'But to accompany you must be sufficient pleasure in itself.'

117

She finally agreed, but most unwillingly. I arranged to borrow a horse from the inn, and we eventually set off, moving from cobbled streets to open country. She rode beautifully, but I was still conscious of a strangeness. As we slowed to a walk, I said, 'Perhaps riding with a mere brother might bore you. Perhaps there is some other man you might prefer?' Her blush at this was so extreme that I pulled up the mare, in consternation. Had I stumbled upon the reason for her strangeness? Could Georgiana, young as she was and sheltered as she had always been, possibly have fallen in love already? – It was almost unimaginable to me. Not that a young man might admire her – not at all! – but that *she,* at a mere fifteen…

There was a silence before she turned to face me, her face the colour of paper. I jumped down, thinking, 'Could it be still worse? Could she possibly have been compromised? In short, could the bloom that I had noticed evidence something too appalling to put into words?'

She cried, 'Oh Fitzwilliam!'

'Tell me,' I said, as steadily as I could, 'what has happened – and who has hurt you.'

'Oh! He has not hurt me!' she cried anxiously. 'Indeed, I love him dearly!'

'But – which you have not said, but which I can surmise – he is either unwilling or unable to declare his honourable intentions. Can – whoever it is – truly be as low as *that*?'

'No, no!' she cried, distressed. 'He is not low – he is all that is kind, charming and amiable but – but he fears you, for you have never liked him!'

And in that moment my heart seemed to stop, for she could mean no one beyond Wickham. I turned her around to face me, for she was sobbing bitterly. She and Wickham had always been friendly, even close. But surely not even Wickham could be capable of taking such advantage of her as – as this? 'Georgiana. Tell me that you do not speak of – of Wickham.'

'I do! He loves me and we are engaged!'

'Engaged! What! – without my consent?'

'I – I could not help it. I always loved him so!'

I pulled her to me and sought her averted gaze. 'But he has never dared – he has not –'

'Oh, never! – only my hand.'

I steadied myself and said, 'And by engaged you actually mean – engaged to him?'

'I mean, that I have agreed to marry him. I have agreed to – a secret engagement.' Adding, with so heady a mix of pride, exaltation and misery that not even I could discern which was strongest, 'Why, had you not arrived, we should have left by now!'

This was a blow, worse than all the rest!

That Georgiana had fallen in love could not astonish – she has the tenderest heart – she can rarely follow even a hunt to its conclusion without dismay – and, God knows, Wickham has never had any difficulty in attracting women. But that someone of so naturally timid and doubting a disposition could have been mad enough, not merely to pledge her troth, but to consent to an elopement! (Though perhaps her very timidity had stood his friend? – allowing him to soothe her nerves and sway her reason?) In short, this was no mere maiden fancy. They would have left together, presumably for Scotland, without my unheralded arrival! There was not a moment to be lost.

The instant we returned from the stables I rang the bell and, in tones I attempted to keep steady, requested that the landlady attend us. 'You are, I beg, to take my sister to your own rooms and to keep her there with a guard upon the door,' I said, handing her ten guineas. 'Release her to no one, beyond myself. She is in very great danger.'

'No! no, you *cannot*!' cried Georgiana. 'I beg you!'

'I can and I shall,' said I. 'Please to recollect, Georgiana, that I am not only your brother, but your guardian, as well. And I vow, on my honour, you shall not leave this place, but by my side!' As she dissolved into tears, I guided her into her room and saw her there, the door locked, and a footman standing by it, before ordering Mrs Younge to attend me in the lounge.

Perhaps she had already guessed what had happened, for her eye was almost sardonic as I said, 'I am astonished that you have sufficient nerve to face me.'

'Is it my fault the silly creature lost her head?' she asked, almost crossly.

'That is not the point, Mrs Younge. She ought never to have been left alone with any young man long enough to lose it!'

'What, your father's own godson? Who could have denied him?'

'Did he bribe you to see her alone?' I demanded – but she denied it. 'In that case, he probably took you in. However, it is of no importance. You are, I believe, paid monthly. I cannot recall the precise amount, but you will find here, in this purse, about three times your fee. Your services, I need hardly mention, will no longer be required.'

She opened the purse, eyed its contents and then said, almost wheedlingly, 'I thank you, sir – thank you kindly! But given Mr Wickham's privileged position, and the long affection between himself and Miss Darcy, I cannot think –'

'You will find the door to your right, Mrs Younge. And should you ever attempt to approach my sister again, you shall find me in a far harsher frame of mind.' I turned away then, towards the window. She hesitated, I am sure, twisting the envelope this way and that, because it took her a very long time to finally shut the door behind her.

With Georgiana secured and Younge dismissed, I next sought out Wickham in town, where I found, as I had supposed, he was not unknown. He was leaving a coffee house with a friend. A look of concern crossed his face upon sighting me, but then he smiled, 'Why, what brings you to Weymouth, Darcy? – Surely nothing as frivolous as pleasure!'

'I must speak to you alone, should your acquaintance be good enough to permit it.'

My purpose gained, I guided him into a nearby graveyard. The irony of the setting was not lost on Wickham, who made some ribald jest, but he was certainly not at his ease. I turned to face him and said coldly, 'Mr Wickham, you have defamed your name, your honour and your house!'

'Nay,' said he, with a laugh, 'she would have confessed to you, I am convinced, before anything serious could have occurred. She has a deep affection for you – quite rare, and even touching, in these sorry times!'

'She told me, not two hours hence, that you and she would – would have eloped tonight! Do you dare to deny it?'

He said not a word, but the look which he darted at me was ugly and somewhat sly. Indeed, well-looking a fellow as he is, he looked almost plain in that moment, recollecting the prize I had torn from his grasp. (And what a prize: young and pretty, gentle and accomplished – and with £30,000 of her own! Any man in England would have thought himself fortunate!)

How I longed for the feel of his jaw against my fist! The violence of my fury shocked me, especially as it could have ended in something still more serious. (*That* would indeed have encompassed his victory!) Perhaps the same thought was in his own mind – that an affair of honour might represent his last best chance – as he swore, 'Your sister loves me!'

'And you?'

'And I, well – why, who could not –'

'And Mrs Younge? Is she in love with you, as well?'

'Her kind heart only wishes Georgiana happy!'

'With such a man as *you*?' I longed to say, but bit it back. Instead: 'Did you follow her to Weymouth?'

'Never, upon my word!'

'Upon your word? Why not your honour!'

'Upon my word of honour, Darcy, I had no more notion she was here – we met at the play.'

I could perfectly imagine Georgiana's pleasure at such a meeting, the alacrity with which she would have fallen in with anything her childhood friend suggested! It might even have been blameless enough, at the beginning. He might even have fancied himself being kind, before so irresistible an opportunity arose before him!

I had previously understood that he intended to seek his fortune abroad. But he had long been furious at me – and he had never ceased regretting choosing the money over the living my father had promised. But what a perfect vengeance he had struck upon! Thank heavens my trip to Weymouth had not been delayed!

I said, as well as I remember, 'Mrs Younge conceived that some latitude must be allowed my father's godson. I entirely disagree. For that reason, I give you this warning. Should you ever speak to Georgiana again – should you ever write to her, approach her, or contrive to send her a message – you shall answer to me! She is not merely too good for you – she is ten thousand times too good for you! – And, in your heart, I believe you know it. Goodbye.'

Upon my return, I found that a maid had replaced the man guarding Georgiana's door. She told me, 'They brought up some victuals, sir, but she would not have any.'

I thanked her and entered. I found poor Georgiana curled up on the bed. At first, I thought her asleep, but her breathing was uneven and, as I approached, she opened her eyes. Her eyelids were swollen, her face desperately pale.

I sat down and waited, as patiently as I could, for I was still angry at her. I could not help thinking, 'Of every man in the world – How poorly does this testify to her sense or judgement?' I had to force myself to recollect that she was only fifteen and far from unusual in being entranced by Wickham – whom Lady Diana herself had once called the most delightful man in London. This thought did not improve the state of my temper.

'What did he say?' she begged. 'Tell me!'

'Does it matter?'

'Yes, it does matter!'

'He has resigned all aspirations to your hand.'

'What!'

I repeated my statement but was still unprepared for the flood of tears that followed. She would listen neither to me nor to reason, and in the end I said, 'Georgiana, I beg that you attempt to reason yourself into a calmer state of mind. I shall return.'

I also ordered the maid to remain in the room, in case she was desperate enough to become a danger to herself. Returning to my own quarters, I attempted to write to the Colonel, who, of course, shares with me in her guardianship, but found it strangely difficult. I kept fancying that I heard her weeping, though she was quite at the other end of the hotel. Yet the sound of her weeping seemed, almost, to follow me.

Chapter 31

London

'It was so good of you to call,' said Miss Bingley. 'I had not the slightest notion you were in town!'

'I have not been here above a week. I believe that I saw you at the Little Theatre?'

'Very likely. The weather has been particularly clement, for the time of year.'

'Indeed,' said Jane.

'I understand that it may turn, quite shortly.'

'Perhaps it may.'

'A pity. Though I understand that the crops need rain.'

'The crops?' inquired poor Jane.

'The crops,' said Miss Bingley, 'are, or so I understand, greatly in need of rain.'

(Excerpt from a letter from Jane Bennet in London to her sister)

My dearest Lizzy will, I am sure, be incapable of triumphing at my expense, when I confess myself to have been entirely deceived in Miss Bingley's regard for me. But, my dear sister, though the event has proved you right, do not think me obstinate if I assert that – her behaviour being what it was – my confidence was as natural as your suspicion… I am very sure that anxiety for her brother is the cause. If I were not afraid of judging harshly, I would almost be tempted to say that there is a strong appearance of duplicity in all of this. But I will endeavour to banish every such thought, and to think only of what will make me happy…

Chapter 32

(From Mr Darcy's diaries)

Rosings is much as usual, though that tiresome Collins fellow, cousin to Mr Bennet, is indeed ensconced at the Hunsford rectory. He called, almost the moment we arrived, in order to abase himself, and at such length that I wondered my good aunt could bear it. I marvel at what, besides his tireless toadying, so appealed to her as to give him the preference, for the living is rather a good one. To his credit, however, he has very recently married Sir William Lucas's eldest, Charlotte. She struck me as a young woman of sense, which is fortunate for, as my aunt has always patronised the local clergy, we are likely to see a good deal of her.

Also at the rectory, though only visiting, is Miss Elizabeth Bennet, the young lady whose swift wit so intrigued me when Miss Bennet was taken ill at Netherfield. I felt almost guilty upon learning that she was at Hunsford, because of the plot to detach Charles Bingley from her sister – though, as *she* will know nothing of it, the discomfort will be entirely my own.

For the first few days, my aunt was perfectly content with the Colonel and myself, in addition to her daughter – and the Colonel had a new horse to teach, which occupied some energy and time. There was the usual nuisance of my aunt's wishing me to engage with Miss de Bourgh, but we were all accustomed to *that.* ('Why do you not play at backgammon with your cousin Darcy?'… 'Have you shown your cousin your exquisite sketching of pond lilies, my dear?')

But by the weekend, even Her Ladyship wished for an addition, and summoned the Collinses. With them, in addition to Elizabeth Bennet, was Mrs Collins's sister Maria – breathy, youthful and almost overawed, not only by the grandeur of Rosings, but by Her Ladyship – and possibly, even by myself. Miss Bennet, by contrast, seemed entirely composed. She even set down my aunt, on one or two occasions.

'And so, Miss Bennet, has your governess left you?'

'We never had a governess.'

'What! No governess? How was it possible? Five daughters brought up at home without a governess! I never heard of such a thing! Your mother must have been quite a slave to your education.'

'She was not. In fact, we managed rather better without her.'

'Well! And are any of your younger sisters out, Miss Bennet?'

'Yes, ma'am, all.'

'What, all five out at once? The youngest out before the eldest is married? How very odd! Your younger sisters must be young indeed!'

'Yes, my youngest sister is not yet sixteen. Perhaps *she* is full young to be much in company. But really, ma'am, it would be hard for younger sisters to miss their share of society and amusement because the elder might lack the means or inclination to marry. Surely the last has as good a right to the pleasures of youth as the first! And to be kept back on *such* a motive – it would not be likely to promote sisterly affection or delicacy of mind.'

'Upon my word! You give your opinions very decidedly for so young a person. Pray, what is your age?'

'With three sisters younger than myself, you can scarcely expect me to own it,' said Miss Bennet. My aunt's expression! – the Colonel and I were much amused.

When Fitzwilliam petitioned her for some music, Miss Bennet performed, and rather better than I had recollected. Her voice is not well-trained, but unusually expressive. She sang 'My mother bids me bind my hair' with an elegance that my sister might have admired, though Georgiana has a polish that most young ladies fall well short of. The Colonel seemed very much struck, saying to me, once we were alone, 'How piquant Miss Bennet is!'

'Quite. I saw something of her in Hertfordshire.'

'And Mrs Collins is an astute and well-judging woman. What a pity she found it expedient to wed that Collins fellow!'

'Expedient is probably exact, for the Lucas family is numerous and not well-off.'

'Well, I enjoyed them both. Perhaps tomorrow afternoon, we might call at the rectory, after taking out the dogs?'

I made no objection, as it would make a change and the walk was a lovely one. As for Miss Bennet, she is well enough, but she has none of Giuditta's mischief. For all her quickness, there can surely be no danger in the acquaintance, either to myself or to the Colonel.

Chapter 33

(From Mr Darcy's diaries)

Possibly because I had been looking over my previous diaries, I dreamed strange dreams in the night, and woke up recollecting scenes long past.

Wickham, of course, was always there. One of my earliest memories is of the two of us playing with the puppy I received on my fourth birthday. My father, who was kind to a fault, gave

Wickham a puppy, too. In fact, his kindness to George was such that I remember quizzing him, 'He is not another cousin, then?'

'He is no relation at all.'

'I could *pretend* he was my brother, however, as I have none?'

'You *could* pretend, but that would not make it true. Someday, perhaps, you will have a brother.' And I fancied a shadow on his face.

Of course, the wished-for brother never came, and I was ten when Georgiana did. By then I had outgrown my affection, both for the notion of a brother, and for George Wickham, himself. I was very well-pleased with the pink bundle my mother cradled – and not at all jealous. Though I *was* – if I am honest – occasionally jealous of my father's regard for George Wickham, who had, even at ten, a knack for judging tone, and a knack for pleasing.

'You do not like Mrs Shipley,' I accused him, 'yet you told Mama that she was the most charming of all her friends!'

'That was only to please your mama, however.'

'And so then, it was a lie?'

'Papa says that, in society, people are obliged to lie. It is called manners there and matters more than anything!'

Secretly, I doubted, for my own father had never told me this, and my father was very much better educated than George's. I could also not help wondering, given his untruths, how far I could depend upon George's protestations of regard. Meanwhile, my father astonished me, after I had already been a year at school, by telling me that George would be joining me the following term.

'But can Mr Wickham afford it?' I asked him.

'He cannot. But George is my godson, and I promised to do all I could for him. I could not manage the estate, you know, without his father.'

I knew this already, for my father was of impulsive rather than intellectual temperament, and I had sometimes assisted him with figures, myself. Even my mother sometimes grew impatient with his mathematics, saying, 'Really, it is not complicated!' And yet she was never entirely well after Georgiana's birth, and a little shortness of temper was to become habitual thereafter. (Her sister, Lady Catherine, was famous for it. Even Father did not care to cross Lady Catherine de Bourgh, when she was displeased.)

Thus George and I began travelling to school together. I took a great deal of trouble in hopes that he would not feel as unhappy as I had, when I first began to board, but George never seemed to suffer from homesickness at all.

Wickham had a mixed time at school. He was casual and lazy, and the teachers proved immune to his charm, so he was near the bottom of every class, and obliged to endure extra Greek and Latin. However, his sporting skills won him genuine acclaim – acclaim amounting to adoration, where some of the youngest lads were concerned – and he was eventually accepted into a rather rakish senior set. We saw less of each other at school than we did at home, where my father relished tales of Wickham's cricketing prowess almost as much as the marks I received in class. At school, I avoided him as much as I could. One day, however, I could not, for the headmaster summoned me.

'Darcy,' said he, 'first, I must commend you. You have done excellently well as prefect this year.'

I thanked him. It was a distinction I could have dispensed with, for ordering younger boys about held no fascination for me – still, it was an honour. He continued, 'Indeed, I considered you as head of your year next autumn, but preferred Roberts in the end. If I have any complaint of *you*, it is this: you are a natural leader, who does not take the trouble to lead.'

I thanked him for his good opinion and promised to try harder to lead – though grateful that Roberts had been selected, all the same.

'And now for the reason for your being summoned. I grieve to say that the matter is serious. It concerns your father's protégé, George Wickham.'

'Is he failing?'

'In one respect, undoubtedly. He has got a young girl into – into difficulties.'

Here I wished to pretend to be shocked, but the cricket team often hung about the town – where there were any number of girls – and I had witnessed the potency of George's appeal from my earliest years. Still, to have seduced a young girl might be considered extreme. I said, 'I am grieved to hear it, sir.'

'But not astonished, I perceive… I wrote at once to your father, who begged my pardon, and who sent me *this*, to pay off the lady. It is exceedingly generous of Mr Darcy, in my opinion. Of course, Wickham is to be sent down.'

I had guessed that much already. One required noble blood to get away with something of this magnitude, and Wickham was a charity case. I could already see where this was tending. No member of staff would deign to take money to a young lady, for fear of scandal, while Wickham himself could not be trusted to do it. I said, 'Of course I will go, sir.'

'Good man, Darcy,' he said, and rose, actually rose, to shake me by the hand. 'You are, and always have been, a credit to the school.'

I did not feel much of a credit to the school as I arrived at the address – a dingy house in a dingy row, its windows dark with soot and its front stoop unbrushed. I could not imagine the dandyish Wickham in such a place – but perhaps their trysts had been in town, instead? Everyone in the street seemed to be eyeing me, as I knocked on the door. A serving girl answered it, curtseying as low as she could. I said, 'I am here on business, with regard to a Miss Amelia. I would be obliged if you would fetch her.'

'Yes, sir. Jus' a moment, sir.' And I heard her calling, 'Miss 'melia! A toff here to see you, from the school!'

The moment she appeared I understood better. Miss Amelia had wide-set eyes, a perfect complexion, red-gold hair and a lovely figure. To my youthful gaze she resembled Botticelli's goddess on the seashell… Having previously believed her a fallen woman and deserving of her misfortune, I suddenly found myself desperately sorry for her. A single moment's weakness, perhaps – and now, how deeply regretted! She blushed as she met my gaze, which made her look still prettier – then I recollected myself.

'My father, who is Mr Wickham's godfather, has begged me to give you this,' I said, handing it to her. 'He wishes me to say that he is extremely sorry.'

'And – and Mr Wickham?' she asked, in a low, tremulous voice.

I hesitated, then, 'I am afraid he has been sent down.'

'Sent – where?'

'I mean, he has been expelled. He will not trouble you again.' She had meanwhile slit open the packet and gasped. Curtseying again, she murmured, 'I thank you, sir, most kindly. Are you – are you his brother, then?'

'Ah, no. I am no relation at all. I wish you good day, Miss Amelia.' I would have liked to have said something consoling but could not trust myself. She watched me leave, as did the maid, peeping round her shoulder. Indeed, I should think half the street was not even pretending to hide their curiosity at the 'toff from the school's' visit to Miss Amelia.

By the time I returned, George was already gone. To my mind, he had already ruined his life, for what reputable school would accept him, even should my father prove persuadable? But all too soon I had something still deeper to ponder, for I too was obliged to depart before the end of term... for my mother's funeral.

She had been taken ill one morning – but then, she was so very often ill, that perhaps not enough was made of it. She complained of weakness, and the surgeon was summoned – but by the time he arrived she could barely speak or lift up her arm. My father rushed to her bedside, and I was sent for – but even my father was barely in time, while I was two days too late. Not even her sister, Lady Catherine, could bid her farewell before the funeral (which ladies of course were not permitted to attend).

I recall mostly shock, a disassociated feeling. There had always been a barrier, not only between my mother and myself, but – I now believe – between my mother and every other person. And, as was the case too with Lady Catherine, perhaps the rest of us tended to feel faintly judged, vaguely disapproved. ('Georgiana, do not lisp – it is most annoying'... 'Fitzwilliam, I beg that you be still. You know I have a headache'... 'I would have loved to attend, were it not for the ache in my back from lifting the child.')

In short, while my father was everywhere beloved for his willingness to celebrate the best in everyone, almost every memory of my mother is tainted by querulousness. I once heard Wickham's father say: 'The Leighton temper is never easy, but Mrs Darcy suffered for being continually expecting, and continually disappointed, and continually sharp with the offspring of others, before finally having children of her own.'

I disliked the notion that George's father knew more about my mother than I, but mostly I was shocked by his information. So, my mother had carried children before me, who had never been born? Perhaps she had been nervous lest Georgiana or I die likewise? –

Perhaps she had even feared that she had somehow failed, by not carrying her other children to term?

I was considering my mother's life – so blessed in some respects, so unlucky in others – on the night following her funeral, while Father and I were sitting near the fire. Greatly daring, I asked about the babies. My father looked up, startled, passed a hand across his brow and said, 'Yes, yes, it was a grief – to her particularly. A famous physician once examined her but could find no explanation.'

'If I might ask, sir, how many were lost?'

'Three' – and then, recollecting – 'and then another between yourself and Georgiana. An affliction, indeed! But who are we to comprehend the workings of fate?'

I tried to imagine being the fourth, instead of the first, and failed. I had always been so accustomed to being the first – and to being alone. Recalling my headmaster's words, I could not help wondering if I might have developed into more of a 'leader' had I not been. Father rose then and said, 'Your mother was never strong. In short, I cannot help but wonder –' but then he halted, and spoke of something else, and the chance passed.

I spent many hours grieving for my mother. Despite being born to wealth and ease – and blessed, not only with my father, but with all the elegance and beauty of Pemberley – she had never seemed very contented. Her face, in repose especially, had something of Lady Catherine's discontent about it, though she was both slimmer and prettier than her sister. She and my father shared almost no interests in common, for she loved embroidery, music and *objets d'art* while he much preferred books – books of philosophy especially. Secretly, I hoped that my own marriage would be less of an alliance, and the lady concerned more of an intellectual equal.

I was yet to meet with a woman who interested me, let alone fascinated me, but I was too young to despair of it...

The Colonel arrived soon after the funeral, gripped my father's hand, and blinked away a tear. (What was there about Colonel Fitzwilliam that spoke to people so? Young as I was, I had always felt it!)

'My condolences, my dear sir! She was a wonderful lady – artistic, caring, beautiful.'

'She was,' said my father.

'But her end was mercifully swift, I understand?'

'It was swift indeed,' said my father, with a sigh.

After Father had left us alone together, I noticed a difference in my cousin. Though never interested in clothes – he favoured the same waistcoat for years – I had never seen him in such a state. His boots had not been cleaned, nor his hair cut, and he had several days' stubble on his chin. Perhaps he had been too distraught about my mother to care about his appearance? I could not resist asking, 'Have you been well, Fitzwilliam?'

The Colonel sighed. 'The truth is – but nay, 'tis far too soon to... And yet, you will hear soon enough, I believe – for, soon enough, all London will know!' Then he turned, looked at me, and said, 'I have killed a man.'

At this, my puzzlement only increased, for my cousin held a commission, and had twice seen service on the continent. In other words, I had simply assumed that he had already killed Frenchmen, in the service of the King. 'In France?' I offered, but he sighed and said, 'No – in a duel.'

'I am very sorry,' said I, feeling exceedingly young and ill-equipped to understand. 'I suppose some matter of honour was at stake.'

'There was none – almost, none at all! There was only my pride and my stupidity, and now I can neither forgive nor excuse myself! True, Smithson was an idle, impudent, arrogant fellow, and insulted me before my men. But I should have treated him with the contempt that he deserved, instead of… And now the poor fellow is dead, leaving wife and child behind him.'

I was secretly shocked but said nothing. He cried, 'Oh, Darcy, how I wish that I was more like you – calm, logical, self-contained!'

In fact I was, and perhaps remain, something of a puzzle to myself, in terms of temperament. I have often been called cool and yet – inside – what do I *not* feel? – In other words, I instinctively believed the Colonel and myself far more similar than we might appear. I even thought, 'Perhaps the only difference is that I am a mere actor, while you are an honest man!'

But all I said was, 'Will there be repercussions?'

'Nay, for my superior stands my friend. But so many misfortunes, and all at once! Your poor mama! – And this business of young Wickham looks ill, indeed.'

'It has been hushed-up, however – and the girl bought off.'

'But how terribly Wickham must feel it, after all your father's goodness!'

I was silent, partly because I doubted that Wickham *did* feel it, and partly because of a sudden recollection of the girl – those tendrils of red-gold hair. I thought, 'It is *her* life, not Wickham's, which has been ruined.' And it seemed to me in that moment that simply to be born a woman was to be born lacking agency, and very nearly powerless.

We agreed not to mention the duel to my father. There was nothing that he or anyone could have done. And the Smithson fellow, after all, was dead.

Chapter 34

(From Mr Darcy's diaries)

It is difficult for me to write this, even to myself – the only person with access to these papers.

But how I wish that I had not agreed to come to Rosings this year! The reason is Miss Eliza Bennet. How ironic is this? – For was it not I, along with Louisa Hurst, who prevented Bingley from engaging himself to her sister? How is it possible that I – clear-eyed, unimpulsive, self-contained – could be guilty of a similar error of judgement myself?

There is, I believe, some magic at work in the Bennet household. The father is clever, witty, sardonic and possesses a certain elegance of mind – but he is very nearly a recluse and utterly regardless of society. His wife is noisy, garrulous, scheming and entirely without disguise. Yet combined, they have contrived to produce two near-magical beings: the first gloriously gentle, sweet and lovely, the second nearly as beautiful and very much more brilliant.

I was walking my new pointer in the woods only yesterday, when I encountered Miss Bennet, seated upon a log, a book on her lap, staring into the middle distance.

Were I an artist, I should have yearned for such a subject! – the contrast between the feathery greenness, the dappled light, her pale gown and those long-lashed eyes was so striking! But my approach, or perhaps the dog's, broke the spell. She started and half-rose.

I said, 'Do not disturb yourself, I beg. I did not intend to interrupt.'

She resumed her seat with a little laugh. 'Why, how you startled me! I was miles away!'

'A novel?'

'No, a poem. Cowper. On so golden a day, I could not resist fleeing the rectory, in order to read it.'

'I greatly admire Cowper,' I was obliged to admit.

'My father's favourite. "*So life glides smoothly and by stealth away / More golden than the age of fabled gold.*"'

I completed it for her: '"*Renown'd in ancient song, not vex'd with care / Or stain'd with guilt, beneficent, approv'd / Of God and man, and peaceful in its end.*" You chose wonderfully well, for today is golden indeed.'

The day, her aspect, the poem, were all in such sweet accord that I expected her to rise and to join me. She did not, however, merely saying, 'This is a favourite spot of mine – perhaps, my favourite walk.'

I could not fault her taste – nor her wish to flee the rectory either, for Mr Collins was generally there. 'Do you intend to linger, Miss Bennet? Or might I be useful in escorting you back?'

'Oh! I should hope to stay another hour, unless the wind rises as swiftly as it did yesterday. And besides, you will have birds to kill or something equally tedious to divert you – men always seem to!'

'But not your father, I think?'

'True – but Papa is an original, and such men are exceedingly rare.'

'You think us trivial, do you?'

'If by trivial you mean addicted to pursuing foxes, chivvying hares, or instructing dogs in curious behaviours – many men can seem trivial indeed! But my father is addicted to ideas, instead.'

'And to Cowper.'

'He does not read a great deal of poetry, but he does admire Cowper.'

I bowed and walked on – thinking, with unwilling admiration, 'What a surprising creature – I should never have suspected her of having a poetic turn!' Though, as I glanced behind, she had already bent her head over her book and was forming as pretty a picture of youthful elegance as one could wish for, one dark curl just detached from all the rest. Not even her sister Jane could have appeared to greater advantage.

I could not wonder that the Colonel, without having mentioned any such intent, called at the rectory that afternoon, and spent an hour with Mrs Collins and herself. Later that evening he said, 'What a clever, thinking creature Miss Bennet is! We had a most amusing discussion, about Mrs Collins's hens – not to mention the fall of the Roman Empire and the family Bennet! How droll her father must be!'

'And his daughter likewise. But what a mixed collection he has sired: Two young idiots, a scholar of terrifying pretentions, one unusual mind and one lovely young creature!'

'She is indeed lovely!' said Fitzwilliam fervently.

Taken aback, I inquired, 'Do you refer to Miss Elizabeth? For *I* was referring to her elder sister, the toast of Hertfordshire.'

'What! – There is a sister still more beautiful?'

'She is generally so regarded,' I said drily.

Though – disconcertingly enough – I found, even as I said it, that I no longer believed it. Eliza's eyes had always been superior, and the pointed chin, the delicate nose and her swift light grace much more to my taste. In short, Eliza possesses all Giuditta's flair – but with intellect and a most ladylike charm appended.

Nor could I imagine her throwing her little shoe at me.

✦

138

DARCY

The next time our aunt summoned the Collinses to Rosings – really, Mrs Collins can scarcely call her life her own – Colonel Fitzwilliam relished Miss Bennet's conversation to such a degree as to draw Her Ladyship's displeasure. 'Of what do you speak, Nephew? For if it is of music, I assure you, I shall have some opinion to share!'

'We were speaking of books, madam,' said Miss Bennet. 'Of *Evelina*, by Fanny Burney.'

'A lightweight, sensational and trivial production, do you not agree, Fitzwilliam?'

'I understand that it has enjoyed a renewed vogue, ma'am, at least at court.'

'Has it? Has it, indeed? Well! I always fancied Lord Orville to resemble you, my dear Darcy – and Evelina my sweet Anne.'

It was perfectly clear where this was tending, so I hastened to turn the subject. 'I can never imagine my acquaintance as being characters in novels, myself.'

'And though I *can,*' said Miss Elizabeth, 'I prefer to imagine characters in books, instead. Although, as Lord Orville is remarkably handsome, and Mr Darcy famously possesses no flaw, the casting in this case might be allowable.'

'No flaw?' inquired the Colonel, surprised.

'Miss Bennet,' I said, 'having determined in Hertfordshire that I conceive myself to be all perfection, will have her little joke.'

Fitzwilliam laughed. 'I have yet to meet a man without a flaw, though I have a most sincere regard for Darcy. Speaking for myself, I am mostly constructed of them!'

'Your modesty must disarm reproof,' said Miss Elizabeth, 'despite its being "the only sure bait when one angles for praise."'

'And *that* was Lord Chesterfield's, was it not?' said I, but received only an arch glance in response.

'Lord Chesterfield!' cried my aunt. 'I could never abide him. For was it not he who remarked, of ladies, that a man of sense must humour them, as he does a sprightly, forward child?'

'He did,' said I, 'though I always suspected, like *one* in present company, that Chesterfield was often in jest.'

'While I find him – like *another* in our present company – without defect,' said Miss Bennet, with a laugh.

Soon afterwards, the Colonel reminded Miss Bennet that she had promised to perform. Lady Catherine listened to half a song and then began to speak to me of politics. As I found this somewhat rude, I moved nearer to the fair performer. At the song's conclusion, Miss Bennet addressed me, almost saucily, 'You mean to frighten me, I expect, by coming in all this state to listen. But I refuse to be alarmed, even though your sister *does* play so well. There is a stubbornness about me that never can bear to be frightened at the will of others. My courage rises at every attempt to intimidate me.'

'I shall not say that you are mistaken,' said I, 'as I have had the pleasure of your acquaintance long enough to know that you occasionally enjoy expressing opinions which are not your own.'

She turned to the Colonel again. 'Your cousin will teach you not to believe a word I say! I am peculiarly unlucky in meeting with a person able to expose my real character in a place where I had hoped to pass with some degree of credit. Indeed, Mr Darcy, it is ungenerous in you – and impolitic besides – for it might provoke me to retaliation. Such things may come out that might shock your relatives to hear!'

'I am not afraid of you,' said I, with a smile – though perhaps I should have been.

'Pray continue,' cried the Colonel. 'I should like to know how Darcy behaves among strangers!'

'Very well, then. The first time of my ever seeing him was at a ball – and at this ball, what do you think he did? He danced only four dances! I am sorry to pain you, but so it was, though gentlemen were scarce, and more than a few ladies in want of a partner. Mr Darcy, you dare not deny it.'

Embarrassed – for I remembered it perfectly – I said, 'I had not the honour of knowing any lady in the assembly beyond my own party.'

'True, and nobody can ever be introduced in a ballroom. Well, Colonel, what will you have next?'

'Perhaps,' I said, 'I should have judged better had I sought an introduction, but I am ill-qualified to recommend myself to strangers.'

'Particularly strangers who are only *tolerable*,' she said, with an amused glance at me. So, she still remembered my ill-temper at the Meryton ball! (I *had* wondered – and had hoped that she did not.) Then, addressing Fitzwilliam again, 'Shall we ask your cousin the reason? Shall we ask why a man of sense and education, who has lived in the world, is ill-qualified to recommend himself to strangers?'

'No,' said he, 'I can answer your question, without applying to him. It is because he will not give himself the trouble.'

'I certainly have not the talent some people possess,' I said, thinking of Wickham, 'of conversing with those I have never met before. I cannot catch their tone of conversation, or pretend interest in their concerns, as I often see done.'

She laughed. 'My fingers do not move over this instrument in the masterly manner which many women's do. They have not the same force or rapidity and do not produce the same expression. But

I always supposed it to be my own fault, because I would not take the trouble of practising. It is not that I do not believe my fingers as capable as anyone else's of superior execution.'

Bested, indeed! Each phrase so elegantly turned, so deftly duelled! – and each delivered with a verbal dexterity that made my head spin. And her air – so effortlessly balanced between flirtation and – and what? – I cannot be sure, though I have wasted some time in trying to decide. But there is a bewitching lightness in it.

It seems to me, as I write, that I am becoming as ridiculously susceptible as Bingley. First my passion for Giuditta – and now this absorption with Miss Bennet, though there is of course no comparison, for Giuditta could scarcely be said to be a lady at all, while Miss Bennet is very ladylike indeed. But they are equally impossible: an Italian genius boasting neither birth nor breeding, and an Englishwoman with uncles in trade, an entailed estate and scarcely a penny to her name!

So why do I think of her so constantly? – why do I recollect her every word, her every glance, her every turn of phrase? Why is it that I dwell on that glimpse of her in the glade, the light on the leaves, the line of her gown? How is it that I cannot help suggesting to my cousin Fitzwilliam, day after day, time after time, that we walk to the rectory, in preference to every other possible direction? Why was I so perversely tongue-tied, only yesterday, when admitted to the rectory in error – when we were, though only briefly, alone? (I still blush to recall, after I asked how attached she was to Hertfordshire, her look of surprise!)

Perhaps I should leave now – just as I fled Rome – before I find myself in the same straits as was Bingley, last November – and for almost exactly the same reason! But – the truth is – I cannot bear to!

There, I have written it. I cannot bear to leave Miss Bennet.

'Just one more week,' I told Fitzwilliam, as lightly as I could, for the third week in succession. 'There is nothing in town that will not keep for another week.'

Chapter 35

Hunsford Rectory, Kent

'But Lizzy,' protested Charlotte, 'he must be in love with you! To have even *entered* the rectory, after being told that I had been called away to Mrs Greene's, is rather extraordinary. Whatever could he have meant by such behaviour otherwise?'

'Had you been there you would never have said so! Why, he did nothing but look at the paper. He said scarcely two words to me!'

'And yet I still believe that there is something in it – for he watches you.'

'Only to see if I do something that he can ridicule.'

'I think not,' said Charlotte thoughtfully. 'It is a curious expression and I sometimes doubt that there is admiration in it – perhaps you puzzle him, somehow. Whereas Colonel Fitzwilliam –'

'Oh, *he* is absolutely my beau!'

'You laugh but truly, Eliza, you could have him, just by stretching out your smallest finger! He forgot to pass the butter twice the other night, for looking at you. And he is, beyond comparison, the pleasantest man – clever, thoughtful, kind, well-read.'

'Indeed, he is as infuriatingly flawless as his cousin affects to be.'

'The Colonel's manners are such as *must* please. And towards you, still more so.'

Eliza laughed. 'My dear Charlotte, your partiality does your heart the greatest credit – what a pity the same cannot be said of your head! Me, wed the son of an Earl? Not even Mama would think it possible!'

Yet secretly, it did not seem to Eliza to be *quite* impossible. The Colonel so clearly admired her – and even her music! She was nothing like as gifted as he imagined her to be, but the quality of his attention was still gratifying.

She unexpectedly encountered him in the woods the next day and – relieved that it was himself and not Mr Darcy – agreed to be escorted back to the rectory. 'And so, do you truly leave on Saturday?' she inquired.

'If Darcy does not put it off again. But I am quite at his disposal.'

'I know no one with more power of choice than Mr Darcy.'

'He likes to have his own way very well,' said Fitzwilliam, 'but then, so do we all. It is only that Darcy has better means of having it than most, for he is rich, and many others are poor. I speak feelingly. A younger son, you know, must be inured to self-denial and dependence.'

'In my opinion, the younger son of an Earl can know very little of either. Seriously, when have you been prevented by want of money from going where you chose, or procuring anything you had a fancy for?'

'These are home questions, and I cannot pretend that I have experienced hardships of that nature. But in matters of greater weight, I may suffer from the want of money. Younger sons cannot marry where they like.'

'Unless they like women of fortune, which they very often do.'

She had expected to amuse him, but he said, very seriously, 'There are not many of my rank who can afford to marry without some attention to money.'

'Is this,' thought Elizabeth, with a blush, 'meant for me?' Recovering her poise, she asked, 'And what, pray, is the usual price of an Earl's younger son? Unless the elder brother is very sickly, I suppose you would not ask above fifty thousand pounds?'

He did laugh at that. 'There are few tolerable young ladies in London, Miss Bennet, with fifty thousand pounds!'

'Perhaps one of the *intolerable* ones might do for your cousin, then – though his sister might be sufficient for his purposes, at present. And as she is under his sole care, she must do exactly as he pleases!'

'No, that is an advantage he must divide with me. I am joined with him in the guardianship of Miss Darcy.'

'Are you, indeed? And does your charge give you much trouble? Young ladies are sometimes difficult, and if she has the true Darcy spirit she might like to have her own way.'

To her amusement, he looked concerned. After a moment he inquired, 'Why should you suppose Miss Darcy likely to be troublesome? Have you ever heard anything to her disadvantage?'

One way or another, Eliza believed, she seemed to have hit upon something near the truth. Therefore, she said at once, 'Do not worry. I never heard a word against her – I daresay she is one of the most tractable creatures in the world. She is a particular favourite with some ladies of my acquaintance, Mrs Hurst and Miss Bingley. I expect you know them?'

'I know them to speak to. Their brother is a pleasant, gentlemanlike man – and a great friend of Darcy's.'

'Oh, indeed,' cried Eliza, 'Mr Darcy is uncommonly kind to Mr Bingley, and takes a prodigious deal of care of him!'

'Yes, I believe Darcy *does* take care of him, in those points where he most wants care. I have reason to think Bingley greatly indebted to him. But I ought to beg his pardon, for I have no right to suppose that Bingley was the person referred to. It is only conjecture.'

'What do you mean?' inquired Eliza, her curiosity all alive.

'Nay, I should go no farther, as it is a circumstance Darcy would not wish generally known. Were it to get round to the lady's family, it would be an unpleasant thing.'

'You may depend upon my not mentioning it,' said Elizabeth.

'In that case… well, it was merely that he congratulated himself on having lately saved a friend from a most imprudent marriage – without mentioning any particulars. I only suspected it was Bingley from believing him to be the kind of young fellow likely to get into a scrape of that sort, and because they spent the whole of last summer together.'

Eliza frowned. 'Did Mr Darcy give you any reason for this interference?'

'I understand that there were some very strong objections against the lady.'

'Were there? And what arts did he use to separate them?'

'He did not speak to me of his own arts,' said Fitzwilliam, smiling. 'He told me no more than I have told you.'

Elizabeth made him no answer, but only walked on, her heart swelling with indignation. When asked why she was so thoughtful, she said, 'I have been thinking of your tale… Your cousin's conduct does not suit my feelings. Who was he to be the judge?'

'You are inclined to consider his interference officious?'

'I cannot see what right he had to decide upon the propriety of his friend's affections, or to determine in what manner that friend was to be happy. However,' she continued, more mildly, 'as we know none of the particulars, it is unfair to condemn. It is not to be supposed that there was much affection in the case.'

'That is not an unnatural surmise,' said he, 'but it is lessening the honour of my cousin's triumph very sadly.'

She could not trust herself to respond to this and said, 'My dear Charlotte has this much consolation for marrying Mr Collins. I think the Kentish woods put even Hertfordshire's to shame.'

The Colonel responded in similar style and did her the further courtesy of pretending not to notice her want of spirits, which was suddenly extreme. It was not only that Mr Darcy had been disclosed as the principal actor in detaching Bingley from her sister. It was the recollection of discovering Jane in tears in their bedroom. It was the remembrance of all her sister had been obliged to endure from their mother, when it finally appeared certain that Mr Bingley was never intending to return… It was the ruin, at least for a time, of all of Jane's happiness.

She ran upstairs at once to consider all that he had said – and the longer she thought, the angrier she became. It was all thanks to Mr Darcy's pride – a pride denigrating anyone with relatives in trade – a pride presuming *his* closest friend as deserving someone higher in rank – even, perhaps, a desire that his own sister Georgiana might capture Bingley. As if anyone could be superior to Jane – her temper delightful, her mind improved, her manners captivating! Elizabeth could acknowledge no excuse for Darcy's behaviour. No! – it was nothing but pride, a pride too abominable to give even her father credit, a pride too abominable to rate any woman without a fortune, a pride abominable enough to deceive his mind and to distort his judgement!

Well, *she* was not going to Rosings, to play and sing for the amusement of such a man and his relations, not she! Instead, she told Charlotte that she was unwell – and it was not a lie, for her emotions, or the need to disguise them, had unleashed a raging headache. And once the others were gone to Rosings without her, as if wishing to exasperate herself as much as possible against Mr Darcy, she undertook to read again each of Jane's recent letters, in which almost every line seemed to speak either of stoical resignation or of the crushing misery of disappointed love.

Chapter 36

(From Mr Darcy's diaries)

When Mr Collins mentioned, almost fearfully, Miss Bennet's indisposition to Her Ladyship, Lady Catherine civilly wished her a swift recovery, but Fitzwilliam cried, 'Ill! She was well enough earlier or, at least, she seemed to be! I hope that it is nothing serious?'

And, as Mrs Collins assured him that it was not, we sat down to one of the dullest evenings I have ever endured. As time wore on – and it wore on intolerably, with no Miss Bennet to lift it – I excused myself and went to the stables. There I borrowed the only horse still saddled and bridled and rode down to the rectory.

It is only a short ride from the stables at Rosings to Hunsford parsonage but, as I rode, I saw my gradual progress in feeling to have been a series of turns. The turn when she had so impudently refused to tell my aunt her age... The expression she had put into her singing... The afternoon when I had surprised her in the glade... The Colonel's utter disbelief ('What, there is a sister still more beautiful?')... The moment when she had teased me about considering her only 'tolerable' when first we met... So many moments, so many tiny revolutions in feeling, since first I heard, with a stab of guilt, that Jane Bennet's sister was visiting at the Collinses, and wished that she was not!

The revolution in my opinion of her looks had started much earlier: from her being 'tolerable' to her possessing 'fine eyes' – to my admiring her light figure in the Netherfield rose garden – to my relishing her dancing at the ball. At Rosings though, my fascination had ripened: from appreciating the piquant variation in her complexion to obliging myself – unwillingly – to tear my gaze from her countenance as she sang. Until I recognised – humbled – nay, humiliated, by my earliest judgements – that she was not merely a beauty, but the most beautiful woman I had ever seen.

I was also convinced that, despite her modesty, she was perfectly aware of my passion. (How could she *not* be? Women boast intuition we men are without, and she is uncommonly clever besides!) No, she would not be astonished at receiving my addresses. She might *appear* to be surprised, but her quickness must have long since penetrated where my wishes lay.

I knocked on the door. The maidservant curtseyed, mentioning that 'the master and missus are both out.'

'But Miss Bennet?'

'Miss Bennet is still in the parlour, sir, unless she has gone upstairs already.'

With what sudden access of nerves did I follow the servant down the hall! I scarcely knew whether I more wished Miss Bennet to have retired, or to be relieved from the burden of hiding my deepest feelings and of claiming her hand at last!

She was seated at a table, a little pale, her beautiful hand to her brow, a letter before her. She rose to receive me in apparent confusion. Given her usual composure, I could not help thinking this more promising than otherwise. Indeed – God save me – I

149

secretly believed myself, in that moment, almost secure of her, as I apologised for my intrusion. I imputed my visit to a wish to learn that she was feeling better.

'Indeed,' she said, recollecting herself. 'A great deal better. Shall I ring for a coffee, against the Collins's return?'

'Not for myself, I beg.'

I sat down, but almost immediately rose again, for I needed movement – I was working on my courage. Finally, I decided that directness was best. I said, as I recall, 'Forgive me, but my feelings will not be repressed. You must allow me to tell you how ardently I admire and love you.'

Here, she coloured in pretended shock… Still, I continued, and with resolution, 'Almost since the first moment I perceived you, I found something so piquant, so captivating, in your air, in your quickness, in your beauty – I found something, in short, I had never met with before.' She modestly averted her gaze – I went on. 'Once I realised the strength of my feelings, I did my utmost to overcome them, as I was perfectly conscious that such an alliance could gratify neither my family's nor my own notions of fitness – that such an alliance would be a source of embarrassment and concern to my every connection. In Hertfordshire, I avoided you as much as I could, yet something kept drawing me back. When we danced together at Netherfield, I was astonished by your grace and fire. While the evenings at Rosings blessed by your presence here in Kent have made it impossible for me to leave. Week after week I have put off our departure, week after week I have felt ever more powerfully that… that, in brief, the inferiority of your connections – the unfortunate condition of your nearest relations – none of this is of importance! Nothing is of any importance, beyond my feelings for you! Instead, I have felt, every day, every hour, more and more

convinced that we are destined to be together. And so I have come
this evening to put myself – hand, heart and fortune – at your feet.'

I am unaccustomed to speaking the language of feelings – nor
did I imagine that I had done so very adroitly. Yet I was still secure
as I turned to face her. I was anticipating not only a pretty confusion
but a modest amount of gratitude, besides. Instead, it was precisely
the opposite!

The instant she lifted her eyes to mine – that smouldering gaze –
I realised how appallingly I had mistaken her. Her words, scorched
into my memory, were laced with contempt: 'I am sorry to
unwittingly cause pain to anyone. It is usual, in such cases, to feel
grateful. I wish that I could feel grateful, but I have never sought
your good opinion, and you have certainly bestowed it most
unwillingly. I am sure that any pain incurred must be of short
duration, after this explanation.'

I had never been more profoundly shocked. My mortification
was complete. Not only had Miss Bennet been sublimely
unconscious of my regard – but she disdained it! It would have been
better, perhaps, had I abruptly apologised and, as abruptly,
departed. Instead, once I had caught my breath, I said, 'And this is
all the response that I am honoured with! I might well ask why –
with such little attempt at civility – I am rejected. But it is of small
importance.'

She might have been Giuditta as she lifted her chin. 'I might as
well inquire,' she returned, 'why you should tell me that you liked
me against your will, against your reason, even against your
character? Was not this some excuse for incivility, if I *was* uncivil?
But I have other provocations – you know I have! Had not my
feelings long since been decided against you, do you think any
consideration sufficient to tempt me to marry the man who has
ruined the happiness of a most beloved sister?… Oh! I have every

reason in the world to think ill of you! You dare not deny that you played the principal, if not the only part, in dividing them from each other!'

'I cannot deny that I did everything in my power to separate my friend from your sister – or that I rejoiced in my success. Towards *him* I have been kinder than towards myself.'

'But it was not merely this affair on which my dislike was founded. Your character was unfolded to me, months ago, by Mr Wickham himself. On this subject, what have you to say? In what imaginary act of friendship can you defend yourself in *this* regard?'

(Wickham, yet again! Throughout the whole of my life – and such warmth in her tone, as well!)

I forced myself to say, 'You take an eager interest in that gentleman's concerns.'

'Who that knows what his misfortunes have been can fail to take an interest in his concerns?'

'His misfortunes! – Yes, his misfortunes have been great indeed!' – and Georgiana's ashen face rose before me as I spoke.

But she responded with energy, 'And of your infliction! You have reduced him to his state of poverty – of relative poverty, at least. You have withheld the advantages designed for him. You have deprived the best years of his life of the independence which was his due. You have done all this – and yet you can still treat his misfortunes with contempt and even ridicule!'

'And this,' I said, striding about again, 'is the estimation in which you hold me! I thank you for explaining it so fully. My faults here appear heavy indeed – and yet perhaps these accusations might have been suppressed had I pretended to be impelled by unqualified inclination, by reason, by reflection, by everything! But disguise of every sort is my abhorrence. Nor am I ashamed of my feelings; they are natural and just. Can you expect me to rejoice in the inferiority of your connections? – or to congratulate myself upon the hope of relatives whose condition in life is so decidedly beneath my own?'

Her colour rose throughout this speech – while the turn of her countenance – I believe – will never leave me, as she said, 'You are mistaken, Mr Darcy, if you suppose that the manner of your declaration affected me in any other way than in sparing me the concern I might have felt in refusing you, had you behaved in a more gentlemanlike manner. You could not have made the offer of your hand in any possible way that could have tempted me to accept it. From almost the first moment of our acquaintance, your manners – impressing me with the fullest belief of your arrogance, your conceit, and your selfish disdain of the feelings of others – had formed the groundwork of so immoveable a dislike that I had not known you a month before I felt that you were the last man in the world whom I could ever be prevailed upon to marry.'

My humiliation by this point was indescribable: I longed to be gone. Gathering about me what scraps of dignity I could muster, I apologised for trespassing on her time. She – just – inclined her head in response, while I fled the rectory with the most disordered feelings. Never could I have imagined so mortifying an interview! Of course, I understand that there are people who dislike me, but that anyone could hold me in such evident *contempt* was, and remains, unbearable. I was not only disdained and rejected, but despised! – I writhed as I recalled her eloquence – and her heat. I had never even conceived it possible for an offer to *offend* – but offend her I had!

And never, in all my life, have I endured such powerful regret. Not merely because I had assumed – although I *had* assumed – that every gentlewoman must desire me, but because she believed me to possess so despicable a combination of pride and arrogance. The last man in the world that she could be prevailed upon to marry! The very *last*!

It was small consolation to imagine the gratification of others – Lady Henrietta, Miss de Ramolles, Miss Bingley – upon receiving a similar assurance of my regard; for, having dreamed of seeing Elizabeth Bennet's glorious gaze across the dining table at Pemberley, of Elizabeth Bennet's arriving at some ball or concert on my arm, no other woman seemed endurable. Indeed, my desire, now that I perceive its hopelessness, was, and remains, all-consuming. Far from contriving to despise her in my turn, I can only recall that exquisite lift of chin, that curl of lip, as she dismissed me. Never had she appeared more alluring, despite her state of health, than while delivering that perfect rebuff, 'had you behaved in a more gentlemanlike manner'! And so restless and miserable did I feel afterwards that, upon returning to Rosings, I found my cousin questioning my health and my aunt my sanity.

'Are you quite all right, Darcy? Really, you appear almost *distrait*!'

'I am sorry to be leaving you so soon, ma'am, but I am perfectly well.'

The Colonel, very discreetly, when only we two remained: 'We missed you, earlier?'

'I felt the need for a little fresh air.'

'Ah. Fine evening for it. I just thought you looked a trifle upset. I am very glad to have been mistaken.'

Still, I was impatient to retire, for I had conceived a plan. As soon as I could I went upstairs, and there – alone at last in the Blue Room – I began to write the letter that had been forming in my head throughout the evening, a letter of excuse – more, of self-justification – that I doubted I would ever be able to send. For how could I rebut Eliza Bennet's belief that I had betrayed Wickham (and, it seemed, her equally passionate admiration of that gentleman) without betraying my sister's secret?

I struggled with this for some time. But finally I determined that, though hopeless of ever marrying her, I owed it to my character to clear my name from the most unfair and egregious of her accusations, at least. She would never be my wife, but I vowed that she would still find, in my letter, some matter for regret – regret at least for the *strength* of her expressions, if not for the actual sentiments that she had – and with such energy! – expressed.

There was, in fact, no risk in entrusting her with Georgiana's secret, for her integrity was such that she would never betray it. Instead, the only risk was that she might learn to think still *less* of me, in that I had not guarded my sister as I ought and – perhaps – think rather less of Georgiana herself for having come so perilously close to disgrace. (But what did her opinion of Georgiana matter, when I could no longer imagine their ever meeting?)

But unless Miss Bennet discounted my word entirely, the truth must – at least – demolish something of her admiration for Wickham. I perceived yet a further advantage, in the Colonel's presence. I could authorise her to request his testimony, in the event of any lingering distrust of my own.

I might even be protecting her from Wickham. The sudden softness of her countenance as she named him had suggested – not for the first time – that she might be as susceptible to his powers as Georgiana had been. Of course, the paucity of her expectations might well afford her sufficient protection, for I knew Wickham intended to marry high. But as I had learned from Georgiana's experience, he was opportunistic in the extreme, as well as being – unlike myself! – impossible to resist.

Thus resolved, I embarked upon my task. Begun in a fury – principally towards Wickham – it was a relief to write yet, having completed it, I instantly tossed the letter into the fire. There was too much suppressed fury – it torched even myself – and I wished to appear as rational as possible. My second draft – how late it had grown! – was very much better. It was calm, reasoned and almost dignified. It would assuredly make her hesitate to link her fate to Wickham's.

But how to get a letter to her? – My time was so circumscribed: there were so many last duties to be performed, so many final visits to be accomplished! But I had perfectly memorised her favourite haunts – and it was with relief that I secured the briefest exchange with her as she emerged, on our last full day in Kent, from the woodland path. How unconvinced, how hesitant, she looked, as she accepted the envelope from my hand! – I could read nothing in her expression beyond doubtfulness. There was, assuredly, no touch of that softness that could so transform it, but neither was there any suggestion of that flash of fire when she had rejected me.

I said as little as I could, for fear of saying too much. And as I turned on my heel and strode away, I thought with a catch in my throat, 'That, then, will be my last glimpse of her!' And even, 'Where shall I find such another?' But enough! It was done – it was over, and, with a final cringe from Collins and a final curtsy from my cousin Anne, we were swirled away in a crunch of gravel, from Rosings and Hunsford both. Too late, altogether too late! And as I cast a last glance down towards the rectory – I heard Fitzwilliam sigh.

'Would you have preferred to stay longer, cousin?' I asked.

'Nay, it was time to be gone.'

'She never alters,' I said lightly.

'Whom do you mean?'

'Our aunt, of course.'

'Ah,' said he, rather sadly, 'I was thinking instead of – of someone else.'

Then it smote me. What a fool I had been, to imagine Fitzwilliam's heart untouched! I had to bite my lip as he continued, 'You must have observed the progress of my affections, Darcy. I only hope that *she* remained in ignorance!'

'I assure you that, if you might be supposed to mean Miss Bennet, I never suspected that your affections were engaged.'

'Truly?' he asked.

'Truly.'

'Well, *that* is a relief, for I had believed you to have surmised the whole! I even feared for our aunt's perspicuity.'

'There, you must have been safe.'

'But how she brightened the entire visit, with her wit, her music and her laughter! When the rectory party was visiting, there was a different atmosphere – an atmosphere of lightness and charm – and all because of Miss Bennet, for though I have a great regard for Mrs Collins, she possesses not one single ounce of charm. And then, to walk with her, to hear her play, to listen to her droll responses to Her Ladyship… Oh! Such arch sweetness! I have never been half so happy at Rosings before – or indeed, anywhere! And, for that reason, it was well past time to be gone. Given another day or two, I should have thrown myself at her feet!'

'But why should you not, if you liked her?' I forced myself to inquire.

'Liked her! Oh, it went far beyond liking, Darcy! I was, I remain, entirely smitten! And yet, a mere younger son, well above thirty, with my leg injury, and my wounded lung, not to mention that duel – I am utterly unworthy – though thinking, as you might imagine, of little else! You must have noticed my distraction.'

I acknowledged as much, though, in truth, I had noticed nothing. And guessed nothing either, so light and easy was his manner in company.

'I still feel that she might have accepted you,' I forced myself to add – thinking, with a pang, that she would never have accepted me.

'You think so, do you? – I do not. She was as charming to Collins as to me! But what a face, and what a figure! I have not met her famous sister, and I doubt I ever shall, but I have never encountered a woman as entrancing as Eliza Bennet.'

'Her sister's beauty is – different. You will recall Louisa Hurst's plot to extricate Bingley from his own entrancement.'

'I do – though before tonight, you never named him. But now – by the heavens – I feel such sympathy for Bingley. A woman superior to Eliza Bennet must be bewitching indeed!'

'I did not say *superior* –' I began uncomfortably.

'And yet, you know, one does not marry an impossible father or an outrageous mother, but their daughter, instead… And, after our every encounter, I kept finding myself relishing, over and over, those clever turns of phrase, her quickness, that dark level glance – turning them over and over in my head, like the pages of a book one so admires that one must re-read it, over and over again!'

For a moment I could not speak, for this, of course, was precisely what I had been doing. How displeased our aunt would have been, were she aware that the entire charm of Rosings, that Easter, had been comprised in the company of Miss Eliza Bennet!

Yet still, I could not help thinking that – had I been in the Colonel's place – I would never have hesitated. I could not imagine Mr Bennet refusing the second son of an Earl for any one of his daughters, as long as the daughter in question was persuadable, and I had once or twice considered her partial to my cousin. His bad lung and his wound, received honourably in the King's service, and even the duel would – in the eyes of society – have been balanced by her poverty. While as for his age, there are marriages of greater disparity agreed in the City every day.

I was still struck, however. I felt ashamed to recall that *my* only scruples about offering to Miss Bennet had involved the disgrace of her connections – whether I might be demeaning myself. How much more self-effacing Fitzwilliam was than I! The light was beginning to fail as I said, 'Well, I believe you rather too modest.'

'Perhaps.'

'You might have another chance,' said I – though thinking, 'But so will Wickham, for she will soon be returning to Meryton.'

'She might come to town, I suppose – likeliest, as the wife of another.'

After that, we travelled for a long while in silence. I could not help wishing, then as now – as I write – that we had had this conversation sooner. Had I known the depth of his feeling, I might have judged hers better – I might even have addressed her in a 'more gentlemanlike' fashion. But still, she would have refused me. She had been clarity itself when saying, 'You could not have made me the offer in any possible way that would have tempted me to accept it.'

But just in that moment, I envied my cousin, for at least he had left Rosings with his dignity intact.

Chapter 37

Hunsford Rectory

Her head was aching, and her mind restless. Determining sleep to be impossible, Eliza rose, lit a candle, and read Darcy's letter all over again.

The tone of the letter was curious. Some of the phrases needled her, reassuring her of Darcy's conceit, arrogance, and self-satisfaction, and making her pleased to have told him so. The sections about Jane, on first reading, were insufferably patronising, and she did not believe one single word of what he had written of Wickham. She thought, 'How dared even he to spread such untruths?' and vowed to burn it.

But a second reading proved more unsettling. He was still – of course – entirely wrong about Jane, but had not Charlotte always said that she had a complacent air? And could anyone dare to say quite such horrible things of Wickham, if they were *entirely* unfounded?

In fact, the oftener she read the letter, the more credence she was grudgingly obliged to give to its author, and the more doubts she had of Wickham. Mr Darcy's *style* might be stiff – at times, it was stiff indeed! – but, unless he himself was deep-dyed in villainy, in its *matter* she was obliged to acknowledge that – rather than Wickham being blameless and Darcy's behaviour quite outrageous – she had been deceived.

First, because the risk of lying was simply too great – and

second, because he had authorised her to inquire of Colonel Fitzwilliam. And no one had ever said a word against the Colonel, who thoughtful probity she greatly admired. There was corroboration too, in the Colonel's clear discomfort when she had inquired about Miss Darcy's being difficult to manage… How it all tied together, having learned the whole! And however could she have been so comprehensively misled?

The answer was clear: her infatuation – and really, it was very little less – for George Wickham. She could summon him up in an instant: those powerful shoulders, those confiding – almost secret – smiles, his unobtrusive gallantries, his warmly expressive voice. But were not such advantages common in the kind of men who lived by exploiting the goodwill of others? Wickham was certainly captivating – there had been few women in Meryton who had remained uncharmed – but what if such captivation was based on nothing more substantial than pleasing manners and fine looks?

Cudgel her brain as she might, she could not recall a single selfless act or charitable impulse of his that might give the lie to what Darcy had described as the reckless profligacy and selfish wickedness of many years' duration. It was mortifying to have been so taken-in! – and to be obliged to admit that the softness of his manners and his admiration of herself had equally entranced her taste and overridden her judgement.

Also, what right had Wickham to tell her anything of his private business at all? They had scarcely known each other one half-hour! As for his assertion, 'I could never dishonour the son, for the sake of the father' – which she had thought so fine – why, had he not done exactly that, not five minutes before?

Wickham had not only squandered his inheritance with gaming, gambling and low living, but had so imposed himself on the ardent sympathies of the youthful Georgiana as to almost succeed in eloping with her! Small wonder the Colonel had uneasily inquired whether she had ever heard anything 'to Georgiana's disadvantage'!

In the light of these shocks, she was reluctantly forced to reconsider the rest of the letter – during which Darcy's attempt to detach Charles Bingley from so disadvantageous a marriage gradually became at least comprehensible.

While in the beginning Lizzy had furiously dismissed 'the ill-behaviour betrayed by your mother, your youngest sisters and even by your father', cooler consideration reawakened all her own previous disgust. Her mother's triumphing over Mrs Lucas ('When dearest Jane is settled here at Netherfield')... Mr Collins' fatuous imposition upon Mr Darcy ('While I, and I alone, have the honour to be able to assure you that Her Ladyship was well, last sennight!') And then, Mary. ('For my next selection, I have determined to offer the company nothing less than Giardini's *Voi amante!* The translation, if I might be permitted to paraphrase...') How vividly, too, she recollected her father's detached amusement and Lydia's hysterical laughter.

Darcy had mistaken Jane's feelings, but Jane's placid demeanour never varied, while Darcy had 'often seen Bingley in love before.' It was equally undeniable that, though Mr Bennet was assuredly a gentleman, he was a gentleman of entailed estate, who had frittered away his assets and neglected to educate his children. His wife and youngest daughters were empty-headed and gauche. And while there was no actual *disrespect* expressed towards either herself or Jane, whom Miss Bingley herself had so conspicuously befriended, the unspoken implication remained that Jane could never be perceived as Bingley's equal. And how inexpressibly depressing it was to learn that her sister's misery had been caused by her nearest relations!

Darcy's praise of herself soothed her, but though he had successfully demolished Wickham's chances, he had done his own no service. Eliza felt sorry for him, grateful for his high opinion and was – albeit unwillingly – obliged to grant him some powers of judgement, but she could never love him. He was not the villain she had thought him, but he was still superior, cold and arrogant.

Yet still, he must have felt something for her beyond anything he had felt before. The expression in his countenance as he had said, 'You must permit me to tell you how ardently I admire and love you' had robbed her of breath. It was gratifying to have unconsciously inspired so powerful a passion – and astonishing that she had never even noticed! But even had there been no Wickham to compare him to, Colonel Fitzwilliam had been so delightfully conversable as to prejudice her, in comparison, against his handsomer cousin. True, Mr Darcy *had* used to regard her, but *that* might so easily have been as an excuse for not looking at his aunt, or for not encouraging Miss de Bourgh. She tried to imagine how so stately a man would flirt, had he a mind to flirt, but could not… And then her head was aching again.

She bathed her temples, picked up the letter, re-read a few more paragraphs, and put it down, thoroughly dissatisfied with herself.

She was only entirely certain of three things. First, that she had made herself look ridiculous over Wickham. Second, that she had chastised Mr Darcy entirely unjustly – almost rudely, indeed! – She blushed to recall the strength of her expressions. Third, if even *half* of what he had written about Wickham was true, he had every right to disdain her taste. But then, his lack of remorse about Jane, his glorying in his manipulation of Mr Bingley ('To him I have been kinder than towards myself'…)

When she recollected this last, she felt better. Oh, he was not worth another thought! She was glad she had told him that he was the very last man that she would marry! Perhaps it would be a turning point in his life. Perhaps from that horrible evening onwards he would behave rather more politely: to women at balls, to tenants at Pemberley, to members of his London clubs… But surely, any such notion was ridiculous: he was not about to change his manners because some penniless young lady had disdained him!

But she wished some words unsaid with all her heart. She had very nearly admitted that she admired Wickham. (As Darcy had noted at the ball, 'You take an eager interest in that gentleman's concerns.') Why, he had – very nearly – accused her of being in love with Wickham, and she had – very nearly – deserved it! Should he desire revenge, he could tell everyone of their mutual acquaintance that she was partial to Wickham – and yet, she could not imagine him doing it. It was not in his character which – though not to her taste – she must respect. And moreover, had he not entrusted *her* with his own sister's reputation?

'From this day forwards,' she vowed, 'I shall never again tease Jane for her candour. Had I only been more like Jane, I should not have to endure such shame that it wakens me in the night! Truly, it is not only Darcy whose eyes should be opened, for I was as secretly proud of my discernment and swift wit as he is of his high breeding and of his famous seat in Derbyshire. What a miserable pair we should have made had I accepted him! Though at least I cannot be accused of ambition or else I *should* have, in spite of all!'

Chapter 38

(From Miss Mary Bennet's private papers)

Query: Of what possible good is it for Parliament to choose to house a militia in a small village, where their presence might be expected to play havoc with their rural inhabitants?

As it is, I assure you, half-Meryton is in unrelieved mourning, even before the militia have all removed to Brighton. Mama and her sister themselves seem absolutely distracted and now, to crown all, comes an invitation for Lydia – Lydia, of every creature in the world! – to go to Brighton with Mrs Forster, who is at least as silly as she, and very nearly as young.

Mama, of course, was charmed. She cried at once, 'Oh! How delightful! How very, very kind of good Mrs Forster! And what a charming chance for you, my dearest Lydia!' Upon which poor Kitty burst into tears and fled up the stairs, bewailing that she had not been chosen, for she 'is two years older!'

Now I – as well as Jane and Lizzy – am still more senior, but I have no wish to go to Brighton – or hardly any, for there might, I suppose, be some vicar there I might aspire to marry. No one pretends that there is anything at Brighton beyond the superficial delights of a vulgar watering-place. However, Kitty continues to feel the injustice most strongly. It would have been better-natured of Mrs Forster to have offered to them both, but she is as thoughtless as Lydia, and dresses rather inappropriately for a married lady.

As it is, our peace is cut up for some time. Kitty is inconsolable, while Lydia rushes about, gloating, and laughing, and enumerating the advantages of Brighton to Mama, who would gladly go herself, I believe, if someone would but offer her a place in their carriage. Our father amuses himself with droll comments. Today it was, 'Mrs Bennet, were you to wear a gown cut like Mrs Forster's I believe that Col. Forster would give *you* the preference, and remove you to Brighton in her stead, for your figure might be superior and, I am sure, your complexion is better.'

Kitty cried, ''Tis I, Papa, and not Mama, who should have been preferred!'

'No, for *you* cannot be spared. Who is to keep Mary up to the mark in her music, if not you? – You see how she fears being overtaken!'

And this was almost cruel, for Mama has vowed to teach Kitty no longer, as she can never recollect her fingerings. Kitty began to cry again, for which I could not blame her, for musical genius is far from common, and our family not overburdened with it. (Really, Mama should find us another master, but it is not everyone who will travel to Meryton for a pittance... thus, Lizzy and I have been obliged to teach ourselves.)

Lizzy, since her return from Kent, seems out of spirits. I suspect that visiting the man whom she so precipitately rejected has taught her to regret – as well she might – all that she has so hastily thrown away. In truth, Mr Collins would have made her. All that she lacks, he could have provided: solid reflection, a more earnest philosophy and a more serious purpose. I saw a look of sorrow cross her face as Mama was quizzing her about the Collins's drawing-room. Even *I* must admit to thinking of Mr Collins at times: I tried for him, but flirting is no talent of mine – and how nimbly Charlotte Lucas haunted his footsteps at the Netherfield ball!

I have writ down what Charlotte Lucas did, for I am fully purposed to utilise my observations, the very first chance that I get.

DARCY

1. She refused to join in going to Meryton, in order to play raucous round games at my Aunt Philips's.

I was convinced at the time, and I remain convinced, that despite a most resolute politeness, Mr Collins was entirely bored, by the games and the officers both. His manners were a pattern of courtesy, particularly towards Aunt Philips – but it is unlikely that her gaucheness escaped his notice.

Lesson to be learned: *I should have stayed at home, as Charlotte did.*

2. On the day when Lizzy refused him, Charlotte displayed a sweet womanly sympathy that was – I suspect – balm to his wounded sensitivities, walking with him, chatting to him, and engaging him towards herself. This was most cleverly done.

Lesson to be learned: *Extend the sweet blessing of womanly sympathy, where possible.*

3. At the ball, while Lizzy rashly attempted to dissuade him from introducing himself to the superior Mr Darcy – I cannot imagine why, for he has every right, as a clergyman, to introduce himself to anyone at all – Charlotte pretended to sudden deafness.

Thus, Lizzy did ill in failing to defer to Mr Collins's good judgement – and Charlotte did well by being discreet.

Lesson to be learned: *If a man is determined upon a certain course of action, it is better to pretend not to notice.*

4.   Whilst I was charming the company, Charlotte was particularly assiduous in her attentions. She was clever enough to realise that *I* was the clearest impediment to her schemes, as our cousin had conceived the heroic notion of marrying amongst the Bennet girls.

Thus, she distracted his attention away from the quality of my performance, and towards herself. At the time, I found this quite annoying but now, I must concede the art in it.

Lesson to be learned: *Do not scruple to distract a man from the talents of your rivals.*

As far as Hunsford and Rosings are concerned, Mama's curiosity is boundless. But Lizzy is so impatient! When Mama began to ask her about Lady Catherine's plate, she cried, 'Oh heavens, Mama! You cannot imagine how many sets she possesses! Gold-edged, French, with tiny flowers adorning them... I cannot conceive why anyone could wish for so many, beyond the purposes of show. I suspect it takes nine scullery maids and twelve footmen to preserve them from tarnish. And had you seen Lady Catherine preening as Charlotte admired them, and with such perseverance, you would have blessed yourself!'

She was equally dismissive with regard to Lady Catherine's lace, her daughter's evening gowns, and the marbled glories of Rosings itself. She positively laughed at Charlotte's affection for her hens, though Lizzy herself once told me that she intended to keep hens and to embroider most tediously besides, so that she might become a proper, dull, little spinster and a credit to our parents' notions of child-rearing – although perhaps that might have been a joke.

In short, though it is sometimes difficult to tell where Lizzy's seriousness ends and her joking begins, there is no doubt in my mind that she is most heartily wishing that she was in Charlotte Collins's place and, should she have her time again, she would not say him nay. But I must return to my essay and cease to be distracted by such petty concerns – for what would either Fordyce or our cousin Collins think of such frivolity as that?

Chapter 39

Longbourn

The day came when Lizzy could resist no longer. She *must* speak of it to somebody – and of course, that somebody must be Jane. After preparing her for something surprising, therefore, she opened her heart – suppressing only the part relating to Bingley and Jane – and told her of Darcy's proposal, his letter to her, and all that she had learned about Mr Wickham.

What a stroke this last was for poor Jane, who would willingly have gone through the world without believing that so much wickedness existed throughout mankind, as here existed in one individual!

'I do not know when I have been more shocked!' said she. 'Wickham so very bad – it is almost past belief! And poor Mr Darcy! Imagine his disappointment – and having to mention such a thing of his sister, too! It is really too distressing! I am sure you feel it so.'

'Not at all. Seeing you do him such ample justice makes me feel, each moment, more unconcerned. If you lament over him much longer, my heart will be as light as a feather!'

'Lizzy, when at first you read his letter, I am very sure that you could not treat the matter as you do now.'

'Indeed not. I was uncomfortable, even miserable. Oh, how I wanted you!'

'And it is most unfortunate that you chose to use quite such strong words about Mr Wickham to Mr Darcy – for they *do* seem completely undeserved.'

'Certainly. But the misfortune of speaking with bitterness is the natural consequence of the prejudices I had been nurturing. From my first meeting with Darcy, I had detested him, while Wickham's manners seemed so delightful! I was equally prejudiced, against the one and in favour of the other! But there is still one point on which I would wish for your advice. Ought we to make our acquaintance understand Wickham's true character – or not?'

Jane hesitated, then, 'Surely there can be no occasion to expose him so dreadfully. What is your own opinion?'

'That it ought not to be attempted. I am not authorised to make his behaviour towards Miss Darcy public and, should we endeavour to remove the public distaste for Mr Darcy otherwise, who would believe us? Given the general prejudice against him, it might be the death of half the good people of Meryton, to attempt to place him in an amiable light. I am unequal to it. Wickham will soon be gone – and then it will not signify to anyone here in Hertfordshire what he really is.'

Eliza's mind was much eased by this conversation – though increasingly exercised about Brighton. And thus, the next evening, as her father's usual hour of retiring approached, she put down her book and moved to the library. He answered her knock with a surprised, 'Who is there?'

'It is only myself.'

'Why, Lizzy, whatever is the matter?'

'I have come, my dear father, to tell you something, and to beg that you will not share it – not even with Mama.'

'Very well, you have my word. Sit down, I beg.'

'I wish to be as direct as possible. I am here, Papa, on Lydia's account.'

'Ah.'

'I believe, and fervently too, that Lydia ought not to go to Brighton.'

'And I feel that she must. Lydia will never be easy until she has made a fool of herself in some public place or other, and we can never expect her to do so with so little expense or inconvenience as the Forsters have offered.'

'Wait! First, Lydia is completely untamed. She says what she thinks – she behaves as her high spirits take her – she attends to no rebukes, not even from yourself! I have long believed that she required guidance, but since the regiment's being in Meryton –'

'A most malicious arrangement on the part of the War Office.'

'Say rather, pernicious – but, at any rate, since the regiment's being in Meryton, she has grown very much worse. And now she will be leaving the family, for the very first time, at just sixteen. She will be attending a woman scarcely older than herself and not noticeably wiser and – though the Colonel is more reliable, he will be principally engaged elsewhere. The temptations of Brighton must prove still stronger than those of Meryton – while Mrs Forster is likelier to encourage Lydia's volatility than to repress it!'

'My dear, I do not believe it possible to repress Lydia. I gave up the attempt when she was three or four.'

'But Papa, if you were only aware of the great – the very great – disadvantages which have already arisen from Lydia's behaviour, you would reason very differently.'

'What, has she frightened away some of your lovers? Poor Lizzy! But such squeamish youths as cannot bear to be connected with a little absurdity are not worth a regret. Come, let me hear the list of pitiful fellows kept aloof by Lydia's folly.'

Tears rose to her eyes as she said, 'Indeed, you are mistaken – I have no such injuries to resent. But our respectability must be affected by the volatility, boldness and disdain for all restraint which mark Lydia's character. Forgive me – for I must speak plainly. If you, my dear father, will not take the trouble to check her exuberance, she will soon be beyond reach of amendment. She will, at sixteen, be the most determined flirt who ever made herself and her connections ridiculous, and wholly unable to ward off that contempt which her rage for admiration will excite. Can you suppose it possible that she will not be despised, even ridiculed, and that her sisters will not be involved in her disgrace?'

Her father was moved. He said, very seriously, 'Do not make yourself uneasy, my love. Wherever you and Jane are known, you must be respected and valued – and you shall not appear to less advantage for having some exceedingly silly sisters. We shall have no peace if Lydia does not go to Brighton. Colonel Forster is a very sensible fellow, and she is luckily too poor to be an object of prey to anyone. At Brighton she will be of less importance, even as a common flirt, than she has been here – the officers will find women better worth their notice.'

'I cannot agree, Papa – and I beg that you will think on it.'

'Goodnight, my dear.' And with that they parted.

Upstairs, Jane asked if she was well.

'I am tired,' said Eliza. 'Tired of Lydia's triumphing and of Kitty's whining, and of Mama's nerves, besides! Although, were it not that I had the Gardiners' trip to the Lakes to look forward to, I suppose I should be equally annoying in my turn!'

Chapter 40

'She is a right one,' said Mrs Hill, to Bessy, 'It is "Hill here" and "Hill there" and never a please nor a thank you, nor a "if it might be convenient!"'

'I wish,' said Bessy fervently, 'that she would go to Brighton and never come back again!'

'But *that* would be too much to hope for.'

'And that Miss Kitty will never leave off a-moaning and a-groaning!'

'Not she, for she was born to complain.'

'The one I worry for is Miss Bennet. She might worry herself into a decline, and she always so kind!'

Mrs Hill said, 'She was an angel put down on earth, on purpose to suffer. 'Tis a wonder she has not died young, or not yet.'

'Nay, do not wish it on her!'

Mrs Hill said darkly, 'I would not wish it on her. There's *some* as I might wish it on, but Miss Bennet – never!'

Just as Lydia was preparing to depart for Brighton, Elizabeth was greeted at the top of the staircase by Mary, who said, very soberly, 'I am glad you are come, Lizzy, for she is weeping!'

'What, again?' asked Lizzy in resignation, for Kitty had been sulking for a fortnight. But Mary only indicated the door of the room Lizzy shared with Jane and returned to her practising.

Lizzy entered, entirely disbelieving – for whatever could Kitty be doing in her own room? But she had not given Mary the credit she deserved, for she found Jane there instead, in tears by the armoire.

'Oh, Lizzy!'

'Why, what has happened?'

'Nothing! Oh – just leave me to my own foolishness, I beg!'

Instead, Lizzy stood, irresolute, just inside the door.

She was almost certain that her sister's misery related to Charles Bingley. She had already confessed both Mr Wickham's real character and Mr Darcy's proposal to Jane – but the rest of the letter remained her secret. But surely confessing that Bingley *had* indeed loved Jane – but had still been argued or finessed out of pursuing her – would only make matters worse?

Finally, she said, 'Jane, I am as convinced as I ever was that Mr Bingley loves you.'

'No one less partial than you could believe it!'

'I cannot help believing it. From the first moment of his meeting you, at the Assembly ball, he looked at no one else!'

'But Lizzy, he could return to Netherfield tomorrow, if he chose. What, beyond inclination, could keep him in town? A week or so might pass in business perhaps – for what could we know of his business? – but it has been months, not weeks!'

'A thousand things might have arisen.'

'I did fancy that he liked me… but no longer!'

Lizzy sat down beside her distraught sister, thinking, 'Oh, Mr Darcy! You have no notion what pain you have occasioned!'

She took a deep breath, but Jane forestalled her. 'I beg you, say nothing, do nothing. You are only too good! – but I shall recover quicker alone.'

Once outside, Elizabeth shut the door and leaned against it. Mary poked an inquisitive head outside her own room, saying,

'There! Did I not tell you?' – but Lizzy only shook her head and moved downstairs.

In her own room, Mary picked up her pen and wrote: *Fordyce instructs us thusly: 'Need I tell you, that men of the best sense have been usually averse to the thought of marrying a witty female? You will probably tell me that they were afraid of being outshone; and some of them perhaps might be so. We are never safe in the company of a critic – and almost every wit is a critic by profession. But to suffer this restraint at home, what misery! From the brandishings of wit, who would not flee? But when that weapon is pointed at a husband, is it to be wondered if from his own house he takes shelter in the tavern?'*

After deep thought, she added: *From Fordyce's pithily turned passage – above – one ineluctable truism emerges, to wit, that wit itself, far from being sought after in a helpmeet, can be viewed as detrimental and even deleterious.*

(In brief, how silly the witty Elizabeth had been, in disdaining the excellent Mr Collins! How deeply she must regret it!) But then Mary thought: 'And yet, if this was true, then surely it is *Elizabeth* who should be weeping, and not Jane?'

And, 'So why is Jane in tears? *She* has no wish to be at Brighton, I am sure – and certainly it could never be anything to do with Netherfield and Bingley, after such a passage of time!'

Meanwhile, Kitty said to Maria Lucas, 'I thought your brother might come, to talk to Mary.'

'Perhaps he might, but for his coughing spells.'

'I cough a great deal in the spring, and sneeze as well. And Papa is so disagreeable when I do.'

175

'La, but your cough is not like Timothy's for,' and Maria Lucas lowered her voice, 'for *his* is serious!'

'I assure you, my cough is also serious,' said Kitty, affronted.

'While your sister Mary is a bit – odd.'

'La! She is so dull! She was born with no sense of fun. You can have no notion how tiresome she can be! But your brother is bookish too, I think?'

'Yes, but there is nothing in *that,* I assure you,' said Maria.

'But he seems intrigued by Mary?'

'I think he finds her rather a curiosity. He likes Mrs Long's niece, Alice, very well – but *she* would never have him.'

✦

Eliza lost no time in alerting Mr Wickham to her change in sentiments. He greeted her exuberantly at her aunt's saying, 'And so, you visited at Rosings! I expect Lady Catherine lost no time in advising you to study your fingerings on the pianoforte?'

'She did.'

'And equally, in acquainting you with the astonishing talent of Miss Anne de Bourgh, who is so musically gifted that practice and performance must be alike superfluous?'

Elizabeth acknowledged as much coolly, saying, 'The dullness of our company was, however, much enlivened by Colonel Fitzwilliam's being of the party. I have rarely met so agreeable a man!'

'The Colonel! Was he there, indeed? And Darcy with him?'

'Yes.'

Wickham shook his head. '*His* manners, of course, one dare not vouch for.'

'Not to the same degree – but I think that Mr Darcy's manners improve upon acquaintance.'

'Indeed! And pray, may I ask, is it in address that he improves or in civility? For I dare not hope' – this in a more serious tone – 'that he has improved in essentials.'

'Oh, no,' said Eliza archly, 'in essentials, I believe, he is very much as he ever was.' The alarm that crossed his face was most diverting as she added, 'When I say that he improved upon acquaintance, I did not mean that his manners were in a state of improvement but that, from knowing him better, his disposition might be better understood.'

Wickham's concern was obvious, but it was not long before the party broke up, with Lydia riotously assuring her sisters – including the still-sulking Kitty – that she would be very sure to write from Brighton, if she had a moment, but that *they* were to write to her directly.

And within a week, Elizabeth was also saying her farewells, and attending the Gardiners northwards.

''Tis not that I expect anything,' Kitty said plaintively the next evening to Mary. 'Nothing beyond my due, I mean. But it does seem most unfair. Jane and Lizzy deserve no less than their expeditions – Jane's to London in January and Lizzy's to Derbyshire – but you and I should have been the next to have our chance, and not Lydia, who is scarcely sixteen! Why, in most houses, she would not even be in society – yet it was *she* who was invited to Brighton!'

Mary objected, 'But Papa cannot afford for us to visit London, or to wander about the rest of England, either. Were Jane and Lizzy not invited by the Gardiners – which *we* might be next year in our turn – they would both still be here. I acknowledge that Lydia has had fortune on her side, to be Mrs Forster's favourite, but perhaps the Colonel believed one guest sufficient for the space that they were offered.'

'The difficulty in making you understand,' said Kitty bitterly, 'is that you find nothing to regret in not going to Brighton, at all!'

'Many philosophers have astutely observed that man is born to suffer, and that such suffering is not only entirely unavoidable but can actually prove beneficial, in terms of a strengthened mind and conscience. The early Stoics –'

'I care nothing for Stoics, whether they be early or late! All I know is that I have been made to look pitiful, in the eyes of all Meryton, and all because Mama allowed Lydia to come out at least a year before she ought!'

'Oh Kitty, I am sure that no one in Meryton pities you!'

'You think not? Then why did our Aunt Philips say, "La! To think of poor Kitty, left behind with – well, never mind what." Poor Kitty, indeed! And no one left in Meryton worth the visiting!'

Chapter 41

Pemberley, Derbyshire

Eliza stood before his portrait feeling odd indeed.

The oddness had begun the previous evening, at Lambton, when her Aunt Gardiner had first mentioned her desire to see Pemberley again. Dismayed, Elizabeth had instantly said, 'Oh, but we have already seen so many splendid houses!'

'But it is not only the house, Lizzy! The woods at Pemberley are famous and the setting, and, taken altogether, it is the loveliest place I have ever seen – Besides, Wickham spent all his youth there, you know.'

Elizabeth, greatly distressed, considered acknowledging to Mrs Gardiner everything that had transpired, between the owner of Pemberley and herself, to make any meeting between them unendurable. Instead, she had asked the maid at the inn whether the family was down for the summer.

'No, ma'am. It is empty,' had been the most welcome response, enabling her to give a properly indifferent answer to the Gardiners the next morning.

To herself she admitted to a little curiosity, as the carriage rolled through the glorious approach to Pemberley, and to a little awe, upon first beholding the house from a distance. ('And of all this I could have been mistress!' she could not help thinking – before recollecting, 'but I could never have arrived with my dear aunt and uncle, for *they* would never have been welcomed.')

It was a useful reminder, as it saved her from anything like regret.

They were shown around by the housekeeper, a woman much less fine, and much less proud, than Eliza had expected to find her. And though the property was immense, and very grand, she was impressed by its quiet, classical, lack of show. There was a more understated elegance within than in any other great house she had ever seen.

The housekeeper seemed exceedingly proud of it. Upon noticing Mrs Gardiner pointing out a miniature of George Wickham to Elizabeth she remarked, 'A favourite of the late Mr Darcy's. He is gone into the army. But I am afraid he has turned out rather wild.'

Mrs Gardiner sent a little smile towards her niece, which Eliza found herself entirely unable to return. Another trial awaited her in the long gallery, however, where she observed a painting of Mr Darcy, with such a half-smile on his face as she remembered.

'It is a handsome painting,' said Mrs Gardiner, 'and a handsome face! – but Lizzy must tell us whether it is a good resemblance or not.'

'Does the young lady know Mr Darcy, then?' asked the housekeeper respectfully.

'A little,' said Eliza.

'And is it not very like?'

'It is very like, indeed,' said she – for it was just such a smile as he had sometimes directed towards her, when she had subtly mocked Her Ladyship. And she stood regarding the portrait for so long that she failed to notice when the Gardiners followed the housekeeper into the next room.

Chapter 42

(From Mr Darcy's diaries)

London being more than usually irritating, and Miss Bingley more than averagely fawning, Pemberley's woods called to me, as they so often do when the weather is set fair. I made some excuse to the Bingleys of business I had to attend to – though I had none – and made good time on the road. How freeing it is, to have no one else's convenience to consult beyond one's own! I left the chaise behind and rode the last seven miles by myself. By the time I reached Pemberley it was late afternoon, the light almost amber on the leaves, pools of sunlight just dappling the stream. I slowed down to admire it, though the mare – scenting her favourite stable – sawed at the bit. For a moment it was as if the wind – or the colours, or Pemberley itself – had lifted every concern from my shoulders.

My new tranquillity was tested almost immediately, however. As I dismounted, my first sight was of Jacobs, limping towards me, just ducking his head. 'Master! Why, we was told –'

'I could wait no longer,' I said. 'The others arrive tomorrow. But – Good God – could it be –'

'Why, what is it, sir?'

But I could not answer him because – or so it seemed – I was suffering some form of hallucination. The number of times I had imagined it! – but that must be impossible. I moved a step closer. It *was* she – her form, her swift way of lifting her head, that sprightliness of movement. Her complexion might be somewhat more tanned, but that dark flash of eye was unmistakeable. She was accompanied by an older couple – not her parents – they were just strolling from the house towards the principal woodland trail. Elizabeth Bennet was walking along the path at Pemberley, just as she had, a thousand times – ten thousand times – in my imagination!

Our eyes met, and she blushed very deeply – as did I, I was quite convinced. The wave of heat almost dizzied me. I bowed, and asked what brought her into the country, or something like it – I hardly knew what I said! She answered – I cannot recall how. Then, collecting myself, I begged leave to be introduced to her companions. Her taunting expression informed me, before she did, that these were some of those very relatives I had so derided on that memorable night at Hunsford. The introductions accomplished, I had to admit that there was certainly nothing to justify contempt in the Gardiners. Her mother's brother has a most pleasing address and the remains of unusually good looks: his wife is petite, elegant and beautifully dressed.

How I might have disgraced myself, had she been alone, I do not know. All I could think was that she was at Pemberley, and surely she would never have come, even to look about the place, if she loathed the very thought of myself? Farther than *that*, though, I dared not venture. I cannot recall above half what was said – I suspect that I asked her, more than once, how long she had been in the country, and how long she intended to remain. Then they embarked on the walk, and I removed indoors... After half an hour inside however, I resolved to find them and to correct any impression I had given upon beholding her that I had lost my wits when she rejected me.

I chose a path designed to intercept their own, still marvelling.

Was she still angry? – I could not tell. She had seemed more confused than angry, I considered, though there had been that mischievous glance as she named her aunt and uncle. She had certainly been as astonished to see me as I had been to see her. She even started as I intercepted their party, as if our previous encounter had never occurred. I fell into step beside her uncle, along the path by the stream.

'I expect you have excellent fishing here?' he inquired.

I acknowledged as much, adding, 'Should you wish to try your luck, I would be most happy to loan you some fishing tackle, and to direct you to some of the likelier spots.'

'I should like nothing better,' said Gardiner, with a laugh, 'but I am inexpert enough to do your rods a mischief.'

'And if I am engaged, my gamekeeper – a most excellent fellow – will assist you.'

'Really, it is most exceedingly kind of you.'

I could not see Miss Bennet's reaction, for she was walking ahead of us with her aunt, but I trusted that such an attention to her uncle could not fail to be agreeable. Gardiner and I then spoke of the City and of various acquaintances we had in common. After half-a-mile, with Mrs Gardiner declaring herself in need of her husband's arm, I silently took her place beside her niece. Miss Eliza seemed anxious to assure me that meeting me was no part of her plan.

'We had no notion that you would so soon be here! Your housekeeper assured us, as she showed us around the house, that you were not expected.'

'Mine was a last-minute decision, to precede the rest of my party, who will arrive tomorrow. Some of whom will claim an acquaintance with you – Mr Bingley and his sisters.'

I was convinced, by her confusion as I named him, that she was also recollecting the last time we had spoken of Charles Bingley, but I continued, 'However, there is another member of the party who particularly wishes to be known to you. Will you allow me – or do I ask too much – to introduce my sister to your acquaintance while you are at Lambton?'

This *did* succeed in confusing her. She said, 'I should be delighted,' but was perfectly silent afterwards.

I would have been happy just to observe the variation of her countenance – how could I ever have thought Giuditta's superior? – but felt obliged to speak. I could not decide whether this new consciousness was promising or otherwise – I was only convinced that *something* had altered, and that my letter – which I had often wished never written – had so far imposed itself on her goodwill that she no longer despised me.

It was not enough, however. I had walked beside her for only a few minutes before all my previous longings were rekindled!

The walk – the radiance of the day, the proximity of her beauty – still held a hallucinatory quality. I was also privately frustrated in my attempt to get a fuller view of her countenance than she seemed to wish to allow. I could hardly take in what she said for wondering about deeper things! And at the conclusion, though I invited her relatives to return indoors, for I wished to show them every possible attention, I was relieved by their refusal. I needed space and time in which to absorb the strangeness of it all. All evening, I could not stop thinking of her. My impatience for the arrival of the rest might be imagined, for the excuse Georgiana afforded to call upon her.

Of course, I could not help recollecting that Miss Bingley would be among the party and that Miss Eliza was perfectly acquainted with the role she played in separating Charles from Jane Bennet. But I can rely on her discretion. I can also depend upon Georgiana, if prompted, to make the proper invitations. How fortunate it is that the Gardiners have but just arrived in Lambton! – There is much that might be attempted – and attempt it I shall.

At least she no longer seems to despise me. There is a great gulf fixed between detestation and love, and her feelings seem somewhere in the middle, but I cannot rest until I *know*, one way or another, whether there is the slightest chance for me. Because, if today has taught me anything, then it is this: *she* must have a thousand choices, a thousand men who would long to marry her – but *my* only hope of happiness lies in that swift dark glance and that light, graceful form. Should she refuse me twice then I shall be obliged to marry – as I vowed I never would – for dynasty alone.

For I can only ever love Elizabeth Bennet.

Chapter 43

Lambton, Derbyshire

Eliza was still shocked upon wakening the next morning. She thought confusedly, 'How am I to understand such behaviour? He seems not only kinder and gentler, but genuinely resolved to pay the kindest attention to people he would normally disdain! And to wish me to know his sister, as well!'

At breakfast, her uncle seemed similarly struck. 'I cannot understand it. His previous acquaintance with Lizzy was very trifling. As for my own experience, I cannot see how his manners could be improved upon. How ever could he have so offended the Skinners?'

'And yet the Skinners, you know, are easily offended,' said Mrs Gardiner. 'And it is not uncommon to misinterpret those whose manners differ from one's own. But how came you to tell us, Lizzy, that he was so disagreeable?'

'I hardly know myself,' said she. 'And yet – I know how unutterably foolish this sounds – I found him pleasanter in Kent than in Hertfordshire, and never more pleasing than here in Derbyshire.'

'He may be mercurial,' suggested her uncle. 'Your great men often are. Yesterday he offered to loan me fishing tackle – tomorrow, he might warn me off his grounds!'

'Not he,' said Mrs Gardiner. 'It is not only his looks – though he is nearly as handsome as Wickham, himself! – There is something very pleasing in his countenance. It is surprising that he has not married, though what lady would be fit for a man with so much to recommend him?... But wait, is not that the Pemberley livery on that carriage door?'

'It is,' said her husband, 'but it will pass by, I am sure. I cannot think that *he* would be coming here.'

Elizabeth watched the carriage roll to a stop on the cobblestones. Then she said, in some confusion, 'In fact, my dear Aunt, they might indeed be coming here. Mr Darcy did just mention, yesterday, that his sister wishes to meet me.'

'Did he, indeed? And she must have only just arrived, as well. How I wish I had chosen my other gown!'

While her uncle said, in an undertone, 'You must greet them, Lizzy. For it must be in compliment to *you* that Miss Darcy – if it is she – pays us such attention.'

Elizabeth moved away from the window, attempting to compose herself before encountering the formidable, supremely accomplished Georgiana Darcy. But there was scarcely time for more before Mr Darcy, Miss Darcy and Miss Bingley entered, and the introduction she had been dreading took place. But – she could not help wondering – could this *truly* be Miss Darcy? There seemed almost no resemblance between herself and her brother! She was tall, full-formed and elegant, to be sure, but so quiet as to seem almost timorous! She seemed still less at ease than Eliza herself, who felt so conscious of Mr Darcy's presence as to be most uncomfortable.

Under these circumstances, Bingley's late arrival counted as a relief. They had hardly disposed themselves when he bounded in, moved directly to Eliza and shook her hand in so unembarrassed a fashion as to claim her as a friend.

He said, 'Darcy is so annoying! You will not credit it, Miss Bennet, but he only just deigned to mention at breakfast that you were at Lambton, and even doubted whether I could be troubled to meet you! Darcy, you know it is true!'

Miss Bingley said, 'You must forgive him, Mrs Gardiner. My brother never travels in a civilised manner. Really, one almost despairs. Even when offered a place in as charming an equipage as Darcy's – and never was there one half so comfortable – he *will* take his horse, in order to appear in a suitable state of dishevelment.'

'What!' cried Bingley. 'Who would choose to be cooped up in a carriage, when one might ride! What say you, Miss Bennet?'

'As I am no horsewoman,' said Eliza, 'I can have no opinion. Except that your appearance seems entirely unexceptionable to me.'

Later, he said, with a hesitancy that told Elizabeth where his thoughts were tending: 'Are all of your sisters at Longbourn, Miss Elizabeth?'

'My youngest sister is visiting at Brighton – and my eldest has but just returned from town.'

'Has she, by Jove?' cried Bingley.

'Yes,' said Mrs Gardiner, 'Jane is so great a favourite with our children that she could not be spared. She is the only person little Edward will always obey. Were Mrs Bennet only persuadable, we would adopt Jane entirely!'

'It is unfortunate for you that London would appear to hold no great fascination for her,' said Darcy with a smile. 'Am I correct, Miss Elizabeth?'

'My sister prefers the freedom of the country,' said Elizabeth, still marvelling at his complaisance. His cordiality at Pemberley had been astonishing enough, but this! – and nor was that all. He soon prevailed upon Georgiana to invite them to dinner. As Eliza was too embarrassed to respond, her aunt, after ascertaining her husband's perfect willingness, accepted on behalf of all their party. Shortly afterwards, the Pemberley set departed, amidst bows from the gratified landlord, his wife, and their servants.

Eliza, both distressed and flattered, returned to her room to compose herself. The moment she was gone Mr Gardiner said to his wife, 'There is more to this business, my love, than meets the eye, I am convinced.'

'In what respect?'

'You are not as accustomed as I to the behaviour of your great men, but Mr Darcy's attentions are decidedly out of the common way. In fact, I can only account for them by assuming that he admires our niece. How his eyes brightened upon seeing her!'

'But so did Mr Bingley's. He is still more charming than your sister's description! So genuine, so unaffected – so open a temperament – I can easily imagine Jane's loving him! But Darcy! Only think, if it were true! It is almost inconceivable. With all our own partiality, to imagine Lizzy at Pemberley – and in town, come to that!'

'I do not say that it is so – and yet I do suspect it,' said Mr Gardiner.

'How your sister would bless herself – Netherfield would be as nothing in comparison! But admiration is not the same as love; and a little fever of admiration might not be sufficient to overcome all the obstacles to Eliza Bennet becoming mistress of Pemberley.'

'And little fevers can also burn out,' added her husband. 'We must not permit our imaginations to overrun either logic or probability. But who would have guessed that we should find ourselves in such circles! I must get my cravat seen to before tomorrow.'

Chapter 44

(From Mr Darcy's diaries)

For the rest of the morning I kept wondering whether Eliza's very evident surprise in the inn at Lambton augured well or ill. In the carriage, Caroline Bingley could find nothing to say of *her* but admitted to being astonished by the Gardiners ('One might suppose him to be a country gentleman, while she has real breeding! Remarkable indeed, for one related to the Bennet family!')

Eliza herself had been, I thought, quieter than usual – I noticed, too, that she had spoken with less reserve to Bingley than to myself. There had been a glow upon his appearance, which had made me almost jealous… I also found myself missing her impertinence. She is so quicksilver, as a rule! But they have agreed to dine with us on Wednesday and, just before we parted, I arranged to fish with Gardiner and Bingley in the morning.

I had no dread of the expedition. From the first moment, I had felt an affinity between myself and Gardiner, and I am not as averse to fishing as I am to many sports. But from the moment I heard that the ladies of their party had judged so well as to repay my sister's visit, I left the others by the stream and headed towards the house. And as I walked, I saw everything with jaundiced eyes, as if Lady Catherine herself had been criticising them: the flowerbeds, the gravel path, the view across the lake… *Nothing* to me looked worthy of being seen by the swift dark eyes of Elizabeth Bennet. I knew – even as I felt it – that this was mad, yet still, I must feel it!

I had been careful, with Georgiana, not to say too much, only that I particularly wished her to be cordial to Miss Bennet, to whose family I owed a great deal. The moment I entered the saloon, Miss Bingley began to tease me. 'Dear, dear! Were you then so unsuccessful?'

'Your brother,' said I, 'has done even better than Mr Gardiner. The rest of us displayed rather less skill.'

'But I am very sure that you left the best of the river to Charles! 'Twould be just like you!'

As I had nothing to say to this, I did not reply.

'What a delightful aspect you have,' said Mrs Gardiner.

'My plan was to continue along the lines laid down by my father. Whether I have succeeded might well be doubted, but it was done in his honour and in his memory.'

'He was renowned as the most delightful man!' cried Miss Bingley.

'He was a very good man indeed,' said Mrs Annesley, Georgiana's companion. I looked encouragingly at Georgiana, in hopes that she might speak – but she was silent. She is too often silent, yet how I wished Miss Bingley more like her, at least in that respect, for she chose that moment to say, 'Tell me, Miss Bennet, is it true that the —shire regiment have left Meryton? What a loss that must be for *your* family!'

Georgiana turned scarlet, but Miss Eliza was not the least discomposed. 'I expect,' said she, 'that my youngest sister's existence will continue. More than that must not be expected, as she is only just sixteen.'

I swiftly turned the conversation, attempting, as far as I was able, to forward her acquaintance with Georgiana, who gradually recovered her poise. How ill-bred it had been of Miss Bingley to taunt Miss Eliza with the regiment – and how mortified she would have been to learn that she had embarrassed Georgiana instead! But then, Miss Bingley – fortunately – knows nothing of Georgiana's past with Wickham.

As our visitors left, I chose to accompany the Gardiners and their niece to their carriage, taking the chance to thank Eliza. 'It was very good of you to come.'

'Not at all. Your sister is charming,' said she. 'How I long to hear her play!'

'Thank you, but I hope to hear *you* play again, as well.'

'I fear *that* would be only an embarrassment, as I have not touched an instrument this long age.'

'But the voice can surely not have altered? Colonel Fitzwilliam said, only the other day, how it had brightened Rosings last Easter.'

She turned to look at me, as if contemplating some swift rejoinder, misjudged the depth of the marble step beneath, and slipped, with a little cry. Taking three steps in one, I caught her round the waist, secured her against the balustrade and released her. So strange a moment – locked close, a third of the way down the marble staircase – time itself suspended!

Her aunt, following, heard the cry and rushed to the head of the stairs. 'Lizzy! What has happened?'

'Why nothing at all! I fell, I cannot think how, but Mr Darcy caught me – for which I am most grateful,' she said to me, with a private smile. 'I am sorry to have alarmed you, Aunt, for I am rarely clumsy, as a rule.'

After assisting them into the carriage, I watched it roll away, still thinking of that little smile. How I wished I could have prolonged that instant on the stair! I was then obliged to return to the saloon, where Miss Bingley was saying very spitefully, 'How very ill Eliza Bennet looked this morning! I never in my life saw anyone so altered. She is grown so brown and coarse!'

'I can perceive no difference,' said I, 'beyond her being rather tanned, no very remarkable result of travelling in the summer.'

Poor Miss Bingley tossed her head. 'Well, I must say, I could never see anything to admire in her. Her complexion has no brilliancy, her face is too thin, and her features nothing out of the common way. And as for her eyes, which have sometimes been called so fine, they have a sharp, shrewish expression, which I do not care for at all. I recall that once, in Hertfordshire, you said, "Her, a beauty? – I should as soon call her mother a wit!" – But after that she grew on you, and I believe you considered her rather pretty at one time.'

191

This was too much for my feelings. I said, 'True, but *that* was only when I first knew her, for it has been many months since I have considered her one of the handsomest women of my acquaintance.'

At this, Miss Bingley actually flinched. How far I had made real inroads into Caroline Bingley's heart is something I have never quite determined. Yet, in that moment, I regretted my warmth, and felt sorry for her.

I could not sleep that night, for recollecting that moment on the stair.

Chapter 45

Longbourn

Mary called from her room, 'Mama, the Lucases are come! Lady Lucas, Maria, and Timothy.'

'Well then,' said Mrs Bennet, '*you* must receive them, for my nerves are in no fit state to come down.'

'But I must practise, Mama.'

'Heavens! Need you practise the whole of the day? – Maria will not stay long, only as long as I shall be obliged to see her mother.'

'But Maria is *Kitty's* particular friend, and all she cares for is clothes and quizzes. She is entirely useless for the purposes of conversation.'

'No more arguments, I beg! You do little enough for the family, after all! Oh, if only Jane was not calling on the Longs! – she is the only one not continually in dispute. And not even your father has the slightest respect for my nerves!'

Mary wished to observe that her own nerves could very ill bear the giggling of Miss Maria Lucas, but she held her tongue. She was struck as they entered by an improvement in Master Timothy's height since his recent illness. Just as she had feared, their two sisters fell to giggling and so, putting aside her book, she offered him some tea. He said, 'Thank you, Miss Mary. What is your book?'

'I doubt that you would care for it. It is by Rev. Fordyce.'

'The sermoniser, you mean?'

'The writer and theologian,' said Mary coldly. 'I am doing a scholarly critique of his sermons for young ladies.'

'A work,' said Timothy, 'which always struck me as being rather poor form.'

'By which you mean –?'

'Simply that as, by common consent, Fordyce himself is neither young nor a lady, who is he to lay down the law to those who might be?'

'Perhaps you prefer his *Addresses to the Deity* instead?'

Timothy shook his head. 'I should have different objections, in that case. For who is Fordyce to address God?'

'Well, he is a Doctor of Divinity, something neither you nor I can claim!'

'And yet you are writing a book. That shows some ambition.'

'I am not,' she acknowledged, 'entirely without it.'

'And do you take the good doctor to task in your researching? Do you examine his theories with an unprejudiced eye?'

Mary hesitated. 'I hope I do. Such indeed is my purpose.'

'Well then, I should like to see it.'

'Why, whatever do you mean?'

'Make a trial of me. Permit me to see a page or two of your *magnum opus*.'

Mary lifted both eyebrows. 'What! Show *you* my essays?'

'Unless you intend them for yourself and yourself alone, you will have to show them to someone at some point, Miss Mary,' he observed, with dancing eyes.

Mary was most discomfited, for no one had ever wished to see her work before. She said, 'Well – that is, I do intend to publish, at some point, but –'

'Then I cannot comprehend your objection. It is not as if I have no knowledge of Fordyce – nor, for that matter, of young ladies, since *I* can boast as many sisters as you can, yourself.'

'Why, whatever are you two speaking of?' asked Kitty, from the other side of the room.

'Of books, silly.'

'How dull you are!' cried Maria Lucas, with a laugh. 'For *we* were discussing whether, in Scotland, all the castles are haunted, and how we should contrive, if one of us fell in love with a Scottish baron and must live there. And Kitty says she could not, but I think – for I have visited at Rosings, oh! ever so many times – that it would be worth it, for the gold plate alone. I would consider a spectre or two quite endurable, in return for owning such views as those from Rosings' windows!'

'Well, *I* should not,' said Kitty, with a shiver. 'I remember one All Hallows' Eve…'

'I should of course be obliged,' said Mary to Timothy, in a lower tone, 'to write out a fair copy.'

'What, with your neat hand? I daresay I could manage well enough! But please yourself, by all means. Only remember, you have promised me first sight of the manuscript.'

'I do not recall a promise!'

'But you *will* promise all the same, for your desire to convert me is perfectly obvious,' said Timothy, with a smile.

'I do not know about converting, but you do Fordyce such scant justice!'

'Not at all. Who can argue, for example, with his advice to read widely? "Whatever kinds of reading may contribute to your general improvement and satisfaction will deserve your attentive regard." Or with this, perhaps my favourite, "No woman in the world ought to think it beneath her to be an economist." Would that my own mama had taken *that* lesson to heart, Miss Mary, when first she wed!'

'And my own mama as well,' Mary was forced to acknowledge. 'For if she had, why, our lives now would see the benefit of it. But still, you take him in such mischievous spirit!'

'It is a grave weakness,' said he, 'but my only one. And perhaps, after reading your dissertation, I shall see the light?'

'Let us play a round game,' said Kitty, 'all together,' but Mary excused herself, and in some perplexity of mind, for Timothy had surprised her. Imagine his having read Fordyce enough to have an opinion, and he only eighteen! Or was he nineteen? She could not recall. She found it difficult to concentrate on her work once they had gone.

'He likes her,' said Mrs Hill. 'I am convinced as he likes her.'

'Nobody,' said Bessy, ''as ever liked Miss Mary. For she puts her nose up with such an air! And Master Timothy is what I call a nice young man. He says, "Thank you, Bessy," and "That is kind of you, Bessy," which is more than any member of the militia ever did! And that Mr Denny tweaking my bottom!'

'So you have said, oh, many a time,' said Mrs Hill heavily. 'But remember, Master Timothy has a fever in his lungs, so it is not of much use his liking Miss Mary or Miss anybody else, either. There are two small graves in the churchyard with Lucas on them – God rest them! – I cannot bring to mind their Christian names.'

'Perhaps it will be like one of those songs where the singer tends the dying sailor on his deathbed,' said the sentimental Bessy. 'Miss Lizzy sings those so sweetly!'

'Nonsense,' said Mrs Hill. 'I have known Miss Mary since she was five and if tears rolled down her cheeks, why, she would roll them right back up again! But I still say as he likes her.'

Chapter 46

Lambton

Lizzy was greatly relieved to be handed two letters at breakfast. 'A note from Jane, at last, and from – but wait, they are *both* from Jane. And I had dared to think her negligent!'

'Why should you not enjoy your letters in solitude?' asked Mr Gardiner. 'Sarah, you and I might take our walk now, as we are due at Pemberley this afternoon.'

His wife agreed, and Lizzy moved to the Pembroke table to read about the state of her mother's nerves, about Kitty's spirits being in a state of modest improvement, and of Timothy Lucas – Timothy Lucas! – being permitted to read Mary's famous essay. Then she suddenly began to read more intently.

... Since writing the above, dearest Lizzy, something has occurred of a most unexpected and serious nature – but do not be alarmed – be assured that we are all well. However, an express came last night, just as we were all gone upstairs, from Colonel Forster, to

inform us that Lydia was gone off to Scotland with one of his officers – to own the truth, with Wickham. Imagine our surprise, shock and disappointment. So imprudent a match, on both sides! But perhaps his character has been misunderstood. Thoughtless I can believe him, but this step – and let us rejoice over it – marks nothing bad at heart. He must know that our father can give her nothing. How thankful I am that we never mentioned what you heard against him – we must forget it ourselves. They must have passed within ten miles of hence. Colonel Forster should soon be here, with a note Lydia left for his wife, informing her of their intent. I must conclude, though I hardly know what I have written.

Hands trembling, Lizzy slit open Jane's second letter.

By this time you must have received my hurried note – I wish that this may be more intelligible but I am so bewildered that I cannot answer for this being much more coherent. Dearest Lizzy, I have bad news for you. Imprudent as a marriage between Mr Wickham and our poor Lydia would be, we are now anxious to be assured that it has taken place for there is but too much reason to fear they are not gone to Scotland. Colonel Forster was here yesterday, with her short note to Mrs F. Though the note mentioned Gretna Green, something was dropped by Mr Denny to the Col., to the effect that Wickham never intended to go to Scotland, or to marry Lydia at all. The Colonel, instantly alarmed, set off from Brighton, in hopes of tracing their route. This he did, as far as Clapham, where they apparently removed into a hackney-coach, taking the London Road. I know not what to think! After that, the Colonel came into Hertfordshire, renewing his inquiries at every turnpike and at every inn in Barnet and Hatfield, without result – no such people had passed through. With the kindest concern he came here to

Longbourn, breaking his apprehensions in a manner most creditable to his heart. I am sincerely grieved for him and Mrs F. Our own distress, my dear Lizzy, is very great. My father and mother believe the worst, but I cannot think so ill of him. Many circumstances might make it more eligible to marry in London than to pursue their first plan – and even if he could form a design against a young woman of Lydia's connections, which is not likely, can I suppose her so lost to everything? – impossible! I grieve to find, however, that Colonel F. is not disposed to depend upon their marriage: he shook his head when I expressed my hopes and said that he feared W. was not a man to be trusted. Our poor mother is really poorly, and keeps to her room, and as to Papa, I never in my life saw him so affected. Poor Kitty has anger for having concealed their attachment, but as it was a matter of confidence one cannot wonder. I am glad that you have been spared these distressing scenes but now, may I own that I long for your return? I am not so selfish as to press for it, if inconvenient. Adieu! I take up my pen again to do what I told you I would not. Circumstances are such that I cannot help earnestly begging you to come as soon as possible. I know my dear uncle and aunt so well that I am not afraid to request it, though I have something still greater to ask of the former. Papa goes to London with Colonel Forster shortly. What he means to do there I know not, but his distress is not promising; and the Colonel must be again in Brighton in the evening. My uncle's counsel would be everything in such a case, and I rely upon his goodness.

'Oh heavens, where is my uncle?' cried Lizzy, rushing to the door. But just then it was opened by a servant, who admitted Mr Darcy – and Darcy alone – into the room. He was, perhaps, the last person she would have wished to see at such a moment – but she had no time for embarrassment or indeed, for anything.

She said, 'Forgive me, but I must go to my uncle, and directly too. There is not a moment to lose!'

'Good God! Whatever is the matter?' he asked, but then, recollecting himself, 'You must send a servant, or advise me where your uncle might be found. You must not go – you are not well.'

Elizabeth hesitated, but she did, truly, feel somewhat faint and trembling. Recalling the servant, she implored him to go by the lane towards the river and to return with her relations, as swiftly as might be, for the matter was urgent. Then she sank back in the chair, looking so miserable that Darcy could not leave her.

Finally, she said, 'I have just had a letter, with news that nothing can conceal. My youngest sister has left her friends and has put herself into the power of – of Mr Wickham. *You,* who knows who and what he is, can guess the rest. She has no money, no connections, nothing that might tempt him to – oh! She is lost for ever! And when I consider that *I* could have prevented it! Oh, if only I had said something! Had I explained even a part – had only Wickham's true character been known! Wretched, wretched mistake!'

'I am grieved indeed – grieved and shocked! But is it absolutely certain?'

'Oh, yes! They were traced as far as London, but no farther. They have not gone into Scotland.'

'And what has been done in order to recover her?'

'My father has already gone to London, and we shall have left, I hope, within very few hours. But how is such a man to be worked on? How are they even to be discovered? It is in every way horrible!'

Darcy seemed scarcely to hear her: he was pacing across the room, frowning.

Eliza perfectly understood it. Her power was sinking – indeed, must sink irredeemably, under proof of such family weakness, such assured disgrace. She could neither wonder nor condemn – any man would have felt the same! But the irony was not lost on her that this thought oppressed her almost as greatly as Lydia's danger – and that she finally believed that she might have loved him when it was clear that any such love must be in vain. Burying her face in her hands, she began to weep.

Finally, he said, in a tone that spoke of compassion, but also restraint, 'I fear that you have long been desiring my absence, nor have I anything to plead in my excuse beyond a real, if ineffectual, concern. Would that I could offer consolation to such distress! – As it is, I fear that my sister will not have the pleasure of seeing you at Pemberley today.'

'Oh, yes! Do, I beg, make our excuses. Disguise the truth as long as you can – I know it cannot be long.'

'You may depend upon it. My compliments to the Gardiners, if you please.' And, with one steady, serious, parting glance, he was gone.

As he quitted the room, Eliza considered how improbable it was that they should ever meet with the freedom that they had enjoyed in Derbyshire – or perhaps at all – and sighed at the perversity of mourning a relationship that she would once have rejoiced to see the end of. At any rate, she saw him go with regret – and with foreboding too, as an early indication of the results of Lydia's infamy.

As to its outcome, never, since reading Jane's second letter, had she permitted herself a moment's hope. Only Jane, she thought, could have flattered herself with any such expectation. While the first letter had been running through her head, she was all astonishment, and how Lydia could have attached him had appeared incomprehensible. But for such an adventure as this she might have sufficient charms, and, though she hoped that Lydia would never have embarked on the affair with such an end in view, she doubted that either her virtue or her understanding would prevent her from falling an easy prey.

She had never perceived that Lydia had much preferred Wickham to Denny, Pratt and the rest, but Lydia only wanted encouragement to attach herself to anybody. First one officer and then another would be her favourite, as their attentions raised them in her opinion. The mischief of mistaken indulgence towards such a girl – how acutely did she feel it! She was wild to be at home and, until her aunt and uncle returned, the misery of her impatience was severe.

When her aunt entered the room, alarmed, on the servant's testimony, for her niece's state of health, Lizzy rushed to her and wept on her shoulder, entirely unable to speak. After a moment, Mr Gardiner said, 'I shall send for the local surgeon, without loss of time.'

'No, it is not I but *all* my family who require assistance!'

'Heavens! Whatever has happened?' cried her aunt.

'Lydia has eloped and – worse still – with Wickham.' And, as Mrs Gardiner exclaimed in horror, 'My father is gone to town and Jane writes in hopes that *you,* my dearest, kindest uncle, might meet him there!'

'Oh, Lizzy!' whispered her aunt, just as Mr Gardiner said, 'But is it true? Surely not even Lydia could do so wild a thing!'

But after Lizzy had, with trembling energy, read them the second half of Jane's letter, he instantly became active. 'First, my dear, I must settle with the landlord – and you will have letters to write to all your local connections. I daresay we can procure assistance to pack and be on our way as expeditiously as possible.'

'But – what must I write?' and 'You are too good!' burst from wife and niece in the same moment.

Mr Gardiner hesitated. Then, 'We will say that family illness draws us back. It is no one's business to own the truth, at this point. And something might still be salvageable in town.'

'But what of Pemberley? We were expected – and was not Mr Darcy with you, just now?'

'He was, but *that* has all been dealt with,' said Lizzy. 'I must, of course, write our apologies to Miss Darcy, but this evening is taken care of.'

And as she ran off, her aunt murmured, 'And are they are on such terms for her to disclose the truth? How I long to know!'

Chapter 47

(From Mr Darcy's diaries)

It has been a long day and may prove a still longer night.

As soon as I could reason, as soon as the sight of her anguish had ceased to unsettle my brain, I had decided. I told the others that business requiring an immediate decision had arisen, and that I was needed in town. Georgiana was excessively disappointed – but she is neither alone nor friendless. Mrs Annesley may be depended upon, and the Bingleys do not propose an immediate removal.

After that, there was all the tediousness of letters, along with business to postpone or to conclude at Pemberley; but I was off within three hours, and write this at an inn in north Buckinghamshire, using as deplorable a pen as anyone can conceive.

DARCY

From the moment Eliza mentioned his name, there was never a doubt in my mind as to what I must do. Her anguished self-rebuke applies far more truly to me than to herself for, had I only mentioned his behaviour at Weymouth, he might never have been accepted in his regiment, might never have gone to Brighton, and might never have been in a position to ruin anyone's sister!

At least Georgiana possessed no sisters whose prospects her own elopement could have ruined! By contrast, every Bennet daughter is now in danger – Elizabeth not least – and Wickham must be found, and bribed or bullied into a marriage I cannot imagine him ever intending to fulfil.

Instead, he will have needed to flee Brighton – for some reason all too easy to conjecture – and, finding Miss Lydia of such a position and such a temperament to be taken advantage of, could not resist… My recollections of the girl herself are few. I can only recall her shrieking with laughter at the Netherfield ball, and, once, teasing her father with regard to his receding hairline, and being perfectly set down – 'God, my dear Lydia, made only a few perfect heads. The remainder he covered with hair.'

Nevertheless, she must and *shall* be saved, for Elizabeth's sake. The recollection of those lovely eyes, still wet from her little storm of tears, drives me onwards. It was all I could do not to clasp her to me – as on that startling moment on the stair. Whatever happens, I believe that the white misery of her face, at the inn in Lambton, will remain with me forever.

If only I had secured her already! Wickham's timing could not have been worse for, allowed the possibility of a second chance – the heaven-sent visit of Mrs Gardiner to her childhood home – I had hoped that Elizabeth might be softening – or at least, that if I again applied and was again rejected, it would not be with quite such resolution and dispatch. (That private smile upon the stairs!) But still, I am sure that she does not love me, and she may never do so. For that reason, my current errand may only serve to ease my conscience.

The first thing is to meet with Jameson, for I might need funds – the second is to discover Wickham's closest acquaintances. That debt collector, Morcombe, may well know something, or Brunswick of the Guards. And I wonder – it is not impossible that Mrs Younge might know. They were as thick as thieves before.

Chapter 48

London

Two days later, Mr Gardiner wrote to Mrs Bennet to say that he had met with Mr Bennet and investigated the principal inns, and that they intended shortly to go farther afield. He could not be as open in an express destined for public consumption as he might have wished, but secretly he felt very nearly hopeless. Mr Bennet was low – Gardiner had never seen him so low before. After his initial energy was spent, he seemed to have given in to despair. He would take out a book and sit by the window of his bedroom, as if in his library at Longbourn, from which he would only reluctantly stir to eat or to sit in a coffee house for an hour. While he was thus engaged, Mr Gardiner would be going from inn to inn and from club to club.

From several he was shown the door, but at one a helpful member said, 'Wickham, in town? Nay, he is sporting at Brighton, with the —shire!' and at another, where Wickham was a member, a young fellow undertook to canvass the current inhabitants, though without result. Mr Bennet was so despondent at dinner that night that Mr Gardiner took pity on him and said, 'You may as well go back home, my dear fellow, and leave this to me.'

There was hope in Mr Bennet's eyes, but he said at once, 'No, it is my fault, and I should be the one to suffer for it! What business is it of yours, that her mother has spoiled her?'

Mr Gardiner hesitated, then, 'That she has turned out so unruly might be down to many factors. Your other daughters –'

'No, no. For she has spoiled her, and let her run wild, and allowed her to think of nothing of importance but officers! While as for Brighton – Lizzy read that aright. She warned me that Lydia should not be permitted to go.'

'She warned you!'

'In my own library. She told me – and I laughed at her! I said that Lydia would not be content until she had made a young fool of herself, at some place or other. Lizzy begged me to reconsider – and I laughed at her! And so, cannot you see, our misfortunes are as much my fault as my wife's? For I was given fair warning, only to make a joke of it! I tell you, I have used humour as a weapon for the whole of my life, but I never thought I should see a day when it turned round and bayoneted me! For who will marry even Jane after such infamy as this?'

Mr Gardiner grasped his hand. 'My dear fellow, I know how deeply you feel it – and I honour Lizzy for her sagacity – but there is still hope! Tomorrow, I shall make a circuit of the money-lenders – I have a list, from Squires, for the purpose – and bribe the truth out of them, if need be, for if there is one thing upon which all are agreed, it is that Wickham will be in want of money. And if nothing comes out of that, I *shall* be astonished!'

'But it is I – and not you, who –'

'You are not fit for it. You are tired – you are depressed. You must go back to Longbourn, and trust in me. I shall not fail, I promise, at least in terms of endeavour!'

Mr Bennet was overcome. Once he had steadied himself, he said, 'How can I ever repay you, whatever the end might be?'

'You can repay me by assisting my poor sister, of course, and by guiding her.'

'Guiding her! When she will never listen?'

Mr Gardiner thought – not for the first time – about the difference between his shallow, silly sister and the warm-hearted, thoughtful and intelligent woman he himself had wedded. Sarah was a tower of strength in such a crisis, while Mrs Bennet took to her bed with the depth of her self-pity. Poor Bennet! – he had deserved better, but there was nothing to be gained by dwelling on it. He said, 'Perhaps the word "guiding" was ill-chosen. But she is as much in need of comfort as any and she will be thinking, and bitterly too, of the part she may have played in Lydia's troubles.'

'But you will not take any pecuniary measures upon yourself? Promise me that you will not!'

'But in case of immediate need –'

'If the need is indeed immediate, I shall repay you, of course.' And he went to write to his wife of all that had occurred.

Chapter 49

Longbourn

Mrs Hill said, 'Aye, that is as much as she will do. The first day she ate nothing, she was too busy squealing about the ruination of her life. And the second day it is, "He must fight Wickham!" And on the third day, "He must never fight Wickham, for then he shall die, and then Mr Collins will turn us out before his body is cold, and – oh then – whatever shall we do?" But ever since Wednesday, she has been eating for England – cakes, mostly, she seems to have a craving for them.'

'My mother was just the same, when she lost that cow,' said Bessy. 'Cried her eyes out, and then craved cakes and cream. She must have put on half a stone.'

'Well, at least it calms her, for a bit. But then it is, "The best girl in the world!" – which Miss Lydia never was, for *that* would be Miss Bennet herself – and then "Mark this, Hill, she was neglected – she must have been neglected, for she was the last creature in the world to do such a thing, were she properly looked after" and "That flighty Mrs Forster! I always said she was empty-headed, and so it has proved!" And sometimes just, "Ruined! Ruined!"'

'I do not know that they are ruined,' said Bessy doubtfully.

'Well, even Miss Bennet – once the Netherfield fellow learned that £1,000 was her lot – he was off as if a highwayman was after him! A sweet face and a sweet manner will never catch such a dandy as *that*. While as for Miss Eliza, she should have taken her only chance.'

'Nay, the parson should have picked Miss Mary, instead. She was born to be a parson's wife and oppress the poor, as Mr Bennet says.'

Mrs Hill sniffed. 'But had Miss Eliza an ounce of family feeling, she would have done her duty by her family.'

'Well, what I say is, had Miss Lydia not come into society at fifteen, 'twould never have happened. That's what *I* say, Mrs Hill!'

'Truer words were never spoken. 'Twas not a year ago the missus says, "Hill," she says, "there is no harm in the world in the poor child's having a little fun. 'Tis no fault of hers that she is quite the last!" And I said, "I only hope she will not get into mischief, ma'am." She should have marked my words! Ah well, I shall take up a slice of fruitcake and hear her talk about the ruination. And you must see to the stew, that it does not burn – else Miss Lydia's will not be the only ruination we hear of.'

Chapter 50

(From Mr Darcy's diaries)

Confident as I am that Wickham had never intended to face the inconvenience and expense of travelling to Scotland on Lydia's account, I did not trouble to investigate the roads going northwards. Instead, I began by touring the better-known money-lenders – from whom I learned nothing. As I could not help suspecting that a group of still less reputable money-lenders existed, I inquired of acquaintances at my club, a few of whom were disposed to be witty at my expense.

'What is this about, Darcy? Need to mortgage Pemberley, do you? Eh? Eh?'

Such sallies failed to amuse, but I smiled in case Thorpe, for it was he, might yet prove useful. The Thorpes, after all, are known to live beyond their means. It was possible that Thorpe might know any number of such people. And so I said, 'No, I am trying to trace someone who might be in quest of a mortgage, instead.'

'I daresay it is George Wickham,' said another acquaintance knowingly. 'We had an older gentleman inquiring about him only yesterday, but not a soul has clapped eyes on him for weeks – not at the Argyll Rooms, nor at Vauxhall. If he is indeed in town – ha! – he must owe a good deal.'

'I expect he does,' said I, as indifferently as I could. 'He generally does, in my experience. Yet it is not he whom I seek but a man called Clive Morris, who may be in still lower water. Do you know him?'

But no one did – unsurprisingly – since I had imagined the fellow, fearing lest someone warn Wickham that I was seeking him. My other inquiries proved equally frustrating, but at least I had the comfort of my own London house to consider them in. Though I spent just as much time thinking of the last view I had had of Eliza Bennet, those expressive eyes black with tears.

She had just implored me to keep her sister's secret 'as long as possible – I know it cannot be long.' What was it in her expression, in that tremble of lip, that has stayed with me? – on the road, at the inn, while returning to Grosvenor Street, while investigating Wickham's least-reputable acquaintance? I also find myself constantly imagining her: returning to Longbourn, enduring the neighbourhood gossips, soothing her distraught mama, while Miss Mary lectures upon the evils surrounding them, and Miss Bennet is certain that all will be well. (I doubt she ever thinks of me.)

At any rate – as I silently promised her – I shall find them. I have Mrs Younge's address, and I intend to go there tomorrow, early, in hopes that they might still be there… Until tomorrow!

Chapter 51

(From 'The loss of virtue in a woman' – being part of *The Wisdom and Wit of Mary Bennet*, part the twentieth)

There is no question that the loss of virtue in a woman is no minor matter. It might be considered a matter of exceedingly great moment indeed. Fordyce himself calls it 'irredeemable'. He also remarks, and justly, 'Remember how tender a woman's reputation is; how hard to preserve, and, when lost, how impossible to recover.'

Unfair as it might seem, the woman who strays from the straight path is cast out – from polite and pleasant society, at least – whilst a man is merely regarded as a rascal. We women are held to a higher standard – arguably, unfairly so. Certainly, more is expected of us than of mere males, particularly where meekness is concerned. As Fordyce himself avers, 'Meekness, cultivated on Christian principles, is the proper consummation, and highest finishing, of female excellence.'

At this point, Mary put down her pen, thinking, 'And one does not, frankly, cultivate meekness on Christian principles in the tents of watering places such as Brighton – but there! I must not permit myself to become distracted.'

Then she heard her mother cry, 'Oh, heavens! Kitty! Lizzy! The Lucases are come, they are indeed. I pray you make my excuses to Lady Lucas. I myself – my poor nerves – cannot bear to go down. The ruination of all my dreams and hopes are the true reason, but I beg that you mention only my aching head, which I shall never get the better of unless I lie, as quietly as may be, on five separate pillows.'

'Why is it always we who are obliged to do the duties of the house?' complained Kitty. While Lizzy said, under her breath, 'And why do they come here at all? Neighbours, in such a case, should commiserate – if possible, without gloating – at a distance, instead!'

Thoughtfully, Mary rose. The Lucases, of late, had included Master Timothy, and she had permitted him a glance at two of her essays. He was not without a certain superficial acuity, and it was only neighbourly to improve his conversational skills.

Observing the discontented Kitty, she said, 'I am willing to assist, Kitty.'

Kitty did not seem over-grateful. She said, 'Lizzy is so ill-tempered these days! And Mama favours Jane so! *You* have your studying and your practice, and *I* wish to read the novel Jane has lent me, but no, we are to be inconvenienced, and all because Lydia was silly enough to run away! Had only I been Mrs Forster's choice, none of this would have happened, for I would have behaved a great deal better than Lydia!'

Timothy, Maria and Lady Lucas were in the drawing-room. Kitty gave Lady Lucas the message from her mama with a little smirk which perfectly betrayed her own opinion.

'Ah! I am sorry to hear it,' said Lady Lucas, removing her bonnet very firmly, 'but your mama will be all the better for a visit from me, I am sure. And, as she is so very fond of my Charlotte, she must long to hear her latest letter to us all.'

'Do not think of troubling yourself, ma'am,' urged Lizzy in some alarm, for her mother's nerves might, by such a letter, be rent in twain, and the peace of the house broken up for some time. But Lady Lucas was in no mood to be denied. She sailed up the flight of stairs like a ship, her prow jutting out before her.

'I hope Charlotte is well?' asked Kitty resignedly of Maria, as Lizzy departed, to do what she could.

Maria said significantly, 'She is indeed well – she is better than well. Come, let us go into the garden, where I will tell you all!'

Mary then assisted Timothy to a cup of tea. After thanking her, he added, 'I enjoyed your last essay, Miss Mary.'

Caught by surprise, Mary blushed and said, 'What aspect of my essay most diverted or informed you?'

'The most amusing passage,' said he, with mischief in his expression, 'referred to Fordyce's opinion of English novelists I gather that he wished them all, with the exception of Mr Richardson, at the bottom of the English Channel.'

'I never wrote such a thing!'

'No, but you quoted it. For here is Fordyce: "Beside the beautiful productions of Richardson's incomparable pen, there seem to me to be very few, in the style of novel, that you can read with safety, and yet fewer that you can read with advantage." He is addressing earnest young ladies, of course, not men of the world –'

'And you would consider yourself one of the latter?' said Mary coldly.

'I shall be twenty next month.'

'Will you?' said she, pleased, without knowing why.

'Indeed, and so, I do. But what of those writers which your hero casts into outer darkness, where there is wailing and gnashing of teeth? What of Daniel Defoe, or Burney? What of Smollett and Sterne?'

'Sterne,' observed Mary, 'is rarely quite serious. Or even quite sane.'

'But he is unarguably brilliant.'

Mary hesitated. She wished to defend Fordyce but was secretly unwilling to abandon Miss Burney. Finally, 'I cannot recall a passage in Fordyce where he wished *Miss Burney* to be at the bottom of the Channel.'

He laughed. 'You are exceedingly literal, Miss Mary.'

'Am I?'

'I find you so. There are two sections in your essay – I marked them in pencil – where your literal point of view caused you to slightly miss the point. If you read less philosophy, and a bit more poetry, that might not happen.'

Mary retorted, '*Religious Musings*, by Coleridge, is most poetical. And I am extremely fond of Cowper's "Far from the world, O Lord, I flee/From strife and tumult far…"'

'There is a great deal of tumult at Longbourn at the moment,' he interrupted, very seriously. 'And I am sorry for it. I pray it all ends as well as possible.'

There was a youthful dignity in his expression. Mary, touched and somewhat flustered, was gathering her scattered wits when Hill entered.

'There is an express come from Mr Bennet,' said she. 'He is returning!'

Chapter 52

(From Mr Darcy's diaries)

I have succeeded, so far at least. Which is to say, they are found!

It was an unimpressive house in a part of town I had never ventured into– utterly different from but somehow reminiscent of the grimy backstreet where I had encountered Wickham's first lover. An alarmed Mrs Younge – thinner than I had remembered – was summoned by her maid. She said sardonically, 'Why, Mr Darcy, sir! Who would have thought it, indeed!'

'Do not play the innocent with me, madam. You must suspect why I am here.'

'I cannot, for the life of me, imagine –'

'Is Wickham within?' I interrupted.

'Mr Wickham? Heavens! Whatever gave you such an idea?'

She was an educated woman, or I would never have engaged her in the first place – a Derbyshire gentleman's daughter who had fallen on hard times. Still, the whine in her voice made me wince. 'Madam, I have no time to waste. Is he within, or not?'

'Nay, I assure you –'

'I have no wish to threaten you. Will five guineas do?' She moved away, as if fearing she might take it against her will. 'So, he has bought you off, has he? You should know, ma'am, that I have not come alone, but with a police officer, who has remained in the carriage. You had best admit me and show me to his room.'

'He has no room. He is not here.'

'I will believe *that* on the evidence of my eyes, alone.'

'Search where you please! – He is not here.'

'But he *was*.'

She was silent. 'Another five,' she said at last.

Contemptuously, I threw ten upon the rug, and she scrabbled to collect them.

'And now, with no farther loss of time! Where are they?'

'Number 142, Wimpole Street,' she muttered.

'Louder, if you please.'

'142, Wimpole Street.'

'Thank you, and farewell.'

'Do you know what it is like, to have no money?' she demanded harshly.

Startled, my hand on the gate, I said, 'No.'

She laughed. Then, 'And are you in love with the lady?'

In love with Lydia Bennet! I left without a bow. Wimpole Street was not far off, and I was almost certain she had not lied – as I had lied about the policeman. Though I could not help thinking, 'Would it not be as well to secure the services of some such person before confronting Wickham?' But I was too impatient and went directly to Wimpole Street. The door was opened by a sullen maidservant.

'No one is here,' said she, and tried to shut the door on my boot.

'I suspect that Mr Wickham is.'

'Micky!' she called, and a heavy fellow appeared behind her.

'Nobody is here,' he said, but his eyes drifted apprehensively from myself to carriage.

I handed him my card. 'I believe that Mr Wickham will see me,' I said, with a confidence I did not feel.

In truth, I was gambling on the probability that Wickham must wish the situation resolved. I have known him, after all, for 27 years – and I knew that to be holed up in Wimpole Street would never suit his notions of comfort. The fellow disappeared with the card… the maid gave me a nervy smile.

I had no sooner removed my gloves when I saw Wickham in the doorway – unshaven, his hair in disorder, his clothes likewise. But such a relief, not to be denied!

He said, as if amused, 'Why, Darcy! We are honoured, indeed!'

'Where is she?'

'Upstairs.'

I moved towards the stairs, but he blocked my way. 'She has no wish to see *you*.'

'In that case, distasteful as it is, I must address you, instead.'

'Wait! Who told you where I was?'

'Mrs Younge, of course.'

Wickham sighed. 'Loyalty is dead.'

'There was no question of loyalty – only of the highest bidder.'

'Well, *there* I was never likely to triumph, was I?'

'Are you married?'

'What right have *you* to know that?'

I said, 'So, it is as I supposed – you are not.'

'What is your interest here? You are not engaged to the sister, are you?'

'I am not engaged to anyone. As for my interest in the business, I have none, except that your infamous imposition on the Bennets has awakened my own guilt, at having permitted you to appear more respectable than you are. My object is to persuade Miss Lydia to leave you. If she refuses – why, you must either marry her, or else return her to her friends. Even *you* must see that you have ruined her else!'

'I like Lydia,' said Wickham reflectively. 'She is a creature of spirit, and exceedingly good company, but marrying her would ruin *me*. She has no dowry to speak of – nor do any of that family – and I am in the most damnable want of money. I seem to run through the stuff with the most confounded speed – as does Lydia, come to that. Even while still at Brighton –'

'I supposed you were in debt.'

'My dear fellow, have you ever known me not to be? The gaming in Brighton was the worst – when it was not the best. Ah – we had some famous nights! Such a pity you missed them!'

'How much do you owe?'

'Nay, that would be telling!' and Wickham wagged his finger at me. It occurred to me that, early as it was, he might not yet have become sober. I said, 'Surely you must know?'

'Not – precisely.'

I assembled my thoughts. Then I said, 'I shall return tomorrow, Wickham, in order to pick up the full and complete list of your debts. Should you wed Miss Lydia Bennet next Friday, I promise to make them all good, not excluding your debts of honour.'

He laughed. 'Nay, we are too alike, Lydie and myself. The woman I marry should have a good deal of money and be far warier than I in the spending of it!'

I crossed to the window, where the grubbiness of the street did not reward me. Finally, I said, 'I could give you – something – in exchange.'

'Not the living your late father promised?'

I bit back a sharp response – for her sake.

I said, 'I could give you enough to live upon, for the beginning of your marriage. Think of it: your debts lifted, yourself restored to some commission or other, a devoted young wife – a fresh start.'

'But why? Why should you take the trouble?' I said nothing, and he said meditatively, 'She is lovely, Miss Bennet, but far too languid. The one with a touch of fire is Elizabeth. I suppose it is *she* to whom I owe –'

Her name on his lips disgusted me – but I would not give him the satisfaction of seeing it. I said, 'I shall return tomorrow, Wickham, by which time you should have made up your mind. Good day.'

Yet despite my seeming assurance, even before entering the carriage, I had already begun to doubt. All I knew was that Wickham's insolence was more than I could bear. (Though how odd that he too had seen 'that touch of fire' which was surely all that Elizabeth Bennet shared with Giuditta!) My other concern was, and remains, had I given him enough hours to itemise his many debts? Though time is of such importance!

But I believe that he will at least consider my proposal. I know his language – I can follow every twist of his brain – he is my own dark twin. I also hope that, along with *some* genuine affection for Lydia, Wickham's natural indolence might assist. He might, at this very moment, be seeking to locate all those bills he has not a prayer of paying himself, and all without the effort and disruption of attempting to captivate some foreign heiress… In short, I have hopes of finding Wickham less insolent and more rational in the morning.

The man is slippery as a fish! But, his debts repaid, he would likely be accepted into the regulars, and the military life is not a bad fit for him – he is incomparably better-suited to loosing firearms than to composing sermons. Against it is the possibility that he might simply disappear, leaving a desolate Lydia behind. I try to imagine a desolate Lydia, but cannot – in my recollection, she is forever shrieking with laughter at the Netherfield ball... Instead, my imagination keeps reverting to Elizabeth, and to that moment on the stairs. A touch of fire, indeed!

Chapter 53

Longbourn

Mary turned the page and suddenly noticed a note in pencil. Timothy had marked a paragraph, 'Perhaps pedantic? T.L.'

Was it possible? Could that paragraph of hers, perchance, be perceived as pedantic? For that matter, might not 'perchance' be considered a touch pedantic? In short, could Timothy possibly be right? Mary stood up and then sat down again, suddenly shaken.

She recollected him saying, with sudden seriousness, 'There is a great deal of tumult at Longbourn at present, and I am sorry for it. I pray it all ends as well as possible.'

Despite being entirely alone, Mary blushed. Whatever was she thinking of? And then she wrote, in her firm, upright hand, 'Not pedantic in the least! See Fordyce page 212.'

Five minutes later, however, she had crossed that out, fiercely enough to almost break through the paper.

'All this business with Lydia,' she told herself, 'has made me less stoic than one would hope. Perhaps, it might be so for us all. Jane is more depressed, Lizzy sharper, and Kitty sorrier for herself than usual… We ought, perhaps, to be rather kinder to each other. I think I will go and see if Mama might like to be read to. Just for the moment, Fordyce can wait.'

＊

The express from her husband had made Mrs Bennet more dissatisfied than ever. She cried, 'But who is to fight Wickham, if Mr Bennet comes away?'

'But only lately, Mama, you feared that Papa would fight Wickham, and be killed, and that our cousin Collins would throw us into the street!'

'I never said that I wished him to fight!'

'No one, my dear Mama, thinks of fighting Wickham,' said Eliza, as patiently as she could. 'My uncle will find them, if they are to be found, and then he will either persuade Lydia to return, or else – or else, he will persuade Mr Wickham to wed her.'

'But if Mr Wickham is unpersuadable then *someone* must fight him, and *then* I must lose either my husband or my brother! Oh, Lord! If only we had all gone to Brighton, as I said at the time – but there it is, *my* advice is never attended to!'

'It is too late, Mama, for us all to go to Brighton – and would serve no purpose, besides,' said Jane.

'As for that Mrs Forster – well! I never liked her – she has a *most* satirical eye. And she is far too young to be a proper Colonel's wife – why, the Colonel himself is most likely repenting. He would have done far better marrying a woman of a sensible age. I always said – did I not, Jane? – that she was too frivolous to be trustworthy. And her fichu so often slipping, besides!'

Jane agreed – it was simplest to agree – and left in time to see Timothy and Maria walking up from Lucas Lodge. Thank heavens Lady Lucas had stayed away! It had taken a great deal of time and patience to calm her mother's nerves after that lady's last visit, when, as far as Jane could tell, she had said everything she could to destroy their mother's comfort. But Kitty was generally glad to see Maria – despite their arguments – and Mary and Timothy had of late found much to say to each other, though little of it intelligible to any other person.

'Kitty, Mary!' she called, 'the Lucases are come!'

In the vestibule, the party soon decided that they would walk, venturing as far as the lake, if the dirt was not too bad. Kitty took Maria's arm, for they had not had a dispute for several days, while Timothy offered his to Mary.

'It is a great deal less pedantic,' were his first words.

'Pedantic!' cried she, much affronted.

'Nay, you know very well that such is your only weakness. And that your hero Fordyce is equally culpable.'

'*That* he is not!'

'Why, no man more! Take this, "Nor do we condemn those writings only that, with an effrontery which defies the laws of God and man, carry on their very forehead the mark of the beast." With an effrontery which defies the laws of God and man, forsooth! While, as to carrying on their very forehead – where, pray, lies the forehead of a book? As for the mark of the beast, great heavens! And, to cap all, he then admits to never having read them!'

'Fordyce,' said Mary sharply, 'in the passage to which you refer, is merely trying to warn young ladies against lewd novels – the kind of novel which neither of us could ever approve! And he is not obliged to read such books as *that*, to disapprove them.'

'I believe it the height of unfairness, to condemn any work unread.'

'But he is a clergyman!'

'As a clergyman, he is – I concede – entitled to an opinion on the Bible – though it would require a fairly reckless clergyman to criticise it. But to pontificate against works of fiction which he concedes that he has never opened, must be reckoned entirely outrageous!'

'However, you said it was improved?' she asked, attempting to keep the interest from her voice.

'What, your essay? – It is transformed! – and certainly publishable. The points you made on female virtue were excellent.'

'Excellent,' thought Mary. Secretly, she conceded that she had underestimated the Lucases. First Charlotte, displaying near-brilliance, had deprived her of Mr Collins – and now her eldest brother was displaying a startling intelligence with regards to her own work. Her thoughts were interrupted by Timothy saying, very quietly, 'I assume that there has been no word?'

'Our father has returned. Our uncle persists.'

'Is your uncle of a persisting nature?'

'Exceedingly so.'

'Then I am glad of it. Your father, I know, despises London. You are rather like him, I think.'

'A house in town is Kitty's dream, not mine.'

'But were you to marry such a fellow as your uncle –'

'Oh! I do not suppose I shall every marry! But I would like to think that my essays might prove instructive to some readers, at some point.'

'As long as you forebear to use seven words where one will do, I am entirely convinced of it!' said he, and looked at her so merrily that she could not resist smiling back at him.

Chapter 54

(From Mr Darcy's diaries)

As soon as I was admitted, I guessed that Wickham had chosen to accept. Until that moment, I had not realised how tautly strung my nerves had been, but I merely said, 'I hope that you are well. Have you decided?'

'We need to discuss the figures, of course. But yes, assuming that all is as it should be, I have decided to accept your proposals. I have not yet told Lydia, however.'

'Not told her!'

'Nay, in case all should go awry. It would be a great pity to disappoint her.'

'It would, indeed,' I said drily. 'Shall we go elsewhere, then?'

'That is not necessary. The papers are here, and I told her not to come down.'

I doubted that this, to one of Lydia's impetuosity, might prove sufficient, but all I said was, 'Do you not have a desk?'

'This table will do. Shall you want tea?'

'Not at present, I thank you.'

We had just settled the date for the following Friday when there was a soft step upon the stairs. 'I am sorry, Wickham,' said Lydia, but I have such a tangle in my hair! – Oh Lord! You never told me that it was Mr Darcy!'

'What I told you,' said Wickham in annoyance, 'was to remain!'

'Nay, but so old an acquaintance! How ever could you have not told me? Well! And so you see, Mr Darcy, how snug and cosy we are, and in London besides! Do not you admire our establishment most immoderately?'

'I do,' said I, for lack of an alternative.

'And you have not even offered him one of Annie's muffins! Whatever will he think of us? I shall ring for Annie and –'

'Do not trouble your cook, I beg.'

'But what are all these papers, Wickham?'

'They are our debts, my sweet,' said Wickham, with a rather fixed smile.

Lydia looked from one of us to the other, in the greatest astonishment. Then, bursting into rapturous tears, she ran to me and threw her arms around my shoulders. 'Oh, you are angelic! You are assisting Wickham with his debts!' I extricated himself from her embrace, as she added, 'I always *said* that you were charming, when Mama was abusing you! But why did you not tell me, my dearest, darlingest creature, that Mr Darcy was to be our good angel? – Only think how delightful it will be, when all the debts are cleared and we might think about clothes for the wedding! – For, would you believe, my dear Mr Darcy, that we are yet to visit a single warehouse? All that I have secured for our wedding day is my shoes!'

Wickham passed a fevered hand across his brow. 'Lydia, when men are involved in business – which we are, and which I told you I should be – *you* must be elsewhere. You shall learn all, once it is over. Until then, not a word, not a syllable, for my head is aching!'

Lydia kissed him, saying, 'My poor cross darling! I shall go upstairs then, till I am wanted!'

There was a silence as she skipped up the staircase. Had I been Wickham, my embarrassment would have been extreme, and I was about to address some minor point when Wickham said thoughtfully, 'I do not suppose, in all Christendom, there is a better-hearted creature, but she is, without a doubt, somewhat impulsive.'

'Indeed.'

'I never intended to wed her. I always thought, once I returned abroad, that I might marry – but there is something to be said for one's native country – and then, who is to say that I would have succeeded?'

Even though I had suspected as much, his tone still astonished me. He had 'never intended' to wed her – he had just wished to enjoy 'the best-hearted creature in Christendom' and then – what? Discard her on the street? My temper rising, I even considered getting up and walking out. Such a man deserved all the opprobrium society could throw on him! And, by continuing, was I truly doing Miss Lydia a favour? But then my head cleared. No – marriage to Wickham was the best that she could hope for. She had made her bed and must lie in it.

'May we continue?' I inquired.

'Ah! You always were a miserably cold fish, Darcy!' said Wickham – and so we did.

I had only just completed writing this last when Colonel Fitzwilliam arrived. He said, without preamble, 'I was surprised to learn from Thorpe that you were in town. Was there something amiss at Pemberley?'

'Nothing at all,' I said, because I did not wish to discuss the negotiations I was embarked upon, not even with Fitzwilliam, till all danger was past.

'Good, for I grieve to tell you that something is very much amiss in Rome.'

So intent had I been on saving Eliza and her sister, that I had completely forgotten Giuditta. She seemed to belong, in fact, to a part of my past as far away as school! My heart sank at the thought that my own reputation had *this* much in common with Miss Lydia's – it was imperilled. And I heard again, inside my brain, those casual thrusts, only with my own name appended: ('I hear that Darcy has lost his case'… 'Who could have imagined *Darcy* such a fool?'… 'I imagine his Lordship will be withdrawing all pretensions to Georgiana Darcy's hand, now that her brother has been so cruelly exposed.')

I squared my shoulders then and asked, 'She persists, then, in her suit against me?'

'She does. It is your word against hers, in fact – or so Jameson says. He advises that you go to Rome, without loss of time, and quieten the lady.'

I thought, 'Go to Rome? – impossible!' Though all I said was, 'But – I cannot!'

'What! But you must! What of Georgiana?'

'I am in the midst of a – of a – certain business, that cannot proceed without me.'

'But Darcy, your entire *reputation* – the family's, likewise – might depend upon it!' He was looking, not only aghast, but even shocked – and with reason, for he is party to all my business, as a rule. After a moment, he asked, 'Perhaps I could assist you?'

'With this, no, I thank you. No one could assist. It is exceedingly delicate.'

That silent promise I had made to her, in the inn at Lambton. No! Even if it meant the end of my reputation, I must remain.

Fitzwilliam did not say, as most men would have, that a breach of promise suit was also delicate, impossibly so. Instead he said, but more hesitantly, 'In that case, Darcy, might I travel to Italy, and negotiate in your stead?'

I could say nothing. I was too near tears, for here was the brother that fate had denied me! Wordlessly, I clasped his hand, and we embraced.

'I can set off tonight,' said he, after a moment, 'but I will need a letter admitting me full authority to negotiate. My carriage –'

'No, no, take my principal carriage,' I said. 'I insist!'

'Very well, I thank you. In that case, all I need from you is the letter, which must be as explicit as may be. There is a lawyer there, very highly recommended, whom I have ventured to secure in the family interest. Have you any sum in mind?'

'None at all. The *money* is of no concern,' said I, as I moved back to the desk to write the letter.

As I write this – for it is late, very late – he will have already left, on a business still more critical to me than all my efforts on Eliza's behalf. Should he fail, my reputation will be destroyed, as surely as was Bunyan's and Sir John's – but I have faith in Fitzwilliam's loyalty. Assuming that Wickham does not change his mind – which is my responsibility – Friday should see Lydia wed and Elizabeth saved.

Tonight, my own salvation must be reckoned less secure.

Chapter 55

London

The Gardiners enjoyed a wide acquaintance, so wide that, upon their return from walking around Hyde Park, the notification from their butler that 'a gentleman had called on business and would call the next day' conveyed nothing. The children were asleep, and they were deep in discussion the following evening, when the gentleman in question returned.

Mr Gardiner said, 'I am afraid, my dear, that I am nearly hopeless. I have tried, and Bennet has tried – tried exceedingly hard, if only for a short while – but, if Lydia is indeed in town, it is beyond our wits to find her.'

'You have tried every club?'

'Even the glee-singers. Not to mention every coffee house or tavern where any acquaintance of his might recall encountering the fellow.'

'And the hackney coaches?'

'I suspect I have spoken to the driver of every such vehicle in London – and all for nothing! I must admit, I begin to share Bennet's own despair.'

'No, no,' said Mrs Gardiner, in distress. 'They might still have gone to Scotland!'

'Such an elopement would be a blessing, by this point, and yet, it has the *feel* of an affair, to me. He may well have promised –' He broke off as the butler entered with a card.

'The same gentleman, sir, as called yesterday.'

Mr Gardiner inspected the card and started. 'Great heavens, it is Mr Darcy!'

'Mr Darcy! Whatever can he want with you?'

'We *did* speak, whilst we were fishing, of his possible interest in – but wait! Is not Darcy connected to Wickham, himself?'

'Well, Wickham was born on his estate, at least… but you must not keep him waiting. I shall be upstairs.'

When Darcy was admitted, he looked, Mr Gardiner thought, very serious even to his waistcoat, which was embroidered in dark gold and black. Mr Gardiner rose at once. 'We are honoured! Make yourself comfortable, I beg, and permit me to offer you a little wine. I doubt it will impress you but some of my friends consider it not displeasing.'

'Thank you, Mr Gardiner, but I am only in need of your time and your patience.'

After a moment he said, 'First, you must know that your niece entrusted me, at Lambton, with the real reason for your leaving the country.' Mr Gardiner half-bowed, as he continued, 'I left Pemberley myself only a few hours later, for town.'

'Indeed!'

'Yes, and with good reason. I have had, in the past, serious – issues – with Mr Wickham, my father's godson, which, out of loyalty to my father, I refrained from making public. The fact that I spared his reputation will always be a source of intense regret to me. In brief, I believe that my ill-judgement, while not the *cause* of your youngest niece's predicament, permitted it to happen.'

'No, no! Neither you, nor myself, nor any other man –'

'I believe it to be true. Why, in terms of the regiment alone – but that is by the bye. For that reason, I conceived it my duty to attempt to locate Wickham here in London. I believed that I had means of finding him that no one else possessed – and I *did* find them.'

228

'What, they are found!'

'They are, yet still unwed. However, I have since brought sufficient pressure and persuasion to bear that a marriage has been agreed and should take place – in fact, on Friday.'

'My dear sir – this is the most remarkable – I cannot begin to express, in fact… What do we *not* owe to you?'

'You owe me nothing, Mr Gardiner. I only acted as my conscience dictated – and was blessed with good fortune, besides.'

'Mr Darcy, I have spent many hours and expended great effort, and found not a trace of them. I believed all hope was at an end!'

'I hope not – I trust not,' answered Darcy, 'but he is unsteady indeed! Thus, I have come to beg a favour from you, with regards to Friday. It would be unsuitable for them to be wed from my own property –'

'My house, and my coach, are entirely at your disposal.'

'Thank you, I was hoping that you would allow it. I also believe that your wife's good influence might be beneficial.'

Mr Gardiner answered for his wife's assistance and then said, 'But first, I must discover what you have promised, for – as you have likely already surmised – I am appointed to act on Mr Bennet's behalf in the business.'

With a faint smile, Darcy rose, saying, *'That* can be of no importance. Perhaps you might acquaint your wife with our deliberations, and I return tomorrow?'

And, in a moment, he was gone.

Mr Gardiner stood in the same position for a moment, too moved – too stunned – to act. That Darcy had done so much! Left Pemberley in their wake – confronted Wickham – and then negotiated, planned and presented the result only once almost every anxiety was passed! Surely, *surely* feelings for Lizzy had played some role in this? – but his wife must not be left to wonder when such news was to be shared.

Greeting her joyfully, he said, 'I have an amazing tale to tell, but first, you must know, Lydia is saved!' And caught her, as she wept, and held her tight.

Chapter 56

Rome

Col. Fitzwilliam had never objected to travelling alone. Far harder for one of his temperament, had been the relentless camaraderie of the regiment. As he travelled, in Darcy's very comfortable coach, across the Channel and through France towards Rome, he fought a certain jealousy of his cousin.

Miss Eliza Bennet's light comment ('Surely, the son of an Earl can know nothing of hardship?') had obscurely upset him for, to him, it had rung true. He had not suffered more than most, indeed! And he had done his best to serve his family, his country and his King, but in what other respect could he be considered useful, instead of privileged? In some ways, this blackmail business was almost a comfort – for he could be of use, while Darcy could scarcely have undertaken such a trip without inspiring gossip.

Yet he still felt expendable, even unnecessary. Unnecessary as the second son of the Earl. Unnecessary in terms of the succession, since his brother's wife had given birth to twin sons. Unnecessary, to the point of familial embarrassment, in respect of the duel.

Naturally, his own brother thought this nonsense, as did Darcy.

In *their* reckoning, he was irreplaceable indeed. And yet… he could not shake the sense that, were he to die on his errand, no one beyond these two would be much affected. Though Georgiana – yes, Georgiana's gentle heart would mourn him.

And at Easter he had been felled by love, and for the first time. How well she moved – how mischievously she had led on his poor aunt – he had never met a woman combining Elizabeth Bennet's ease and spirit with such ladylike manners! If only she had possessed even £3,000! – But he would never have dared ask so rare and glorious a creature to give up – the *prospect* at least – of so much more, on his account!

The heat steadily increased as he travelled south, while the standard of the inns fell and steeply too – with one so filthy that Fitzwilliam elected to sleep in the coach, while his coachman snored on the leads. (Though the fellow seemed cheerful enough: 'With this weather, sir, one is really as well-off outside as in!') There were other compensations. He found that he had forgotten the stepped levels of Italian landscapes, their stalwart cypresses, the characteristic rows of vines, that watercolour quality of light.

As they approached Rome he felt a quickening – how long it had been – with the liveliness of the streets, the vagrants (so much darker and handsomer than the waxen waifs of London), the fishing boats on the river Tiber. In Rome, every woman seemed a beauty, and a beauty too in the Eliza Bennet mould – slim, mischievous and clever, with pitch-black hair and dancing eyes. The central section was dirtier than he had remembered, but just as characterful, the Colosseum more impressive, the opera house still more brilliantly lit.

He had never met the lawyer from Rome, but guessed that it was he, upon seeing his black cloak and leather folder.

'Torelli?'

'Colonel! You are early!' He was in fact a trifle late, but had travelled enough to know that, in the south, this would be considered early. 'I beg you, follow me!'

It was scarcely more than a hole in the wall but cosy, a coffee house smelling equally of stale ale and warm-baked bread.

'And your cousin?' asked Torelli.

'He could not come.'

'Perhaps afraid to risk his heart again?'

'What, are you acquainted with the lady?' asked Fitzwilliam, with a smile.

'I am not. I have not even seen her. I do not care to be robbed at the opera.'

'Robbed?'

Torelli shrugged. 'I refer to the ticket prices. In the best seats, of course.'

'Has she a reputation, here in Rome?'

'Not such as would amaze an Italian – an Englishman, perhaps. Here we manage things more sensibly. There is the wife with the money, and the mistress without!'

The Colonel – secretly somewhat shocked – laughed politely and said, 'As I wrote, I know nothing of the law, and I am content to leave the interview in your hands. All that I insist upon is that you not leave Miss Menotti and me alone together. To be clear, she would be as secure with me as with the Holy Father – but who is to say that she might not sue me for breach of promise in my turn?'

'I shall remain,' said Torelli.

'Also, Darcy *did* suggest, in his note, that the lady's maid might perhaps be bribed.'

'All maids can be bribed. I shall find out – from her, or from a

footman or from a neighbour – what hour would be best and tomorrow, we shall see!'

The next morning the two men were shown into a room of startling beauty and eccentricity by a pert maid. While Fitzwilliam was admiring an ebony sculpture, he heard a noise and swivelled round.

His first reaction was one of pure astonishment. Had he been asked to imagine the woman who would attract Darcy he would never have imagined this! Giuditta Menotti was beautiful but dishevelled, her wrap almost diaphanous, her eyes blazing, her hair – which was glorious – wild. She appeared to have a natural self-consequence and, or so it seemed, a complete disdain for appearances.

She dimpled at him. 'You are cousin to the English milord?'

'If you mean Mr Fitzwilliam Darcy, I have that honour.'

'But you are also Fitzwilliam!'

'It is my surname, ma'am, and his given name.'

'How strange! And you a soldier! You have come to command me, I suppose?'

'I do not give orders to ladies, ma'am.'

'*Bene* – because this lady will not be ordered. Who is your companion?'

'Antonio Torelli, madam. A lawyer.'

Giuditta pirouetted into a chair, pouting. 'A lawyer? How dull. And so, why did your cousin leave me?'

'I was informed,' said the Colonel, 'that you left him.'

'No, no. I had agreed to marry him,' said she, tapping her tiny foot upon the floor.

'If you would be so kind,' said Torelli, 'might you tell us when he first made you the offer?'

He had opened his writing case and was carefully selecting a pen.

'At least once a week, sometimes more. As my maid will attest.'

'Did you ever agree a date for the wedding?'

She said, with a toss of her head, 'In the spring. I always wished to be married in the spring!'

'And you were,' said Torelli, making a note on his paper.

'Were? Whatever do you mean?' cried the startled Colonel.

Torelli ignored him. Instead he said, very calmly, 'You were married in the spring, madam. In the spring of 1806, to be precise.'

'What!' cried the Colonel, new hope stirring. 'She is married already?'

'To Giuseppe Silvestri, a distinguished physician. They parted several years ago, but remain wedded to this day.'

The little shoe missed Torelli's head by several inches.

The Colonel rose, appalled, as she screamed, 'How do you dare? *Che creatura disgustosa e spaventosa! Lei menti!*'

'I think, Colonel,' said Torelli, calmly replacing his papers within his case, 'that we might be said to have concluded?'

Later, Fitzwilliam wrote a short note to his cousin.

Dear Darcy, I am relieved and delighted to inform you that our business is resolved, and without the loss of a single guinea to the lady! The lawyer only two days ago discovered a previous marriage, not yet annulled, to one Giuseppe Silvestri, an older fellow and one rather distinguished in the medical field. The lady was less than pleased! Yours etc. Fitzwilliam

Chapter 57

Longbourn

Mrs Hill, seeing Jane and Lizzy walking in the garden, could contain her curiosity no longer. She walked out to meet them, saying, 'If I may ask, what news has come from town?'

'News from town!' repeated Lizzy.

'Why, did not you know that an express has come from Mr Gardiner? I took it to your father a half-hour ago!'

The girls instantly rushed back to the house, where they found their mother returning downstairs for the first time since the blow from Brighton had descended. A single glance was sufficient: the very ribbons on her cap were bobbing jauntily. Kitty was meanwhile pouring tea for Mary and for Timothy Lucas.

'There you are, at last!' cried Mrs Bennet. 'And now you can share in the good, good news! Your sister is to be wed and on next Friday, too! There's for you – and for all those people, Master Timothy, such as your own mama, who never believed that it would happen!'

Timothy's eyes danced as he assured her that his mother would be the first to rejoice, upon which she said, with a sniff, 'Well, I can only trust that Lady Lucas will be more agreeable now – but, dear heavens! Here it is Monday already and nothing yet done about the wedding clothes! For you all must have new gowns of course, and, as for my dearest Lydia, there is nothing that she does not deserve!'

Jane said, 'As I understood it, Mama, our uncle must have embarrassed himself on Lydia's behalf. I doubt that Papa will send her money for new gowns, or new shoes, or indeed for anything!'

'Oh, nonsense! Should he have said such a thing then he was jesting – which he does, between ourselves, altogether too often for my poor nerves – though 'tis lucky that Mrs Gardiner is in town to advise, for Lydia knows nothing about the business. But still! She will be married, and at just sixteen! How I long to see her with a ring upon her finger! – But what about linens? We must see – without loss of time – about the linens, and the silver, as well!'

'I am convinced, Mama, that Papa would not wish you to order anything immediately,' said Elizabeth.

'But *that* is only because he has not thought of it, for men never do! Ah! You girls can have no notion how much goes into the setting up of a house! Clothes, bedlinen, furniture, cutlery… There are so many things to think of! How I hope that he chooses to settle close by, or no farther than Harpenden, at least. Oh, how silly I was to have fretted so! – I should have had more faith in my brother Gardiner! And how fortunate that Lydia attended Mrs Forster to Brighton, after all!'

She continued at dinner in the same triumphant strain: 'I was saying, Mr Bennet, how charming it would be should the Wickhams settle close by. Just think of the advantages for our girls! For example, Mrs Wickham – Mrs Wickham! how well it sounds! – must be of *such* assistance in enlivening the neighbourhood, in the wintertime, particularly. Why even Mary, I believe, would not dislike an occasional evening party – while as for myself –'

'Mrs Bennet,' said Mr Bennet, the moment the servants had disappeared, 'before you take any or all of the houses hereabouts for your son and daughter, let us come to a right understanding. Into *one* house in this neighbourhood Lydia and her husband shall never have admittance. I will not encourage the impudence of either, by receiving them at Longbourn.'

'That is a joke still more tedious than your usual, Mr Bennet. Do not be so absurd, I beg.'

'I have not the slightest intention of allowing either of them here. Lizzy, could you pass the salt?'

'The salt! The salt! Here you are, heartlessly turning your backs upon your own daughter –'

'No, for I have only one back to turn. But, if I did have several, I assure you that they would all be turned, and heartlessly too. Absolutely heedless of the results which could well have occurred – not only to herself but to each of her sisters – Lydia chose to elope with a fellow of whom even his own Colonel speaks ill, a fellow of no family and no reputation –'

'Well,' cried Mrs Bennet, 'he has sat at this table often enough!'

'He has, I acknowledge, but he shall do so no more. Think on it! – Without your brother's intervention, Lydia might have come upon the town! She will get not a penny from me.'

'But – but – why, Mr Bennet! She can scarcely be properly wedded without a new gown, a new – or nearly new – carriage. Not to mention the clothes, shoes, bonnets –'

'My dear madam, are you still to understand that she will *never* be properly wedded? *That* is all gone by!'

'But 'tis as if she was not properly married at all!'

'Good heavens,' said he mildly, with one of those swift shifts of mood so much a part of himself, 'you have understood some part of the business, at last.'

His wife burst into a fit of weeping as she left the room.

'My own opinion about this sad business –' began Mary.

'Hush!' said Lizzy fiercely. 'For here are the servants.'

Later, she and Jane discussed the news in their bedroom. 'We must believe that Wickham has changed,' said Jane earnestly, 'or hope so at least, for Lydia's sake.'

'What, you believe Lydia's deep maturity likely to influence the fellow for good?'

'I never said so, but Wickham would never have agreed to marry her without caring for her. He had other courses open to him, which she was without. He could have volunteered for the regulars – or even become a mercenary.'

'No, for *then* he might have come to harm! Instead, he took, as he prefers, the easiest way out of his difficulties. For the moment, Lydia has been of use – she has cleared all his debts. By misbehaving so abominably, she has increased her dowry many times over!'

Jane cried, 'Increased her dowry! In what respect?'

'Why, by settling his debts, of course! I am not entirely sure of the figures, but Papa *did* say that Wickham would be a fool to take her for less than ten thousand pounds – and that he should be sorry to think so ill of him, at the very beginning of their acquaintance.'

Jane was appalled. 'Ten thousand pounds! But how is such a sum to be repaid? – Our good kind uncle! How could he afford half ten thousand pounds? He has children of his own – and may have more!'

'I do not know,' said Eliza, and lay down on her bed.

Lydia was saved – for the moment – and she ought, she knew, to feel grateful. But she had few illusions that it would last, or that irredeemable damage had not been caused. She fervently wished, as she wished at least twice a day, that she had never confided in Mr Darcy. Worse still, she found herself continually blushing at all the tender thoughts that she had wasted on George Wickham. How could she have been so deceived, and by nothing more than fine looks and fine manners? – Truly, had she not been nearly as foolish as Lydia herself, and four years older besides?

The wavering glow of moonlight through the window reminded

her of the carriage-lamps when she and the Gardiners had been travelling down from Derbyshire. She had been half-asleep, half-waking for most of the journey, but then, the whole period in Derbyshire had taken on the quality of a dream. She recollected it in parts – that shaft of sunlight piercing the stream at Pemberley, her aunt preferring her uncle's arm and Darcy stepping forward to take her own, the speed with which he had caught her against the marble steps, and – oftenest of all – his long and serious glance as they had parted. Whether it had been more powerfully comprised of promise or of regret she could never be certain; yet still it felt as if the whole of her life had led up to those few moments – at Pemberley, in Lambton – after which everything felt entirely different.

'What must he be thinking now?' she kept wondering. Perhaps that last look – that serious look – had been some variety of farewell? She had thought, while in Derbyshire, that he might still care, even that she might – someday – receive an assurance that he still loved her. Had Lydia taken away that hope, for hope she must now call it, too?

Yet his behaviour in Derbyshire had been so different! From his astonishment at perceiving her to his respectful treatment of her relations, from his wish to introduce her to his sister to his apparent grief for Lydia – surely, either *he* had fundamentally altered or – at least – he had wished to be perceived as a very different kind of a man! Surely so great a change could never have resulted from her ill-judged tirade at Hunsford? Surely, he could not have so patiently borne the petulance of her rejection as to still wish to marry her? Surely, surely – he could not still love her?

A wild notion, perhaps – but at the time she had thought so. She had thought so as they stood by the carriage at Pemberley, waiting endlessly for the Gardiners to join them. She had imagined then that he was wishing to… She had thought so with Miss Darcy – how, from the moment he entered the room, he was attempting to forward their acquaintance. She had certainly thought so in that blinding moment on the marble staircase… And she had thought so even during those first moments of misery and humiliation at the inn, when he had spoken of his shock and grief. Surely it was not impossible that he *might* still care? ('Allow me to tell you how ardently I admire and love you.')

But this was madness! He might regret her – indeed, she suspected that he might have been already regretting her, even as he strode around the room at Lambton. And with reason, for there had been some opportunity for the renewal of his addresses… before that horrible day had demolished it. The irony was that she so longed to see him, just when seeing him must be impossible – that she so admired him, now that his once-passionate admiration of herself had ended! She had been obliged to bite her tongue when Mama had bemoaned – and truly – the fact that Jane's hopes of Netherfield were gone. Her mother would never know that her own hopes of Pemberley, frail as they had been, had been still more effectively struck down!

Again and again, she repented her misfortune that Darcy had arrived just as she was rushing to fetch her uncle. He, who she would have wished to have been the last, had been the *first* to know of Lydia's disgrace! They could never have hoped to hide Lydia's marriage – from anyone, indeed, as it would soon be in the papers – but at least its disgraceful prelude would never now be advertised. And yet, Darcy's presence had been a comfort, in that moment. His eyes had been so warm – he had seemed so deeply moved. And that last, long, steady gaze had felt – yes, at times at least, she believed that look to contain a promise.

It was long before Elizabeth slept.

Chapter 58

London

'Oh, Lord!' cried Lydia. 'Here I have a pimple on my nose, and on my wedding day too! My dear, good, sweet aunt, have you any hawthorn? For see, I have a pimple, just here!'

'Good gracious, Lydia, it is tiny – never mind, I shall go and see.'

'Thank you, my dear aunt! 'Tis not every day that one is wed, after all! How I wish Kitty was here, to see my dress. Is it not pretty? – but such a rush! I would have preferred, you know, to have more than a week to look about me… but still, it was sweet of Wickham to be so urgent about the matter.'

'My dear Lydia, please remember that you are extremely fortunate to be marrying at all!'

'Nay, I know that very well,' said Lydia more seriously, 'for quite a few had set their caps at him, including Mary King herself! 'Twas said, indeed, that she had accepted him, but her guardian sent her back to Wiltshire instead. While Lizzy herself –'

'That is *not* what I meant, Lydia,' said Mrs Gardiner patiently. 'Instead, I meant almost the opposite. For it is not every man who will wed a girl foolish enough to elope with him. In such cases, men, having received what they most wished for, often abandon the girl and then – and then that is the end of all her chances! *That* is what I meant by your good fortune!'

'Oh, la! As if Wickham would ever have done such a thing! I do wish you would not make me laugh, Aunt, when I am having such difficulties with my hair. Can you assist me with this curl?'

'Well, he has not abandoned you, as it happens, but who knows what might –'

'Just as I said! Of course, there are always young girls silly enough to fly away with some fellow of ill repute. I pity them – I do indeed! – but they should have judged better in the first place, I vow… It will *not* be pinned, Aunt – it *will* fly about! Do you observe the curl I mean?'

'Is that better?' inquired her aunt, making an adjustment.

'Oh, why *that* is perfection! How clever you are! Now, do I not look charming? Cannot you imagine me, promising away before the rector, with Wickham – so tall, so handsome – beside me? You did say that he was to wear his blue coat, did you not?'

Mrs Gardiner began to tidy the detritus on her dressing table. She said, 'I know nothing of Wickham's coats, Lydia. He could scarcely be wed in his uniform however, under the circumstances.'

'Why, what circumstances? Whatever can you mean?' asked Lydia.

'Well! He left his regiment, without informing a soul, at dead of night, and thus, technically at least –'

'Oh heavens, there is nothing in *that*! It is as often done as not! He had no wish to disturb the Forsters, was the reason. Although there was the most unpleasant fellow who *would* keep following him about in Brighton and making the queerest threats you ever heard!'

'Why, what kind of a fellow?' asked her aunt.

'Mr Quigley – yes, that was his name – a perfectly horrid man, with the most appalling clothes, simply reeking of snuff and ale. At first, I thought him only a quiz, but then my dear Wickham told me that he was perfectly vile. And *he* is the reason Colonel Forster will have understood why my poor love had to leave – and swiftly, too. But – la! – 'twill not be long before Pratt and Denny and I will all be reunited, and then, just think how merry we shall be!' With a sudden access of nerves – 'as long, my dearest, my most delightful aunt, as we can procure a little hawthorn. For this pimple deforms my pretty nose, and on my wedding day besides!'

Her aunt went downstairs in search of the hawthorn. And as she did, she comforted herself with the recollection that Lizzy and Jane had gently and rationally persuaded their father into receiving the wedded Wickhams at Longbourn after all, in order to dampen any gossip. And it *was* her niece's wedding day…

She was surprised to find her husband and Wickham already downstairs. Wickham, she noted with relief, was wearing his blue coat, for his uniform might have been a provocation too far. She had to admit too, that he looked very handsome. 'You are ready,' she said, 'but Lydia is not!'

His bow was very nearly a burlesque as he responded, 'The bridegroom complete, my dear Mrs Gardiner! And you are looking delightfully!'

'Oh, I have done nothing for my own appearance! But forgive me, I beg, for I am in quest of something for Lydia.'

Her husband said, 'We are expecting Mr Darcy at any moment.'

'What, does he intend to accompany us?'

'So he said.'

Wickham laughed. 'If he said so, then he will accompany us, for Darcy is always to be depended on… It is a hopeless defect, and quite irredeemable!' Just then, a knock was heard at the door.

Mr Gardiner said hastily, 'I shall admit him, and check the carriage.'

Darcy entered, with a nod to Wickham. 'And so, is all prepared?'

'I am prepared, though I dare not answer for Lydia. But is it not the bride's privilege, to be as late as possible?'

'So I understand. In the meantime, I hope that you have thought about the vows that you will shortly be making.'

'Oh, I have indeed – at every wedding I have ever attended. But – ha! – at the times when I have thought about them, *I* was not the one making them!'

Darcy frowned. 'The vows are serious, Wickham – in your case, more so than most. As your bride is so young, you might be said to hold her life in your hands.'

'I am perfectly well aware of that,' said Wickham sharply.

'Good, for that is all that I have to say. Where is Mrs Gardiner?'

At this, Lydia rushed into the room and danced a little circle on the rug. 'There! I am ready! What think you, my darling Wickham? Do I not look charming?'

And Darcy thought that she did indeed look charming, eyes alight, hair perfectly arranged, despite one straying curl, and in those bright dark eyes, glowing as they were, just the slightest hint of Eliza's... In that moment, he almost envied Wickham. Would Elizabeth ever look at him, eyes alight, with such perfect confidence?

Wickham picked her up and half-tossed her towards the chandelier, catching her neatly on her way down. 'Then come, my silly goose, and let us be wed!'

As Darcy took one last look around the Gardiners' drawing-room he thought, 'Georgiana might like such a settee,' and, 'I wonder if I shall ever set foot in this house again?'

Lydia's spirits soared higher and higher as they reached Hertfordshire, late that afternoon.

'I wonder, my dearest love,' she said, 'if anyone knows that we were to be married today. We should have decorated my uncle's coach with ribbands, that everyone should gape as we trotted through the village!'

'The inhabitants of Meryton never cease gaping at anything,' said Wickham lazily.

'Oh look, there is my aunt's maid. Ellie! Ellie!' In disappointed tones: 'She did not hear me, above the rattle of the chaise. I wonder if my Aunt Philips herself might be about – she normally makes her calls on a Friday, but I cannot see her. How dull the street looks without the red coats of the regiment! Scarcely a man to be seen!'

'Let us hope that Kitty has recovered her spirits since we left for Brighton.'

'Oh, my dearest Kitty! How much I shall have to tell her!'

'I daresay. But remember, not a word about Darcy.'

'Of course not, for I promised! But just *think* how shocked Lizzy and Jane would be to know that Mr Darcy – Mr Darcy! – had attended our wedding and been so kind!'

'As I told you already, 'tis nothing to him. Like a normal person giving tuppence to a beggar.'

'And then, to track down that horrid Quigley, too!'

'But *that* was only – but never mind! He might as well be worshipped by you, along with every other woman in the world!'

'La, you are funny. Worshipped, indeed! When he is nothing, compared to *you*! Oh look, there is my aunt, indeed!' And she had descended almost before the coach had stopped and was hailing a most gratified Aunt Philips.

245

Later however, delighting in her mother's pride and in Kitty's pleasure, and elevated to a still higher effulgence of spirits than usual, Lydia forgot her promise. As she was describing the events of the morning to her sisters, she said, 'and my uncle had entirely disappeared, and then I began to fret and fidget – oh! you can have no idea! – but *then* I recollected that, even if he did not return in time, Mr Darcy could have given me away in his place.'

'Mr Darcy!' cried Elizabeth, in the utmost astonishment. 'What! Was *he* present?'

'He was indeed, but – oh heavens! I ought never to have said a single word. It was to be such a secret! – Ask me no more, I beg, for I promised so faithfully!'

'Of course we shall not,' said Jane at once, and Lizzy agreed. However, her curiosity was such that she was obliged to run away. The breeze in the garden cooled her face, but she was unable to stop wondering, or to think of anything else. What possible circumstance could have persuaded Mr Darcy to attend such an event, when even being in company with Wickham disgusted him? Could they have been reconciled? Or – could Darcy have been enlisted to persuade Wickham to do the honourable thing? Had he reasoned, had he bullied, had he – was it possible – had he even assisted Mr Gardiner in bribing him? Could he have felt something of the guilt she herself had endured, of knowing what Wickham was and of failing to expose him?

This last, she thought, was not impossible. Mr Darcy might have possessed sufficient influence to have seen Wickham expelled from the regiment, but never used it. That long, steady look in the inn: had there truly been a promise in it – not to herself, but to Lydia, and to their family? He was so steadfast, so honourable a man!

She burned to know. One chance of discovering the truth still remained to her, and Elizabeth sat down that afternoon to write to Mrs Gardiner, with a heart strangely fluttered. Against all logic, all reason, all sense, *Mr Darcy had attended her sister's wedding.* (Still, she could not quite believe it.) But her aunt must know the reason, and she herself could bear such uncertainty no longer.

Lizzy quietly took her place – unluckily, beside Wickham's – at dinner that evening. He, however, was as lively as his bride, and even leaned down to say to her, in a manner almost conspiratorial, 'I do hope, my dear sister, that you are not annoyed at me. I shall never forget your generous kindness when first we met, when I knew almost no one here in Hertfordshire.'

The startled Elizabeth hastily assured him that she was not. After a moment, he marvelled, 'You look as lovely as ever, by Jove! Lovelier, if anything – and Jane, as well. How your father must bless himself, to have *four* such beauties in the family!'

This was too much disrespect – towards Mary, as well as herself – for Eliza's temper and she turned her back to him to address Kitty's plans for the morrow, showing him no more of her vaunted loveliness than the turn of her shoulder. She felt an uprush of pity for her sister, thinking, 'Poor Lydia! Imagine, such gallantry, almost flirtation, and on his wedding day!'

$\oint$

The next afternoon, Elizabeth, having received her aunt's long and ample letter of explanation, sat transfixed, staring out of the window but seeing nothing – not the robin, not the clematis, not the arc of ash trees nor the sweet curve of grass.

... I do not speak to be thanked, so I beg that you say no more about it, but your uncle would most readily have settled the whole, and he and Darcy argued about it for some time, which is more than the lady and the gentleman in the case deserved! At last, your uncle was forced to yield, and merely to take the probable credit for it, which sat so very ill with him, that I think your letter today gave him much pleasure, as it required an explanation that would rob him of his borrowed feathers and leave praise where it was due. No doubt you know, pretty well, what has been done for the young people. His debts, amounting to a thousand, settled and another thousand settled on him, and his commission purchased... And the supposed reason this was to be done by Darcy alone, was because it was due to his reserve and lack of proper consideration that Wickham was able to impose upon a gentleman's daughter – though I cannot believe that his reserve, or indeed <u>anyone</u>'s, can be held responsible for such an event. But be assured that your uncle would never have yielded had he not given Mr Darcy credit for <u>another</u> interest in the affair...

'Another interest!' thought Eliza. Her aunt was implying – in fact, both the Gardiners seemed entirely convinced – that she and Darcy were in love. Mr Gardiner had conceded to Darcy's paying the whole – and such an amount – for no other reason. Had her uncle *not* been entirely convinced, he would have divided the amount with Mr Darcy, or even owned the whole!

To be fair, theirs was no unreasonable assumption, given the Gardiners' partiality. Darcy's half-courtship in Derbyshire had probably sufficed to persuade them that he had feelings for her, never guessing that these were only the tattered remnants of rejected affection, rather than fresh young love, itself! Her aunt knew but half the tale for, just as Elizabeth had never admitted Wickham's wickedness, she had never told her aunt of Darcy's proposal.

The letter finished:

Will you be very angry at me, dear Lizzy, if I take this opportunity of saying, which I was never bold enough to say before, how much I like him? His understanding, manners and opinions all please me – he only wants a little more liveliness, and that, if he marry prudently, his wife might teach him.

Oh! This was almost as intolerable as not knowing at all! Her wildest imaginings had been proven true – he had done more, far more, than she had dared to guess – but only her affectionate aunt would have assumed, from his honourable actions, that passion was at the root of them. He had provided an alternative motive which – knowing him as she did – she found entirely credible. His sense of honour had been roused – and his sense of honour was formidable. He had known Wickham's character all his life and had still permitted him to take advantage of others. He had never exposed him, even with exposure in his power. (What Wickham had once said to her – 'Out of respect for his father, I could never expose *him*' – had been far truer of Darcy, instead!) Finally, he was one of the wealthiest men in England. What would have been hardship – even sacrifice – for the Gardiners would be far easier for Darcy of Pemberley to encompass.

The fact that she and her sisters would have been so grievously affected had doubtless played some part – yet four innocent young ladies might have roused the chivalry of many. And might it not have been some secret satisfaction to Darcy, with her burning rebukes perhaps still ringing in his ears, to have so honourably salvaged her youngest sister's reputation? He had answered her ungraciousness by rescuing, not only Lydia, but her own prospects, besides!

He would never have done it for Wickham's sake – nor probably, for Lydia's. Her heart did whisper that he had done it for her. It had whispered it from her first reading of her aunt's letter, though she had silenced it. However, the possibility – though it was only a possibility – that her aunt and uncle might have reason for their confidence, would not be silenced. Mr Darcy might have confided in her uncle… Mrs Gardiner was intuitive. That last deep look of his… could its promise possibly have been – to her?

In any case, how heartily did she regret every ungracious act, every saucy speech she had ever directed towards him! She felt humbled – but she felt proud of him, proud that in a cause which would never be public, he had so generously overcome detestation of Wickham, disdain for Lydia, and the grimness of the entire business, in a just cause. She read her aunt's commendation again and again. It was not enough – it was nowhere near enough – yet still it pleased her.

It also gave her pleasure, though pleasure mixed with passionate regret, to re-read her aunt's conviction that affection and confidence – very nearly, *an understanding* – endured between Darcy and herself. 'Oh!' she thought, 'If only it had – if only it did!'

She only turned, unseeingly, from the window upon hearing the door being opened. It was Jane, looking exceedingly pale. Hastily pushing her aunt's letter into her pocket, she cried, 'What has happened?'

'Oh Lizzy,' said Jane, 'our Aunt Philips is come – and *he* is returning to Netherfield!'

'Mr Bingley, you mean?'

'And Caroline.'

Lizzy roused herself to comfort her sister. 'But Jane, *you* have nothing to fear. You have not been at fault in any way… He chose to go to town, and now – and *now* he chooses to return. Which he has every right to do, surely, as he has lease of the place?'

'But it will be impossible to avoid seeing him, and I cannot dissemble – I cannot ignore him, or be aloof, or be anything, beyond what I am! And then, to see Caroline again, after her treatment of me in London, her cruelty – oh, you were not there, you never saw! But just to be under the same roof will be so difficult! It will be so difficult to appear as if nothing has altered, after all that I felt before he went away, and all that I endured in town!'

'I accept,' said Eliza, 'that you feel all this, and deeply too, for you feel everything deeply. But there is this much to be said – for Charlotte has always said it – that you never *appear* to feel, but instead possess that calmness so generally admired. I have confidence that you will not display any unwarranted feeling. And if he *should* be returning on your account – for it is not impossible – such modesty as yours will never betray you into any excess.'

'Oh Lizzy, how I wish that this was true!'

'It *is* true, I promise you. Indeed, the danger is all on his side. He will probably fall in love with you all over again, and his poor sisters become too distressed to bear it!'

But all the while she could not help thinking, 'Mr Bingley and his sister – probably the Hursts. But is there not just a chance of Mr Darcy, too?'

Chapter 59

London

'I am going to Netherfield,' said Bingley.

Caroline looked up in alarm. 'To Netherfield! Why, I thought you had given up the lease, months ago!'

'I had some thought of doing so, but did not, in the end.'

'And when did you think of going?'

'Next week, certainly. Probably Thursday.'

'And for what reason?' asked Louisa keenly.

Bingley looked self-conscious. 'I have not,' he said, 'been there for some time. And I wished to see about the new plants, and the new greenhouses. There should be some decent shooting, as well.'

'Do you wish us to attend you?' asked Louisa.

'Not necessarily, though you would be more than welcome, of course. I believe Darcy is coming.'

'In that case,' said Caroline quickly, 'I might, perhaps, see my way to assisting.'

'Thank you. I advised Mrs Emmerson to ready all the rooms, in any case.'

Once the sisters were alone – Mr Hurst, drowsing upon the settee, could be discounted – Louisa lifted her eyebrows and said, 'Well!'

'You think it rather concerning?' asked Caroline.

'Nay, I *suspect* that it is all over.'

'But he never once saw her, while she was in town!'

'True, though we were fortunate. At the Little Theatre, for example.'

'But I think he did observe –'

'Yes, yes, but if you recall, I persuaded him that he had been mistaken. While you, on Bond Street, practically pulled him into some jewellery shop upon observing her approaching with her aunt. And when she called on you, you discussed the weather till she grew too discouraged to persevere. But I am almost certain that he is still thinking of her. And if *Darcy* attends him, why even the rumour about Mr Darcy and the other Bennet girl might contain at least a little substance.'

'There is nothing to *that*,' said Caroline. 'Had you been at Pemberley, as I was –'

'But he left, and so abruptly, the moment after her departure!'

'Indeed. But *she* went back to Hertfordshire, while *he* went straight to Grosvenor Street, for the Thorpes met him there, just afterwards.'

'Well, it still seems very odd, and Charles excessively self-conscious. I believe that he is going to Netherfield on purpose to see Jane Bennet. Which is extraordinary, considering that it was only last week, after hearing of Wickham's marrying amongst the Bennets, when we were congratulating ourselves on our escape!'

'Darcy,' said Caroline, 'would *never* marry Wickham's wife's sister, never! – but we must attend Charles, all the same, and protect him as best we can.'

'We can try,' said Louisa, 'but I fear it is a good deal too late.'

Chapter 60

Longbourn

The intervening time sped by and, in testament to Aunt Philips's reliability, Mr Bingley was certainly returning. Lizzy could not help thinking that his visit must signify renewed hope for Jane, but their mother's lack of restraint proved a severe trial for both.

'Jane, come with me a moment, I beg, for it has occurred to me that the antique lace from my own mama just requires the smallest amendment to be quite perfection… Jane, there is a concoction Cook has heard of, which is of use in brightening the hair. Yours is so fair already that you scarcely need it, but Cook's cousin swears by it, and we could make a trial of a single wave, perhaps… I know how fond you are of that green gown, my dearest Jane, but the hem is so completely frayed from when you turned it that I should not advise you wear it after Saturday – I *believe,* at least, they come on Saturday. And when they do, Mr Bennet, you will call on Mr Bingley, of course.'

Mr Bennet said, 'I have no such intention. You promised me only last year that, should I call upon Mr Bingley, he would marry one of my daughters. Mr Bingley is a very pleasing fellow, but I will not be sent on a fool's errand a second time. As it is, I see not the slightest hope of disposing of even one of our daughters much before luncheon.'

'He will think you abominably rude!' she cried, but then she brightened. 'And yet, 'tis true, we do not now require an introduction, and we have owed the Longs for weeks.'

'Perhaps we might include the Lucases,' said Mary.

'Nay, for Lady Lucas's nose is still out of joint that Lydia is every bit as wedded as Charlotte is – and Kitty is not speaking to Maria, besides.'

'But perhaps,' said Kitty slily, 'Mary might be speaking to *Timothy* Lucas?'

'Nay, the Longs and the Gouldings will do perfectly – I wonder, Jane, how soon we might learn whether the Hursts are also expected at Netherfield?'

Jane, having no information, left the table as soon as she could. As the days crept by – the Netherfield party had arrived, but *they* had seen nothing of them – she lapsed into a quiet depression. Lizzy thought, 'She cared for him even more than I feared,' and, 'But surely Bingley cannot remain much longer without calling? That would be an insult beyond most, and his temperament is so open and friendly!'

When Bingley finally chose to ride over, it was Mrs Bennet who recognised him from her dressing-room window. She rushed down the stairs crying joyfully, 'Girls, girls! Here is Mr Bingley come at last! Come and see! Come at once!'

Jane instantly seated herself, but Eliza came to the window, to quieten her mother – saw Darcy with Bingley – and sat down beside her. She had always thought it possible, but not even Aunt Philips had mentioned Darcy.

Just then Kitty cried, 'La! There is another man as well. It looks like Mr what's-his-name, that tall, proud man.'

'Mr Darcy! And so it does, I vow! Well, any friend of Mr Bingley's is welcome here, but otherwise, I must say, I hate the sight of him.'

Lizzy picked up her work, embarrassed and confused, while Jane bent over her own. Kitty was just repeating something their Aunt Philips had told her when the gentlemen were announced.

Elizabeth instantly met Darcy's gaze, but then confusedly dropped it. After Bingley had complimented Mrs Bennet on the fineness of their garden, Mrs Bennet said, 'It has been so long a time, Mr Bingley, since you went away! Some people hereabouts did say that you would never return, but *I* never believed it. Netherfield is as charming as ever, the shooting is quite excellent at present while, as for the society – well!'

Bingley pronounced himself properly convinced of Hertfordshire's delights, while Eliza dared not make another trial of Mr Darcy's gaze. She felt his presence. Despite saying as little as he could, he seemed – to her at least– to dominate the room.

Mrs Bennet said, 'There have been a great many alterations, my dear Mr Bingley, since you were last here. Miss Lucas is married and settled down at Kent and, more recently, my own Lydia was wed in London. It was in the *Times* and, I believe, the *Courier*, though not drawn up as it deserved to be but only, 'lately, Mr George Wickham to Miss Lydia Bennet' – without a syllable of where she lived, or who her father might be. It was my brother Gardiner's work, too, and I wondered how he came to do it so ill! Did you see it?'

'I did, ma'am, and I wish her very happy,' said Bingley handsomely, while poor Lizzy dared not lift her head.

''Tis a delightful thing, to be sure, to have a child well-married, but they are gone down to Newcastle – a place quite northwards, it seems. Perhaps you heard of Wickham's leaving his regiment and joining the regulars? He still has *some* friends – thank God – though not as many as he deserves!'

Eliza, who could bear no more, glanced up and inquired, 'Do you intend a long stay in the country, Mr Bingley?'

'A few weeks, I believe, for the pheasants.'

'And when you have killed all your own birds,' said Mrs Bennet graciously, 'you must come here. I am sure Mr Bennet will be vastly pleased to save the best of the covies for *you*.'

At this, her two eldest exchanged dismayed glances. To Elizabeth's heated fancy it seemed that not even Bingley could fail to be disgusted and, once the gentlemen departed, they would never come back again.

Jane then asked Mr Darcy if he was not missing Pemberley, for her uncle and aunt had never seen any place half so beautiful.

'They are extremely kind,' said he. Elizabeth longed to say something of Pemberley – how strange that it felt easier to speak to Bingley! – but persuaded herself that Darcy would understand. At one point, she glanced up and found him regarding her, as if doubting that he had ever found anything worth admiring.

It was only as the gentlemen rose to depart that her mother recalled her hospitable intent: 'Oh, Lord, I had almost forgot! Mr Bennet was *most* insistent that you come to dinner while you are in the country. You had absolutely promised to come before, and a date agreed, but you fled to town, instead!' Bingley looked slightly embarrassed at this, but both young men declared themselves disengaged in two days' time.

As soon as they were safely away, Mrs Bennet thought to consult her cook, though she paused at the door to apologise to Jane, 'My dearest Jane, I did think of asking them to stay tonight, but the pork is left over and there is not fish enough for more than *one*… And who could have imagined that disgusting Mr Darcy would return? Has he not six or seven homes of his own to dwell in?'

Jane assured her that the young men would never have expected to be asked and went upstairs to muse over Bingley's every expression, every smile and every glance… and to hope that he had not been embarrassed by her mother.

Meanwhile Eliza – who secretly thought Bingley as smitten as ever – was obliging herself to delight in Jane's prospects and mourning her own, while scolding herself roundly for imagining that Darcy would ever repeat his declaration. So proud as he was, and as he had every right to be! What man of his estate would stoop to offer again to a woman who had so summarily rejected him! – Most likely, the ease and warmth she had perceived in him in Derbyshire had been due to the familiarity of his parish, his estate and his sister. As for his politeness to the Gardiners, why, who could fail to like the Gardiners? – her aunt all elegance, her uncle everything that was just, considerate, well-judging and well-informed! Perhaps Mr Darcy had only attended Bingley into the country to compare herself with someone he was considering offering to in town?

And then, his almost puzzled look towards her, as if marvelling that he had ever been so entranced! She had probably disappointed his expectations: she had been so silent, so timid, so dull!

She recalled Charlotte Lucas saying, 'A woman ought ideally to betray, if anything, more than she feels.' She herself had betrayed far *less* than she had felt, upon seeing Darcy again. Had hers been a fatal error of judgement? Was it even possible, in this instance, that her own pride might prove her undoing?

Chapter 61

(From Mr Darcy's diaries)

I have just returned from riding around Netherfield, having promised to give Bingley my own estimation of its value, should he determine to make the Ibbotts an offer. However, my mind was so occupied that every shed, every greenhouse, and every line of timber made no impression at all. I could think of nothing beyond each glance vouchsafed to me by Eliza Bennet – the same task that had occupied much of the previous night.

I could not interpret the state of her feelings. As she curtseyed to us – we had entered together – she glanced at Bingley rather than at myself. When she spoke, her voice was as pretty as ever, and the turn of her countenance as bewitching, but there was not the faintest shadow of mischief in it – quite the opposite. I even believed myself to intercept a swift glance of concern towards Miss Bennet, as if fearing that our visit might upset her.

Mrs Bennet, at least, was entirely unaltered. She was at once disputatious and officious, obsequiously ingratiating towards 'dear Mr Bingley', and coldly ceremonious towards myself. At one point she mentioned Wickham's still having 'a few friends, though not as many as he deserves' – this sword-thrust, of course, aimed at me. At that point, Eliza's beautiful eyes did flash, before returning to her work (could she have been recollecting her own warmth in Wickham's defence, at the Hunsford rectory?)

There was another moment when she betrayed some fire, when Bingley mentioned his pheasants, and her mother invited him to treat the Longbourn covies as his own. Or did I imagine the glitter in that swift-dropped gaze? How I longed for just one glance of warmth or understanding! – but these were denied me. As at Pemberley, as at Lambton, Eliza spoke to Bingley far more than to myself… Could she have been so embarrassed by our last encounter that she can no longer bear to see me? Could my unexpected appearance have reminded her of that terrible day beyond her capacity to dissemble? In short, might my errand in Hertfordshire prove as bootless as my application in Kent?

Back at Netherfield, I had Bingley's delight, and my own jealousy, to endure. Bingley jubilantly told his sister, 'I have never, in all my life, received such gratifying attention… There was not a shadow, in Miss Bennet's air, of anything beyond pleasure at seeing us, and you cannot imagine how delighted she was to be assured that *you* would call!' He had been so welcomed, so distinguished – Miss Bennet had been so modestly charmed with him – that, as Louisa Hurst complained, he was intolerably above himself.

But all that I can think of is that corner of her father's house – her room, his library – where *she* might be, her head so beautifully poised, those dark eyes so unreadable. Every woman in her presence seems lacklustre – even Miss Bennet seemed predictable, prudish – and very nearly plain. Oh, I am very far gone, indeed!

I can only hope for better things from Thursday. Surely, if I have any chance at all, she will give me some hint of it? – and, if there is *not*, out of charity, teach me to hope no more?

The evening at the Bennets' was almost unbearable. The partridges were perfectly rendered, but I could scarcely touch mine. There was no opportunity of speaking to Eliza beyond the most formal exchange, as she assisted with serving the coffee. She asked after Georgiana, and I responded, but could think of nothing to add. How I longed for a return of her little barbs, her sardonic asides! The music was heavy likewise, though Miss Mary was – at long last – persuaded to give way to Elizabeth. She played and sang some air I did not know – her voice more enchanting that ever, as Bingley alone was bold enough to mention.

Upon our return to Netherfield, the sisters and Hurst turned in immediately, but Bingley asked me to have a glass with him. I was in no mood for it but could hardly refuse.

'Darcy,' he said, 'I want advice.'

'You may depend on me, as far as I am able.'

'I – I am still very much in love with Miss Bennet, as you have probably surmised.'

'Indeed.'

'Last year you told me that you believed Miss Bennet to be uninterested. Your exact description – how it has tormented me! – was of her being "the acknowledged beauty, complacently accepting the admiration of the company." And what I must know is, do you still believe this? Is this still your opinion?'

'Not at all,' said I.

Bingley seized on this with delight. 'So, your opinion *has* altered! For what reason? Do you truly think it possible that she is not indifferent?'

It was hard – with my own feelings in such disorder – to have to deal with his! However, I took a deep breath and said, 'No. I think, instead, that she was never as indifferent as I wished to believe. In short, I suspect that I was comprehensively wrong about her feelings for you – and about a great deal else, besides!'

'What, you now suspect that she – that she *did* care for me last year?'

'I might be wrong,' I said, not wishing to admit that Elizabeth's reproaches during that tempestuous proposal were the source of my information. 'But my reasoning is this, that the two eldest Bennet daughters do not wear their hearts on their sleeves. Miss Elizabeth, like her father, uses wit to keep feeling at bay, while Miss Bennet uses correctness, instead. With *her,* every move, every comment, every gesture is beyond reproach – voice and manners, grace and mien. There seems no difference in her manner, whether she addresses her sister or her housekeeper! Yet, when she speaks to *you*, there is – a brightness, a glow, about her. Her eyes, already soft, grow softer. Her complexion, always exquisite, deepens. She

261

probably still hopes that her *manners* might shield her from discovery, but I am quite certain she loves you.'

Bingley turned aside then, to brush his eye with the back of his hand. 'Oh, Darcy! I cannot tell you what a relief this is! For I had thought the same, but believed it to be only my own wishes, my own longings! I kept doubting – and truly, I am still doubting! Why should so rare a creature, acknowledged as everything that is gentle and lovely, clever and kind, care for me?'

'You are too modest, Bingley. Why should she *not,* indeed?'

'Oh – ten thousand reasons! And yet, my dear fellow, as I am as convinced as ever I was that I have never seen her equal – or indeed, any creature who could bear the comparison – I believe that I shall try for her – if I dare! But how?'

'How?' I inquired.

'I mean, in what manner? In what fashion should I make my addresses?'

I could not help smiling. That he should ask *me,* who had so excelled at my single attempt at offering my hand that I had deeply offended the lady concerned! Finally, I said, 'How ever ineptly you might word it – however nervous you might feel – the *verdict* will be in your favour, I am sure.'

'But she has never said anything to bolster my resolve!'

'Miss Bennet is far too modest to encourage – would that her mother might emulate her! – Instead, she regards you with a warmth and a confidence she bestows on no one else. Your slightest jest seems to resonate with her – everything you do she appears to approve. Despite her natural diffidence, I truly believe that, tomorrow, you will be answering the dearest wish of a deeply affectionate heart.'

He gripped my hand almost painfully. 'No man ever had a better friend than you, Darcy!'

'Not at all – but I hope you might believe me.'

'And I wish you would come with me tomorrow!'

But this would be too much, with all the uncertainty I was enduring. Instead, I wished him Godspeed, using a meeting in London as my excuse, but undertaking to return once it was over. With that, we parted.

Chapter 62

Longbourn

The next afternoon, upon observing Jane alone in the drawing-room, Bingley dared to enter.

She rose at once.

'Oh, forgive me,' said he, 'I did not intend to intrude.'

'But you are not intruding. Lizzy was just here, but Mama called her. Is there anything you need?'

He hesitated, then rushed on. 'As it happens, Miss Bennet, I do have something particular to ask you. Have you a moment to spare?'

For a moment, Jane almost wished that Lizzy would return. There was something in his tone – she prayed that she would not disgrace herself by fainting. She failed to meet his eyes, but she had never heard his voice quite so soft before. He came closer… he was capturing her hand – he was kissing it. How warm his lips were!

'Miss Bennet – Jane. You must have some suspicion of – of the ardent admiration and esteem in which I hold you. Ever since we met, I have felt – I have thought – oh, there is no one like you! And so, what I am asking – though doing it very ill – is whether you might be willing to marry me. I know I am unworthy – but then, who could possibly be worthy, of so sweet, gentle and lovely a woman? But I have loved you, I believe, ever since I first met you, at the Meryton ball. And whatever you answer, I truly believe that I will love you for the rest of my life.'

She could not speak, but her radiance as she raised her face to his set his heart in a glow. It was all he could do not to clasp her to him. 'Oh!' he cried, in ecstasy, 'you do care for me? You do assent?'

'My dearest,' she whispered, and just dared to stroke his cheek.

'I have never been so happy!' he cried. 'I shall make you so happy! I shall buy Netherfield – if I can, if the Ibbotts will sell it. I shall make up a drawing-room for you, in green and cream, the colours you love best. I shall plant your favourite roses along the drawing-room windows –'

'Oh, *my* preferences must be of no importance!' cried Jane, almost distressed. 'Nothing is of importance, as long as we might be together!'

At that moment, Lizzy returned. Startled, she froze, as the lovers separated, her sister blushing, Bingley ablaze with happiness. She began to retreat, just as Bingley whispered, 'Tell her, tell your sister – I go to your father, this instant!' and, just acknowledging Eliza, passed her into the hall.

'Oh Lizzy!' cried Jane, embracing her. ''Tis too much! Oh, why is not everyone as happy?'

'No one could be better than you,' said Elizabeth fervently, 'and no one more deserving of happiness. While your husband-to-be is so peculiarly well-tempered that you may have your nearest rival in England, for generous goodness, beneath your own roof!'

'Oh never, never – he is a thousand times my superior, in every respect! But I must go to Mama – he is gone to our father already.'

And once she had gone, Lizzy felt – so many things! – satisfaction, delight, and perhaps most of all, relief. So this was the end: the end of their mother's scheming, of the Hursts' pride, of Caroline's sisterly ambition, of Darcy's error of judgement – the happiest, wisest, most reasonable end!… She could not help suspecting that Darcy's absence had been on purpose, that he might have chosen to go to town to give Bingley a fairer chance of catching Jane alone. Surely someone of his acuteness must have penetrated Bingley's wishes. Why even Mary had observed how swiftly Jane's beauty had rekindled his admiration!

She imagined Jane as the mistress of Netherfield, greeting the company, directing the servants, gathering nosegays from the garden, supervising the nursery… It was a delight to imagine it, and no more than her sister deserved, not only for her sweetness but for her fortitude. She recalled interrupting Jane in tears in their bedroom… She imagined those endless mornings she had endured in town, hoping in vain for Caroline Bingley to return her call… She recalled her generous support of their mother's nerves when the blow from Brighton fell.

But then, when had Jane *not* been admirable? When had she ever whined, as Kitty could, or rebelled, like Lydia? When had she ever embarrassed the family, as Mary had at the Netherfield ball? Mr Bingley – rich, friendly and good-tempered – had been born fortunate, but never more fortunate than to have been loved by Jane!

And yet, throughout the evening – an evening of no common satisfaction to them all – her mind could not help drifting to town, to where Mr Darcy was, could not help wondering what he might have known of Bingley's intentions, and what he might be thinking.

But the *last* person Eliza herself was thinking of, either then or during the days following, was the next important visitor to Longbourn.

Chapter 63

Hunsford Rectory

'She is gone,' said Charlotte, troubled. 'And in such a state!'

'The question now,' said Mr Collins heavily, 'is whether we should warn Mr Bennet that Lady Catherine is utterly and irrevocably opposed to such a match. My inclination – I must confess – would be so to do. But would my cousin Bennet heed such a warning? I confess that I rather doubt it, but you know him better than I!'

Charlotte hesitated. 'Mr Bennet is a man of uncommon abilities, who prefers to perceive the world as a matter for laughter, lest he weep.'

'This is not to the point, Charlotte,' said Mr Collins fretfully, 'and I must beg that you keep to the point!'

'Very well, then. Were you to propose that he upbraid his favourite daughter for daring to attract Mr Darcy, Mr Bennet would, I believe, be divided between taking offence and overt ridicule.'

Mr Collins strode up and down before saying, 'I confess myself confounded! Who could have ever imagined that Mr Darcy could be interested in Eliza Bennet? The gap between their importance in the world – the gap between their intellects – for, though she is not deficient, *he* possesses such superiority! Did you ever imagine, whilst she was residing with us, that such a catastrophe might occur?'

'Once or twice,' she ventured, 'I –'

'For we, as you must appreciate, might never hear the end of having invited her!'

'Well, as I recollect, I teased her once about his liking her – but she only laughed at me. The person *I* considered to be in danger – of marrying beneath him, I mean – was Colonel Fitzwilliam, instead.'

'Exactly! Well and justly said!'

'It was *he* who was forever drawing Her Ladyship's ire, for chatting to Eliza. And it was he who, speaking as a lady, would be generally considered the more pleasing and amiable acquaintance. And then, Eliza liked him – she *confessed* to liking him. Indeed, so agreeable did he make himself – so well-judging was his tone and so enjoyable his company that she once laughingly told me, "I sometimes find myself wishing, my dear Charlotte, that the Colonel was rather less well-born!"'

'Great heavens! Is no man safe from such ambition?' he inquired, perturbed.

'Oh, 'twas only a joke! And yet, we might perhaps have been misled, by her utter detestation of Darcy in Hertfordshire, to assume that it would endure. He is unusually well-looking, and their encounter in Derbyshire most excessively ill-timed – from Her Ladyship's perspective, at least. Had Lizzy been a day – even half-a-day – earlier, she would likely never have seen him again. The circles in which they move are so distinct!'

'Well, they *would* be, of course.'

'But she was not trying for him, that much I can vouch for. When they first met, he disdained her, and she ridiculed him. It was all I could do to persuade her to behave civilly, indeed! And while she was visiting here, I sometimes suspected that he was only paying attention to Eliza in order to avoid Miss de Bourgh. Her Ladyship is convinced that he adores his cousin, but, if he does, *I* have never seen it.'

Mr Collins shook his head mournfully. 'Nevertheless, it happened. She met him again at Pemberley, and *there,* at least, she seems to have liked him well enough. Might she have been jealous of Jane and determined to outrank her?'

'Oh, never! Especially as Jane's hopes of Bingley *then* seemed so completely at an end! But I can only say that she detested Darcy in Hertfordshire as heartily as Lady Catherine herself could have desired – and had not much better an opinion, while staying in this house.'

'It is some comfort, at least, that we are not to blame,' said he, unshipping a great sigh.

'No one can ever be blamed,' said Charlotte, 'for someone's falling in love!'

'But did she not write to you, while in Derbyshire?'

'No. Her next letter to me was after Lydia had eloped. And my fear then was that she had been forced into a position where no man of reputation would marry her. For as Lady Catherine told us, "Who would ally themselves with so disgraceful a house?"'

'How ironic that her own nephew… though this rumour, of course, may not be true.'

'But it may be true. Her Ladyship would never have rushed to town without serious cause of alarm.'

'And 'twas *we* who invited her!'

'But how could we be blamed for inviting a friend to visit?'

Mr Collins shook his head. 'Ah! You do not know Her Ladyship as well as I!'

Charlotte, stifling a sigh, reflected that she *did,* indeed, know Her Ladyship. 'Well, husband, perhaps your notion of a letter to Mr Bennet is a good one. It could at least stand as evidence that *you* did nothing to forward the match, if it ever *is* a match. Write to Mr Bennet, advising him that such a match is unsanctioned by Mr

Darcy's connections, and *you* cannot be blamed. Although I can –
all too vividly – imagine Mr Bennet's amusement at receiving it,
should you keep a fair copy, you might persuade Her Ladyship that
you always kept her best interests at heart. And she did look *most*
unwell as she departed!'

Chapter 64

Longbourn

As an unknown chaise and four was reported to have drawn up
outside the main entrance, Jane and Mr Bingley instantly chose to
escape into the garden, leaving Lizzy and Kitty with their mother.
However, Mrs Bennet's surprise was only equalled by her
gratification once their visitor was announced.

'Lady Catherine de Bourgh!'

Mrs Bennet rose and curtseyed rapturously, murmuring, 'Your
Ladyship!' Elizabeth curtseyed likewise, though her own surprise
was more than equalled by her misgivings. She thought, 'Whatever
could have brought Lady Catherine to Hertfordshire?' – while Her
Ladyship and her mother were a most unlucky conjunction! Indeed,
how long could it be, before Mama made some foolish or
embarrassing comment?

The silence that followed was almost unendurable – it was a
relief when Lady Catherine broke it. 'I trust you are well, Miss
Bennet. That lady, I suppose, is your mother.'

'She is.'

'And *that,* I suppose, is one of your sisters?'

Mrs Bennet said, with the greatest alacrity, 'She is, ma'am, my
youngest but one. My youngest is very lately married, while my

eldest is walking somewhere about the grounds with a young man whom we expect will soon become a member of the family.'

Lady Catherine sniffed. 'You appear to have a very small park here.'

'It is nothing in comparison to Rosings, ma'am, but, I assure you, it is a great deal larger than Sir William Lucas's.'

'This must be a most inconvenient sitting-room in the summer; the windows are full west.'

'They are, ma'am, but we never sit here after dinner... If I may ask, did you leave the Collinses well?'

'Yes, the night before last.'

'And might you honour us by taking some refreshment?'

'No, I am not in need of anything. Miss Bennet, there appears to be a prettyish wilderness to one side of your lawn. I would be grateful if you might honour me with your company.'

'Yes, my dear,' cried Mrs Bennet, gratified. 'Do show Her Ladyship the fountain. And she might be pleased with the hermitage.'

Elizabeth went into the hall for her parasol, returning in time to hear Lady Catherine rather grudgingly declare the dining parlour and drawing-room to be 'decent-looking rooms'.

She thought, 'Heavens, how lofty her tone is! – "A very small park... a prettyish wilderness... decent-looking rooms!"' And whatever could she mean by appearing – without the faintest excuse – at a place with which she was entirely unconnected, and in such evident ill-humour?

Her Ladyship did not keep her long in suspense. As soon as they entered on the gravel walk: 'You can be at no loss, Miss Bennet, as to my errand here.'

'Indeed, you are mistaken. I have been entirely unable to account for the honour of seeing you here.'

'Miss Bennet,' said her visitor, very heavily, 'you ought to know by now that I am not a woman to be trifled with! But however insincere *you* choose to be, you shall not find me so. My character has long been celebrated for sincerity and frankness and, in such a moment, I am unlikely to depart from it… A report of a most alarming nature reached me, two days ago. I learned, not only that your sister is to be most advantageously wedded, but that you – Elizabeth Bennet – are widely expected to marry my own nephew, Fitzwilliam Darcy! – Though I would not injure him so far as to believe so scandalous a falsehood, I came to be assured that there is not a particle of truth in the business.'

'If you believed it so impossible,' said Eliza, colouring, 'I wonder that you took the trouble of coming so far! Whatever could you hope to gain by it?'

'Why, to insist upon having such a report comprehensively contradicted, of course!'

'Your visiting Longbourn might rather confirm than quash such a rumour, if it is indeed in existence.'

'What! Do you pretend to be ignorant that such a report is abroad?'

'I never heard that it was.'

'And can you declare, likewise, that there is no *foundation* for it?'

'I do not pretend equal frankness with Your Ladyship. *You* may ask questions that *I* may choose not to answer.'

Lady Catherine stopped, turned, and said, very sharply indeed, 'This is not to be borne! I insist upon knowing the truth! Has my nephew made you an offer of marriage?'

'Your Ladyship has already declared it to be impossible.'

'It *should* be so, while he retains use of his reason. But your arts, your allurements, might have drawn him in.'

'If I *had,* I should be the last to confess it.'

'Miss Bennet, are you aware that I am almost his nearest relation in all the world? I am entitled to know his every concern! – Very well, let me make it still clearer. This match – to which you have sufficient presumption to aspire – can never take place. Never! Mr Darcy is engaged to be married to *my daughter.* Now, what have you to say?'

'Only this – that, should that be the case, there is no reason to suppose that he could ever make an offer to me.'

Lady Catherine looked away. 'Their engagement is… of a rather peculiar kind. From their infancy they have been intended for each other. It was the favourite wish of his mother, as well as myself. Whilst they were in their cradles we planned their union and now, when it is on the threshold of accomplishment, is all this to be overturned by a mere chit of a girl, of inferior birth, of no importance in the world and wholly unallied to the family? Can you be lost to all sense of delicacy or propriety? Have you not heard me say that he is destined for his cousin?'

'I have, and I had heard it before. Yet what is that to me? If there is no other objection to my marrying your nephew, am I to be deterred by the knowledge that his mother and his aunt would have preferred him to wed Miss de Bourgh? If Mr Darcy believes himself unconstrained in his choice, then why should *I* be constrained? You and your sister did as much as you could, to forward the match, in planning it. The *completion* of such a scheme must depend on other people.'

'Yet honour, decorum and prudence – yes, prudence, Miss Bennet! – all forbid it. You shall never be noticed by his family and friends. You shall be censured and despised by us all!'

'These are heavy misfortunes,' answered Eliza, 'and yet, on the whole, any wife of Mr Darcy must have such causes for happiness as to make her unlikely to repine.'

'Obstinate, headstrong girl! Is this your gratitude for all my attentions of last spring? Is *nothing* due to me, upon that score? I wish you to understand, beyond any doubt, that I intend upon carrying my point – and I am not in the habit of brooking disappointment.'

'That makes *your* position more pitiable but can have no effect upon *me*.'

'I will not be interrupted! You must hear me out! My nephew and my daughter might have been formed for each other. They are descended from the same noble maternal line and, on the father's side, from extremely ancient, though untitled, families. The fortunes on both sides are splendid. They are destined for each other, by the unanimous will of every member of their respective houses. Is all *this* to be upended by the pretensions of a young lady with neither family nor fortune? How is this to be endured! Surely you are not so unreasonable as to wish to quit the sphere in which you have been raised?'

'Should I wed your nephew, I should not consider myself as quitting that sphere. He is a gentleman; I am a gentleman's daughter. So far, we are equals.'

'You *are* a gentleman's daughter, I concede. But who are your uncles? Do not imagine me ignorant of their condition!'

'Whatever my connections, if Mr Darcy does not object to them, then they can be nothing to you.'

Lady Catherine hesitated, then, 'Tell me, once and for all, are you engaged to him?'

After a moment's deliberation, Elizabeth felt obliged to say, 'I am not.'

'And do you promise never to become so?'

'I am not to be intimidated into any condition of the sort! And, even if I *were,* would it make it any likelier that Mr Darcy would choose to offer to Miss de Bourgh? – Allow me to say, madam, that this application has been as frivolous as it has been ill-judged. How your nephew might regard such interference in his affairs I cannot tell, but you have no right to involve yourself in mine.'

'Wait! I have not yet done! I am no stranger to the particulars of your youngest sister's infamous elopement, and that it was only a patched-up business, at the expense of your relations. Is such a creature to be my own nephew's sister? Is it possible that the shades of Pemberley should be thus polluted?'

Elizabeth said resentfully, 'You can now have nothing further to say – you have insulted me in every possible method. I must beg leave to return to the house.' As she turned, her companion followed her, crying, 'Unfeeling, selfish girl! Cannot you see how an alliance with you must demean him in the eyes of the world?'

'Lady Catherine, I have nothing further to say.'

'You are, then, resolved to have him?'

'I have said no such thing. I am merely resolved to act in that manner which best serves my own interests, without reference to the opinion of someone entirely unconnected to me.'

'And this is your real opinion – this is your final resolve! Very well! I shall know what to do. I had hoped to find you reasonable, Miss Bennet – but, depend upon it, I shall carry my point!' And, as she turned towards her carriage, 'Mind, I take no leave of you, Miss Bennet. I leave no compliments to your mother. I am most seriously displeased!'

Her mother greeted Eliza anxiously in the vestibule: 'What, would she not rest even a half-hour?'

'No, she would go.'

'What a prodigious fine-looking woman! She is on her way elsewhere, and chose to call in passing. I suppose she had nothing particular to say to you, Lizzy?'

'Nothing at all,' said Eliza. It was a lie, of course, but better a lie than the alternative. She went at once up to her room, there to recollect every moment of the recent scene, and to consider the part she had played, with deepening doubts and strong misgivings. Had she been rude? Yet how could she have been ruder than Her Ladyship, herself? – It was a rational scheme, to be sure – to travel all the way from Rosings to Longbourn in hopes of prevailing upon a comparative stranger to act against her own interests!

But it was Lady Catherine's final threat that most concerned her. Might she be contemplating an application to her nephew? Her last statement could mean little else… and Eliza could not help feeling that if – as had sometimes seemed likely – Mr Darcy was combatting an inclination in her favour, even the slightest intervention might cause him to abandon the idea. He might even suppose such reasoning as Lady Catherine's to contain much common sense. After all, had he not admitted, 'Could you expect me to rejoice in connections so inferior to my own?' and, 'I cannot deny that I did everything in my power to separate my friend from your sister – Towards *him* I have been kinder than towards myself.'

It was true that he seemed to have altered, but *that* might be in manners rather than in fundamentals. His civilities on his most recent visit had been so correct! If he had unbent with her aunt and uncle in London – as Mrs Gardiner's letter had suggested – meeting with them, dining with them, almost charming them – why was he still so chilly here in Hertfordshire?

But the truth would soon enough become evident. If she discovered that, despite his intention to return to Netherfield, he remained in town, she must presume that Lady Catherine had triumphed. Then, most likely, she would never see him again, or not till he was himself wed – not to his cousin, she suspected, but to someone of far greater pretentions than herself. *That* thought was unendurable. 'Is it possible,' she thought, 'that I am in love with him, after all? – and that the man, who began by pronouncing me not handsome enough to dance with, the man whose proposal so upset me, is the person likeliest to make me happy?'

※

Mary heard her weeping and mourned for her sister most sincerely.

'As Thomas Paine opined, "These are the times that try men's souls,"' she wrote. 'Lizzy is, I am sure, deeply divided at present, between joy at Jane's betrothal and at Mrs Collins's being with child, and a deep and abiding sorrow that she rejected our cousin, herself. She is weeping for her lost hopes – and truly, I cannot blame her!'

Chapter 65

(From Mr Darcy's diaries)

'Lady Catherine de Bourgh,' said the butler, and I put down my book, astonished, displeased, and almost alarmed. First, it was not my aunt's usual time to be in town; and second, because she would doubtless find the house ill-prepared for her inspection. Third, I had already instructed my staff that I would dine at one of my clubs, so there was almost nothing to eat in the kitchens.

'Refresh the tea,' I ordered, under my breath, just as she swept in. I took her hand and bowed. 'Your Ladyship! I little thought to see you here.'

'I should rather think not,' said she, very crisply.

'I fear you find my staff and myself unprepared – I am only staying for a few days, on business. Is this chair to your taste?'

'I should prefer one somewhat higher, if you please. I am a trifle weary.'

'But surely you have not come all the way from Rosings today?'

'No, no, from Lady Alexa's. But only yesterday I travelled, with my companion, to Hertfordshire and back.'

'In one day! To see the Swanleys, I suppose?'

'No. No,' – fixing me with that gimlet gaze – 'I was visiting at a place I had never been in all my life. A place called Longbourn, near Meryton.'

I was silenced. Luckily, Fredericks appeared with fresh tea, and a few tiny biscuits and cakes. While he remained – how long he took! – nothing, of course, could be either said or done, beyond ascertaining whether my aunt might prefer a teacake to a scone. The moment he had discreetly closed the door, she resumed: 'You can imagine my errand there, I am sure.'

'I fear that I cannot,' said I, though I had already conjectured the nature of the case, and steadied myself, besides.

'Surely you cannot be the *last* to know that your name has been linked – and in the eyes of all the world! – with that of the second Bennet girl?'

'I have never heard a syllable of this,' I said, truthfully. Then I turned to observe the view from the window, where it threatened rain. Indeed, as I watched, the clouds seemed to thicken.

'But so it is – Mr Collins himself has assured me of it. And Lady Alexa most certainly heard someone say, at the Earl of

Weybridge's, that Charles Bingley was to wed *one* sister, and Darcy of Pemberley the other!'

I thought of refusing to answer. But then it occurred to me that the truth might serve a double purpose: quashing any society gossip and calming my aunt's agitation besides. I said, 'I fear, ma'am, that your information is deficient. The rumour-mill is, in this case, only half-true. Bingley is indeed engaged to Miss Jane Bennet: I had a note from him to that effect, only yesterday. However – and between ourselves – I made my own proposals, in due form, last spring at Hunsford Rectory –'

'What!'

'Permit me to finish, I beg – to her sister Elizabeth – and the lady would not have me.'

'She *refused* you?'

'She did. Leaving no possibility of doubt.'

'Refused you? *Refused* you!' I acknowledged it again, and she cried, almost affronted, 'Great heavens! Refused you, upon what plea? For what reason?'

'I am not at liberty to tell you.'

'What utter arrogance! And from *such* a family! – Yet surely, after so signal an insult, you can have no notion of trying for her again?'

'That, ma'am, is a question which I am not prepared to answer.'

'You must not, you *shall* not! Fitzwilliam, you must be aware that I am never one to throw my weight about. I would be, I daresay, the last, the very last to lay down the law to any person. In addition, you know how I pride myself on weighing up the evidence before entering upon any judgement! However, *this* much I must and *will* say… I interviewed Miss Bennet at Longbourn – we walked about her garden – and I found her utterly obdurate. Not to mention unmannerly, obstructive, resolute and impossible!'

'If I might ask, in what respect was she unmannerly?' I inquired.

'In every respect! She disdained me! When I demanded that she own whether or not she had engaged herself to you, she refused to say! When I reminded her of my own kindness to her down in Kent, she did not even acknowledge it. And when I described the accord as to your destiny that your dear mama and I had reached – that accord which likely softened the pain of her death-bed – she said, "You both did as much as you could, in planning the marriage. Its completion must depend upon others." Have you ever, in the entire course of your life, heard anything likelier to offend?'

How my heart leapt at this intelligence! For I could not but think that, had Eliza truly decided against me, she would have owned it to my aunt, without disguise. I forced myself into calmness, however – for I was also exceedingly angry. Once I recovered myself, I said, 'Aunt Catherine, first, I accept that the ownership and destiny of Pemberley must appear of prime importance to you.'

'Precisely! Exactly! Just as it is to Georgiana and to Colonel Fitzwilliam and to our every other relation. It is of paramount importance to us all! It is the primary seat of –'

'Indeed. As I said, I appreciate that such is the case. However –'

'And that is not all, Fitzwilliam. You must have realised that Anne is devoted to you. Devoted!'

'And I am equally devoted to your daughter. She is a kind and gentle young lady, and one whom I hold in particularly high regard. And yet though I love my cousin, and have, ever since she was a child, I could never become her husband. I know that such an idea has been recommended; my father himself, and more than once, begged me to consider it. But Anne is like a second sister to me. I could no more wed Anne than I could wed my dear Georgiana!'

Truly, I do not believe that anything I could have said would have made the slightest impression on such obduracy… except this.

She was not only silenced; she looked miserably stricken and suddenly rather old. It was as if, till this truth had been released – and, to me, it did *feel* like a release – she had succeeded in flattering herself that the brotherly fondness I had always felt for Anne was – love!

And yet, why should she *not* have so schemed, and so hoped? Many mothers would have, for amongst the aristocracy, cousins are allied as often as not. No, I had to accept that I had suddenly deprived my aunt of the fondest wish of her heart, and for her only child, besides. In that moment – perhaps for the first time in our long acquaintance – I pitied Her Ladyship. But I had only half a heart available for pity, all the same, because the rest of my soul was bounding with a sudden access of hope, on my own account.

Elizabeth Bennet had refused to tell her that she would never marry me. In her mind, therefore, marrying me remained an option. It did not mean that she *wished* to marry me – not in the least – but she had not ruled it out, as she had, and so emphatically, before. In other words, her opinion of me must have altered.

I still felt far from secure. But – in that moment, for the first time – I suspected that she might be yielding and that my behaviour at Pemberley had shaken her conviction of my arrogance, pride and disdain for others. Even during that scene which still possessed such power over my imagination – her tears at the inn at Lambton – had she not betrayed some level of confidence in me? ('Hush it up, I beg, for as long as you can. I know it cannot be long.')

Meanwhile: 'I am weary, Fitzwilliam. A glass of wine and water, if you please.'

Rather than summon a servant, I procured it for her myself, and she took several sips, frowning faintly before pronouncing, 'It is a blow, Fitzwilliam. I cannot deny it. It has long been the first wish of my heart – as it was of my sister's – that the two estates be united.

But if it is not to be, then that is the end of it! – Anne will still marry, as well or even better, perhaps. While there is still time for you to learn to see through the ambitious pretentions of Miss Bennet.'

'I cannot see, myself, what she has pretended,' was all I could trust myself to observe.

'Though it is far from my nature either to hector or to impose,' said she, in more of her usual style, 'I would strongly advise that you think, not merely about the personal attractions of your potential wife, but about her class and breeding, also. You should not rashly imperil dear Georgiana's chances by allying yourself to a woman of inferior rank, pert manners and a lamentable level of accomplishment, whose mother is less than genteel, and whose sister is a disgrace!'

'She is no more like her sister than –'

'Hear me out, I beg! You have decided – in defiance of the wills of your extended family, and all sage advice – against my daughter Anne. So be it! But there are other well-born young women, besides Anne! Do not, I beg, disgrace yourself in the eyes of the world by pursuing Elizabeth Bennet, whose ambition, upon seeing Pemberley, has apparently so worked on her dislike as to make it not inconceivable that she might accept you.'

This was too much. As I rang the bell I said, as politely as I could, 'My dear aunt, you are tired, you are unwell. I recommend that you return to Lady Alexa's. Fredericks, I should be most obliged if you would assist Lady Catherine to her carriage.'

Perhaps she was indeed tired, for she made no objection, only lifting her finger at the door to say, 'Reflect on it!' And once she was gone, I returned to the window, and watched the carriages pass, one after another, and listened to the rain, wondering what *she* might be thinking, some miles north, in Hertfordshire.

Chapter 66

Longbourn

Elizabeth was stopped by her father at the foot of the stairs.

'I was just coming to look for you,' said he. 'Come with me into the library, if you please. I have had a letter.'

Full of foreboding, she followed him. 'What if Lady Catherine has written to him?' she thought, dreading the explanations that might ensue.

Her father said, 'I had no notion that I had *two* daughters on the brink of matrimony. Allow me to congratulate you, therefore, on a very important conquest.' At this, Eliza coloured and was silent, wondering whether the letter might be from Darcy himself, instead of from his aunt. 'You look conscious. Young ladies have great sagacity in such matters, but I think I might defy you to name my correspondent. This letter is from your cousin, Mr Collins.'

'Mr Collins! What can *he* have to say?'

'Something very much to the purpose, of course. What relates to yourself is as follows, "Having offered the sincerest congratulations upon the nuptials of your eldest, allow me to offer a hint about another. Your second daughter, Elizabeth will, or so we understand, not long bear the name of Bennet after her sister has resigned it, and the object of her choice might be considered one of the most illustrious personages in the land, being blessed with splendid property, extensive patronage, and noble kindred." Whoever can he mean, Lizzy?'

'I – have no notion!'

'He continues, "Yet in spite of these temptations, I advise my cousin not to take advantage of this opportunity. My motive for cautioning her is that we have reason to believe that his aunt, Lady Catherine, does not look on the match with a kindly eye." Mr *Darcy*, you see, is the man! Now I have surprised you! Could he – or the Lucases, from whom he presumably gained such gossipy intelligence – have chosen anyone less likely? Darcy! – who never looked at any woman but to see a blemish – and you, who have always detested him! Is it not diverting?'

'Oh!' cried Lizzy, 'it is indeed, and yet so strange!'

'Precisely. *That* is what makes it so amusing! Really, I would not give up Mr Collins's correspondence on any account. And so, Lizzy, did Lady Catherine call the other day to refuse her consent?'

Eliza forced herself to laugh when she would far rather have wept. Never had her father's wit been deployed in a way likelier to upset her. Mr Darcy 'never looked at any woman but to see a blemish'? Was this how men spoke when they remained at table after the ladies had departed? And if the *Collinses* had been informed, was it not likely that Lady Catherine had carried her point? She had still heard nothing about Darcy's returning to Netherfield.

Upstairs, she thought, 'It is over, he will not come. He will be at Bingley's wedding, perhaps – it would look rather odd if he was *not* – but, after that, I shall never see him again!'

Chapter 67

Mrs Hill said to Bessy, 'Master Lucas did not come. They say at Lucas Lodge as he is ill.'

'What a pity. But then, he is so often poorly,' said Bessy.

'He had a chill, they all did, but he cannot shake off his

coughing, and Sir William has sent Thomas to town, with four horses, on purpose to bring back a surgeon.'

'Why, whatever is amiss with Mr Jones?'

Hill sighed at such stupidity. 'Nothing is amiss with him, but *he* is only an apothecary. And there are some clever men up in town who might know better.'

❖

Mary heard the news from Kitty. 'He just lies in bed, reading, and his brother reads to him, when he grows too tired.'

'But what ails him?' asked Mary, reflecting how, on the night of the ball, he had gradually wearied while dancing.

Kitty looked thoughtfully at her. 'They are concerned for his lungs.'

'Not – consumption?'

'Maria never said so,' said Kitty, 'but I fear that it might be. Their sister Esther, if you recall, when she was five –'

'I do recall,' said Mary abruptly, and left the room. Upstairs, she could not work. She opened Fordyce to this: 'Happy beyond the common condition of her sex is she who has found a friend indeed: open-hearted yet discreet, fervent yet steady, thoroughly virtuous but not severe, wise and cheerful at the same time.'

It was F major/minor day, but she found that she could not practise, either. She suddenly put her head down on her pianoforte, thinking, 'He cannot die.'

And then, as if struck by some deep blinding light, she realised why.

Chapter 68

(From Mr Darcy's diaries)

I returned to Hertfordshire from London, not only to wish Bingley joy, but secretly determined to give a trial to all my hopes – and my fears, also. Eliza had refused to tell my aunt that she would never marry me. At times this seemed unsurprising: she had been importuned, and likely lectured – she had not wished to give Her Ladyship any such satisfaction.

But at other times it seemed of remarkable significance. Her silence and discomfort of the week before might have been embarrassment (for I had been embarrassed, too). Our stiff exchange over coffee might have been my own fault, rather than her own.

Mrs Bennet – who did not appear particularly gratified at my reappearance – proposed that Kitty and Lizzy accompany me on a long walk to the Ridge, and thus it was agreed. However, as we took in the best part of the view, and just as I was meditating how we might escape from Kitty, she told her sister, 'I wish to call on Maria Lucas.'

'Why, I thought you were annoyed at her?' inquired Eliza, startled.

'Oh! I was – on Thursday, excessively – but she sent me a card with a pressed flower on it, and *now* we are as good friends as ever. She was worried for poor Timothy, is why she was so horrid.'

'The friendship between yourself and Maria,' observed Lizzy, 'perfectly replicates that between your mamas. You are at odds on Tuesdays, Thursdays and Saturdays, and the dearest of friends on

285

Mondays, Wednesdays and Fridays… On Sundays, it might depend upon the quality of the sermon.'

'That is nonsense, Lizzy,' said Kitty, walking off rather crossly.

I was delighted to see her depart, of course. I was just meditating upon how best to begin when Elizabeth said, 'Mr Darcy, I am a very selfish creature and – for the sake of relieving my feelings – care not how much I must be wounding yours. I can no longer restrain myself for thanking you for your unexampled kindness to my poor sister – Were it known to the rest of my family, I should not have only my own gratitude to express.'

'I am astonished and sorry,' I said, taken aback, 'that you were ever informed of what might have given you unease. I had not imagined Mrs Gardiner so little to be trusted.'

'You must not blame my aunt. Lydia's thoughtlessness first betrayed it to me and, having heard only a part, I could not rest till I had learned the whole. But how can I ever thank you?'

I stopped and faced her, saying, 'If you *will* thank me, let it be for yourself alone. Your family owe me nothing. Much as I respect them, I believe I thought only of *you*.' She turned aside – but, or so I believed, from embarrassment rather than displeasure. I then added, more feelingly, 'You are too generous to trifle with me. If your wishes are the same as they were last spring, tell me at once. My own hopes and wishes remain unchanged, but one word from you will silence me on this subject forever.'

She looked up – those beautiful eyes! – and said, 'Mr Darcy, the recollection of that evening has – and for many months – been an embarrassment to me. *You* have nothing to reproach yourself for, having been treated with such unwarranted disdain! Indeed, it has been many months since I have learned to think that everything that I said of you was unjust, and that everything I said of another was untrue!'

This was the moment. I shall never, if I live to be a hundred, forget her expression, as she looked up at me – very upright, with a heightened colour, utterly courageous, utterly certain. I longed, more than anything on earth, to embrace her, but did not dare. Instead, I took her hand – she almost *offered* it me – and kissed it. I said, 'Can you possibly mean that your opinion of me has truly altered?'

'Yes – oh yes!'

And then it was as if there was no one else, and nothing else, and she half-gathered into my arms, and I felt – just for a moment – that strong, sweet, heart beating against my own, as truly as I had so often imagined it. And long, very long, we remained, with her nestled against me, like a storm-tossed seagull who had come to rest. And the very woods seemed – but this must only have been imagination – to come closer, the birds to hush, the sky to grow brighter and brighter above that canopy of greenness above. 'I am dreaming this,' I murmured at last.

'No, it is I who is dreaming!'

'And you are truly willing to marry me?'

She looked up, eyes wet with tears, and said, 'It is the first longing of my heart.' Then she took my arm, and we walked on, with too much to be said for words. There was such perfect accord between us! Finally, she said, mischievously, 'And so, did Lady Catherine truly call on you, in London?'

'She did.'

'And order you not to marry me?'

'That was certainly the substance of it.'

She laughed. 'And so, you agreed?'

'I did not. I offended her, instead – though grateful to her all the same.'

'Grateful!'

'Intensely grateful. I could have blessed her, indeed, for it was she who taught me to hope. I knew enough of your character to believe that, had you truly decided against me, you would have owned it, honestly and openly.'

Elizabeth laughed. 'Indeed, after abusing you to your face, why should I have scrupled to abuse you to your near relations?'

'But what did you tell me that I did not deserve? For though your accusations might have been ill-founded, my behaviour was such that I cannot bear to think of it!'

'Let us not speak of the greater shame belonging to that evening,' she said lightly. 'The conduct of neither, I fear, could bear the strictest examination – but I hope that we have both since improved in civility.'

'I cannot be so easily reconciled to myself. Your reproof, so well-delivered, "had I offered in a more gentlemanlike fashion" – how it tortured me! While that turn of your countenance as you said that there would have been no possible way I could have made an offer of my hand –'

'Oh! No more, I beg! I have long been so heartily ashamed of it! Indeed, as soon as I read your letter –'

'Truly?'

'Well, *almost* as soon as I read it. At first – I must confess – I did not believe a single word. But it was not long before I accepted that I had been as partial, foolish and ill-judging as any woman in England. And, although I could not recall all the furious expression with which I confronted you, your courtesy, in comparison, made me feel as uncomfortable as I have ever felt in all my life!'

'I hope you have burned the letter. Though I believed myself, at the time, to have been writing with perfect calmness and self-possession, I fear it conveyed little beyond bitterness, instead.'

'The letter shall be burned, if you consider it essential to the continuance of my regard, but you do it great disservice. Though it might have *begun* in displeasure, the end was charity itself. You finished by writing, "God bless you."'

So I had; I had forgotten. After a moment we resumed walking, while I thought, 'No, instead God has blessed *me*, by throwing you in my path!' But all I said was, 'Indulged, for the whole of my life, with all that anyone could wish for, and spoiled by women hoping for my favour, I had grown arrogant, indeed! Oh, what do I not owe you, my dearest, loveliest Elizabeth? By you I was properly humbled. You taught me how unlikely I was to please any woman worth pleasing!'

'Had you persuaded yourself that I should?' she asked.

'I had. What will you think of my presumption? I believed you to be wishing, even expecting, my addresses!'

'My manners must have been at fault – but, truly, had *anyone* offered to me at Hunsford, I would never have thought of *you.*'

'You mean the Colonel, I suppose.' But, with her leaning on my arm, how could I possibly be jealous? And, when I recollected all his generosity on my behalf, I added fervently, 'He is the best of men! Might not we marry him to Mary or to Kitty?'

After she had finished laughing, she cried, 'But whatever did you think, upon seeing me at Pemberley? My own mortification was extreme, and my shock as well, for we had been so confidently assured that you were not expected!'

'I felt nothing but surprise.'

'No more surprise than I, at meeting with such unlooked-for generosity. My conscience told me that I deserved no particular attention. Imagine my shock at receiving so much more than my due!'

'At first, I only wished to prove that I had taken your rebuke as seriously as it deserved. But upon seeing you again – your skin just touched by the sun – oh, I will never forget how you looked, standing by the Gardiners, the sunlight brightening your hair! Like a hallucination, or a dream!'

I had lost all sense of time, or indeed of anything beyond the ecstasy of having her on my arm and so, I suppose, must she, for it was late indeed before we thought to consult our watches. Only then did she mention Jane. I instantly admitted that I had not only misjudged Jane's feelings for Bingley but greatly mistaken the warmth of her feelings in general. Elizabeth instantly forgave me, but then questioned, 'Did you ever feel that Bingley might have suited your sister, then?'

'I do not know, but can imagine no more generous-hearted husband than Bingley. Your sister is fortunate indeed!'

We were by then almost at the edge of the forest. I recollected the path, the widening arc of trees, everything, from hours before… Had it been that same day when we had first set off? – it felt a lifetime! I pulled her closer, but she laughingly warned me not to tempt her. Reluctantly, I released her entirely, and we left the woods with a most respectable number of yards between us.

And now? Well, it is two o'clock, yet I still feel no desire to sleep – it may elude me for the whole of the night. But instead of worry, it is joy that keeps me sleepless, joy above all, that – despite all my self-doubts and weaknesses – she loves me. What man on earth, as violently in love as I, would not feel the same?

But for me there is a still deeper gratitude, a gratitude that, by humbling me, forgiving me and accepting me, she has freed me from being isolated, separate, alone. In society's cold-blooded estimation, I might perhaps be lifting her – but Elizabeth Bennet has, most assuredly, saved me.

Chapter 69

Longbourn

Jane was utterly incredulous.

'Oh, Lizzy, you are joking… Engaged to Mr Darcy? – impossible!'

'This is a wretched beginning indeed! My sole dependence was on you! But I am indeed in earnest. He still loves me, and we are engaged.'

'Good heavens, is it really so? My dearest Lizzy, I would – I do – I do indeed congratulate you! But are you quite certain that you can be happy with him? Oh Lizzy, do anything rather than marry without affection! Are you sure that you feel all that you ought?'

'Oh, yes! You will only think I feel *more* than I ought, once I tell you all.'

'Why, whatever do you mean?'

'I must confess that I love him better than I do Bingley – I am afraid you will be angry.'

'Now, you must be serious. Will you tell me how long you have loved him?'

First, Eliza shared all that he had done for Lydia. Her sister was hardly less incredulous at this information, which was entirely new to her, but still pressed her about Darcy.

'How long? Oh, I hardly know! When he offered to me before, I did indeed detest him – but my respect for him increased shortly afterwards, because of his letter. I told you of the letter.'

291

'I have never seen it – but you did indeed tell me of it, and that, when she was only Lydia's age, Wickham attempted to elope with Mr Darcy's sister. In other words, he was never truly the delightful young man all Meryton admired… And then we argued about whether it was our duty to mention it.'

'And – most unfortunately – decided against.'

Jane nodded. 'Perhaps it might have been better. But *I* believed that Wickham might have repented – and you joked that it would be the death of half the good folk of Meryton to overturn their ill opinion of Darcy!'

'I did. But since I had so roundly abused Darcy for ruining Wickham's chances, he went to some trouble to convince me that Wickham had wasted his own chances, instead. And, in the end, I was obliged to admit that Darcy had indeed behaved honourably, and to regret my fiery expressions.'

'But what of your refusal?' asked Jane, after a moment. 'Did you regret that?'

'I did not. I respected him, at that point, but could not like him. To me, he still seemed rather heartless, superior and arrogant. He had referred, when offering to me, so dismissively to our rank, and to our sisters' behaviour at the ball! But in Derbyshire – oh! from the first moment of encountering him, he was so altered! He did not disdain the Gardiners but entreated our uncle to fish at Pemberley and begged leave to introduce his sister to me. His manners possessed warmth and thought for others – he even seemed to treat servants with greater consideration!'

'I never found his manners at fault,' said Jane, 'in that regard – or indeed, in any.'

'Our aunt kept marvelling, "How came you to say he was so disagreeable, Lizzy?" While our uncle kept expecting him to find someone better worth associating with. And it was *my* ill-tempered rebukes, that evening at Hunsford, that had altered him!'

'Heavens! – and you might never have known, had not the excursion to the Lakes been curtailed, and Derbyshire substituted!'

'True. But I had no more notion of his taking my words so to heart – especially as I felt particularly ashamed of them! But in Derbyshire, every day brought more kindness and greater attention, from his sister as well as himself. And I kept thinking that, had I met such a man here or even in Kent, as he appeared to be in Derbyshire –'

'You would have accepted him?'

'Well, I should have asked for time in which to consider, at least. For he is quite ridiculously handsome.'

'He is handsome indeed. It is difficult to see how he could be *more* handsome.'

'Well, if you recall, I would never concede his good looks, once he had so disdained my own, and in public besides, but I will confess that in Derbyshire, with his manners so softened, I *did* concede them, if only to myself. It was only there that I finally understood why, when he entered the room, even Georgiana's lady companion seemed fluttered, and why even Aunt Gardiner admired his countenance. In short, my pride – at being reckoned not pretty enough to dance with – had blinded me to what must have been obvious to every other woman in the world!'

'So in Derbyshire, you *would* have accepted him.'

'Yes – no – I do not know! It had been but a few days since the revolution in my own opinion and an – an attraction is not enough to build a marriage on. But then… there was a moment at Pemberley when I tripped upon the staircase and might have fallen, but he caught me and in that instant I felt… And then at Lambton, as he took his leave, there was something in his expression that might have been… But when he returned here, I doubted again. He claims now that I gave him no encouragement – and I did not – but there remained a – connection, that I could not get the better of. And so today, once Kitty had walked on to the Lucases, I dared to thank him for all that he had done for Lydia. And then he told me, "I was thinking only of you." Which I had sometimes imagined might be the case, but never dared to believe.'

'Oh, Lizzy! So he never stopped loving you, in spite of all!'

'I believe not,' said Eliza, half-laughing. 'Not even my ill-temper was sufficient to deter him.'

'And you have accepted him!' cried Jane, embracing her. 'Now I have nothing left to wish for! I always had a value for him. Were it for nothing but his love of you, I must have esteemed him – but as Bingley's friend and your husband, there can only be Bingley and yourself dearer to me. Forgive me my slowness – and my doubts – you have made it so delightfully comprehensible!'

'It was my own fault, for mocking him so often, and so cruelly – but I did not know him then.'

'But how sly, how reserved you have been with me, Lizzy! How little you told me of all that passed at Lambton – I owe all that I know of it to Bingley, not to you!'

Eliza then admitted the motives of her secrecy. She had feared to mention Bingley while Jane was suffering, while her own unsettled state of mind had led her to avoid mentioning Darcy. All was acknowledged, and half the night spent in conversation.

Chapter 70

Mary heard the babble of converse in her elder sisters' room with some indignation.

'At so late an hour! And so much laughter – it is very heartless, when you consider that, not far away, poor Timothy is so unwell!' – For everyone had heard of the surgeon's visit, and how he had remained for five whole hours – and how another expert was to come from town upon the morrow.

'How I wish that I could see him!' she thought. 'Even if... especially if...'

But *that* could never happen, for she had never prayed harder, in all her life.

✦

When Mrs Hill announced Lady Lucas, Kitty and Mary both looked up, as did their mother, in some surprise, for Lady Lucas had departed, rather ruffled, after a minor dispute only the previous afternoon. As she entered, with sombre mien, Mrs Bennet cried, 'Why, is something the matter?'

Lady Lucas said stiffly, 'My dear Timothy has told me that he would like – that he wishes to see Miss Mary.'

'Mary!'

'If she would be so good, of course.'

With every eye upon her, Mary rose.

Her mother said, 'Well! I am sure Mary can have no objection, though –'

'I am ready to come at once,' interrupted Mary, though she was not, because her heart was beating so suddenly and painfully that she suddenly wondered if she had not inherited her mother's palpitations, though not her famous nerves.

'You are a good girl,' said Lady Lucas. 'He *will* be grateful. My poor Timothy! They *say* he should get better, but he is so unwell that I cannot help worrying! I came in the carriage, so you need not change your shoes.'

'In the carriage!' thought Mary. 'Matters must be desperate indeed!' and rushed to fetch her bonnet.

Lady Lucas had never been alone with Mary before, but as the carriage moved off, she seemed moved to unusual communicativeness.

'You are a sensible girl, and nothing like Lydia,' said she, 'so I need not tell you to speak quietly. I expect he wishes to talk of books, but it might only be a whisper, for sometimes… But I know how fond you are of books. He is a trifle thin, just at present. He does eat, but not a great deal, or with much interest. Perhaps you might encourage him, for he has doubtless heard me to the point of exhaustion… He mentioned that you are writing a book. A novel, I suppose?'

'I am attempting a scholarly consideration of Fordyce's sermons,' said Mary, thinking, 'A novel! I should hope not!'

'Gracious!' said Lady Lucas. 'Timothy has read him, I believe.'

'And to some purpose,' thought Mary, and again, her pulse sped.

'It is important,' said Lady Lucas, in a lower tone, though there was no one to hear beyond their coachman, 'that he remains calm. His brother sometimes reads to him, which he likes. You might do the same, should he ask you.'

'I shall be very calm indeed,' said Mary fervently.

'Thank you,' sighed Lady Lucas. 'Luckily, you are nothing like Lydia, or indeed Lizzy, for such spirits might oppress many invalids.' ('Is he then an invalid?' wondered Mary.) 'I am glad that you are a sensible girl.'

Mary thought: 'It might be my epitaph. Not beautiful or witty or silly… a most sensible girl.'

And then, almost before she was prepared, his mother was ushering her into Timothy's room. Timothy and one of his brothers', perhaps, for there was another bed by the wall. He looked at her, and smiled, but with eyes like flames of coal. Shaken, she crossed to the bed and took his hand.

'I am so sorry you are unwell,' she said, as steadily as she could.

'But I shall be better, now that you have come.'

'My dearest, will you have a glass of water?' asked Lady Lucas.

'No, I am no longer in need – of anything,' said he. 'Except for a word with Miss Mary – alone.'

His mother shot a glance of warning at Mary, but reassured by her quietness, left the room.

'You are good to come,' said he, 'when I have tormented you so.'

'You have never tormented me, but encouraged me, instead.'

'I am grateful all the same, for your forbearance.'

'No forbearance was required. Your thoughtfulness captured me. And set me thinking clearer.'

He closed his eyes then and said, 'I can have no right, and yet, and yet – should I come through this, Miss Mary… Should I come out the other side, I – I cannot help myself, selfish as it might be! – Should I come out of this, might you possibly be willing to consider –'

297

'Yes,' said Mary, as the tears coursed down her cheeks, 'yes, yes, yes!'

He took her hand, and laid it against his hot cheek, and whispered, 'Thank you! And now, if I should die, I shall not die unloved!'

But Mary said, and fiercely too, 'You shall not die.'

Chapter 71

(From Mr Darcy's diaries)

As Kitty declared herself too tired, we enjoyed a second rapturous walk together the next afternoon. At the end of it I said, 'With your permission, Eliza, I would like to speak to your father tonight.'

'So soon!'

'But how long can it be before he guesses? He is no one's idea of a fool!'

'It is not my *father's* reaction that concerns me, Fitzwilliam.'

'Well, she must learn the truth, at some point. Perhaps he might be persuaded to tell her?'

Elizabeth straightened her shoulders in the manner I loved, and said, 'No, I shall do it. I shall go to her dressing-room tonight, and tell Mama, and *you* must tell my father that I will.'

I never feared for the outcome, for Eliza had assured me that Mr Bennet would do whatever she wished, as he had perfectly proved when she refused the hand of Mr Collins. However, as I rose to find him in his library – to which he was accustomed to retreat after dinner – I still found myself nervous, something I attributed to his mordant wit. I did not fear a *refusal* – instead, I feared being laughed at – an odd sensation, and one that vaguely reminded me of being back at school. At any rate, I knocked and was admitted.

Mr Bennet looked most disconcerted. 'Mr Darcy! This is an unlooked-for honour. Have you come in search of any book in particular?'

'No,' said I. 'I have come for quite a different purpose... Mr Bennet, I have come to ask for the honour of your daughter's hand in marriage.'

He turned quite white and was entirely silent for a moment. Then he said, 'I presume – I suppose – you must mean my daughter Elizabeth?'

'I do, sir.'

'And – if I might ask – has she then, *accepted* your offer?'

'Several days ago.'

He passed a hand across his brow. Then, his expression clearing, he shook my own, saying, 'In that case, Mr Darcy, I can have nothing more to say. Except, of course, that we are gratified and delighted by so unanticipated an honour. And also that you might ask Eliza to come and see me, that I might congratulate her for myself.'

Yet he looked neither gratified nor delighted. Instead, the poor fellow looked – much as my Aunt Catherine had done – suddenly depressed and rather old. I knew not how to reassure him – so I merely bowed, thanked him, and departed. In the drawing-room I whispered to Eliza, 'Your father wishes to see you, in his library.'

She nodded, made some excuse, and left us: myself to fret, the rest to discuss how Timothy Lucas's recovery was progressing after yet another setback – and whether or not Jane Bennet ought to return to the Gardiners', to give Mrs Gardiner's fine taste free rein in the warehouses of London.

Chapter 72

Longbourn

Mr Bennet was pacing the room as Lizzy knocked.

He said, and at once, 'Are you mad to be accepting this man? Have you not always hated him?'

'I did not always love him as I do now – but I have never hated him!'

'In other words, you are determined to have him. He is rich, to be sure, and you will have more fine clothes and fine carriages than Jane. But will they make you happy?'

'Have you any other objection, beyond your belief of my indifference?'

'We all know him to be a proud, arrogant sort of a man – but, if you truly like him –'

Quick tears sprang to her eyes. 'I do! I do like him – I love him! Indeed, he has no improper pride. You do not know what and who he really is – pray do not pain me by speaking of him in such terms!'

'Lizzy,' said he, 'I have given him my consent. I now give it to you, if you are resolved on having him. But let me advise you to think better of it. I know your disposition, Lizzy. I know that you could be neither happy nor respectable unless you truly esteemed your husband. Your lively talents would place you in the greatest danger in an unequal marriage – you could scarcely escape discredit and misery. My dearest child, let me not have the grief of seeing *you* unable to respect your partner in life. You know not what you are about!'

'Oh, Papa! How can I make you understand? – It is true that, at first, I did detest him. He wounded my pride by disdaining my looks, when first we met. And his manners at Netherfield prevented me from understanding him. I teased him for his apparent self-satisfaction – which was imaginary, by the bye – but all the while, at Netherfield and at Rosings, he was learning to love me. Mistaking my mockery for flirting, he even proposed to me in Hunsford – and was refused.'

'You refused him, did you? There you did well!'

'Nay – I still blush at the recollection! I lost my temper and blamed Mr Darcy, most unjustly, for blasting Wickham's chances… But instead of disdaining me afterwards, he wrote me a letter.'

'A letter, did he?'

'Yes, a long letter, detailing such evidence of Wickham's ill behaviour as shook all my belief in him, and compelled me to esteem Mr Darcy, though still, I could not like him. I lost all respect for Wickham, and gained in respect for Mr Darcy, but was in love with neither… But in Derbyshire, Mr Darcy unexpectedly arrived at Pemberley just as the Gardiners and I were viewing it, and he had entirely altered – towards my relatives, towards myself, towards everyone! He was modest, courteous, thoughtful – he had taken my every reproach to heart. And when I first learned about Lydia and Wickham, oh! – how kind he was!'

'*That* was a black day for us all,' said he feelingly.

'A black day for Mr Darcy too – for he believed his forbearance partly to blame. The moment we left, he followed us – in his case, to London. It was he who found Wickham, not my uncle. It was he who prevailed upon him to wed Lydia. Lydia was wed from my uncle's house, but it was Darcy who paid his commission, Darcy who bribed him to go through with it, Darcy who arranged the whole!'

Mr Bennet almost jumped from his chair with shock. 'What! And Edward Gardiner –'

'He longed to assist, but Mr Darcy would not have it. Apparently they argued, again and again, but Mr Darcy prevailed. He believes, you see, that by not denouncing Wickham for having tried to seduce his sister, he had colluded in making Lydia –'

'Good heavens! This is evening of wonders, indeed! And so, Darcy did everything – made up the match, gave the money, paid the fellow's debts and got him his commission! So much the better! – it will save me a world of trouble and economy. Had it been your uncle's doing, I must and would have paid him – but these violent young lovers carry everything their own way. I shall offer to pay him tomorrow – he will rant and storm about his love for you, and that will be the end of the matter! While as for Collins's pompous letter of warning –'

'I could not enjoy it,' said she, 'for *then* I was still in uncertainty!'

'And *now* I fear I gave my teasing gave you pain.'

'But you never intended to, Papa. And it is now of no consequence at all.'

He put his hands upon her shoulders and said, very quietly indeed, 'Well, my dear, I can have nothing more to say. If all this is true, then he deserves you. I could not have parted with *you*, my Lizzy, to anyone less worthy.'

And with that he kissed her on the brow.

She could not quite trust herself to answer, but a moment later he had seated himself and continued, in almost his usual tone, 'If any young men come for Mary or Kitty, send them along, for I am quite at leisure!'

❖

DARCY

(From Mr Darcy's diaries)

When Eliza returned, I dared to ask, 'You convinced him?'

'Heavens,' she whispered back, with a comic expression, 'this is a lesson to better guard my tongue! He was entirely convinced of our mutual detestation. I only hope *you* were not offended?'

'How could I, or anyone, be offended by a father's love?'

She said wisely, 'Time. Time will do it. He will live to see us happy, and to rejoice – not merely that my uncle's business prevented us from venturing as far as the Lakes, but that you were generous enough to persevere, despite the abuse greeting your first application!' That soft mockery in her gaze… How alluring she was! But, as we were far from alone, I comforted myself with the recollection that soon everything would be as open as I wished it to be.

I admitted my engagement to Bingley before we retired – and thoroughly shocked him – for, though Jane Bennet has known for several days, she had sworn not to mention it, and kept her promise.

'Nay, you should not jest on serious matters, Darcy!'

'I never jest. She refused me at Easter, but I have prevailed at last.'

'Refused you!'

'She did. I have been in love with Elizabeth, I believe, as far back as Miss Bennet's illness, here at Netherfield, but said nothing till after we met at Rosings. When first I perceived her walking about the avenue at Pemberley, I thought I was hallucinating – but it was she, and she is now engaged to me.'

'Well! I was never more confounded! What a dark horse you are! – though, to be sure, I cannot blame you. She is not like my sweet Jane, but there is a brilliance about her – while, for a brother, I could wish for nothing better! Let us toast to being brothers!'

I did not mention Caroline; he never named Georgiana. But brothers – *brothers* we have always been. Only Fitzwilliam is closer to me.

Chapter 73

(From Mr Darcy's diaries)

My wedding morning, only five o'clock, and my mind in turmoil. Not from doubt – for I have no doubts at all – but from doubts about these diaries. After this morning is past, and the celebrations over, and the night – tonight! – concluded, what good are these volumes, to me or to anyone?

I should not wish even my beloved to read them.

Ought I to burn them?

Perhaps I ought, yet somehow, I cannot. Even my doubts – my despair, the letter I struggled to write at Rosings, the time of suffering in Rome – might there not be a time when I would wish to recall them? Do I write so ill that I should be ashamed?

Yet there is no one – not even the Colonel – to whom I would wish to entrust them. Perhaps I shall build a secret place at Pemberley and leave them there, for someone decades, even centuries on, to uncover?

For now, there is only the glory of this new dawn – the glow of hope, of gratitude indeed, within my soul.

Fitzwilliam Darcy

✦

'I saw it the day she come to Pemberley,' said Jacobs in the servants' hall, well-pleased with having the attention of the entire company. 'He give her a look and looked again, as if he was a-seeing things. And she looks at him. And I jus' *knew!* I thought as how all the folk who said as how he was too proud to marry was wrong!'

＊

'So then, it is over,' thought the Colonel.

In his hand was Darcy's letter: it was typical of Darcy to be kind. There was nothing jubilant about it, he merely stated that he had recently been fortunate enough to secure the hand of Miss Elizabeth Bennet, and that the marriage would take place, together with Bingley's marriage to Miss Jane Bennet, in Hertfordshire on the twelfth.

He recalled Darcy inquiring lightly, 'But why should you not offer to her, if you liked her?' And his quiet, 'I still feel that she might have accepted you.'

How blind he had been, last Easter, not to notice that Darcy had also fallen in love with Elizabeth Bennet! Then, he had been too involved with his own feelings to notice his cousin's. But now, the pieces of the puzzle had clicked together: Darcy's continually putting off their date of departure, his depression on the eve of their final day, his frequent visits to the rectory, his unusual preoccupation.

Might Darcy have been right? Might she, truly, have accepted him? – He had doubted it at the time and found that he still doubted it – but it was of no consequence, in any case. But what a match for Miss Bennet! And what a triumph of inclination over ambition for his cousin – for the Bennets were even less well-off than most gentry. And how could he have perceived nothing?

In retrospect, a man entranced by Giuditta Menotti would be very likely to fall in love with Eliza Bennet. Though one was quite mad and the other perfectly ladylike, they were both dark and beautiful, charming and vital... He looked down the avenue of years, imagining a marriage for Georgiana, fine-looking children, Christmas balls at Pemberley... He was glad for Elizabeth, who would soon be his cousin by marriage, but there was still a pang of regret, that he had never dared to try for her.

He suspected that there would be, to the end of his life, a little regret.

However, the Colonel had never wanted for courage. He sat down and wrote:

My dear Darcy, Your letter gave me a great deal of pleasure. Permit me to congratulate you, and most warmly, on your good fortune – and hers, besides! She could not have chosen better as I beg you tell her, on my behalf. Wishing you joy with all my heart, yours etc. Fitzwilliam

⸙

'Oh heavens, no!' said Caroline Bingley. 'No one, I assure you, could be more delighted than I! Mr Darcy is well enough to look at but quite a stick, and completely humourless besides! He never actually offered to me – I rather discouraged him, when he was likeliest thinking of it – but, *had* he done so, I should have been obliged to decline. He is not at all the sort of man I like. There has always been a chilly side to Mr Darcy – but I wish them very happy, all the same… No, not a beauty, for *that* would be her sister – *such a friend of mine* – but Miss Eliza is well enough. She is often said to have rather *fine eyes*.'

✦

'Have you heard the gossip about Darcy?' inquired Thorpe of Sullivan, at the club.

'Nay, what about him?'

'He is marrying low – low indeed! – the daughter of some penniless Hertfordshire gentleman, of no particular lineage or distinction. And after Giuditta Menotti herself set her cap at him in Rome!'

'Nay, there was nothing in *that*! You could find no one who knows more of the matter than I, for I introduced them myself. She could not have been less interested in Darcy, I assure you. Were she intrigued by either of us, it was I that she favoured! But what a glorious voice – and such a presence upon the stage!'

✦

My dear Aunt, I have news that can no longer be delayed. I am sure that you will rejoice in my happiness, in that I have prevailed upon Miss Elizabeth Bennet to marry me. The wedding will take place in Hertfordshire, on the 12th inst. but very quietly. However, both my bride-to-be and I would be most honoured should you consider attending a private dinner to mark the occasion next September…

✦

307

'And so,' said Mr Gardiner, 'it seems that we are all to go to Pemberley for Christmas! And your fond farewell to Derbyshire as we departed seems somewhat premature.'

'I did wonder, even then, if we might not return,' said his wife, 'but I never thought of Pemberley. That glorious walk by the stream!'

'And that glorious day's fishing by it.'

'How very curiously it has happened! We little knew, by asking Lizzy to accompany us, that we were altering the entire course of her life.'

'When things are meant to be,' said Mr Gardiner, 'they are meant to be. Even Lydia played some part in the business.'

'Not to mention your goodness in attempting to find her.'

'And your patience on her wedding day.'

'Oh, heavens, yes! The hawthorn, and the curl!'

'The curl?' asked Mr Gardiner, in bewilderment.

'Never mind, my love,' said she. 'Really, the curl was of no significance at all.'

✦

'A double wedding! La! Were I Eliza,' said Lydia, 'I should prefer to be the only bride on the day.'

'Were I Eliza,' said Wickham lazily, 'I should not marry the fellow at all, for a colder fish never existed than Darcy!'

'I suppose they *were* rather thrown together, with Jane's engagement.'

'And he has no other friends to speak of, for only Charles Bingley is good-natured enough to put up with him. Though Bingley is friend to all the world!… I do wonder, by the bye, if the Bingleys might not prove useful.'

'Useful? In what respect?'

'Well, what is his income?'

'I never heard. But he is very rich for, the moment he came to Netherfield, not only Mama but Lady Lucas and Mrs Long and every other lady obliged their husbands to call, without loss of time.'

Wickham stroked his chin thoughtfully.

'And then, *she* says, "And the wedding day almost here, Bessy, and I am going half-distracted! For Jane and Lizzy are both in town for the wedding clothes, and dear Lydia and Wickham so soon to arrive, and Mary gone to read to poor Timothy Lucas – they say he is failing by the bye – and a thousand things left to contrive before the twelfth! My poor nerves!"'

'*Her* nerves!' cried Mrs Hill.

'And 'er palpitations. Do not forget 'er palpitations!'

'I am not likely,' said Mrs Hill heavily, 'to forget her palpitations.'

'A boy,' said the midwife. 'And as fat and thriving a little dumpling as was ever seen!'

Mr Collins cried, 'I am, indeed, the happiest of men! We shall call him William.'

'A lovely tribute,' said the midwife, 'to her grandfather Sir William!'

'Oh… ah… quite,' said William Collins. 'Just so, indeed.'

'No, no, you were misinformed, my dear Alexa,' said Lady Catherine sharply. 'My daughter never cared for Mr Darcy in *that* way, never! They were always exceedingly close, and naturally he admired her, but cousins do not always make for healthy alliances, and I advised him most strenuously against it, when he seemed to be thinking of it. As for Miss Bennet – I *believe* the name is Bennet – I cannot approve his choice. I would, between ourselves, have been better-pleased had he married higher – but *Anne,* I assure you, is not in the least affected.'

'Mark my words,' cried Aunt Philips, shaking her head so emphatically that her ribbons wobbled, 'there never was, in all creation, a more fortunate family than the Bennets. Young Bingley comes to Netherfield – and every girl in Hertfordshire is setting her cap at him – but 'tis Jane who marries him. Then Lizzy visits Derbyshire – takes Mr Darcy's fancy – and *he* as rich as the Prince Regent! And then, Lydia was not in Brighton more than a month before being spoken for, while Miss Kitty will not be long upon the shelf. Truth to tell, 'tis a mercy that Miss Mary is plain as a pikestaff or my poor sister would have no one left at home at all!'

'May we waken Mr Hurst?' asked Caroline Bingley.

And, as Mrs Hurst had not the smallest objection, Miss Bingley sat down to the pianoforte, pushed back her sleeves, and began to pound upon the instrument.

'Save the women and children!' cried Mr Hurst. 'Whatever is happening?'

It was over, and they were in the same bedroom at Netherfield that had previously been his own and looking over the same sweep of country. It had been so tiring a day, and one of such heightened emotion – but, at long last, they were alone together. He had thought so much – there was so much that he wished to say – but he understood, and instantly, that it was not the moment for words, upon meeting that beautiful dark gaze.

Just for the moment, words could wait.

Looking pale and thin but exceedingly steady, Timothy knocked on the door to Mr Bennet's famous library.

'Who is it?'

'It is I, Mr Bennet – Timothy Lucas.'

'Good heavens,' said Mr Bennet to himself. 'Could it possibly be…?'

❖❖❖❖❖

Please consider leaving an honest review of this novel on Amazon or Goodreads.

And… Alice's prizewinning *Susan* is an imagining of Austen's 35-year-old Lady Susan, when a young lady of just sixteen. Here's the opening…

Susan: A Jane Austen Prequel

by Alice McVeigh

Susan Smithson was the kind of pupil Mrs Ansruther detested: pretty, impertinent and – worst of all – poor. Yet she had still never supposed that she might be obliged to send her away. On that Tuesday morning, however, Susan was summoned, but not invited to sit down.

'I am sorry to tell you, Miss Smithson, that you will be leaving my establishment.'

'For what reason?'

'I believe you know the reason.'

'And yet I do not.'

Mrs Ansruther rapped her pen upon her desk. 'Miss Smithson, such pretence at innocence will not do. Miss Priscilla was most explicit, and the music master – Mr Maggini – himself did not deny the occurrence.'

'What you term the *occurrence* had nothing to do with me.'

'That does not signify, for you did not rebuke him.'

'I did indeed.'

'Miss Priscilla denies it.'

Susan attempted to summon bright tears to her eyes. 'My poor aunt! And her brother only dead last Christmas!'

'Last Michaelmas, you mean. I too feel for your aunt, yet I cannot allow you to remain at my school after such a scandal – and besides, you are sixteen already.'

Susan was indeed sixteen, and impatient to leave besides, but not in such a fashion – in disgrace! She had mentioned her aunt, but it was her uncle whom she dreaded, for he ranted so. She touched her eyes with her pocket handkerchief, which moved Mrs Ansruther not at all.

'I dare say you will marry,' she said, rising. 'And if you heed my advice, Miss Smithson, you will choose a gentleman of decisive character, who might have some hope of making you behave. I confess myself unequal to it. Good day.'

Outside, Susan instantly collected herself, and then flew to her room to pack, where her friends awaited her. 'I am to go,' she told them. Even Lavinia was sorry, while Anne wept, and Henrietta hung about her affectionately. Miss Priscilla was abused for having told of her, and it did her heart good to hear Mrs Ansruther so abused. 'How could she take his part? – and he only a music master'… 'And to think, it was she who engaged him!'… 'For my part, I shall never let him touch my fingers again, though he plays divinely, but he *is* so very plain!'

Susan said nothing, taking care to fold her gowns neatly, for she had no maid to tend them, and the school maids were dreadful. As she folded, she recollected that she too had thought Mr Maggini plain, before he had amused her with tales of Florence and entranced her with gossip of the Prince Regent's violoncello performance. Still, it had been utter foolishness on her part not to scream for assistance as he pressed her hand to his lips – but she had already vowed never to admit it – not even to herself.

'Do you stay in London?' asked Anne wistfully.

'In Portland Square. You visited me, did you not? – at my uncle's.'

'I suppose you will still have masters for French and music.'

'As to *that,* my uncle will decide.'

'Will your aunt be very angry?'

'Not if she can get the remainder of the fees from Mrs Ansruther – as I suppose she will.'

'You might attend balls,' said Lavinia enviously. 'And concerts,' added Anne, and little Henrietta again wished to know why Susan was leaving and was again denied.

Susan said wistfully, 'Balls and concerts! Those I might look forward to!' – for the regime at Mrs Ansruther's was strict; the older girls complained that they might be buried in the country for all the use that London was to them.

Lavinia said, 'I wish he had kissed my hand, instead. We're never allowed to enjoy anything!'

Susan smoothed down her working muslin. In truth, she had long desired to escape, as she found all lessons dull, except for music. Her aunt had entered her at Mrs Ansruther's only two years before, having despaired of her applying herself at home, and she would be leaving with only the sketchiest notion of Italian, and with French not much more advanced. Her friend Anne, though only fifteen, knew far more than she – yet she still felt ready for the world. London was still, after all, London (Mrs Ansruther's school was also in London, but one might as well be at York as in Russell Square). As Susan smoothed the ribbons of her favourite gown, pleasurable visions of London danced through her head. If she could but manage her uncle!

Though spared another encounter with Mrs Ansruther, Susan had yet to take leave of Miss Priscilla, the mistress who had reported her flirtation with Mr Maggini. Miss Priscilla, far from repenting, dared to fire a little poisoned dart in her direction: 'I trust, Miss Smithson, that you do not intend an early marriage?'

'I do not.'

'I am no advocate,' she said heavily, 'for early marriages, even where great alliances might be in question – which they could never be, of course, in your case. It is my opinion that early marriages are often mistaken ones.'

Susan doubted her authority for this assertion, as Miss Priscilla had never bestirred herself to marry at all, so she assured the lady that she contemplated no such rashness, and then submitted to a lecture on making herself discreetly useful back at home, something Susan had no intention of doing, for what else were servants for?

Finally, there were tears, from Anne and little Henrietta especially. But then it was over – and she was free.

Acknowledgements

First, as ever, I must thank my husband Simon for his unstinting encouragement and his editing, generosity and support – a task made far more complicated by his own book (*Music in Edwardian London*, Boydell Press) being written simultaneously.

Sabrina Rood did her usual marvellous editorial job, assisted by brilliant ARC readers Karen Quigley, Laura Farnsworth Nielsen, Sarah Pope, Carol Briggs, Lester Barnes, Miriam Rheingold-Fuller, Rebecca Fuller, Anne Clark and Vesper Miekle. They all made excellent 'catches' – for which I'm very grateful.

I could also never have managed without the stalwart and sensitive Phil McKerracher, and the gifted team at Design for Writers.

In addition, the encouragement I have received, on social media and otherwise, from friends, family and – yes, fans – is not to be told. A particular shout-out to those who wrote to me so personally after I 'came out' as ADHD – a *very* late diagnosis – in my news-letter. *Thank you!*

Of course, writing any Austenesque fiction is risky, and fiction based on *Pride and Prejudice* perhaps riskiest of all. Mr Darcy boasts a fan club Austen herself might envy, and I'm aware – though I haven't read even one of these, in case of being influenced – that many distinguished authors have already attempted to illuminate Darcy's point of view.

The *temptation* to do so must be obvious: so much of *P&P* favours Elizabeth's perspective, while the reader must guess at Darcy's. And then, the missing scenes are so intriguing! Who hasn't, for example, imagined what happened when Darcy confronted Wickham in Weymouth?

At any rate, I hope that Darcy fans will forgive me!

I write a monthly newsletter (www.alicemcveigh.com), and love to connect on Facebook and Instagram through the weblink linktr.ee/ASTMcVeigh.

Finally, if you liked *Darcy*, an honest review on Amazon or Goodreads would be hugely appreciated!

A.M.